DEATH OF A RADICAL

An early fan of Georgette Heyer's Regency romances, Rebecca Jenkins began collecting diaries and journals from Georgian England as a child. Her passion for the period led her to study history at Somerville College, Oxford, from where she went on to become an accomplished journalist and broadcaster. *Death of a Radical* is her second novel. She lives in County Durham.

Also by Rebecca Jenkins

F.R. JARRETT MYSTERIES
The Duke's Agent

NON-FICTION
Fanny Kemble – the Reluctant Celebrity
The First London Olympics – 1908

DEATH OF
A RADICAL

Rebecca Jenkins

Quercus

First published in Great Britain in 2010 by

Quercus
21 Bloomsbury Square
London
WC1A 2NS

A CIP catalogue record for this book is available
from the British Library

ISBN 978 1 84916 233 3

10 9 8 7 6 5 4 3 2 1

Typeset by Ellipsis Books Limited, Glasgow

Printed and bound in Great Britain by Clays Ltd, St Ives plc

For Bob and Gail Jordan – to Bob for sharing his profound knowledge of the history of objects, and Gail, the best of readers.

PROLOGUE

Ancient walls rose up against an indigo sky. Ice frosted the pavement. In the deserted courtyard the merest sliver of a glow seeped out from between shuttered windows. At this time of the evening, in the depths of February, the college's inhabitants were huddled up within its thick walls. A slight figure lurched out of the shadows. One arm encumbered with a bundle, he carried a lantern shielded against his body.

Favian Vere Adley paused a moment, propping an elbow against the cold stone.

Favian was proud of his name. The father who burdened his offspring with such weight was a gentleman of means whose hobby was classical erudition. 'Favian signifying a man of understanding,' he would rehearse to his only child. 'And Vere – faithful and true. Worthy qualities in any man. Mind you live by them.'

Favian aspired to live up to his name. He was a sickly child; his world was narrow and confined, but amid the sweet smell of oiled leather in his father's library he discovered the enchantment of words. He marvelled at the truths they encompassed in neatly bound lines of print. Young Favian believed in the power of the word to reform the world and make men's souls sing.

So naturally he desired to give the world a poet.

As a boy he set out to instruct himself. He read *The Times* from the age of eight and later the *Manchester Guardian* when he could get it. He read Shakespeare and Hume, Wordsworth, Shelley and Godwin. He was eager to learn meaningful things. But to be honest (and Favian desired to be rigorously honest), he lacked direct experience of the world. Favian Adley had never felt the vital pulse of Life until one April day walking down Piccadilly. He was just a boy of sixteen, still in the care of his tutor. They rounded a corner to find themselves confronted by soldiers, big as life, riding down the pavement. The troopers were herding a crowd with drawn swords. It was not a mob of drunken rabble, as some reported. The boy saw ordinary folk, dressed cleanly – tradesmen and even women; citizens being ridden down by the soldiers of their own king.

They had lined the streets to protest the removal of the people's champion, Sir Francis Burdett, to the tower. Sir Francis was Favian's hero. He had followed the story avidly but newsprint had not prepared him for this: the shrill cries, the ominous percussion of hoof beats, the violence and fear sharpening the very air. A man pushed past him holding his bloodied head and moaning out loud. Favian was stunned and elated and terrified all at once. He could feel his own blood humming under his skin.

His tutor gripped his arm and they were home before he knew it. Taking off his coat in the familiar confines of his own room, Favian found a smear of blood on his sleeve. He knew then, at the age of sixteen, that there were things – real things – to be said. And Favian Vere Adley swore to himself that he would say them.

For months he tumbled fervent words on to the page only to throw them into the fire. Then the day came when his father entered him as a gentleman commoner at Oxford University. Now, at last, he was ready to publish.

Throwing back the wings of his scholastic gown, Favian lowered one knee unsteadily to the frozen pavement. His icy fingers fumbling a little, he unfolded a toy balloon.

'*Fierce roars the . . .*'

The words came out in an undignified croak. His thin back rounded over with a spasm of coughing. The cold was injurious to his chest but he was determined. He had copied his 'Ode on Tyranny' out in his best hand on hot-pressed paper and signed it with a flourish 'Fidel', advocate of the people. He and Studdley had planned the little ritual together. But Studdley had succumbed to brandy punch and was snoring half off the sofa in the rooms they shared.

At the third attempt Favian succeeded in attaching the paper to the balloon.

'*Fierce roars the tyrant's ire, freedom's spirit to consume . . .*'

That time the words came out with a pleasing cadence. What better publication for one's poetry than to send it up into the night trailing fire?

Favian was proud of his poem. At times, the scansion ran a little uneasily (Studdley assured him that the *feeling* carried it through) but it had true dramatic scope. His Muse of Freedom visited Sir Francis in the Tower and the journalist Peter Finnerty in the cell where he languished for telling the horrid truth about the Walcheren campaign. Favian was particularly fond of the stanza that began,

> *Wasted blood shed in Walcheren fields*
> *With tyranny's destiny congeals*
> *And an indignant people raised at last*
> *Redeem their birth right . . .*

His ink-smudged fingers held the wick to the lantern flame. It smouldered, then glowed. The paper sack bellied out delightfully. With a faltering lurch it rose into the dark, trailing its paper tail. Looking up, the notion of his poetical essay on the Existing State of Things floating past the Warden's very windows struck Favian as wonderfully ridiculous. His snort of laughter exploded in the disapproving silence of the frozen courtyard.

It was at that moment that he observed the open casement. For the first time he heard the muffled chime of silver on china and then, more clearly, a disembodied laugh. The balloon seemed to hesitate. With languid malice it curved into the Warden's window and disappeared. There was a soft implosion, a flare, and a woman squawked. With a considerable turn of speed, Favian Adley snatched up the folds of his gown and scuttled away into the shadows.

CHAPTER ONE

Snow had come early to the moors that year. It came on an aching east wind that welded the moderate falls into a thing of torment. As February prepared to give way to March, the winds dropped, leaving curdles of snow in the hollows. Amid the brittle ochre straw new life grew pale green, pliant and vital. Jonas Farr was in good spirits. Thanks to a couple of days' work in the last town, he had a full stomach and his mind was at ease with itself. He was a young man – not yet twenty years old – with a strong, compact body and an open face. He strode over the rough ground, swinging out his staff.

Jonas caught movement against the dull colours of the damp moor. Some way off two boys appeared to be crouching on the edge of an overhang. One stretched up an arm, etching a vicious shape against the white sky. The arm snapped down. The boy's companion scrabbled to gather up more missiles.

The assailants were too preoccupied with their game to notice Farr's approach. 'What's this then?' he demanded, laying a hand on the collar of the nearest wretch. He looked down into a pinched, feral face and glanced over to see what the boys had caught.

Down below, a slight gentleman was cornered on a path running some ten feet beneath the overhang. Eyes peered up between the brim of a low-crowned hat and a mud-spattered scarf held close by a gloved hand.

With an explosion of energy that caught him unawares, the second boy was up and off. His companion twisted out of Jonas's grasp, delivering a painful kick as he rolled away to race after his accomplice. Cursing, Jonas loped a few paces, then stopped. It would be foolish to leave his pack and staff, and encumbered as he was, there was little chance of catching them.

'You are not hurt, sir?' he called out to the man below.

But the man had not stayed. His receding figure was hurrying across the moor towards the horizon.

Perhaps the poor daisy had been too ashamed to tarry. Held at bay by a couple of young ones hurling muck! Jonas surveyed the landscape about him. He was a stranger to these moors and the gentleman might have reassured him that he was travelling on the right road. His best option seemed to be the narrow causeway below.

Climbing down to the road he heard the tinkle of a harness bell. A chapman came into sight, trudging towards the overhang with a string of pack-horses, his lumpy outline mimicking his lead pony's swaying gait.

'Good-day!' Jonas called out.

The chapman cocked his head in acknowledgement

of the greeting without slacking the rhythm of his pace. A man with property had reason to be cautious of strangers met on the moor. Jonas stepped back to give him room.

'Say, goodman, is there a place hereabout a journeyman might shelter the night?'

For a moment he thought the man would pass without answering him, but as he drew abreast their eyes met. With a jingling of harness and bells, and some shoving between beasts and man, the pack-train came to a halt. The chapman planted his weight comfortably.

'Not from round here, then?' he asked.

'No.'

Jonas fondled the nose of the nearest pony, inspecting the line. There were half a dozen little Galloways, shaggy-haired and stoic, each loaded with sacks. The pony pushed its rough head against his chest amicably as he scratched its forehead under the straggling mane.

'Yon pack's shifted,' he commented. 'This jagger's back'll be good for nowt.'

The pedlar came round to look.

'I've had naught but trouble with this poxy crook!'

Shaking his head the chapman lifted the heavy sack to reveal a pad stuffed with heather fastened to cross-pieces of wood. A binding on one of the cross-pieces had frayed, allowing the pad to slip.

'Make do for another trip yet, Enoch, she says. I'll make do her!' the chapman pronounced. 'Told her it was buggered, didn't I? Women!' He jerked his head in Jonas's direction. The young man stepped forward to take the weight of the sack. Muttering to himself, the chapman pulled a couple of strips of leather from inside his sleeve and proceeded to make a rough repair.

'Thanking you,' said the chapman, his good humour restored. 'How do you know nags then?'

'Me auntie Annie's of your trade – carries cloth out Saddleworth way. Spent a summer with her once as a lad.'

'You're never kin to Jagger Annie!'

'You don't know Annie!'

'I do! By heck she's got a tongue on her has Jagger Annie.' The pedlar eyed the young man with fresh interest. 'What brings you this way?'

Farr indicated the pack he had put aside on the ground and the shoe last that hung from it.

'Shoe making's my trade. Had a fair place, but these times . . . The master couldn't keep his family let alone a journeyman – work's so pitiful scarce.'

'Bad times,' agreed the pedlar. He fixed the young man with a mournful look and shook his head. 'Desperate times,' he repeated gloomily. Jonas met his eyes.

'As bad as they've ever been.'

The weather was closing in, charging the air with a fine, freezing drizzle. The chapman fiddled with a buckle, adjusting his leader's harness.

'Militia's out Yorkshire side,' he said.

'Oh aye?'

'Aye. Getting ready for the fairs, I reckon. Haven't the

heart to go far – it's bitter this time of year.' The pedlar added a contemptuous snort.

'Easter Fairs? Hiring fairs, are they? Where about these parts?' Farr asked.

'Woolbridge, in a few weeks' time', the older man jerked his head, 'mile or two that-a-ways, down on the river. Well now,' he gave his pony's cheek a final pat. 'Best be off. Yon track there, that'll lead you to Grateley Manor. Cook there likes company and they've a couple of barns that aren't overlooked.'

With a brief nod and a medley of 'hie!'s and clicking noises, the chapman hauled his train back into motion.

The track climbed up steps of land to a windswept expanse where hardy trees stood within a high stone wall. Drawing near, Jonas saw that beyond the wall a sunken track led into a milking yard. Towering over the yard, with the air of an ancient strongplace, was an old farm house, its deep-pitched roof carried on walls studded with few windows.

A thin gentlewoman of middle age stood at the kitchen door. Straight-backed and arms crossed, she cut an odd figure in an old-fashioned jacket and plain cloth riding skirt. She had a long, narrow face, her pale skin accentuated by the springy black curls of her cropped hair. Her figure radiated indignation. A path curved round to the public side of the house where dirt and pebbles gave way to cobbles. The gentlewoman's attention was fixed on a group that was passing through the whitewashed gateway and down the hill. A man pushed a handcart of belongings, trailing a woman with a baby in her arms. The woman spoke sharply and Jonas caught a glimpse of a sullen boy beyond the cart.

Farr's staff struck stone with a sharp tap and the gentlewoman spun to face him.

'What do you do here?' she demanded.

'Beg pardon mistress. I'm a journeyman. Shoe-making's my trade – but I've a fair hand for carpentry and the like if you've a broken chair, or some other job.'

Jonas braced himself for an abrupt dismissal.

The gentlewoman glanced back into the shadows behind her.

'He can feed in the back-kitchen, cook, but he'll sleep in the barn.' The hot eyes snapped back to Jonas. 'Your name?'

'Jonas Farr, mistress.'

'And *have* you come far?'

'Served my apprenticeship in Leeds, mistress.'

'You can have shelter tonight and in the morning there's a pair of slippers and a chair need attention.' The passionate energy welled up again. 'No fires or tricks, mind. I keep my pistols by me and I do not scruple to use them!' With that, she turned on her heel and stalked into the house.

Jonas Farr found himself facing the substantial figure of a woman who eyed him with the moist gaze of a friendly bovine. She ushered him into the kitchen with a wave of plump, floured fingers.

'Arethusa,' she said. 'That's me given name but Miss Lippett she calls me cook. I'm cook and I don't know what else for I've scarce help about the place – all but none since Betty Tully's been sent off along with her Ben.' She set out bread and cheese on the table and pulled out a chair. 'Take a cup of ale? It's warmed and spiced – just the thing against the cold.'

Arethusa settled herself in a wide country chair by the kitchen range. Resting her trotters comfortably on the grate, she snuggled a pot of warm ale to her pillowy chest and fixed Jonas with the full force of her curiosity.

'Such a day! Dismissed Ben Tully and his family, just like that! And not a chance of hiring until the Easter Fairs – not way out here.'

'Fairs come round soon enough,' Jonas responded, his eyes on his plate. He had never seen cheese like it. It was an anaemic cream colour, sweaty and crumbly. He laid a fragment on the corner of a piece of bread and took a cautious bite.

'And who's to do the outside jobs?' Arethusa demanded, ignoring him. 'Never mind what Betty did about the house – and even that no-good boy of theirs. Miss Lippett, she bowls in all in a fury, pays Tully his wages and turns him out. Wife and bairns along with him. There's no telling what that's all about.' The cook gazed at Jonas as if he might have an explanation of the mystery.

'She has a temper, then, your mistress?' asked Jonas, warming the tip of his nose in the fragrant steam that rose from his mug. Arethusa gave her head a good scratch.

'They all have their faults, don't they? The quality. And she is quality – whatever they might say,' she stated. '*I* say she's got no harm to her. As often as not she keeps herself to herself and her *books*.' Arethusa drew out the last word with a humorous emphasis to underline the strangeness of such a preoccupation.

'She's put up with Ben Tully for more than a twelve-month. Why choose this day to turn him out? Eeah! That's a mystery. Mayhap her boo-ooks carry the answer!'

'I have a taste for books myself,' said Jonas. The cheese had a soft tang about it that was not entirely unpleasant. He cut a thicker slice.

'You canna read!'

'I can.'

'Well now!' exclaimed Arethusa, rolling her shoulders to giggle coquettishly over her plumped-up breasts. 'I'd never take you for a reading lad. So you's looking to settle, then?' Jonas took note of the softening look in the cook's eye. He pushed back his empty plate.

'Looking for work. So these fairs – it's not just wool then?'

'Nay. Leather and sheep and horned cattle too. They come from all over. Second day, mistress gives us the day off. So will you be staying?'

Jonas stood up. 'That was grand. Thanking you, cook. Now, if you'll point me to this barn your mistress spoke of, I'll turn in.'

Arethusa led him to the barn. She was inclined to linger until a girl came with a message that the mistress was waiting on her and Jonas was finally left in peace.

The lantern Arethusa had provided burned with a steady light. Outside the wind buffeted the stone walls of the barn. It had been near a year since he had completed his apprenticeship and left his grandfather's house in Leeds. It was the only home he could remember with any clarity. He had been nothing but a youngster at the time of his father's death, when his mother had returned to her kin. In his mind's eye he could see his grandfather – neatly dressed and strong-looking for all he was over sixty – sitting in his ladder-backed chair reading in the firelight. His calm eyes were looking at him, magnified by the round glass of his wire-rimmed spectacles.

'All men are equal when they can read, Jonas lad. In books a man may find the wisdom of the best of his fellows – living and dead. A reading man's never alone for he has the company of philosophers, poets and other great men.'

Smiling, Jonas rolled himself in his blanket, pulled a leather-bound book from his pack and, stretching out by the lantern, began to read.

The barn door dragged on the floor and a gust of icy air invaded his sanctuary. Miss Lippett entered, windtossed and holding up a lantern.

'Did I not tell you no fires, sirrah!' Jonas scrambled to his feet.

'Beg pardon mistress but the lantern's safe. See. I've cleared a space – and there's water should there be some accident.'

Miss Lippett strode up. In the pool of light that illuminated the floor Jonas noticed that she was wearing a man's riding boots. Her fierce gaze swept his corner. Every wisp of hay had been cleared from a neat circle about the lantern and a bucket of water stood within arm's reach. She saw the crumpled blanket and the book.

'Do you read, journeyman? Far be it from me to stop a man reading his Bible.'

Jonas bent down to pick up the precious book. 'In honesty mistress, this is not the Holy Book.'

'It is not? What does a shoe-maker read, then?' Her thin hand snatched the book from him. 'Mr Gibbon's *Decline and Fall*!' She stared at him round-eyed. 'What matter can a journeyman take from the history of the Roman Empire?'

'The same matter that any man may, mistress.'

She half smiled, then suspicion flooded up.

'Did you steal this? Do you mean to sell it me? You have heard I am a scholar no doubt.'

'No ma'am!' He saw her draw herself up. 'I mean, no, I did not steal the book, mistress – your cook's told me you're a learned lady. The book's mine – it was given to me by my mother's master. A reverend gentleman who's shown me great kindness.'

'Well,' she tossed the book back to him. 'It is but an odd volume of a broken set.'

'So it is, mistress. But to me it's also a precious companion.'

A faint longing softened Miss Lippett's expression. She reached out and tapped the book lightly.

'Indeed, some books are precious companions.' She stepped back abruptly, her back ramrod straight. 'Some fool is forever telling me that a woman's wit is too paltry to benefit from book learning. Who am I, then, to say a shoe-maker may not improve himself so?'

'It was my own mother who first taught me to read, mistress. She's a great reader and a fine woman.'

It may have been the wind chapping her cheeks, but Miss Lippett looked quite pink in the lantern light.

'Well. You mind that lantern. If you suit me, I may have a day or two's work for you here. I happen to be short a man and do not find it convenient to search me out a new hireling this week.'

It was just before ten o'clock on the night of the twenty-seventh of February when Mrs Watson heard the dog barking in Powcher's Lane. She unlatched her window and smelt smoke. She glimpsed a glow through the stripped winter branches of the Bedfords' orchard and raised the alarm. By good fortune, Robert Mouncey, the saddler at the top of the lane, and a couple of his neighbours, weavers laying by stock for the upcoming fairs, were also up late. The response was swift. The Bedfords' home was the one house of substance in the working quarter of Woolbridge. (Mr Bedford – despite his wife's objections – insisted that he reside within sight of his mill.) Had the fire jumped the stable wall it might have ripped through the crowded lanes and caught the better part of the neighbourhood sleeping. As it was, the fire was put out before the stable block was properly alight.

Amid the remnants of a straw mattress the fire fighters found the scorched remains of Michael White, the Bedfords' coachman. He lay stretched out, a brandy bottle by him and an overturned lamp. He had been a solitary drinker and a foreigner, not known in the Dale. Mr Bedford had hired him in Leeds. It was said that White had taken the brandy from his employer's cellar. It had not been the first such transgression. The sinner, it seemed, had suffered the consequences of his sins. Neighbours remarked on the charity of Mr Bedford who, despite the damage and the inconvenience caused by the careless manner of his servant's demise, nonetheless paid for the burial and a stone marker in the churchyard.

Michael White had no family. No one claimed him as a friend. His few belongings were fire damaged and disposed of. Saul, Mrs Watson's youngest, a sturdy, useful lad of eight, was the one person who retained a memento of his passing. While assisting the carpenter summoned to repair the loft, the boy discovered a sooty button with a curious raised cable border. He rubbed it on his sleeve, thinking it silver. He showed it to his master, who advised he throw it away, for what use was a scorched button?

Saul, however, kept it. He called it the Burned Man's button and on occasion he would display it to other boys, his particular friends, and thereby gained considerable credit among his circle.

CHAPTER TWO

Frederick Raif Jarrett strode across the marketplace towards the Queen's Head. There was anticipation in the air beneath the steely skies. The first herd had arrived at Woolbridge. A group of drovers with their broad-brimmed hats, heavy coats and long staffs were gathered around a brazier. The Easter Fairs were approaching, marking the end of winter and bringing trade and diversion to the town.

Jarrett had always considered himself an even-tempered man but he had been cross for days. A few months previously he had assumed management of the Duke of Penrith's northern estates more by accident than design. In his military days he had endured many wet and cold weeks in the saddle in a cheerful spirit. He had survived asinine superiors, incompetent allies and enemy ambush, but that day he could not recall feeling so put out of sorts by anything as one and three-quarter hours spent in the company of Mr Hilton of High Top.

Mr Hilton was a sociable man; a principal tenant of

the duke's and a leading light of the Woolbridge Agricultural Society. He had sought out the duke's agent to enquire whether his Grace might be inclined to contribute to a subscription being raised among agriculturalists in the neighbourhood to engage Mr Colling of Alnwick to bring his fabled bull, Cupid, to stand at Woolbridge and improve the stock in the Dale. That subject had been speedily settled but a good hour and a half passed before Mr Jarrett was able to shake himself free near two whole hours wasted breathing the stifling exhalations of his beasts while Mr Hilton made conversation.

In the Dale everyone knew one another's business. What they did not know, they speculated. Jarrett's head was ringing with snatches about Mr Hilton's preference for fish, soggy bottoms ('that piece down there by the beck, it's a trial'), pockmarked trees, Mrs Anders's arthritis and our Dot's knees ('a canny milker our Dot'). Or was it Mrs Anders's knees and the cow suffering the arthritis? He longed to ride away, set sail, chop some wood – any simple exercise of action: clean, clear, wordless action with direction and a point to it.

And now he was late. The Queen's Head rose before him. The inn had sat comfortably at the southern end of the market opposite the church for more than a hundred years. For the last twenty it had been in the capable hands of Jasper Bedlington and Polly, his wife. The magistrates met there; the Agricultural Society, the Box Society; the Odd Fellows held dinners there and every quarter dances were mounted in the convenient assembly rooms on the first floor. The oppression of respectability seemed to crowd in on him as he marched under the coach arch. He took off his hat to run an impatient hand through his corn-blond hair. Could this really be his life?

'Mr Jarrett! There you are!' Mrs Bedlington, the publican's wife, called out from the kitchen door. 'Colonel Ison's upstairs in my best private, when you're ready.'

'Damn the man,' Jarrett muttered to himself. 'Good morning Mrs B. You didn't hear that, did you?'

She screwed up her face in a comical expression of sympathy. She was a good woman. He smiled back.

Colonel Ison was Member of Parliament and the leading local magistrate. A compact man with restless eyes under heavy black brows, he was ever busy in the public interest – especially in so far as it coincided with his high estimation of his own importance. This morning he was in his costume as Colonel of the Woolbridge and Gainford Volunteers. It was the habit of the commanders of such companies to design their own uniforms. Ison's was not as extravagant as some.

'Am I not to have the pleasure of Lord Charles's company today?' The colonel looked over the agent's shoulder as he greeted him.

'The Marquess of Earewith is out of town,' Mr Jarrett replied. For him this was something of a relief. Charles had been keeping him company for months. He could see, however, that the colonel was disappointed.

'Might I know when his lordship is to return?'

'I am not informed of his plans.' When Charles had left he had been more than usually mysterious. Jarrett suspected he was up to something; as perhaps the marquess's closest friend, he was resigned. Having no duties or responsibilities to speak of, my lord often took pleasure in preparing surprises with which to ambush his intimates.

Colonel Ison expelled a hard little sigh. He was a man who relied upon the security of rank and the rank of Mr Jarrett eluded him. On the one hand, Mr Jarrett was the duke's man of business: a trusted agent but still a servant and as such the social inferior of a magistrate and Member of Parliament. And yet, Mr Jarrett was intimate with the duke's family, in particular with his Grace's son and heir, the Marquess of Earewith. The colonel being a mere public acquaintance, the most aristocratic family in the district and their circle had not seen fit to elucidate the mystery. The ambiguity of the precise nature of Mr Jarrett's connection with the ducal family, therefore, rankled. Whenever he was with his Grace's agent Colonel Ison had the obscure feeling that someone was making a fool of him.

'Domestic peace is most precious in time of war,' the colonel pronounced. He thrust a pamphlet at Jarrett, planting his feet to stand four-square. 'Civilization itself rests upon it. As I told the Home Secretary in the lobby last week, we need decisive action, a firm hand.'

Jarrett took the proffered paper and looked down at it, wondering by what unlucky chance *he* should have been selected for this particular address. The British had been at war with the French for the best part of his adult life, and there was still no end in sight, but Ison was the worst kind of armchair warrior. A part-time soldier, he had never faced a real enemy in his life. He was, in consequence, at the same time loudly bellicose and fearful. Jarrett turned over the document in his hand. It was printed on thin parliamentary paper, GEORGIII REGIS, CAP.XVII in bold print on its cover: *An Act for the more effectual Preservation of the Peace, by enforcing the Duties of Watching and Warding.*

'What manner of action, sir?'

'Disturbances are in preparation for the Easter Fairs, I am sure of it.' The magistrate swayed a fraction towards him, deploying his formidable eyebrows to add weight to his words. 'I am certain of it.'

'I have heard nothing locally, colonel,' Jarrett responded mildly. In his past life Raif Jarrett had had considerable experience of undercover work. He prided himself on his intelligence. Mr Hilton was the greatest gossip in the neighbourhood and as far as Jarrett could recall, his best piece of news had been Mrs Anders's arthritis (that and an obscure anecdote about some newly discovered fungus that pockmarked trees).

'Foreign agitators!' the words were expelled from the colonel's lips. 'It is a matter of outside agents.'

'You can't mean the French?'

The colonel tweaked one gold-braided cuff impatiently. 'You can be sure our enemy will benefit.'

23

Britain being an island, French agents were not that common an occurrence. Jarrett could think of nothing that might tempt them to their isolated neighbourhood. There were no munitions factories, no important barracks or prison camps and Woolbridge was miles from the coast. He wondered briefly if the colonel was drunk. He scanned the polished surfaces of Mrs B's best parlour. There was no liquor in evidence.

'My dear sir . . .' he began.

'Intelligence, Mr Jarrett; I have intelligence!' snapped the colonel. His cheeks flushed red. 'There are rumours . . . Radicals. Insurgents.' He straightened his shoulders a fraction as if bracing himself. The agent's expression was unreadable. He seemed entirely unmoved.

Jarrett was aware of the incidents of machine breaking in recent months. The worst of it had been down in Nottinghamshire. Stockings and serges formed a principal part of Woolbridge's manufacture, but the methods of the local masters were traditional. 'We have no steam-mills here,' he objected. 'Our weavers have no new machines to break.'

He heard the breath rush through the colonel's nose.

'If I could relate to you all that I have been privy to, Mr Jarrett,' Ison exclaimed irritably. 'Only last Friday I was speaking with Yorkshire members in Westminster – manufacturing districts to the south of us have suffered more than the odd broken frame. There is co-ordination sir and the canker is spreading – how else may a stocking knitter in Nottingham find common cause with a West

Yorkshire cropper? They both sing songs of General Ludd! We face a great conspiracy, sir: one that threatens not only property but perhaps the very security of the state!'

Jarrett stared into the wide-opened eyes in the empurpled face. The man seemed genuinely moved. He wondered if the colonel had some particular reason for his concern.

'Is one of our manufacturers bringing in new machines?' he ventured.

'Men of property must be allowed to carry on their business.' The colonel looked away and cleared his throat. His attention fixed on a painted box lying askew on a side table. He straightened it.

'The matter under discussion, Mr Jarrett, is the preservation of the public peace. I have called you here as a courtesy. Please inform his Grace that I am calling on my fellow magistrates to enact the Act. I have already requested assistance. I am expecting a troop under the command of Lieutenant Roberts.'

'You've called in the regulars?' exclaimed Jarrett, startled. The country had been through two bad winters; people were tired of the war and the price of bread was high. But as far as he could tell from his rides up and down, the local populace in this isolated dale were as they had always been – not entirely law-abiding as far as the strict letter but loyal subjects of their king. The only reason he could see to use the Act to call in a troop of regulars to this out-of-the-way district would be to strengthen the magistrate's hand – but to what purpose?

'The Easter Fairs draw thousands to Woolbridge, who knows what villains concealed among them,' the colonel was saying.

'Surely our militia is sufficient to contain any—'

'They are not sufficient to this!' the colonel cut him off.

Jarrett had experience of what a bored troop of battle-hardened regulars could do to a town. He had a profound distaste of martial law.

'But you know how the regulars are disliked,' he persisted.

'We are at war,' the colonel stated fatuously.

Jarrett felt a powerful urge to take a swing at the man. For a glorious moment he imagined the startled look on the MP's face at finding himself on his arse in the hearth. Instead he turned away and leant on the mantel. A log had rolled out. He kicked it back into place with rather more energy than the task required. In selling out he had thought to regain his independence. And yet, here he was again forced to watch the follies of his self-styled superiors unfold. He wanted to leave that room. Ride away and never come back. His eye was drawn to the mirror above the fireplace. The reflection of the self-important little man behind him dominated the scene. The neighbourhood had two powerful magistrates, the one vain and ambitious, the other ambitious and corrupt. Fortunately the pair despised one another. Had it been the latter – Jarrett's old opponent Raistrick – who was seeking to acquire an armed troop, the duke's interest and every other interest in Woolbridge would be at risk. Ison was a blowhard but he cared what other men of standing thought of him. That should keep the colonel within bounds, Jarrett told himself; this was none of his business.

Some way off deep in the bowels of the inn, he heard a woman's voice. It had a cheerful, domestic tone. A vision of Mrs Bedlington and her mild, helpful husband sprang into his mind. His horse, Walcheren, was below in the stables, only a few yards away from where they stood. That made him think of Robert Mouncey, the saddler he patronized in Powcher's Lane who liked to spout irreverent philosophy while he mended your bridle. He liked these people. He was the duke's representative in this out-of-the-way place. He could make it his business.

'If I may make a suggestion, sir ...' he turned back donning his most conciliatory face. 'His Grace has a warehouse in town. It is standing empty and the location is convenient to the markets.' The colonel chewed his bottom lip.

'A military strategist such as yourself, sir,' Jarrett continued, mentally kicking himself for sinking so low, 'will see the benefit in lodging the troop together and I am sure his Grace will be willing to meet the expense.'

The colonel's eyelids flickered. 'A generous offer,' he admitted grudgingly.

'Shall I make arrangements?'

The colonel drew a fat letter out of his pocket and tapped it against the palm of his free hand. 'I have called an extraordinary meeting of the magistrates tomorrow,' he said. 'Should Lord Charles have returned by then his counsel would be welcomed.'

'The warehouse?' Jarrett prompted. Colonel Ison jerked his chin.

'Do it.' The older man unfolded his letter and pretended to absorb himself in its contents. 'I have another appointment, Mr Jarrett,' he said. 'I must prepare. Goodday.'

Jarrett almost laughed out loud. Did the old badger expect him to back out bowing low like a footman?

'I shall wait to hear from the lieutenant when he arrives, then,' he informed the room with a slight bow. As he left, the colonel's voice followed him.

'If the marquess is not available, perhaps you would attend the meeting in his place. Twelve noon.'

The galleried courtyard of the Queen's Head was empty and still. It was that lull in the morning after the deliveries and before the midday customers gathered. Jarrett could smell ale and baking bread. He heard a woman singing. Ringing out in the calm of the yard the voice was enchantingly pure with a heart-catching lilt. He stilled, listening to the song.

> Every night I dream about him,
> Every day I take no rest,
> Every instant thinking on him,
> My heart ever in his breast.

Recognition lit Jarrett's features. He took the gallery steps two by two. He began to sing along in a pleasing tenor.

> *And 'tho long distance may be assistance*
> *From my heart thoughts of love to remove,*
> *Yet my heart is with her altogether,*
> *'Tho I live not where I love.*

He completed the last lines alone. There was a squeal and the trample of bare feet on boards. A door flung open and a female dressed in a shift visible under a trailing shawl propelled herself into his arms.

'Captain Fred!'

The woman swept back a mass of curls to greet him with an open-mouthed kiss. She was slim and wiry, of a height to fit under his chin. He flicked a quick glance about the gallery. There was no one in sight.

'Bess!' he responded as she leant back to look at him. She had the freckled white skin of the true red-head. He smiled down into pale blue eyes in a vivid, knowing face.

'Kiss me again!' she demanded.

'In the yard of a public inn? Bess, I'm a respectable man these parts. Would you have me rob you of your good name?' A lewd hand gripped him firmly on the buttock.

'I give you my all freely, my chuck – as you well know. Come in, come in!'

Bess pulled at his hand, dragging him into her room. 'It's cold enough to freeze the tits off a sow out here.'

Bess drew the edges of her shawl together, leaving the curve of one shoulder in plain view. There was a smudge of soot on her luminous skin, defining the hollow between left shoulder and breast.

'Come sit with me,' she said.

Bess settled herself at a dressing table loaded with half-burnt candles. They huddled on every available surface, melted wax dribbled in curious shapes. A large hamper lay flung open in the middle of the floor. A pair of sky-blue dancing shoes with yellow laces peeped out from beneath a grey hooded cloak lined with red and a profusion of surprisingly long black horse-hair curls that foamed out across the floor. Jarrett held the wig up, examining its length.

'Adela in *The Haunted Tower*,' Bess explained. 'I can scarce keep my mind on my part so in terror I am of setting light to myself in the stage lamps with those damned curls trailing everywhere. Sit down my sweet – don't mind those. They're crushed to pieces anyhow.'

Jarrett laid the curls aside, brushed a pair of taffeta breeches off an armchair and sat down.

'I'm in a rush. I've a meeting with the manager,' said Bess, her voice muffled as she pulled a dress over her head. 'Sugden – that's our manager – he smells a Prospect; a prominent citizen, a magistrate; we've plans to make. Do me up, there's a love.'

She turned her back to him. Jarrett fastened the tiny buttons with expert hands. She gave a delighted shudder and smiled at him over her shoulder.

'Glad to see you haven't lost your touch.' She smoothed her bodice, admiring her freckled bosom in the mirror. 'Sugden plans to have me put the foolish rabbit in a good humour.'

'You're with Sugden's Players?' Jarrett returned to his chair.

'How could you not know it?' The actress was indignant. 'And my name up on all the bills pasted up over this town. Bess Tallentyre there, in full black print! Years it's taken me to get that and you've not even noticed!' She looked at him in mock horror. 'You've never given up the playhouse? You've not turned *that* respectable!'

'Never! You know I am a slave to your breeches parts.'

She trailed a saucy look over his own well-fitting breeches. 'I remember . . .'

He leant back in the chair, stretching out his legs straight before him.

'How long's it been, Bess? Last I heard you were headed for Bath.'

'Bath!' She twisted to face him, her hands to her cheeks in exaggerated dismay. 'Lord God that was . . . No! I shan't name it. Years ago!' She turned back to her mirror. 'And you were off to Spain.'

'Portugal. But I sold out. You see before you the agent to the Duke of Penrith.'

She paused, haresfoot in hand, meeting his eyes in the mirror.

'Fancy that!' she said. She rose in a fluid movement and came to stand over him. 'My soldier boy no more then.' She traced the plane of his lean cheek with a finger. 'You look thin, love.' He smiled up at her.

'Why the prominent citizen, Bess? Surely Sugden must have his licence if the bills are already up.' Bess returned to her mirror.

'We have the licence but players always need patrons.' She leant forward, examining her face critically, a pair of tweezers in one hand. 'Sugden's hoping I can coax a bespoke out of the creature.' She frowned as she plucked a stray hair from one elegantly arched brow. 'We need to make the best of these fairs. Business has been thin, very thin. Town to town there's been talk of riots and combinations. Sugden says he's lucky to get a licence in half of 'em.'

'Does the rabbit have a name?'

'Didn't catch it. The big man, that's all I know.' She shot him a mischievous look. 'Why? Do you know all the great folk these parts then? A pox on it! Where is that rouge?'

The thought of this bit of his past meeting with Colonel Ison MP and Chairman of the Bench was unsettling. He caught Bess looking at him in the mirror. She was smiling.

'Hush now, be easy. You know I'm not one of your loose-mouthed molls.'

'What'll you offer him?' he asked lightly.

'What do you say to a *Beggar's Opera*? My Polly Peachum is always a favourite.' Bess struck the attitude of a soulful coquette. 'My Polly is much sought after.' She insinuated herself on to his lap. 'Sugden and the rabbit can wait.' Her lips hovered above his as her hands busied themselves with his buttons. 'Come show me how much you missed me, captain, for old times' sake.' Her pliant lips closed over his, soft and insistent.

Jarrett closed the door quietly behind him. He took a smart step back as a man in a hessian apron crossed the yard below and went in by the kitchen door. Glancing down, he moved swiftly towards the stairs, straightening his cravat. His footfall was surprisingly soft.

An elegant young buck was standing in the yard looking up at him with worldly brown eyes from beneath the brim of an expensive-looking hat.

'You're back,' Jarrett commented without breaking stride.

'I am,' replied Charles, Marquess of Earewith.

'How was York?'

'Wearisome. We have a letter.'

'We?' With an internal sigh Jarrett gave up on the stables and changed course for the bar.

'It is addressed to me,' Charles admitted judiciously, following him, 'but it concerns you. We are expecting a visitor.'

'We are?'

Since his unexpected assumption of the duties of agent, Raif Jarrett had occupied one of his employer's properties, a manor house a little way out of town, known in the neighbourhood simply as 'the Old Manor'. It was a bachelor household, presided over by Jarrett's valet, Mr Tiplady, a London servant of some pretensions. The duke's son and heir, Charles, finding himself with no pressing engagements, made himself at home there. That, Jarrett thought impatiently, did not give him the right to inflict other guests.

'Don't be such a bear,' said Charles as if he had spoken aloud. ''Tis an act of philanthropy. Grub's in need.'

'Grub? The lad's coming here?'

'His mother . . .'

'Dear God!' Raif winced. 'If she's coming, I have pressing business somewhere a *very* long way off.'

The family tree of the Dukes of Penrith was a tortuous one. It was not widely known, but Charles's great-grandfather, the third duke, had married twice. As an ageing widower he had fallen in love with a pretty young thing glimpsed at church. Her father was forceful and the old duke besotted – so he married her. His Grace's happiness was short-lived. He died a bare four months after the union. His young widow was consoled with a tidy settlement and soon after married a wealthy banker. The couple were blessed with a daughter who grew up to become Grub's fond mama. The pair therefore formed part of the ranks of vague relations known to the duke's family as cousins.

'Have no fear,' Charles consulted a sheet of notepaper crossed over in an untidy hand. 'His mama remains in London. Her spouse, she informs me, is Most Upset at his son's Disgrace.'

'What has Grub done?' Jarrett asked over his shoulder. They were walking down the passage to the bar and it was a narrow one. 'Shouldn't he be at school?'

'According to this he's been up to some mischief, been sent home for a spell.' Charles held the paper up at an angle frowning as he deciphered the lines in the dim light. 'Something about an unfortunate accident; she becomes rather obscure at that point. Anyway, his mama is sending him up here.'

The public bar was quiet. The pair crossed to seats by the fire.

'Why here?' enquired Raif, tossing his greatcoat over the back of a settle.

'So that we may reform the boy by our manly example?'

Raif raised his eyebrows sceptically. Charles perused the scrawled sheets once more. 'Aha! She wishes you to paint his likeness.'

Now that was unexpected. Jarrett was a competent painter. As a lad, living on the continent with his mother, he had studied with Italian masters and had thought once of becoming a portrait painter. His family had dissuaded him from adopting such an ungentlemanly profession.

'She wants me to commemorate his disgrace?'

'No. His birthday. She intends to present the canvas to Mr Adley in the hope of softening the paternal heart. Three-quarter length or full sized, as you think best.'

'When am I going to find time to paint a full-sized canvas?'

'Oh there's plenty of time,' Charles responded cheerfully. 'Apparently the boy is at liberty for the rest of the academic year and his birthday is weeks off.'

Jarrett sighed, trying to calculate how many years it had been since he last saw the lad. He must be in his teens by now. Difficult years. He had been a fetching little chap – despite the sickliness that endowed him with the luminous, sunless pallor that had led his hardier cousins to name him 'Grub'.

'Which birthday is it?' he asked.

Charles squinted at the page, turning it about, then he gave up, tossing it aside.

'She may say but it is smudged. Old enough to travel alone at least.'

'So when are we to expect him?'

'Tomorrow.' Charles grimaced apologetically. 'I know, I know, I should have mentioned it earlier.'

'You've had that letter for weeks!'

'I mislaid it,' said Charles evasively.

'Bollocks!' responded Jarrett, fully aware that Charles had purposely left him with no option but to accept his fate. Charles was determined to domesticate him. He was forever trying to impress upon him the charm of family ties. Mrs Bedlington set down a couple of tankards before them. Her expression was prim. 'I beg your pardon Mrs B.'

'Some of your marvellous hot toddy?' enquired Charles, favouring her with his most boyish grin. 'How delightful.'

'Oh you!' she responded and bustled off swinging her hips.

Jarrett leant forward to pick up his mug.

'Now you're back, you can attend the magistrates' meeting tomorrow. Colonel Ison is most eager for the pleasure of your company.'

'Bollocks!' echoed Charles. 'Why?'

'He suspects evil doings at the fair. He's calling on the magistrates to enact the Watch and Ward. He has a troop of regulars on their way.'

'Really?' asked Charles with a flicker of astonishment. He stretched, cat-like, in his wing-chair. 'I blame the uniform,' he drawled. 'These old homebody soldiers do like their wars.'

'Indeed. I've promised him a warehouse – the one down on the river by Bedford's mill – for a barracks. The estate's paying for it.'

'Why?'

'Because home deployment in time of war is a bad business.' Jarrett's delivery was clipped. 'Troopers are best kept under the eye of their officers.' Charles glanced up at him from under his lashes.

'You know best,' he said soothingly. Mischief returned to his voice. 'But I am not attending that meeting!' His companion didn't seem to hear him. He was staring into the fire. 'Why so solemn?'

Jarrett looked across at his friend. Charles was such a pleasant fellow – the easiest companion in the world –

but he did not waste time on things he did not wish to see.

'The colonel is bringing in a troop of regulars,' he repeated.

'They will keep the peace.'

'Or they will help to break it.' Jarrett adjusted his position restlessly. 'The colonel says he has heard rumours – radicals at work in the neighbourhood. Have you heard anything?'

'They were full of that at York. Talk of – what are they calling those fellows who attack their masters' machines?'

'Luddites.'

'That's it. There was an attack on a mill near Halifax. They caught the villains. They're coming up at the assizes. If there are any of that sort around here ... I'd be the last to know.' The marquess drained his mug and looked around. 'More toddy?' Jarrett shook his head, his mind on his recent interview. 'Mrs B!' Charles shouted.

Mrs Bedlington popped her head round the door. Charles gestured at her with his empty mug, softening the action with his most winning smile. She simpered and disappeared.

'Colonel must have his reasons,' Charles commented, hoping to dismiss a subject that had begun to bore him.

'Indeed.'

'There was that fire the other week,' Charles suggested idly, 'behind the Bedfords' place – might have been malicious. The colonel's friendly with the Bedfords, isn't he?'

'A drunk's carelessness.' Jarrett was curt, his attention elsewhere. 'No. The colonel has intelligence!' he pronounced in a fair imitation of the colonel's manner. 'Makes me wonder where he's getting it.'

CHAPTER THREE

'Ostrich feathers!' the milliner declared, 'worn flat about a little yeoman's hat. And roses are *quite* out – oh dear me, yes. I did see a sprig of laurel on a pleasant lilac bonnet in the Park last Saturday – St James's I mean, of course, where all the *quality* walk. But roses . . .' She gave a dismissive snort. '*They* just will *not* do this season.'

Favian Adley squeezed his eyes shut, wishing he could close his ears as well. Oh, the airless, cramped, freezing misery of a winter journey by public coach! The leather upholstery sweaty with the breath of penned human beings; the ceaseless struggle to find some way of bracing one's weary frame against the constant lurch and sway.

His purgatory had begun with his mother insisting on rising at five o'clock to accompany him to the Belle Sauvage, one of the busiest coaching inns in London. It was a mystery to Favian how his diminutive mama could attract the attention of so many as she orchestrated waiters, pot-boys and even ostlers to do her bidding. She displayed her son centre stage in her comedy, loading him up with such 'comforts' as a stoneware foot warmer – which she twice insisted be filled with freshly boiled water by a sniggering boot-black. And then there was the woollen night-cap she had begged her son, her hands to her breast in supplication, to wear under his hat. (Favian had managed to slip that into a pocket.)

As the vignette of his tearful mother supported on the arm of her servant shrank within the frame of the coach window, Favian closed his eyes in the hope of anonymity at last. Instead the wretched milliner had taken it upon herself to introduce the whole company. There was a sallow gentleman with large bags under his eyes who presented himself as Mr Jones, a retiring curate, a spinster named Price and a neat little girl, perhaps of fourteen or fifteen, with big brown eyes and glossy wings of dark hair peeping out from under her bonnet. Her companion, Miss Price, gave the girl's name as Miss Bedford, but when the spinster whispered to her charge Favian caught the name 'Lally'.

'Mrs Burroughs, milliner to the gentry, that's me – and who might I have the honour of addressing?'

The blasted woman jostled him with her foot. With a great show of reluctance Favian opened his eyes.

'Mr Adley,' he muttered.

'Well, Master Adley, what takes you up north? Returning to school? Been poorly, have you?'

'Madam, I am a collegian! A gentleman of Oxford.'

'Hoity-toity! A *gentleman* of Oxford no less.' Mrs Burroughs cast a knowing look about the company.

'Never mind, my dear,' she said, leaning forward to tap Favian's knee. 'Dorothea Burroughs is not one to take offence.'

Favian recognized the tone. She was setting out to make a boy of him. The situation called for extreme measures. Favian resorted to an exhibition of his most revolting cough. It was a fine example, with a sickening catch of phlegm ending in a dramatic wrench for breath. Generally after such a performance strangers left him in peace. Indeed, he noted with satisfaction that the other passengers looked quite uncomfortable. Dorothea Burroughs, however, was made of sterner stuff.

'Such a terrible cough! Poor young man! No wonder your mother was fretted all to pieces about you. For that was your ma, was it not, that accompanied you at the inn? I said to myself it had to be, so moved and tender she was towards you. Why do you not wear that night-cap she gave you under your beaver? You put it in that pocket, I fancy.'

'I'm not a child, ma'am!' he expostulated, outraged that he had been stung into sounding like one.

Dorothea Burroughs launched into a series of anec-dotes containing intimate details of various acquain-tances who had succumbed to putrid chests through not having sufficient care of themselves. Unnerved by this assault, Favian began to cough in earnest. Mrs Burroughs rattled on as he bent forward, gasping for breath.

The curate sitting next to him blinked at the young man's discomfort. Miss Bedford peeped out from beyond his bulk. Was this what was meant by being talked to death? A surge of terror threatened to overwhelm Favian.

A little gloved hand impinged on the edge of his vision proffering a large red handkerchief. He reached out and clasped the hand. It was warm beneath its smooth casing of thin, polished leather and perfectly steady. His chest felt as if it must crack asunder for straining against the congestion in his lungs. He was growing light-headed. Dimly, against the stream of the milliner's babble, he heard Miss Bedford's soft voice.

'Hush. Try for a shallower breath.'

He hung on to the warm hand. With an explosive retch, he coughed up the obstructing phlegm and air seeped into his sore lungs. He was conscious of the other passengers shuffling in their seats as the crisis passed. Mrs Burroughs alone seemed oblivious to the spectre of dissolution that had glanced up among them. Favian released the gloved hand with a wan smile to its owner. The solemn brown eyes turned mischievous as Miss Bedford smiled back. She had remarkably luxuriant eyelashes.

'You'd do well to mind your prayers, young Master Adley,' commented Mrs Burroughs. 'You have need of the Almighty's aid with that cough.'

Favian turned his head to his clerical neighbour, his voice languid with the exertion of his recent crisis.

'Mr Jones, sir; you are an educated man. I have been much struck by Pliny's arguments in his *Natural History* – I'm sure you know it: *that the supreme being, whatever it be, pays heed to man's affairs is a ridiculous notion.* What would be your opinion?'

'Saints preserve us! Never say the boy is an atheist!' exclaimed the milliner.

'Now, now Mrs Burroughs, I am certain that the young gentleman did not mean to shock you,' responded Mr Jones. He smiled at Favian under the hedge of his eyebrows. 'Now did you, Mr Adley?'

'Indeed Mr Jones, as it happens, I did – but the philosophical question has merit all of its own, do you not think?'

The milliner clamped her lips shut and drew her skirts away. Satisfied that she had excluded him from her presence, Favian leant back gratefully and composed himself to sleep.

The *London Union* rattled to a halt in the cobbled yard of the White Horse Inn, Leeds. Favian tumbled out into the buttery sunshine, wrung out and aching. With a shy smile and a bow to Miss Bedford, he snatched up his bag and made his escape. He turned down Boar Lane, past the imposing edifice of Trinity Church and out into the broad sweep of Briggate. There was a chill in the air. Passers-by hurried with their heads down, preserving a space between themselves and the next man. Across the wide thoroughfare a tight pack of inns jostled for street space, shop fronts for the long yards that lay behind, with their stables and higgledy-piggledy hives of rooms: the Bull and Mouth, the Albion, the Old King's Arms. A group of citizens stood talking, their arms crossed, faces guarded under the brims of their hats. Favian gave the group a wide berth and turned his steps towards the river. Beyond a lumbering luggage wagon, he discovered the comfortable bow windows of the Royal Hotel.

The inn was warm and full of talk.

'Been a row on Briggate,' said the pot-boy, a long stringy youth with bad skin. 'Did you see owt? A hundred or more they say. Could hear 'em from 'ere.'

'I didn't,' responded Favian, sorry he had missed the excitement. 'What was it about?'

The boy caught his master giving him a hard stare and flicked the table with a grimy cloth.

'Apprentices complaining. Wages been cut again. What can I get you?'

Favian asked after the Carlisle coach and was informed that he had two and a quarter hours to wait before its arrival. The pot-boy stood before him, his eyes fixed on his face, his mouth slightly open, waiting. Flustered, Favian ordered the dish of the day.

It felt delightfully robust to eat at the public table in the coffee room. His mother would have insisted he dine in a private parlour. He was not hungry but Favian forced himself to swallow half the plate of broiled pigeon put before him. Then he withdrew to a settle in the bow window to while away his wait with a book.

Favian kept his copy of *Pig's Meat* by the radical philosopher Thomas Spence for his public reading. He had purchased it over a year previously from a bookseller in St

Paul's renowned for the number of times he had been prosecuted by the government. He had so far failed to finish it. He had, however, gained much entertainment from the reactions of those of his elders who happened to notice what he was reading. Mr Spence was one of those free-thinkers condemned by the respectable as a filthy Jacobin who only desired to corrupt honest English persons. Favian, who enjoyed thinking, prided himself on giving a hearing to all philosophy.

Favian arranged the tract before his face in such a manner that the cover might easily be read and slid a look about the room. Much of the company had dispersed. Favian sighed. Word for word *Pig's Meat* made dull reading. His thoughts turned to his visit north.

Favian Adley had never known that careless resilience of youth where vital spirits give the illusion of immortality. As a child he loved to watch any trial of physical ability – whether it be a cricket match or a couple of porters fighting in the street. There was one man among his acquaintance who seemed to him to bring together the two halves of his ideal – to combine physical grace and confidence with the enquiring mind of a gentleman scholar, and that man was his cousin Raif.

They had first met when Favian had been five or six years old. His father had taken Mrs Adley abroad on a trip to Vienna – the very first time Favian had ever been separated from his mother. He had been in good spirits for the first few weeks but then he had succumbed to one of his regular bouts of lung fever. Unable to reach his parents, his nurse had sent word to his most illustrious relative, the Duke of Penrith. The duchess was still mourning the tragic loss of her youngest son and the duke had taken his wife to Brighton, hoping to distract her from her profound melancholy. By return of post the duke had replied that the little boy should be sent to recuperate on his Yorkshire estate. So Favian and his nurse found themselves at Ravensworth with a skeleton staff and the young marquess, Charles, as titular host. Those few weeks might have been as barren and confined as all the rest for Favian, for cousin Charles, then fifteen, shied away from the company, being still raw from the loss of his brother; but that summer cousin Raif was at Ravensworth.

More than a decade later, Favian could recall precisely the sensations and scenes of that magical visit. On the second day, left unsupervised, he had discovered the duke's library, an imposing room, well kept and containing many valuable books. He had climbed to the uppermost rung of the library steps in order to view the collection from a proper perspective when his cousin had entered through the French doors from the garden, a volume of essays from *The Spectator* in his hand.

He had not seen the boy at first. Favian remembered the thickness of his corn-blond hair and the way he moved with a controlled grace that implied a vitality commensurate to any physical challenge. He had sensed another presence and looked up. The boy was used to encountering impatience from adults, but the blue eyes registered a friendly interest as the youth nodded a greeting. They had fallen into conversation. Favian remarked that he was not familiar with Mr Addison's entire work but that he had found himself particularly diverted by that author's essay on ghosts and apparitions. His new friend had agreed it was an entertaining piece. Considering the memory, Favian realized that his companion must have been amused under his courtesy. The boy he then was had been exhilarated to converse with a man of near twenty without being dismissed.

From that moment, young Favian's every waking thought turned to finding the means to be in the vicinity of his hero. Never before had he experienced the vibrancy of such anticipation: ears tuned for the sound of his nurse returning; stretching on tip-toe to look over the high sill of the nursery window, down into the courtyard where Raif and Charles collected their dogs each morning to go shooting. The boy watched Charles and Raif go out where ever they wished. They took their guns from the gun-room, whistled to the dogs, and walked out. His nurse had never thought to take Favian further than the lawns and the narrow paths of the rose garden. He longed to see the wood, to be with the men like a normal boy.

That morning Nurse stepped out to visit the housekeeper's room. Favian was nervous as he edged into the corridor. In the distance a servant was dusting a table. A voice called. The girl answered with a pleasantry. He scarcely seemed to register upon the vastness of the main stairway as he crept down. The door to the library was open. At the end of the vista, sun streamed through the glass of the French doors.

The panes made a dreadful clatter in their frames. He was certain that someone would catch him. As he crossed the lawn every window in the house seemed an accusing eye at his back. Favian was not used to running. He walked as quickly as he could to the white gate that led to the home wood. And there he was. In the wood. He was light-headed with the unexpected exertion and the daring of what he was doing. He had read of woods in print on pages but nothing had prepared him for the vitality and variety of the colours, the smells, the sensations. It was strange and exotic to be so entirely surrounded by living, unconstructed things. There were birds everywhere. He could hear them move about and call to each other in the foliage around him.

A dog barked nearby. That would be the others. He left the path to follow the sound. Cousin Raif would be so surprised to see him walk out of the bushes. He would not imagine that the boy could be so bold.

Then he was lost. The dog moved off and the undergrowth seemed to close around him. He could not see where he was. He was proud and he would not cry for his nurse. He folded himself into a ball by the root of a large oak and despaired.

Charles's dog came across him a few minutes later and his bark fetched the hunters. Charles stood over him cradling his gun, a look of irritation on his fine-cut features.

'What foolishness is this, Grub? Are you determined to catch a chill? Oh my! But there will be such drama back at the house. The servants will be in uproar. And what about Nurse? No thoughtful boy would put his nurse to such distress.'

Cousin Raif silenced him with a look. He crouched down beside the boy, helping him up.

'How do we find you here, Grub?'

'I only wished to go shooting with you and to see the wood.'

'So you get yourself lost?' Charles scoffed. 'What if we had not found you? What if some stray dog had come upon you or a gypsy had carried you off!'

The young marquess pulled a face with wide, staring eyes. He stood there, not particularly tall, but well-made and strong. There was a healthy flush to his fair skin. His boots were worn and there was mud on the sleeve of his shooting jacket. Favian's toes felt damp. The thin pumps he wore were made to tread boards and carpet, not mud and grass. The little boy longed to cross over into Charles's world; to share in his liberty and strength. He could not express the passionate intensity of his feelings. Charles stared at him as the tears welled up. The boy felt his hero's hand warm and steady on his thin shoulder.

'Let him join us. We do not plan to be out long.'

Raif had taken the powder horn that hung over his own shoulder and he had fastened it about him.

'The youngest member of the party can carry the supplies. Only remember, Grub, next time you wish to favour us with your company, join the expedition at the outset. A man is less likely to get lost that way.'

'Oh very well,' conceded Charles. 'Do try to refrain from snivelling; it disturbs the game.'

Favian felt such pride as he trotted after them into the sunny wood. He even felt happy to be in company with Charles.

The sun went in. The brisk March wind had gathered up some clouds. Favian had the impression he was being watched. He looked around. Across the cobbles another wing of the inn overlooked his seat. In a window on the first floor he caught sight of Miss Bedford's neat profile. She had removed her bonnet and was talking to someone beyond her in the room. She turned and their eyes met. Favian glanced away, blushing.

There were two men standing in discussion before the Royal Hotel. The first man, tall with a patrician profile, held himself with the posture of a military man. The second was a fellow with a sharpish nose and a pointed skull barely covered by a ginger fuzz of close-shaved hair. The latter man held his hat under his arm while he fiddled with a pair of bilious yellow gloves. Favian noted that the taller man did not show his companion the courtesy of uncovering.

Favian was intrigued as to what business the men might have with one another. Perhaps the gingery fellow might be a money lender, but then again, he looked too eager. He glanced up. Miss Bedford was still at her window. He was certain she was watching him. He took out a pencil and paper as if seized by inspiration and jotted down a note. He contemplated it. 'Yellow gloves,' it read. He underlined the 'yellow' with a decisive stroke and sneaked a glance under his lashes. Miss Bedford was leaning forward, distinctly looking in his direction.

The two men parted. The man with the yellow gloves slid off. Favian tried to analyse precisely what it was that made the fellow look furtive – something in the line of his shoulders or perhaps it was just his sandy colouring and that ferrety face. The man swung his head round and stared in his direction. Favian flinched back out of sight, startled by the thud of his heart. He caught his breath and slid a glance into the street from the shelter of the window bay. The gingery man had disappeared but his taller companion was entering the inn. Catching a full-face view, Favian recognized the elder brother of a school friend. After the first shock of recognition he recalled that Strickland did hail from these parts. No matter. It should be easy to avoid his brother. There was no need for the fellow to enter the coffee room.

No need, but there he was, standing at the threshold, looking about. Favian hunched himself over his book.

'By Jove! Is that young Adley? Why it is! Still as fond of raspberry puffs, my lad?'

It is not easy to pretend to such studiousness as might render one deaf to so direct an address. The voice was distinct and the rest of the coffee room plainly heard it.

'Don't wish to recognize me, puppy? What, after all those teas I funded you and my scamp of a brother? For shame!'

Favian looked up with what he hoped was a fine performance of the scholar surprised and sprang up, blushing.

'Mr Strickland, how do you do? Forgive me, please. When I read I forget the world. How are you, sir? And how is old Sticks? Haven't seen him in an age.'

Mr Strickland towered over him, crumpling Favian's hand in his hearty grip. With his own kind he was a jovial man.

'He's lounging about at mother's. Mooning over some girl. Mother's pleased. Tells me the girl's suitable.'

As Favian recalled, Sticks had been an early devotee of the charms of the female sex, celebrated among his school fellows as a hero in the dynasty of Venus.

'So, how come I find you here?'

'I am awaiting the Carlisle coach, sir. I'm on my way north to visit my cousin Jarrett.'

Mr Strickland tilted his head back to examine the slender figure before him. Poor Adley could do better with himself. His delicate features and ivory skin were perhaps a handicap he could hardly disguise, but his hair could be better dressed. The silky strands were looped back behind his ears in an untidy way.

Favian held the gaze, feeling his dignity leak away. By some unlikely insight, Mr Strickland divined his unhappy accident.

'Been rusticated, have you! So what was the crime? Climbing in late? Boxing the watch?'

Damn the boy! By what right should the drab squib give him such a supercilious look? Mr Strickland checked himself. Sorry for his lapse in noblesse oblige, he became over-jovial to compensate.

'Always had more mischief in you than met the eye, eh? Remember Hal telling me of the time you blew the top off old Dr Hamgold's desk. Laughed 'til I cried. Should have liked to have seen it. Never fear – you'll not hear a word from me. Good shooting up there. I envy you. 'Deed I do.'

Favian burned with a strong sense of injustice. Mr Strickland's thoughtless words belittled his poetic gesture, reducing it to the unthinking foolery of a schoolboy's prank. It was fortunate for his composure that at that moment a man came to the door to announce the arrival of the Carlisle stage. Favian mustered his dignity in a stiff bow.

'I must be off. This has been a happy chance, sir. Do give my regards to Sticks when you see him next.'

''Deed I will. Give your cousin Jarrett my regards when you see him. A good man. Knew of him in Portugal.'

Mr Strickland smiled after the boy as he left. He looked peaked, poor soul. He remembered his brother telling him that Adley suffered with his chest. He looked down and saw that the boy had left his pamphlet on the settle. *Pig's Meat* – Mr Strickland frowned as he read the dedication. Silly puppy. He was half inclined to go after the boy and give him some sound advice, but then no doubt his cousin would put him right. Good man – excellent riding officer. Mr Strickland looked at the pamphlet in distaste. It was a mystery to him why anyone should be allowed to print such rubbish. It was positively incendiary in these times – particularly in this troubled district. For a sliver of a moment he wondered if he was wrong about the boy. The ridiculous notion of Favian's elfin frame concealing a dangerous Jacobin amused him greatly. Mr Strickland chuckled to himself as he threw the pamphlet into the fire.

CHAPTER FOUR

'Down to the bottom of Cripplegate and up t'hill,' Favian repeated under his breath. On a sunny day, when the sliver of sky above was blue and the sun's rays might slant a little way down the walls, the alley might have been considered picturesque. Today with the slate sky pressing down, there was an air of oppression about it that left Favian breathless. Descending at Greta Bridge he had chanced upon a currier who offered to convey him into Woolbridge. Leaving his trunk for collection he set off in the man's gig. The currier had deposited him at the end of the alley with instructions that a short walk would lead him into the heart of the town and to the Queen's Head, from where he might send a message to his host.

Favian congratulated himself. If a poet was to speak for the people he must acquaint himself with all conditions and here he was, for the first time in his life, in the midst of the dwellings of working men. It was a mercy that all smells were deadened in the cold air, for rotting sewage clogged the simple drain cut through the packed earth. A building straddled the street over a barrel-vaulted arch. Following the curving passageway, Favian saw a flight of stone steps to his left. They rose to a half-court enclosed by several storeys climbing up to the sky. He heard the sounds of a horse entering the narrow alley behind him. He climbed the steps out of its path.

The hoof beats and the clean ring of metal bridle furnishings were amplified within the high walls. Favian watched unseen as a horseman filled the narrow frame of the street, an officer on a black mount. The horse's eye was bright. Its neat head posed proudly on its glossy, curving neck. From the soft shine of the rider's boots to the sky-blue hussar jacket and the tall red-tasselled cap, the lieutenant was the perfect print of the military hero.

Favian felt an overwhelming sense of trespass. The pristine colours of the rider's presence seemed an unwarranted intrusion into the drab reality of the alley. He had an impulse to throw filth at the vibrant blue of the jacket, to rub mud into the insulting scarlet of the sash. The lieutenant seemed oblivious of his surroundings. His features were placid as he passed. The hoof-beats receded. Favian's chest was tight. It hurt. He sat down on the steps. He knew of old that if he could but sit a while and calm himself, he might avoid a full-blown attack.

Time passed, measured by each shallow breath. Favian glanced up to see a woman stagger down the alley towards him. She listed against the weight of a heavy basket, helping herself along the wall with an outstretched arm. She dropped her burden and straightened her back.

'You ill?' she asked.

'Long day. Been travelling,' he managed to squeeze out, smiling at her as cheerfully as he could.

'Come up and sit by the fire.' Leaving the basket on the ground she grasped him unceremoniously by the arm and helped him up. She was a strong woman. Before Favian could protest she was steering him up the steps to her door.

'You sit there,' she said, depositing him in a chair by a scrubbed pine table. 'Sara Watson.'

'Favian,' he croaked, between gasps, 'Adley.'

'That's a fanciful name.' She set a tumbler before him and poured him some water. 'Have a sup of that. I'll be back.'

The room was dim and calm and warm. Although his wheezing was a distraction, Favian was nonetheless thrilled by this novel opportunity. He had never seen the inside of a labourer's cottage before. He looked about him curiously. It took a moment for his eyes to adjust to the gloom. The light from the window was as thick as amber. At first he thought there was parchment in it, instead of a broken glass, then he realized it was patched with newspaper, yellowed and faded in the light. The room seemed well swept and neat. There was a board floor under his feet. He didn't recognize the fuel smouldering in the stone hearth. It gave out a musty smell. There was a rack standing by the fire with some sort of flat cakes on it. Shelves in the corner displayed a collection of earthenware pots and bunches of dried herbs. On the table stood a wicker basket filled to the brim with neatly folded stockings, a bobbin of matching thread balanced on top.

The air felt thick in his throat. He turned his face to the cold air flowing in from outside. The open door was an oblong of light. Through it he heard his hostess grunt as she wrestled her burden up the steps. She filled the doorway: a solid determined outline leaning out in counterweight against her laden basket. Face flushed, she heaved it onto the table with a crash.

'Turnips! They're a weight, I don't mind telling you.' She gave him a shrewd look. 'Any better?'

Favian took a dutiful sip of water and nodded, fighting the impulse to cough.

'I am most grateful to you for your kindness, Mrs Watson. May I . . . ?' He put his hand in his pocket. He paused at the look on her face. The room was so sparse, so bare, he could not help himself. He drew out his coins. They clinked under his fingers resting on the table top. Sara Watson stood very still. He glanced at the turnips piled in her basket and back to her face.

'To buy your family a better dinner,' he pleaded.

'They're for pigs out back!' she exclaimed, outraged.

Favian's cheek burned red hot. He heard a snort.

'Eeeh! Look at your face!' His hostess laughed out loud. 'Where are you from, lad?'

'London.'

'Eat mouldy turnips down there, do they? Times must be bad.'

Favian was overcome with a bout of coughing that bent him in half. Through his fit he felt the firm touch of a human hand. His hostess was rubbing his back. The intimacy from a stranger was startling. It was oddly comforting. He had had a nurse once who would rub his back like that when he was a little boy. He glanced up to see Mrs Watson's face full of warm concern. Dimly he registered the sound of boots with metal rims on the outside stairs.

'Heard they're here already,' a male voice said. 'A couple of days early; no one's sure why. They're resting out of town; at inn on't Carlisle road . . .'

The speaker blocked the light from the door, a young giant with a ruddy complexion. A slighter young man with thick brown hair with a curl to it stood behind him. He peered past his companion's meaty shoulder. He had well-spaced eyes and a generous mouth that looked as if it smiled easily. Favian gasped for breath trying to compose himself.

'Mam,' the first youth said, 'you remember Jo.' He nodded in Favian's direction. 'Who's this then?'

'He'll have to tell you, didn't catch the name,' Sara Watson replied, her hand maintaining its soothing rhythm on Favian's back. 'Found him on the steps. Poorly chest.'

'Can see that.'

'Dickon, my eldest – and his friend Jonas.'

'Favian Adley,' he squeezed out, half extending a hand. The movement caught his throat and Favian spasmed with another hacking cough. His eyes were level with Dickon's waist. He carried a knapsack slung across his chest. A sheaf of papers poked out from its open maw.

Dickon straddled a stool and sat at the table, his arms folded, watching Favian struggle for breath. He was as broad as a young ox. His skin was flushed as if he had been exerting himself. His shirt was open about his throat. Favian found his eye drawn to the triangle of muscular chest visible beneath the handkerchief tied loosely round his neck. The pulse of health seemed to reside in the smooth skin as it rose and fell in an easy rhythm.

'He needs some coltsfoot tea,' said Jonas, watching Favian's narrow back shudder under the racking cough. 'Got any coltsfoot, Mrs Watson?' He walked over to inspect the stand of shelves where some herbs hung drying. She gave him a blank look.

'Coddy foalsfoot, Mam,' her son translated.

'Oh! Foalsfoot. I've some fresh flower heads,' said Sara, pointing to a particular section of shelf. 'Plucked last week.'

Jonas picked out a few yellow flower heads, intent on his task. His brown fingers moved through the neat bundles of herbs, lifting the lids off earthenware pots to check their contents, culling a sprig here, a root there.

'Eh up – elderflowers,' he pronounced with satisfaction. He stepped over to the fire and poured a little water

61

into an iron pot. He hung it on the hook. 'You don't mind?' he said, with a glance at his hostess.

'Feel free,' said Sara, dryly. She seemed amused rather than offended by his invasion of her kitchen. Jonas flashed her a grin, his attention on the ingredients he was adding to the water.

'Coltsfoot and a handful of elderflowers, some mallow root, a bit of liquorice and a touch of honey,' he said with assurance. 'This'll help that cough.'

'I don't want to be such trouble,' Favian murmured, embarrassed.

'Don't look like you can help it,' said Dickon. He took off the knapsack and let it drop down by the table. 'So – what you doing here, then, Favian Adley?' He had a quick ear. He echoed the unfamiliar name perfectly. 'What business have the likes of you in Powcher's Lane?'

'Just arrived from the south,' Favian wheezed as best he could. 'Told this was the short cut to the Queen's Head.' He ran out of breath.

'Let the boy be,' Sara intervened. 'Let him get his breath back. How did it go?' she asked her son.

'Got a couple of days' work building pens for t'markets.'

'Good on you.' Sara pulled her sewing basket towards her, selecting a stocking from the pile. 'Soon as I finish these Mr Foster says he has another hundred. He's building stock for t'fairs.' Jonas strained his brew off into a mug and placed it in front of Favian.

'There,' he said. 'Try that.'

Favian took a dutiful sip. He was fully prepared for it to taste disgusting. In his experience such concoctions generally did. He was pleasantly surprised. For the most part it was sweet and fragrant. He could smell the elder-flowers. He felt the hot liquid seep down his throat, calming it. Jonas stood looking down at him with his arms folded across his chest, like a craftsman waiting for his patron's verdict.

'Good,' Favian told him, surprised by the warm feeling spreading through his chest. He watched Sara's needle as it flashed through the fabric. His shoulders relaxed. The company seemed perfectly at ease with his presence among them. He felt oddly at home. His eye fell to the papers sticking out of Dickon's bag. They seemed to be a sheaf of printed sheets.

'Jo's a singer too, Mam.' Dickon's remark seemed to have some significance Favian didn't quite catch. Sara gave her son a sharp look over her sewing.

'He's brought a new ballad.' Dickon pushed a sheet across the table. Favian leant forward to peer at the title, intrigued. It was a crudely printed ballad sheet, 'The Weaver's Lament'.

'Know it?' Dickon asked. Belatedly Favian realized the question was addressed to him. He shook his head.

'*Your mouth it is shut and you cannot unlock it,*' Dickon sang, completely at his ease. '*The masters they carry the keys in their pocket.*' His voice was tuneful and direct.

'Why, that's poetry!' exclaimed Favian.

'Verses that speak to a man's heart,' said Dickon.

'Poems for the people.' The words just formed themselves. As he heard himself speak them, Favian felt something click into place.

'Poems for the people,' repeated Dickon, considering the phrase. He shrugged. 'If you like. Written by working men – even 'tho they canna risk printing their names on it.' The remark was a challenge.

'And men should speak their hearts,' Favian responded eagerly. 'I believe that.'

'And what do you know of working men's hearts?' Dickon's tone was belligerent.

'Nothing, it's true. But I wish to learn. I am a poet.' Favian felt himself blush at the confession but he carried on bravely. 'I want to speak truths. It is as the poet Wordsworth says: *we must be free or die, who speak the tongue that Shakespeare spake . . .*'

'Speak what?' Dickon cut in. He leant forward and plucked Favian's mug from where it rested on the table top between his hands. He sniffed the contents and put it back with a grimace. 'Don't smell too bad.'

Favian dutifully drank another mouthful.

'Shakespeare,' Jonas's voice caught Favian by surprise. He had been sitting a little back from the table, calmly observant. 'He wrote a play called *Hamlet*. Me grandfather took me to see it once in Leeds.'

'Ham what? To a play about a pig?' Dickon's eyebrows shot up.

'Not a pig. A prince. A foreign prince called Hamlet.

He saw the ghost of his father and had to right a wrong.'

'And did he?'

'Think so.' Jonas considered the matter. 'His lass went mad and drowned, though, and they all died in the end.'

'Don't sound like much.'

'There were some fine speeches in it.' Jonas leant back his head and fixed his eyes on the ceiling. '*Oh that this too, too solid flesh would melt and resolve itself into a dew,*' he said, his mouth taking pleasure in the words. He straightened up. 'Well, you'd have liked the fighting.' Favian stared at him amazed.

'You remember that – though you only heard it once?' he asked.

'Stuck in me head. Words do that sometimes.'

Favian felt a rush of fellow feeling. 'It is the same for me,' he said.

'Well now, Favian Adley, you're looking better,' said Dickon. He rose, his full frame suddenly making the room feel small. 'Jo. We'd best get goin'. They'll be ringing the bell at Bedford's soon.'

Favian got to his feet.

'I will walk out with you,' he said. He addressed his hostess shyly. 'Mrs Watson, I cannot thank you enough for your kindness. I shall never forget it.'

Her smile transformed her face. All at once he saw a young woman before him. She patted his arm.

'You're welcome, lad. You take care o' yourself and that chest. Any time you're passing Powcher's Lane, come visit.'

65

She watched the lads leave together, smiling at the comical contrast between the slim back of the boyish gentleman and her young giant more than twice as broad towering beside him. Favian had his head poked forward as he addressed her son, his expression intent.

'Tell me more about these poems for the people – these ballads; I should like to hear more,' she heard him say as they descended the steps.

CHAPTER FIVE

The smoke rising from the chimneys of Woolbridge hung still against a grey, frozen sky. A couple of drovers stood warming their hands at a brazier near the tollbooth that marked the top of the market. One nudged the other. An eccentric figure was marching up Cripplegate Hill. It was clothed in a gentleman's greatcoat. The hem of the garment swung with the rhythm of each determined step. A drover stepped into the oncomer's path. The crown of a mannish beaver hat bobbed as Miss Josephine Lippett straightened her spine.

'Well, now – what's this, you reckon Michael, fish or fowl?' he said.

Miss Lippett stared beyond the man with a furious intake of breath.

'Buggered if I know,' responded his companion. The warmth of the pair's bulky presence carried in the cold air with the stink of cattle.

'Does your cock stand?' the drover called out as the gentlewoman pushed past. Miss Lippett spun round in fury. Hobbled in her skirts, she lost her balance and fell into the muddy gutter. The spatter exploded around her with the men's laughter.

Nailed boots pounded on the cobbled stone and Jonas Farr sprang between them, pushing the bigger man's chest.

'Ask me if my cock stands, why don't you?' he demanded. He shoved the man again. The drover backed away from his fury.

'She tripped. It was just a lark.' The herdsman was shame-faced.

'I'll give you larks!'

Half truculent, half embarrassed, the drovers retreated behind the tollbooth. Jonas leant down. Miss Lippett gathered her collar about her lower face in a defensive gesture. Her eyes met his, framed between the line of her hat and the mud-spotted fabric she held close in her gloved hand. There was a frozen moment and then Jonas helped her up. As Miss Lippett resumed her full stature she brushed him back, her voice trembling with emotion.

'Leave me!' She looked away to soften her brusqueness. 'Filthy brutes! They are fit for nothing but cattle company!'

'I wish you'd let me walk with you, mistress.'

Miss Lippett gripped her coat to mask her shaking hands. There was a large stain on the cloth to which a cabbage leaf clung. She flinched as Jonas brushed it away.

'It will be a sorry day when a Lippett of Grateley is

afraid to walk through this town in broad daylight. I will not be so insulted.' She stamped her foot. 'Did you mark them? You are my witness! The magistrates are meeting at the Queen's Head. I shall pursue this. Those filthy beasts shall not go unpunished.'

Passers-by were staring at her from the opposite pavement.

'Come away,' Jonas coaxed. 'Your coat is damp. It should be dried and cleaned.'

'Not before I have laid my complaint before the magistrate!' Miss Lippett set off at a furious pace, Jonas following after her.

Across the street Raif Jarrett watched the scene from a shop window. He had been contemplating the composition made by the drovers and the smoke and colour of the brazier. He had been thinking how he might capture it in lake and burnt earth when the drover stepped into the woman's path. It all happened so quickly he did not have time to respond, and when the servant came up he thought it best not to interfere.

'What an extraordinary woman!' he muttered. He supposed from the quality of her clothes that she was a gentlewoman, but to stride about dressed in such an odd fashion was to invite insult.

'What?'

Charles looked up from the counter where he stood with the shopkeeper in rapt attention at his side. The shopkeeper craned his head, watching the woman disappear from view.

'That's that Miss Lippett – Miss Josephine from up Grateley Moor. Gentleman Jo some call her.' The shop-keeper recalled the company. 'Not to her face, mind,' he added hurriedly. 'An old family.'

Charles was concentrating on his task. Three little heaps of gunpowder stood side by side on a piece of white paper.

'See now, if I fire this one and it takes readily ...' Charles struck a flint above the first pile.

'You've piled those too close,' Jarrett remarked.

The marquess ignored him and struck the flint again.

'If the composition is pure,' he continued, 'the smoke should rise upright and the powder burn without firing the other two heaps.'

The flint struck a spark. There was a sharp bang fol-lowed by another, a puff of black smoke and all three heaps burnt merrily. With remarkable alacrity for a man of his bulk, the shopkeeper sprang forward to smother the flames with his leather apron. Charles stood his ground.

'This is bad powder,' he declared, slightly loudly. 'I dare say the manufacturer has mixed common salt with the nitre. You must complain to your supplier, McKenzie. He is rogue to sell you such poor stock.'

'I told you, you piled the heaps too close,' Jarrett repeated, his attention caught by the sight of a familiar face on the street opposite.

His arrival in Woolbridge the year before had not been without incident. Isolated communities are inclined to be suspicious of strangers. For a time, some had cast Raif Jarrett as a murderer. That misunderstanding had been resolved but at his darkest hour a youth called Nat Broom had stolen his boots. Jarrett considered himself a tolerant man and his boots had been returned, but they were his favourites and he remembered the insult. And there was Nat Broom. He seemed to have improved his lot in life. His wiry, insignificant frame was dressed after the fashion of a respectable domestic. He was scurrying down the hill.

'I'm for the Queen's Head.' Jarrett made for the door. 'If you're determined to avoid the magistrates, Charles, don't show your face there before one.'

He pulled the shop-door closed behind him. Cripplegate Hill fell sharply down towards the river. The river itself was obscured by the jumble of warehouses and alleys that made up the working quarter of the town. At the foot of the hill the road divided, the one branch turning in a broad swathe between the gates of Bedford's Mill and the imposing frontage of Mr Bedford's home opposing it. The other branch turned towards the bridge over the river. Nat Broom approached the house.

A herd of cattle was crowding over the bridge harried by a couple of mastiffs. They were a highland breed, with rough reddish hides, wild eyed and snorting as their hooves slipped on the cobbles. Nat Broom did not mount the steps to the Bedfords' front door; instead he turned down Powcher's Lane. Through the movement, beyond the herd, Jarrett thought he glimpsed the man by the stable yard behind the house. The beasts obscured him a moment and then he was gone. A thoughtful look on his face, the agent turned back up the hill.

He was crossing the yard of the Queen's Head when he heard a familiar step behind him under the arched passage leading in from the street. As quick as a scalded cat, Jarrett ran lightly up the gallery steps. Colonel Ison came into view below. Jarrett froze. Ison was wearing his uniform again. His expression was preoccupied. Jarrett took a further stealthy step back up the stairs. The man hadn't seen him. Just a foot or two and ... The colonel looked up.

'Mr Jarrett!'

'Colonel,' the agent responded, descending to the yard at an easy pace.

'I heard Lord Charles was back in town,' the magistrate responded, looking hopefully beyond him. Jarrett couldn't resist following his gaze, turning around to search the stairs and gallery. They were perfectly empty.

'The marquess has asked me to present his apologies. He has been delayed on other business.'

A door opened. The colonel glanced up. Bess Tallentyre stepped into view on the gallery dressed in full battle order. She was followed by a small man with close-cropped hair and dark, expressive eyes.

'Ah, the man of business!' a voice boomed.

The newcomer's presence filled the archway from the street. He was a large man – not overly tall but broad-shouldered in a way that belied his gentleman's clothes.

He carried a drover's stick. The face beneath the sweeping brim of his hat combined the nose of a Greek statue with sensual lips and the heavy chin of a pugilist.

'Mr Jarrett!' The heavy staff swung out as the newcomer sketched a satirical bow. The mischievous gaze appeared to alight on the colonel as an afterthought. 'And the colonel too.'

The powers of Woolbridge faced one another across Mr Bedlington's yard. Colonel Ison was the gentry's magistrate; Mr Raistrick ruled over the rest.

'A word with you, Mr Raistrick,' the colonel snapped. Jarrett reflected – as he had before – that it was fortunate the two men detested one another. Woolbridge would be a dangerous place if ever those two found common cause.

'You'll have to wait,' Mr Raistrick responded blithely. 'I have an appointment.' He looked up at the pair standing on the gallery. 'Sugden, isn't it?'

This was appalling. It had not occurred to Jarrett that the 'big man' Bess had mentioned might have been Raistrick. As a solitary wanderer, free from the connected web of a settled existence, Jarrett had been used to keeping the sole record of the discrete parts that made up his life. It now dawned on him for the first time how the crowded nature of civilian society might shatter that discretion.

The little manager brushed past him, hurrying to greet the Justice. Bess floated down the stairs in his wake, her fingers caressing the wooden balustrade as she might her lover's skin. She paused for the space of a heartbeat by Jarrett's shoulder.

'Have a care, Bess,' he murmured. 'That magistrate is no rabbit.'

She slid him a side-glance from under heavy-lidded eyes. 'No?'

'Raistrick's more of a wolf.'

She paused on the step below, twisting her waist to lean in towards him. Her freckled breasts curved up enticingly above the lace of her bodice.

'Well now,' she breathed, 'it's been a time since I've played with one of *those*.'

They had the attention of the entire company. Mr Sugden watched them with a calculating gleam. Colonel Ison looked constipated. Magistrate Quentin Raistrick advanced, swinging out his staff. He looked up from the foot of the stairs. A crusted stain marked the front of his rich red brocade waistcoat.

'Introduce us, Mr Jarrett.'

'Miss Tallentyre, Mr Justice Raistrick,' Jarrett replied, as shortly as he could and continued by him into the yard.

Mr Quentin Raistrick, attorney-at-law and Justice of the Peace, swept off his hat. His eyes were a smoky grey defined by brown lashes. With sinuous grace Bess extended a hand across the space between them. He captured it in brown fingers and slowly turned the palm up. He pressed his mouth to the inside of her wrist where the white skin glowed through the gap above the fastening of her glove.

'Miss Tallentyre,' he purred.

His eyes fixed on her face in a manner that was at once both masterful and hungry. Her lips parted as if the air had grown thin.

Jarrett watched the colour flush Bess's cheeks. He could not believe what he saw unfolding before him. He had hardly been the duke's agent six months and here he was, confined in this backwater, watching the biggest rogue in the neighbourhood pressing his nose against his past. Colonel Ison was staring at the tableau, his pose of lofty detachment at variance with the avid curiosity in his eyes. Baffled by this unexpected convergence, Jarrett muttered an excuse and fled.

Voices resonated down the corridor leading to the magistrates' meeting room. The top note was angry and female. Occasionally the indistinct murmur of a male voice attempted a counterpoint. Framed in the open doorway, the Reverend Prattman, Woolbridge's most prominent cleric and third Justice of the Peace, sat besieged behind a broad table. His hands gripped its edge as if the oak were his defence and anchor. Before him paced the eccentric gentlewoman who fell by the tollbooth. She held her heavy broadcloth coat in her hands. She spun it out in a vast arc, clipping the tip of the nervous cleric's nose, causing him to start back so violently he almost overset his chair.

'See! See the filth!' she cried, indicating with a grand gesture the stained coat that now lay on the table between them. 'I was pushed into the gutter! I!' She leant over the table towards the shrinking Mr Prattman. 'I, a Lippett of Grateley, pushed into the gutter by a pair of mean vagabonds in broad daylight in the middle of the market!'

Mr Prattman looked upwards for his salvation and saw Mr Jarrett hesitating in the corridor.

'Mr Jarrett! Come in, come in,' he appealed. 'Miss Lippett has suffered a terrible outrage; she is most upset.'

Mr Jarrett winced. He had no wish to make the acquaintance of the absurd creature. Composing his most aloof expression, he stepped into the room.

The woman was dressed entirely in black serge, save for a small ruff of white lawn visible around the high neck of her gown. The curls that framed her face were wiry, reminding him of black lambs' wool. Back against one wall, he noticed the servant who had come to her aid by the tollbooth. He was observing the scene with an easy detachment, as if he had paid his ticket to some mildly entertaining play. Though not a vain man, Raif Jarrett was accustomed to meeting a certain softness in female eyes. There was none in those that regarded him now.

'I regret,' he said, 'I have not been introduced.'

As the words left his mouth he became conscious that there was yet another person in the room; a pair of familiar grey eyes flecked with green observed him with distinct reproof.

'Miss Lonsdale! I did not see you there.'

'Evidently, Mr Jarrett.'

Miss Henrietta Lonsdale was a lady of good family, the companion and stipulated heir of a wealthy aunt. Her borrowed status encased her in a confidence beyond the strict count of her years. They had made one another's acquaintance during the affair that had embroiled him on his arrival the previous year; she had proved an ally in his time of need. Although he never entirely felt he had Miss Henrietta's measure, he considered her a woman of distinction. He did not like her to think badly of him. She always dressed with taste, he reflected. Today she wore a sage green carriage dress of soft cord that set off her eyes. At present those eyes were making him uncomfortably aware that he was not behaving as a gentleman should.

'Miss Lippett,' Henrietta stepped forward. 'You will not have made the acquaintance of the Duke of Penrith's new agent. May I present him to you? Miss Josephine Lippett of Grateley Manor, Mr Raif Jarrett. The Lippetts of Grateley are one of our oldest families, Mr Jarrett.'

'We trace our ancestors back before the Conquest,' Miss Lippett declared.

Mr Jarrett made his bow.

'So this is the man, is it?' The creature looked him up and down. 'You're not a magistrate.' Out of the corner of his eye, Raif caught a flinch of brotherly feeling in her manservant's expression. He seemed oddly independent for a domestic.

'No, no dear lady,' said Mr Prattman hurriedly. 'Mr

Jarrett's opinion is much valued among us – indeed, he is come here today to attend our meeting at the colonel's invitation. Is that not so, sir? You are come for our meeting?'

Miss Lippett made an impatient gesture. A muslin handkerchief broke free from her cuff. It wafted down to rest at Mr Jarrett's feet. Mr Jarrett did what was demanded of a gentleman. He picked it up. It was curiously delicate for so mannish a creature. There was an emblem decorating one corner: blue cornflowers in a sheaf of corn executed in tiny, exquisite stitches. He returned it to Miss Lippett with a small bow. She sniffed.

Up to that point he had been debating whether or not he should confess that he himself had witnessed the incident in question. At that moment he decided discretion was the better part and he would not offer up this information. He disliked strident females. Miss Lippett had her servant's testimony, he told himself; there was no need for his involvement.

'Indeed Mr Prattman, I have come for the meeting,' he addressed the vicar. 'But I fear that Colonel Ison and Mr Raistrick have been delayed.'

A look of pure panic crossed the vicar's kindly, moonish face. 'And Sir Thomas too.' He fixed his fellow man with a pleading look. 'A terrible to-do. Miss Lippett was assaulted by a couple of ruffians, Mr Jarrett.'

'So I understand, sir.'

'Very distressing. In the open street. She is much upset.'

'Indeed, sir.'

Miss Lippett was impatient of such sentiment.

'I wish to make my complaint,' she declared.

'Of course, of course, dear lady; we need Pye, Mr Raistrick's clerk. Pye takes down the complaints.' Mr Prattman's gentle eyes beamed a silent appeal to Mr Jarrett. Instead, it was Miss Lonsdale who came to his relief.

'Miss Josephine, why do we not repair to a private parlour?' she suggested, her tone soothing yet firm. 'Mrs Bedlington may clean your coat for you and I am sure we both should benefit from refreshment. Mr Prattman may send us the clerk to take down your complaint.'

Miss Lippett's face softened. She linked arms with Henrietta and patted her hand.

'You are my friend and a gentlewoman, Miss Lonsdale. I shall go with you. Send Pye to me,' she instructed Mr Prattman with a curt nod. Henrietta Lonsdale piloted her charge out of the room. Jarrett watched them process down the corridor, the manservant following at a discreet distance.

'My man saw them,' Miss Lippett's voice drifted back. 'He saw the outrage.'

Jarrett pushed back his chair, stretching out his legs as Colonel Ison called the magistrates' meeting to order. Mr Prattman had recovered his composure since his encounter with Miss Lippett. He sat looking up at the colonel with pink cheeks, his rounded hands resting neatly on the table top. Frozen in an oasis of reverie, Sir Thomas of Oakdene Hall sat apart from the others, a little back from the table, both hands balanced on his gold-topped cane. Sir Thomas was the district's sole baronet, heir to an ancient line. Although his Catholic faith excluded him from appointment as Justice of the Peace, the Duke of Penrith and his son the marquess excepted, Sir Thomas was the acme of Woolbridge society. Sir Thomas seldom voiced any opinion and it was the colonel's habit to invite him to add the weight of his presence to the magistrates' deliberations.

'Mr Raistrick will be late,' announced Colonel Ison, giving the lawyer's clerk a stern look. 'It is inconvenient, Pye.'

The lawyer's clerk had a face so smooth it might have been fashioned from porcelain paste. He looked back at the colonel through dark almond-shaped eyes with an elfin detachment that might have been contempt. The colonel shuffled his papers.

'We will start without him.' The colonel paused impressively, his eyes travelling from face to face around the circle. 'Discretion is of the utmost importance, gentlemen. This must not be discussed outside this room. I have called us together to invite my fellow magistrates to enact the Watch and Ward.' Mr Prattman pulled a solemn face, expressing a little tutt. Colonel Ison half raised a warning hand. 'I am apprised that secret combinations are organizing in this very district,' he continued.

'But we lack Mr Raistrick and two more,' Jarrett interrupted. 'I understood the Act requires that *five* magistrates agree to enforce its provisions.' And lawyer Raistrick at the very least is hardly likely to agree to supply his rival with an armed troop, he told himself privately.

'I have here the signed agreements of Justices Kelso and Fife, our Richmond colleagues,' responded the colonel, patting a pocket, 'and as for Mr Raistrick, he is merely delayed!' he concluded with a confidence that gave Jarrett pause. His voice quickening dramatically, the magistrate resumed his theme. 'Combinations, gentlemen, and a preparation of hostile weapons! We are facing the winter of 1801 again. Who can forget that fatal hour? Then the troubles in Yorkshire were barely snatched up in time. The peace of this district lies in our hands, gentlemen. We must have the courage to take the necessary measures.'

'Secret combinations in the *Dale*, sir?' Jarrett interjected, braving the colonel's scowl. 'To what purpose?'

'For ill-purpose, Mr Jarrett! You may scoff but I cannot be so easy when I hear what I have learnt of late.'

'Pray tell.'

Colonel Ison looked at him full face. A shutter fell at the back of his eyes.

'I'm not alone in my suspicions, Mr Jarrett,' he blustered. 'I have official reports—'

'Official reports?' repeated Jarrett. The colonel's

temper, it seemed, had betrayed him into saying more than he had intended.

'May I remind you, Mr Jarrett, that you are invited here as an observer.'

'Of course, sir, but I am also his Grace's representative and his Grace, the Duke of Penrith, has concerns as to what might justify the imposition of a troop of regulars on this neighbourhood.' That was a lie, but a white one. Neither Jarrett nor Lord Charles had had any communication with the duke in weeks. However, Raif knew his patron well enough to anticipate his response. His Grace would tilt his head in that charming fashion he had and tell him in a rueful tone to do whatever he thought best.

Colonel Ison resolutely ignored him.

'Gentlemen,' he pronounced impressively, 'I am here to inform you all that disorder threatens. My information is endorsed by the highest authorities. As Chairman of the Bench I tell you that this information must and will be acted upon. The Home Secretary himself has been apprised.'

Mr Prattman sat up with a sharp intake of breath. Colonel Ison bestowed an approving glance upon him.

'Indeed,' he said.

Urgent knuckles rapped the door. It opened to admit the disembodied head of Jasper Bedlington. A tuft of the soft fringe of hair encircling the innkeeper's bald pate stood up, giving him a harassed air. Distant sounds of raised voices filtered into the magistrates' chamber.

'I beg pardon, colonel,' he said, 'if you'd be so kind.

There's a small misunderstanding below. Lord Charles –
the Marquess of Earewith – he sends his compliments
and requests that you and Mr Jarrett might join him
down in the courtyard.'

CHAPTER SIX

An audience had gathered along the gallery. A trio of players from Mr Sugden's troupe stood half dressed, as if just emerged from their beds, exchanging witticisms as they shared a loaf of bread. Jack, the Bedlingtons' young son, hung out over space stretching to gain the best possible view of the action. Down below in the yard stood an officer in a hussar's blue jacket trimmed with silver. He held a slight figure in an undignified arm lock while Lord Earewith looked on, holding a red-tasselled shako under one arm.

The commotion had drawn the ladies out of their ground-floor parlour. Jarrett's attention was caught by the line of Miss Lonsdale's neat figure, delineated by the mustard-yellow shawl of fine wool that draped in fluid folds down her back. Miss Lippett's servant stood by the door, his face turned upwards to the gallery, an expression of frank admiration on his face. Miss Lonsdale caught the look and searched out its object. Justice Raistrick had appeared on the opposite side of the gallery with Bess Tallentyre on his arm, the little manager Sugden bobbing in their wake. The actress showed every sign of being delighted with her escort. When his gaze rested frankly on her bare neckline, she smiled coyly at him. She detached herself with a graceful side-step and took up an attitude by the balustrade. Her bold eyes found Jarrett's and she winked. He took an involuntary step back into the shadow of the wall.

Henrietta Lonsdale was well acquainted with Lord Earewith. She was curious as to his connection to the young man being detained by the lieutenant. She had the distinct impression that the youth had taunted the lieutenant and she was near-certain she had observed him tread on the officer's boot. She was impatient of such behaviour. Lord Earewith was a charming young man but he was not going to stop this by dancing around the pair so ineffectually. She took a brisk step forward.

'I repeat, unhand my cousin!' The marquess's crisp elocution carried up to the gallery. 'Raif!' he called out. 'Come talk sense into this damned Achilles. I beg your pardon, ma'am. Miss Lonsdale, I did not see you there.'

'Lieutenant! What is the meaning of this?' Colonel Ison's martial roar resounded as he thundered down the gallery steps with the duke's agent a close second.

In profile Jarrett observed Miss Lonsdale drop back in a fine counterfeit of maidenly modesty. Her lips were pleasantly red in the chill air.

The lieutenant released Favian abruptly. He turned to the colonel, snapping into a salute.

'Lieutenant Roberts, colonel sir!' His hand went to his jacket and then stilled. 'Beg pardon, colonel; orders are in my saddlebag.'

Lieutenant Roberts was the sort of young hero frequently described as a 'pretty fellow'. He was of taller than average height. His nose was straight. An ill-natured person might point out that his eyes lay a mite close to one another but his figure was good. Grey mud clung to the knees of his white breeches and stained the tasselled ends of his scarlet sash.

'What's this? What's this sir?' the colonel barked. 'Have you been wrestling in a ditch?'

Favian's clothes too were scuffed but his expression was animated. He seemed almost elated. Jarrett's eyes narrowed in speculation.

'Perhaps Mr Adley could give us his account of what has occurred,' he suggested dryly.

'Cousin Raif! How good it is to see you again!' The young man's face lit up with touching affection. Miss Lonsdale's eyes travelled back and forth between the youth Lord Charles had just claimed as kin and the man the boy called cousin Raif, her brain a web of speculation.

'And you,' replied Jarrett with the flash of a warm smile that was so brief and sudden that a moment later Miss Lonsdale wondered if she had imagined it. 'Can you explain this?'

'I've just arrived in town,' Favian responded dutifully. 'I lost my way. There's a wide street down by the river?

There was a group of people gathered there listening to this fellow singing. He was most tuneful and as I have a particular interest in folk song . . .'

Jarrett gave him a hard look. Favian paused, his hazel eyes guileless.

'Well, up comes the lieutenant,' he continued. 'He pushes through the crowd and sets in after the fellow. The singer, he took to his heels – well, I think that's what happened; it was hard to see. I was jostled in the crowd. I was standing by the mouth of an alley. Up comes the lieutenant and somehow we get into a tangle and down we fall in a heap. I was crushed under him – he's a fair weight I can tell you.'

'You little wretch! You tripped me!' exclaimed the lieutenant with heat.

'I did not,' Favian stated calmly. 'You knocked me down.'

'Colonel, I must protest. This – this *boy* – interfered with my pursuit. The song was seditious. The singer had a knapsack; I am certain he was distributing bills.'

'Let me see them,' demanded Ison. The lieutenant blinked.

'I had my hand on one, sir, but I dropped it when this boy tripped me . . . I couldn't find it afterwards. The crowd had scattered. Perhaps he stole it.' He took a step towards young Adley as if he were in a mind to search him. The youth pulled his shoulders back.

'I did not trip you,' he repeated, the picture of injured innocence.

'Could you identify this singer, lieutenant?' intervened Jarrett.

'There is little hope of that.' Roberts was aggrieved. 'He was wound up in a muffler.' Jarrett watched the boy's face, noting that his breath was laboured as if his chest was tight. Charles threaded a hand under his young cousin's elbow. Favian's chin went up.

'Mr Adley,' the agent asked, 'did you get a clear view of this man the lieutenant was pursuing?'

'Not so as I could recognize him again.' He spoke loudly. 'It all happened too fast. Could have been a woman for all I saw.'

'Don't be ridiculous!' snapped Lieutenant Roberts, scowling like a child.

'An unfortunate mistake – don't you agree, Colonel Ison?' Lord Charles appealed to the magistrate, his smile at once both intimate and bashful as if they two alone shared an understanding. The bluster drained from the colonel. He simpered. Charles proffered the shako he held to Roberts.

'Yours, I believe. I am sure that your energy and zeal are a notable acquisition to the forces of law and order, lieutenant.'

'This is the Marquess of Earewith, lieutenant! Heir to his Grace, the Duke of Penrith,' Colonel Ison declared. 'If Mr Adley is his cousin there must be some mistake. Apologies, Lord Charles, apologies. I hope the boy is none the worse for wear?'

'The "boy", colonel, is—' Favian began heatedly. Jarrett

slipped his hand under the opposite arm to that held by Charles, confining him between them.

'Enough, Grub!' he murmured. 'I am sure that Mr Adley regrets any misunderstanding, Lieutenant Roberts,' he continued firmly. Mr Jarrett stretched out his hand. 'A poor welcome to Woolbridge, I fear. Frederick Jarrett, agent to his Grace. I have made the arrangements to billet your men down on the river. Do they meet you here?'

The lieutenant returned his grip with the bewildered look of a man out of his depth.

'They are halted to the north.'

'Let me know when you wish to be shown your barracks.'

'First the lieutenant and I have matters to discuss,' said Colonel Ison, darting a curious look between Jarrett and the marquess. He waved Roberts aside. 'You will excuse us, gentlemen.'

'Grub! What have you been doing?' hissed the marquess, as he steered Favian away. 'Must say,' he interjected, looking the boy up and down, 'you've grown.'

'Delighted to see you too, cousin Charles.'

'How did you give Tiplady the slip?' Charles demanded. 'He was to meet you at Greta Bridge just past noon.'

'The coach arrived an age ago. I made my own way.'

Jarrett followed them, contemplating his dilemma. They were advancing towards that part of the yard where Miss Lonsdale stood with her friend. The ladies were monitoring their approach with frank curiosity. It was not every day that a new relation of the duke's appeared in the neighbourhood. He wondered what the company thought of Grub's greeting him as cousin. That was bad enough, but at the edge of his vision he was aware of Bess Tallentyre craning over the gallery rail adjusting a tendril of her springy copper hair. Given his earlier feelings it was ironic how he now prayed that Raistrick found further reason to detain her.

'I think we should introduce Grub to Miss Lonsdale, don't you Raif?' Charles had recovered his habitual poise. 'She is one of the most charming ladies in the neighbourhood, Grub.'

To reach the ladies they must pass the gallery steps. Jarrett fought the desire to slip away down the archway to the street. He sensed movement above. He was on stage in a farce without an exit line.

A curse on small towns! A gentleman of his experience was bound to enjoy variety in his female acquaintance but that variety was not supposed to meet. Like the wrong colours laid side by side, Miss Lonsdale's gentility was compromised by Bess's presence while the gentlewoman's proximity tarnished the actress's charms.

Bess glided down the gallery steps to his right. She leant over the rail, sweeping her expressive eyes up to Raistrick who observed them from above. 'Your wolf can bite my arse anytime,' she said.

Jarrett winced. Charles was introducing his cousin to Miss Lonsdale.

'That one has an interest in you, lover,' commented Bess. She looked Miss Lonsdale up and down. 'Stiff and starch – though a pretty enough figure. She should smile more.'

'That's no business of yours, Bess.'

Charles was inviting the ladies to accompany him into the inn. Miss Henrietta consulted her companion. Miss Lippett was determined to press her case. She indicated the gallery where Mr Raistrick stood conversing with the vicar and Sir Thomas. Framed in the doorway to the tap, Charles performed a comical shrug for Raif's benefit, pulling a face in Miss Lippett's direction. The eccentric gentlewoman was in full flood once more. With a pair of matched bows, Charles and Favian disappeared into the inn leaving Jarrett marooned.

Henrietta scarcely heard her friend's diatribe. She had a liking for originals and little qualm about the spinster's public eccentricities but her mind was preoccupied. Miss Lonsdale was a self-assured woman. She had had the running of her aunt's not inconsiderable estate for some years and she had long since passed the first blush of youth. She was not, however, unconscious of the demands of reputation – that most fragile and valuable of qualities for a female lacking great personal wealth or the protection of a forgiving husband. She was not certain that she could risk being seen in public conversation with an actress. And yet, her curiosity was overwhelming.

She took advantage of a dramatic pause in Miss Lippett's impassioned monologue.

'I should like a word with Mr Jarrett. Will you walk with me, Miss Josephine?'

'But he is talking to that creature!' cried Miss Lippett, affronted.

'That creature, Miss Josephine?'

'That player! Rogues and vagabonds by the letter of the law alone – and I dare say a deal worse that may not be spoken by a lady of breeding! You cannot mean to speak to that man now!'

Miss Lippett's vehemence made up Miss Lonsdale's mind. She disliked being told what she might or might not do.

'Let it never be said that I compromise my friends!' she said lightly. 'I shall risk my reputation alone.'

'I shall keep you in sight!' Miss Josephine hissed after her in a carrying tone.

She felt rather exposed as she crossed the few yards to Mr Jarrett. She wished that Lord Charles had not gone in. Mr Jarrett had his back turned to her and she was forced to the subterfuge of a small cough to catch his attention.

The actress had very bold hair. It was unruly, curling every which way. Henrietta resisted the impulse to touch her own smoothly confined tresses. Perhaps that was what men liked. Mr Jarrett certainly seemed to approve. In height, Miss Tallentyre was shorter than Miss Lonsdale, and yet the actress contrived somehow to look down on the gentlewoman with a knowing air Henrietta did not like. She straightened her spine.

'Miss Tallentyre of Mr Sugden's troupe? I am Miss Lonsdale.'

Henrietta inclined her head in gracious acknowledgement as the actress sank into an over-elaborate curtsey.

'Players so seldom come to Woolbridge, Miss Tallentyre, we are looking forward to the treat. What do you offer us?'

'*Love in a Village* perhaps, ma'am, followed by *The Way to Keep Him*,' responded the actress pertly. 'To open the fairs, Magistrate Raistrick has bespoke *The Beggar's Opera*.'

'*The Beggar's Opera*! Fancy! And is there a speaking part in it for you?'

'I am Polly Peachum!' exclaimed Bess, stung.

'And does the role please you?'

'I am much applauded in it, ma'am. Although a good Macheath is hard to find. Now this one,' the actress insinuated a hand under the agent's arm, 'he would make a thrilling Macheath, don't you agree?'

'Indeed?' Miss Lonsdale's fine eyes flashed the gentleman in question a fierce look. He was standing quite still with a distant air. She noted that he did not remove the hussy's hand.

'You must have heard him sing?' Bess trilled. 'Why just this morning—'

Mr Jarrett slid his arm free and took a small side step. 'I believe Mr Raistrick wishes to speak to you, Miss Tallentyre,' he said, speaking low. Mr Raistrick was indeed descending the stairs to join them.

Miss Lonsdale was mortified. She had a profound dislike of Mr Raistrick; she thought him a rogue and a bad man. And that hussy had her eyes fixed on him as if he were a fish she was reeling in on her line. Henrietta did not know if she was more furious with herself or with Mr Jarrett: she who had allowed a foolish impulse to betray her into joining such company or the so-called gentleman at her side who betrayed no sign of appreciating the difficulties of her situation. Or perhaps his wooden countenance was an attempt to disguise his disgust at her unladylike inquisitiveness. Tears of frustration pricked Miss Lonsdale's eyes. Pressing her lips together she braced herself for her humiliation.

Bess was throwing out her hip. He could almost see her puffing up her breasts. Of course, that damned lawyer was enjoying the view. What had possessed Miss Lonsdale to join them? Jarrett risked a side glance at the lady. She was in profile to him. The tender curve of a white earlobe peeped out from beneath the smooth wing of her hair, unadorned and pure against the soft skin of her neck. He bent his head.

Henrietta felt the warmth on her cheek. The agent's low-pitched voice vibrated the tendrils of hair that skimmed her ear.

'I believe Miss Lippett waits to speak to you, Miss Henrietta. May I escort you to her?'

His arm was steady under hers. Miss Josephine's expression was a caricature of despairing outrage as she watched them approach. Henrietta suppressed a hiccup of hysterical laughter. She had not thought that the space in the yard was so great.

'You are previously acquainted with Miss Tallentyre,

Mr Jarrett?' The question startled her; she had not meant to speak it aloud.

'I have seen her perform before, Miss Lonsdale,' he replied. Miss Lonsdale glanced back over her shoulder at the vignette of the magistrate and the actress.

'It seems that Miss Tallentyre has won another convert to her *performance*, Mr Jarrett.'

They had reached their goal. Miss Lippett stood tethered to her space as if it had some magical protective properties. She reached out to slip an arm about Henrietta's shoulders and drew her close, throwing the agent a furious look. Jarrett experienced a flash of annoyance. His eyes travelled to the door behind them: the door that led to male company and ease. Damn Charles for abandoning him!

As if his mental summons had been heard, the door swung open to reveal Lord Charles.

'Ladies, you should come in and warm yourselves. I have found the lawyer's clerk for you, Miss Lippett. He is waiting within. Mrs Bedlington has tea made fresh. Will you come?'

'With the greatest pleasure, my lord,' Miss Lonsdale replied with aplomb. The ladies swept past Mr Jarrett with barely a nod and were gone. Charles reappeared a moment later. He shut the door behind him.

'Raif, you have such interesting acquaintances,' he remarked.

Raistrick stood at ease, one arm resting on the balustrade as he towered over Bess Tallentyre. Jarrett watched as the actress threw back her head, showing off the line of her throat in her merriment. Bess had always had a taste for dangerous men. But she was no fool, he consoled himself, and loyal – or had been once.

'Can't say I'd want one of my liaisons consorting with that fellow. Unlucky, eh?' Charles was enjoying this entirely too much.

'Grub?' Jarrett enquired.

'Tea with the ladies.'

'Ah.'

Above on the gallery the Reverend Prattman was addressing Sir Thomas in hushed and urgent tones. They were too far away to catch his words. From the pantomime he appeared to be expressing his concern for the baronet's health in the chill air. Sir Thomas endured these attentions with the air of a stoical tortoise. Down below, Colonel Ison stood across by the stables, his back to them, elaborating his discourse with the occasional gesture. Lieutenant Roberts listened, his expression intent.

'Will the meeting reconvene, do you suppose?' Charles asked idly.

Jarrett's response was interrupted by a clatter of iron-bound wheels and hooves. A gig turned under the coach arch. A well-fed middle-aged woman encased in lilac satin sat up beside a grizzled old man who slumped over his reins. His mistress wore an extravagant hat fixed at an uncomfortable angle on her carefully pinned blond curls. Round, pale blue eyes swept the scene, coming to rest on Magistrate Raistrick. The pale blue turned to ice as they inspected his companion.

Raistrick unfolded himself from his lounge against the gallery steps and sauntered over to the gig.

'What, Amelia, no carriage?' he asked without preamble.

The lady bunched her plump cheeks into a little-girl moue. 'Bedford's abandoned me,' she responded in a flirtatious voice pitched a shade too high for a woman of her years. 'He's taken the carriage to Leeds and left me to shift for myself. He's fetching his niece for a visit,' she added as an afterthought.

'How charitable of you.'

Mrs Bedford cocked her head, her expression blank. How could she miss the irony in that voice? thought Jarrett. The lady produced a stack of white cards from the seat beside her.

'I bear invitations,' she declared gaily. 'I am having a select reception Thursday night to mark the opening of the fairs. Do say you'll come.' She leant towards the lawyer proffering a card, the action offering him a generous *coup d'oeil* of her ample bosom. Raistrick took the card, dangling it between finger and thumb.

'What a shame,' he purred. 'I am sponsoring a performance from Sugden's players that very night. The delightful Miss Tallentyre over there is to give us her Polly Peachum in *The Beggar's Opera*.' Mrs Bedford's mouth dropped open; she closed it with a snap. Raistrick looked deliberately across at the actress who stood preening herself by the gallery steps. 'Shall I introduce you?'

For a moment Jarrett thought Mrs Bedford would respond to the unmistakable challenge but she displayed impressive self-control. A smile extended itself from her mouth, stopping just short of her eyes.

'What a calamity!' she exclaimed. 'And what time does this *affair* start?'

'Eight, I believe.'

'Well, that's settled then!' The lady patted her gloved hands together in a parody of girlish exuberance. 'You shall all come to me for your dessert and wine at six and we shall go as a party to your entertainment. Now, say you will come!'

Raistrick bowed his assent. Jarrett thought he detected in his manner a measure of appreciation at Mrs Bedford's management. The lady extended her hand in a regal gesture. The lawyer, taking his cue, helped her down. Keeping his arm extended, he swung her round in an arc and let her go as if unleashing her upon the company. Whether by chance or design Mrs Bedford fetched up before Miss Tallentyre. The actress contemplated her, a gloss of impertinent amusement on her pale face. Mrs Bedford spun on her heel and swooped down upon the marquess.

'Lord Charles!' she trilled, 'and Mr Jarrett,' she added with a degree less warmth. 'You will come to my party? Say you will?'

'You are kindness itself, madam, but I have a young

cousin just arrived and I fear—' Charles began by way of excuse. Mrs Bedford would have none of it.

'What a treat!' she cried. 'You must bring him. You'll not find better fare. I'm known for my sweets and Bedford never skimps on his wines. And we'll all go on together to Mr Raistrick's theatricals.' She swept gaily on towards the colonel. Her eyes appeared to alight on the young lieutenant for the first time. She advanced upon him with a tigerish look.

'Is this our young defender? You must introduce me, colonel. You will come to my gathering – will you not? You know I'll be mortified if you neglect me!'

'Time we called the carriage,' murmured Charles.

'Grub will be exhausted,' Jarrett agreed.

'Should see him home.'

'Absolutely.'

They made their escape into the inn.

Several minutes later, as they took their places in Lord Charles's carriage, Mrs Bedford still had the colonel and his lieutenant pinned. The carriage swung out into the street. Jarrett caught sight of a new figure in the background of the scene. A man was gazing at the colonel as if waiting to catch his attention. At the last moment, as the carriage passed, Nat Broom turned his face away into the shadows.

Favian settled back against the comfortably cushioned upholstery and gazed happily at his cousins. He fingered the ballad sheet secured safe in the pocket of his coat. He thought of his day's adventures and hugged to himself the promise that there were more and better to come.

Her view of the gentlemen was obscured by the table top. It was confined to four legs, clothed in dark cloth breeches and black stockings, and two pairs of smooth polished leather shoes with silvery buckles – one pair square and sharp, the other rounded and rubbed. The strangers had arrived that afternoon on the stage from Carlisle. They had taken separate rooms. Such details Hester Teward, the daughter of innkeepers, had noted, but her real interest lay in the paper bag protruding from the rounder gentleman's pocket. Being five years old she was of the perfect height to notice such things. Her eyes followed the fingers as they reached in to draw out another piece of cinder toffee from the striped paper. The elegance of the wrapping identified the sweets as Hester's particular favourites – the treat her da would bring her back when he attended the monthly market at Penrith. During the winter months the road across the tops from Bowes was frequently impassable and she had not tasted such sweets for ever so long.

There was a knock on the door and her mother entered.

'There's men asking for you, Mr George. Say they're expected. Hester, you come out from under there! Stop bothering the gentlemen.'

Her mother's hands reached under the table and Hester was unceremoniously swept up into her arms. The sudden change of perspective on the room and its occupants was entertaining. She looked down on the gentleman with the toffee. He had round cheeks and a bald patch at the back of his head. His hair was cut short and reminded her of the fur of Tuffy, her dog – the thick curling fur on his chest. The gentleman's eyes crinkled into slits as he smiled up at her. Hester did not like his companion. He was stringy with hard edges. He had the mean look of a man who did not favour children. As her mother carried her out of the room the first man spoke up.

'Perhaps the little girl would care for some toffee?'

He did not speak like folk Hester knew, but she understood the offer. She reached down and selected the largest piece in the bag with care. It was solid and sticky in her chubby fist. She sucked on it happily.

'Thank the kind gentleman,' her mother's voice insisted.

But the sweetness in her mouth was too good to remove so Hester smiled around it and giggled at her new friend over her mother's shoulder, her curls bouncing about her radiant face.

CHAPTER SEVEN

He never slept for long. It was a habit formed during his military service. Behind enemy lines a man who slept too deep risked being captured or killed. Despite the removal of that imperative, in civilian life the habit remained. He relished the peace of the small hours when the world slept. In the chill half-light he could be himself – self-sufficient, self-possessed.

The stable clock chimed four as he put down the sword he carried and hung the lantern on a convenient hook. Walcheren, his big-boned bay, poked his head over his stall to greet him with a soft whinny. Jarrett ran a hand over the animal's sleek neck. Walcheren's breath misted white from his flared nostrils. Outside there was heavy frost on the ground and stars stood out against a clear sky. The shifting lantern light illuminated a straw-stuffed target suspended from a hook. It was crossed with lines marking out seven segments. A black line of tar ran across the floor from a spot midway beneath the bottom of the target. He picked up his sword. Placing his feet either side of the line, he began the familiar ritual.

It was soothing. He focused on the exercise of muscle and will required to fuse the sword into an extension of his arm. First position, second position, lunge. He moved smoothly, striking the shifting dummy across each segment, body upright, balance correct, his aim true.

It was pure luxury to be alone. Of all the adjustments of civilian life, it was the unrelenting assault of inquisitive society he found the most difficult. Military life might be boring and dangerous by turn but it had a map, a uniformity that allowed self-containment. He had always considered himself a competent man. It was unsettling to discover existence in a provincial town more challenging than life-threatening exertion and the exercise of set tasks.

The stars were fading as he finished. He sluiced off the sweat at the stable-yard pump, the freezing water numbing his skin. Rubbing himself dry with a towel he kept for the purpose, he pulled on a clean shirt. In a few minutes the servants would be waking. Walcheren stamped restlessly in his stall.

They took the western road up into the hills. Dawn had not yet broken. The sounds they made in their progress – hooves striking the hard ground, the creak of leather, the huff of Walcheren's breath – were intimate within the wider stillness. As the track climbed the hoar frost deepened and the moor opened out on either side. This was land pared down to its primitive bones. The pre-dawn light reflected off the white crystals sharpening each shadow. It was as if he and his horse were lone intruders in an ancient enchanted land, a land that might flick them off into oblivion with a shiver of its crust.

The Carlisle road ran straight into the blank luminescent sky. He caught movement in the blurred band of greys and purple at the horizon. A shape broke away: a tiny cart growing in size. Before long he could hear the small sounds of its approach. Jarrett's sharp eyes picked out a single horse and an open cart driven by a mound of cloth surmounted by a hat. A man's voice carried crystal clear across the expanse.

'Step up, Larkin. Go-awn!'

The cart was drawn by a well-fleshed grey mare that picked its way fastidiously over the icy track. As Walcheren trotted up the mound of clothes spoke.

'Mr Jarrett!'

The driver tipped back his hat and drew down his scarf to reveal a man of thirty or so. Jarrett recognized the even features of the landlord of the Bucket and Broom, an inn he patronized further up the road.

'Bless us!' the man exclaimed, 'I'm that glad to see you!'

'Mr Teward! What brings you out so early?' Jarrett responded to this unexpectedly fervent greeting.

'Bad luck, Mr Jarrett, that's what. One of me guests, he's only gone and passed in the night. Found him in his bed barely an hour since, tucked up and cold as stone.

Meg tells me – fetch the magistrate!' He expelled the sigh of a burdened man. 'Need to do these things right.'

'Was this an old man? Did he seem in poor health?'

Mr Teward shook his head – so far as the bulk of his coats allowed.

'Couple of years older than you or me but not what I'd call an *old* man. Mr George, him that's travelling with him, or was, he tells us Mr Pritchard had a troublesome gut. But I had no suspicion.'

'Strangers, are they?'

Mr Teward nodded, distracted.

'Travelled up from Brough a day back. What luck!' He paused, shuffling the reins between his hands as if gathering up his thoughts. 'Mr Jarrett, you'd not be so kind as to call in?' he asked in a rush. 'I don't like to ask, but just while I'm fetching the magistrate? Ruth, Meg's sister that lives with us, she's off on a visit and our man Simon, he's been called out; his gran's had a turn and he'll not be back a while. So Meg's got naught but a silly maid and the bairn in the house. I left the maid all to pieces,' he elaborated gloomily. 'Say the truth, I'm not easy leaving the three of them with a stranger and a corpse.'

'Of course!' Jarrett assured him. He hoped he didn't sound too enthusiastic. He had already made up his mind to stop by. His curiosity was piqued. 'I shall do so directly. I can have a look at the man and talk to his companion . . .' he suggested, hoping the innkeeper would not think him officious.

Mr Teward was more than happy to cede another man authority. His face blossomed with relief.

'I am beholden to you, Mr Jarrett.' Adjusting his scarves and hat Mr Teward disappeared once more behind his swathes of cloth. 'I'll be back as soon as I can.' He slapped his reins on the grey mare's broad haunches and the cart rolled on towards Woolbridge.

The room was cold. The fire in the small grate had burnt down to embers. The furnishings were simple – a window on one wall, a large press against another. A leather travel bag stood parallel to a chair with a man's clothes folded over it and, beneath, a pathetic pair of rubbed shoes with rounded silver buckles. The board floor was dominated by a country-made four-poster bed with heavy curtains drawn around it.

'He's in there,' she said, her eyes fixed on the bed.

Mrs Teward lingered by the open door. She was a little blonde woman with delicate blue veins visible under her translucent skin. Her small features were pinched with anxiety.

'We left him as we found him. I was bringing the shaving water and I could get no answer. I fetched Dan and he took a look and . . .' She shivered. 'He's just lying there with his hands on his chest as if ready laid out. Who sleeps like that?' She swallowed nervously and began again. 'It's my sister Ruth's room by rights but the gentlemen they wanted separate accommodations and we were expecting another party.' She trailed off. 'I'm right glad to see you, Mr Jarrett,' she murmured in an unconscious echo of her husband.

She turned up her face and he smiled down at her, his mouth twisted in a wry expression of sympathy.

'Very difficult for you.'

She returned a wan smile. In different circumstances she was a pretty woman. She shifted her weight.

'Mr George's downstairs having his breakfast. I'd better . . .' She hesitated. 'The maid's not to be relied upon. Not this morning.'

'Of course,' he responded.

He shut the door behind her and approached the bed. His hand poised to draw back the curtain, he was visited by the absurd idea that Mr Pritchard lay in wait on the other side preparing to leap out at him in the manner of a jack-in-the-box. He pulled the heavy fabric back.

Mr Pritchard lay on his back, the bedclothes pulled smooth across his body. The waxy mask betrayed no signs of struggle. As Mrs Teward had remarked, the man looked as if he had been laid out – straight on his back, hands folded across his chest. Jarrett attempted to lift a finger; the hand and arm moved, locked rigid with it. With a silent apology to the soul here departed, Jarrett heaved up the body. The upper torso was stiff but the legs still had some give in them. He displaced the nightshirt sufficiently to glimpse the skin on the back. There were dark purple stains where blood had sunk. The pattern was as might be expected if Mr Pritchard had died peacefully in that position.

He stared down at the bed. There were two pillows. Only one lay under the man's head. There was nothing unusual in that. Why should a man not prefer to sleep with one pillow rather than two? The second pillow had been neatly placed along the footboard precisely at the mid-point of the bed. Mr Pritchard had been a tall man. The pillow touched his feet. Any movement in his sleep would have displaced it.

'That's not where I would have put it,' Jarrett remarked to himself.

He pictured Mrs Teward straightening the pillow. So much for leaving Mr Pritchard as they found him.

The Bucket and Broom was an old house. It had been built to withstand the harsh winds and weather that swept across the tops. Its walls were a good two feet thick. The leaded window attracted his attention. It had a deep sill and that sill was wet. He lifted the latch. The window swung open easily with barely a sound. There was water pooled in the grooved metal of the frame. He looked down. The ground was not too far below. He leant out as far as was prudent, scanning the rough stone of the outer wall. There were windows to either side, the one to the left shuttered, the one to the right unshuttered. The sun coming up behind the house threw a shadow over the foot of the wall below. He closed the window. He examined the boards beneath, running his palm across the surface.

'It is winter,' he reminded himself. 'There's damp in the air but still . . .'

He walked to the door, pausing to straighten the covers he had disrupted. Mr Pritchard's frozen features seemed faintly derisive.

'Of course, I could be imagining things,' Jarrett remarked, 'but I wonder.'

Down below the hall was quiet and the doors were all shut. He heard voices down the passage. A dog yapped and a child laughed. He slipped out of a side door.

The rising sun bathed the moor in buffs and pinks. The inn was of regular, square construction with stables and outbuildings to one side. He took a path around the opposite side of the house towards the moor view he had seen from the room above. He walked slowly, his eyes to the ground. The earth was stony and dry. The frost was beginning to melt close to the house but in the dusting of white he could pick out a man's foot-prints and the paw-prints of maybe three dogs – two fanning out and one faithfully trotting at its master's heels. He identified the three upper windows – the one on the end shuttered, Mr Pritchard's window in the middle and its neighbour to the left with the shutters folded back. Beneath the first unshuttered window he thought he discerned a stray print from another footstep. It was turned in to face the wall, as if a man had stood beneath the window – but with the hoar frost dissolving he could not be sure. Beneath Mr Pritchard's window some animal had dug. At the edge of the soft pile of earth he found a distinct round hole some four inches deep, as if a straight, stout stick had been poked in hard at an angle and then pulled out. He crouched down to take a closer look.

A ground-floor window opened above his head. A chubby hand and a brown velvet sleeve were followed by the round-cheeked face of a man with full red lips and gravy on his chin. Jarrett straightened up, quickly putting his hand in his pocket.

'Dropped it taking out my handkerchief,' he said with an easy smile. 'Careless of me but no harm done. Mr George, I presume?' he enquired. 'Frederick Jarrett. Agent to the Duke of Penrith. I met Mr Teward on the road and he asked me to call by. I was hoping to have a word.'

Mr George wiped his chin with a large linen napkin. He rocked formally from the waist, his expression both conciliatory and solemn.

'Is that so? A sad, sad affair. I am breakfasting in the parlour; do come join me.'

'Such a sad business,' Mr George repeated, waving Jarrett to the table. 'Poor Pritchard. Have you breakfasted?'

The tragedy, it seemed, had not affected Mr George's appetite. A solitary slice of beef lay in a smudge of gravy on a blue and white platter, a napkin-lined basket was empty but for crumbs, and egg shells littered the cloth around his plate. Mr George picked up the coffee pot and gazed at it uncertainly.

'This coffee, I regret, is cold,' he said. 'Shall I ring for the landlady?' Without waiting for a response he picked up the little brass bell by his plate and rang it vigorously.

For good measure he opened the door and called out. 'Mrs Teward!'

A voice responded from down the passage.

'Coffee for Mr Jarrett, if you'd be so kind.' Mr George closed the door. 'Such an obliging woman,' he remarked jovially. He returned to his seat. Pushing back his plate, he brushed away a scatter of crumbs with the back of one plump hand.

'Mr Jarrett, you say? Agent to the Duke of Penrith? And Mr Teward sent you?' Mr George's forehead creased in a puzzled frown. 'You are a magistrate perhaps?' he suggested.

'No. But I am responsible for the duke's properties in these parts,' Jarrett replied, content to imply that Mr Teward might be a tenant of his Grace.

Mr George's lips formed a question but at that moment the maid, a clumsy girl with reddened eyes, came into the room. She struggled with a tray that was almost overbalanced by a large milk jug decorated with hunting scenes in pastel pinks and blues. As she approached the table, it tilted. Mr George rescued the jug neatly. With a startled look the maid abandoned her burden and fled.

'Ah! These country inns!' Mr George remarked cheerfully. He poured coffee into a fresh cup. 'Milk?' he asked, and poured before his guest could protest. Jarrett normally took his coffee black.

'You arrived with your colleague from Brough yesterday, I understand.' Jarrett accepted the proffered cup.

111

'The afternoon before. This is – was to be,' Mr George corrected himself, 'our second day.'

There was a folder on the table embossed with a gilded badge. A sheaf of papers peeped out. The uppermost leaf was a neatly executed list with figures attached.

'You are come to Woolbridge for the fairs, sir?' Jarrett asked. Mr George stilled.

'Filling an army contract perhaps? Wool cloth?' Jarrett suggested.

Mr George gazed at him, his head cocked to one side, his eyes as blank as a bird's. Jarrett nodded towards the folder.

'I recognize a procurement docket,' he explained. '16th Lancers – Portugal – until last year.'

'Ah! One of Wellington's men!' cried Mr George, suddenly good humoured again. 'Lieutenant?'

'Captain.'

'Beg pardon.' Mr George acknowledged his mistake. 'We prefer not to advertise our presence too widely. These are profitable contracts.' He bunched up his round cheeks in an apologetic grimace. 'Don't want to give opportunities for underhand dealing. All fair and above board, you know.'

'A large order?'

Mr George wrinkled his neat nose.

'Considerable,' he admitted. His eyes narrowed speculatively. 'Does his Grace have interests in mills hereabouts?' Jarrett gave him a cold look. 'Forgive me,' Mr George said hastily. 'An unintentional impertinence! His Grace's affairs are a private matter, dear me.'

'This tragedy – will it interrupt your business?'

'No, no, no!' Mr George responded with a dismissive little shake. 'It is my custom to travel alone . . .' He spread out his plump hands, palms up, and trailed off into a shrug that somehow conveyed the idea that he was a man who would do his duty whatever the circumstances.

'Was Mr Pritchard a close friend?'

'A colleague.' Mr George put aside his coffee, his expression oddly prim. 'We have worked in the same department for some years. This was our first tour together.' He checked himself. 'Pritchard had an excellent reputation.'

'And was it known that Mr Pritchard was in ill health?'

'Poor Pritchard!' Mr George wagged his head sadly. 'Forever complaining about some little ailment or another.' He looked up at Jarrett, his chubby face contrite. 'I fear I didn't take sufficient notice. Just thought it was his way. But then when a man's time is come, God's will be done,' he finished, the pious sentiment at variance with his comfortable expression. He picked up his cup and took a sip.

'And last night, did he seem uneasy in any way?'

Mr George's forehead creased in thought.

'He complained of being fatigued from the journey,' he said cautiously. 'But as to anything more . . .' He gestured helplessly with his cup. 'He said he would take his sleeping draught and go to bed.'

'A sleeping draught?'

'He always carried it. He was, by his own account, an indifferent sleeper.'

'What kind of draught was it?'

'I never saw it. I understand he regularly took it.'

Jarrett contemplated the broad, open face before him. Mr George seemed at ease with himself and the situation. He thought of the bird-like expression he had glimpsed a moment earlier and wondered if the man was really so guileless.

'It must have been a shock to find him this morning.'

'Indeed. But I didn't find him,' Mr George corrected firmly. 'The landlord called me after his wife discovered the tragedy.'

Jarrett sipped his own coffee. It was bitter. Chicory. Mr George shot him a sympathetic little grimace and picked up the painted jug.

'A little more milk perhaps?'

Jarrett shook his head. Mr George added a little milk to his own cup. The hunters pursued their merry chase around the jug with the pink hounds at their heels.

'I was awoken by a dreadful wailing in the passage. Our maid, I believe. I was making my toilette when Mr Teward knocked.'

'Your room is next to Mr Pritchard's?'

'To the right down the passage.'

The second unshuttered room, thought Jarrett. Was it Mr George who laid out his colleague in that fashion? If the limbs were still pliable he couldn't have been long dead.

Mr Jarrett gave his companion a rueful smile. 'How times have changed! In my day when we travelled on the

114

king's shilling we were expected to share accommodations.'

Mr George looked displeased.

'I am not a junior, Mr Jarrett,' the civil servant said haughtily and then repenting, added with a touch of humour, 'Besides, poor Pritchard snored terribly. Had I been forced to sleep in the same room I should not have had a wink of sleep.' His eyes widened as if caught by a sudden thought. 'I have heard that such snoring can be a sign of a weak heart. Do you think perhaps that is significant?'

'Perhaps. How did you find him?'

Mr George shifted in his chair.

'I did not go in.'

'No?' Jarrett lifted his eyebrows.

'I stayed at the door of the room,' Mr George said stubbornly. 'The Tewards had already found him. Perhaps you think me squeamish, Mr Jarrett – I'm not proud of it, but Mr Teward assured me Pritchard . . .' he hesitated delicately, 'had gone to a better place.'

'You did not take a moment alone with him, to pay your respects?'

'No!' The denial was energetic. Mr George stood up abruptly and turned his back to stare through the window. He pulled out a handkerchief to dab his face. The fabric dislodged a paper bag from his pocket. It fell to the ground. 'I paid my respects from a distance. Pritchard was a private man. He would have preferred it that way.' Mr George's tone was querulous. 'I did not like

115

to intrude.' He glanced down and spied the bag. With a soft *tsk!* of annoyance he snatched it up and replaced it in his pocket.

'Forgive me. I am moved.' Again he applied the handkerchief to his face. He turned back to his interrogator, his manner infused with an air of martyred politeness. 'If you require nothing else, Mr Jarrett, I should be grateful for a little solitude. I find this sudden loss has affected me more than I knew.'

CHAPTER EIGHT

A line of washing cut across a corner of the kitchen. Behind it a boiling kettle whistled. He ducked under the line and removed the kettle from the range hot plate. A tantalizing smell assailed him. A symmetrical phalanx of tawny currant buns was cooling on a wire rack on a long bench by the hearth. His stomach rumbled. He picked one up. Its absence left a reproachful hole. He put it back.

'Mrs Teward!' he called out.

No answer. A door opened somewhere, admitting a chill draught of air. Voices and footsteps and Meg Teward came into the kitchen bundled up in a large shawl and carrying a basket, with her daughter at her heels.

'Mr Jarrett,' she greeted him. 'We've been collecting eggs.' She put her basket on the table and unwound herself from her shawl. Hester was clutching a grey puff ball of a dog with bright jet eyes.

'You keep him away from those hens,' her mother

advised her. 'Your da catches him he'll not stand for it; he'll fetch his hesslen stick.'

Her daughter pushed out her lips in a mulish look; it was a half-hearted expression. The threat had the sound of one often repeated and never acted upon. Hester marched up to the visitor.

'Tuffy's been biting 'ens,' she informed him. It was a young dog, barely out of puppyhood. It wagged its stump of a tail and bobbed its head at him.

'Has he? Bad dog!' he responded with a straight face.

'Bad dog!' she repeated with relish. 'I give him a kelk to square 'm up.'

The dog bounced up and lapped her on the mouth. Hester grimaced, giggled and departed on some business of her own.

'You've spoken to Mr George, then,' Mrs Teward said. She was cleaning the muck off the barn eggs and placing them in a broad earthenware bowl.

'Yes.'

She surveyed him with an unexpectedly motherly look.

'You've not breakfasted? You must be half starved.'

'That new bread of yours does smell wonderful,' he confessed.

He drew out a chair and sat down while she brought him a warm loaf and butter. She lifted the cover from the large platter standing in the middle of the dark oak table.

'You must try my baked ham,' she said with pride.

'Your husband is a lucky man, Mrs Teward.'

She watched him approvingly as he demolished half a loaf and three generous slices of ham.

'Fancy a curran wig?' she asked as he finished.

'I beg your pardon?'

She laughed and fetched the tray of currant buns.

'Curran wig,' she repeated.

He grinned back. It was good to see her smile. The colour had returned to her cheeks. Mrs Teward sat in a rocking chair by the range with one of her daughter's pinafores and began to mend the hem. He bit into the bun. It was spiced with a sticky honey glaze. He licked his fingers. It was such a comfortable scene he was reluctant to disturb it.

He pushed back his empty plate. Her hands dropped in her lap. He glanced over at the little girl playing in the corner.

'Hester, honey,' her mother said. 'Go up and find Joan for me and ask her how far along she is with the beds.' The little girl danced out singing with the dog at her heels.

'I'm sorry to have to trouble you with this . . .'

She shook her head. 'No trouble – not from you.'

He leant forward, his forearms on his knees.

'You say Mr Pritchard lies now as you found him? Neither you nor your husband laid him out that way?'

'No!' She shivered. 'He was lying like that. 'Twas unnatural.'

'It's certainly odd.' He paused. 'And you don't think Mr George went in – for decency's sake perhaps?'

'I wondered,' Meg Teward responded, her confidence returning as her curiosity came to the fore. 'But he was not going into that room,' she said positively. 'Nearest any of us saw him come was the door.'

'But he might have gone in earlier?'

Mrs Teward sucked her bottom lip. 'I wondered,' she repeated, 'but Mr George is so certain he never went in that room. And Dan said he was shocked when he told him. Went lily white, he said.' She shrugged.

'Was the window open when you first went in and found him?'

'It was!' she agreed eagerly. 'Don't know what he was thinking. He let all the weather in. The room was bitter.'

'The shutters are closed at night?'

Mrs Teward nodded. 'Close them when I go up to put the pan in – to warm the beds like. Mind, Mr George, he's the same.'

'How so?'

'I put up the shutters last night like every night, but this morning both had their shutters back.'

'A hardy pair,' he commented. 'Had Mr George left his window open too?'

'Oh no!'

'But you found Pritchard's window open; you're sure?'

She nodded. 'Wet all blown in. I told Joan she was to wipe the boards . . .' She hesitated, wide-eyed. 'You don't think that's what killed him?'

'Cold air couldn't fell a man tucked up in his warm bed with those weighty curtains around him,' he reassured her. 'Something else did for Mr Pritchard. It's a puzzle.' He stared into middle distance. 'And that second pillow, it was at the end of his bed?'

'Pillow?'

'There are two pillows – the one under his head and the other at the foot of the bed. Did you find the second one like that, resting on his feet?'

She frowned at him, twisting her mouth up. For a moment she looked just like her little girl.

'No.' She spoke slowly, remembering. ''Twas on the floor. I must have picked it up. What does it matter?'

'At the foot of the bed?'

'No, by t'wall; up at t'head.' She started as Mr Jarrett stood abruptly, his expression distant.

'Forgive me!' he said vaguely. 'There is something I must just–'

And he left the room.

The bag stood by the chair where Pritchard had left it. Jarrett's hands moved through the contents. He brought out a small glass bottle. The paper label was handwritten in a thin, faded script: *Sleeping Draught*. The rest was smudged. Jarrett could barely make out '... drops in water'. There was perhaps an eighth of an inch of brown liquid left. He drew out the stopper and inhaled the heady odour of dried grass. Laudanum. He corked up the vial and replaced it. Crossing the room, he picked up the pillow at the foot of the bed and, taking it to the window, inspected it. There were faint stains on the linen. At first he wondered if they were merely evidence of Mrs Teward's lack of laundry skills, but after a quick survey of the other linen on the bed he dismissed the thought. The landlady was a careful housekeeper. The stains were new – pale streaks in the middle of the case, still faintly damp. He held it close and sniffed.

Grasping the pillow firmly in both hands he stood over Mr Pritchard's unlovely head a moment and then he replaced it at the foot of the bed. He returned to the dead face. His movements economical and precise, he lifted each eyelid in turn. Then he bent indecently close. First he smelt and then peered at the gaping mouth. Making a soft, frustrated sound he straightened up abruptly and circled the bed, drawing back the curtains to their furthest extent before resuming his oddly intimate position. Tilting his own head to catch the light, he thought he discerned a faint purple tinge to the skin of the lower cheeks and chin.

'If it's a bruise, it might develop,' he muttered to himself. 'Or it might not.'

The door pushed open and an animal scampered into the room, its toenails clicking on the boards. With an excited snuffle and a bark Tuffy darted under the bed. Jarrett heard the dog's jaws click on something. Hester followed her pet in a flying tackle. She emerged wrestling a caramel-coloured block from between its teeth. Tuffy relinquished his prize and trotted out of the room. Hester popped the square into her own mouth. She looked up at Jarrett with a smug expression.

'One of Mr George's toffees,' she announced. 'He give me one before.' She stared at the shape on the bed. She sucked on her sweet. 'Dead as a door nail, ain't he?' she remarked. Her baby hand reached for his and Jarrett enclosed it gently in his fingers.

'Yes,' he said, leading her to the door. 'He's with the Lord now and we should leave him to his rest.'

'So,' he began conversationally as he closed the door behind them. 'Mr George is generous with his toffees then. Does he give them to everyone?'

'Only me,' replied his companion.

'But he must have given some to Mr Pritchard.'

'He don't like toffees,' Hester replied flatly. She stopped and stood on one leg thoughtfully. 'Happen he give some t'others.'

'Which others?'

'Them that came.'

'Mr George and Mr Pritchard had visitors?' She caught the urgency in his tone. Hester's round eyes fixed solemnly on his with a worried expression. She jerked her head. He stood on one leg.

'When did they come?' he asked. He hopped a step. 'Yesterday?'

She giggled and shook her head, making her curls bounce against her cheeks. She hopped a step and waited.

'The day before?' he asked, balancing easily on his one leg. The little girl stared at him, waiting. He hopped another step.

'The evening they arrived?' he guessed. She nodded vigorously and hopped down the corridor.

As they reached the head of the stairs he took her hand again.

'Two feet now,' he instructed and suddenly felt very old. 'I don't suppose anyone remembers anything about those visitors?' he asked casually as they descended. Hester stopped. She pulled him down to crouch beside her, balancing uncomfortably on the narrow stair. She cupped her sticky hands around her mouth and whispered in his ear.

'So one man had a big cloak,' he confirmed. She nodded and whispered again. She gazed at him, her face inches from his. She smelt of honey and earth. He frowned into her pure blue eyes framed in their pretty black lashes.

'He smelt like what?' he queried.

'Me gran's box,' she repeated clearly. Rolling her eyes at his backwardness, Hester tugged his hand and pulled him back up the stairs. She marched into a bedroom. Looking about he realized belatedly it was her parents'.

'I should not be in here,' he protested, but Hester was standing by a table.

'Me gran's box,' she repeated, pointing to a polished oysterwood box standing on it. She opened the lid. He crossed over to her. The box was lined with sandalwood.

'Oh!' he said, light dawning at last. 'He smelt like your gran's box.'

It had been raining upstream. The river was opaque and implacable, pushing rusty foam frills around the rocks in its path. He followed the bank as the winter daylight faded until he could sense more than see the curves of the open land around him. Walcheren picked his way down the pale path. A bridge came into view and above it a neat stone folly. A rosy warmth glowed through the shutters fastened against the night.

His knock was greeted by a bark. He lifted the latch and entered to be met by a yellow dog with a pointy muzzle and large, upstanding ears. The hound reared up on its back legs. Catching the forepaws with one hand, Jarrett rubbed its head. He nodded to the stocky figure who sat on a stool by the fire mending a rabbit net.

'A damp night.'

'That it is,' Ezekial Duffin responded peacefully.

Seven months previously, when fate had first brought Jarrett to these parts, he had taken refuge in this folly. Then it had been spartan and neat. Now the pungent warmth of the room wrapped itself around him. Racks of drying rabbit skins leant against the walls. A rope was stretched across one corner. On it hung a water-marked coat and a dingy shawl half obscuring a couple of cages. Jarrett caught the lithe line of a ferret behind the mesh.

'Drink?' Duffin jerked his head in the direction of a small tapped barrel.

'You?' Jarrett asked, helping himself to what proved to be small ale. Duffin produced a mug from the floor beside him.

'I'm set,' he said. Jarrett sat down on a pile of sacks and made himself comfortable.

'So what's the crack at the Bucket and Broom?' asked his host.

Jarrett had grown used to it, but it was quite surprising the things that the countryman knew. Had Duffin been with him when he was scouting in Spain, the allies might have been in France by now. He had rarely met a man with a better nose for intelligence on his own ground. Duffin chuckled.

'Wench that does for old George, the tollgate, she was full of as how one of Dan Teward's special guests had passed in the night.'

'A Mr Pritchard. So, it's up and down the Dale already.' Jarrett took a draught of ale. It was refreshing. A 'special' guest, he noted. Duffin stretched out the section of net he was mending and checked his handiwork.

'Oh aye! And how as the duke's man was there on't spot keeping bonny Meg Teward company while her man were off fetching magistrate.'

'What!' exclaimed Jarrett.

'There, there,' Duffin soothed facetiously. 'Many a man would be flattered. You've got a reputation – ladies consider you an 'andsome man.'

'Damn and blast it!'

'Don't tell me you've never been talked about before.'

'Maybe,' Jarrett admitted with a wry twist of the lips, 'but in the past I've rarely lingered long enough to hear it.'

The poacher's eyes were acute under the bushy bar of his eyebrows as they scanned his visitor.

'What's got you started?'

'This Mr Pritchard was an unusually considerate man. He laid himself out decently before he died.' Jarrett swilled the liquid gently around in his mug. 'Then there's an open window in the dead of winter with marks on the ground beneath it and a convenient sleeping draught.'

'And what does the magistrate say?'

'Natural causes. Dan Teward fetched Ison and he brought his pet physician, Parry, along to agree with him . . .' His mind touched irritably on his brief encounter with the colonel. The man was a pompous ass!

'And you think someone climbed in through the window in the night and did for this Pritchard? But who let him in? Someone had to open the window.'

'I have my suspicions as to that – but . . .' Jarrett shook his head as if seeing off a wasp. 'Motive. That's the rub.'

'And why lay the bugger out? It only attracts attention.'

'Does it? Only mine, it would seem. No evidence of anything save God's will, according to the magistrate. The colonel assures me he has many in his wide acquaintance who sleep straight as a board on their backs.' Jarrett gave way to his impatience. 'Only an idiot would sleep that way and he'd choke!' he exclaimed.

'Mayhap that's the answer.' Duffin paused as he tightened the last knot on his handiwork, snapping the line tight between meaty balled fists. 'He supped his draught, laid down straight and, a bit fuddled like, he choked.'

'I wish I could believe it,' said Jarrett in a discontented tone.

Duffin got up and went to his cages. He fetched out a pale cinnamon-coloured ferret and brought it back to sit by the fire. The creature made a clucking sound as he stroked it.

'Good rabbits this season. We're planning a visit up over Grateley Manor way. You like it up there, don't you?' he addressed his pet. 'She's a quick one Queenie is.' Queenie bumped him under the chin with her sleek head. 'More loving than a woman is a good ferret,' Duffin commented fondly. Jarrett shot him a quizzical look. 'And that thought's beneath you,' the poacher added deadpan. 'Thought you had breeding.'

'His eyes had those brownish specks I've seen before in a strangled man,' Jarrett remarked.

'But this one wasn't strangled?'

'Smothered, by my guess. I fancy Pritchard was drugged. I caught a whiff of laudanum on a pillow.' But the smell had faded along with the drying stains. The echo of the colonel's lofty dismissal mocked him. 'And where is the *evidence*, sir, for this extravagant speculation?' Ison, of course, had taken straight away to Mr George with his civil service deference, his official seals and delicate speculations about Mr Pritchard's poorly heart. Duffin was pulling a face.

'There'd still be some thrashing about.'

'So the murderer tidied him up – laying him out as

he was found. I'd say it happened around midnight or before,' Jarrett reasoned out loud. 'It takes a man half a day to stiffen completely and rigor was only half set when I saw him.'

'And no one heard nothing?' Duffin produced a teasel and began to groom his pet, his big hands light and gentle. 'She likes this; it settles her – don't it?' he cooed to the ferret. Queenie looked up at him and made her clucking noise, as if in response. 'Who had reason to want this passing stranger dead?' the poacher asked.

'His travelling companion?' Jarrett thought of the mark outside the second unshuttered window and Mr George's complacent, self-indulgent face. 'He wasn't just any stranger, Duffin. As you said yourself, a special guest. He and his partner came to buy cloth for the army. There's plenty of money to be made on those contracts and where there's money . . .'

Queenie turned on the poacher's lap, watching the visitor with glassy black eyes.

'Anyone been seen about?' asked her master. 'You can't be thinking on Dan and Meg Teward? They're good people.'

'No. There were two men came to see Pritchard and his colleague the night they arrived.' Jarrett pulled a discontented face. 'But the bar was busy and no one recalls anything much about them. It's winter,' he admitted. 'It's not unusual to be muffled up. Mrs Teward says she was called away. She took the slighter one for a local man, though she did not know him; the other she wasn't so sure about – she can't recall why. The only impression was of a sweet-smelling man with a dark beard.'

Duffin cocked his head at that, but he let it pass, his attention focused on the animal between his hands. Jarrett stood up restlessly and walked over to stare into the fire.

'What you got there?' asked the poacher.

Jarrett looked down and opened his fist. Two buttons lay on his palm, one white metal stamped with numerals – 68 – the other silver gilt and embossed with the insignia of the 16th. He hadn't noticed he had taken them out.

'These? I usually carry them with me in some pocket.'

Two regiments. Two fragments of his life. He circled the buttons in his palm.

'Lucky charms?'

Jarrett closed his fist and shook the pieces of metal gently. The movement shifted the hair bracelet he always wore on that wrist. He could feel it slipping against his skin. 'Remembrances,' he said. He put the buttons back in his pocket.

'Word must have got out if there are military buyers in the neighbourhood,' he resumed. 'Have you heard anything?'

'There's been some gathering in corners – and weavers too, now you mention it. With the fairs coming up, I didn't think twice on it.'

'And the fairs open tomorrow. There's something coming, Duffin, I feel it. The colonel's all fired up about agitators and now this.'

'What's up with the colonel?'

'He's enacting the Watch and Ward.' Jarrett cast a side glance at the man sitting beside him. 'It's a newish act. It gives our magistrate the means to call in a troop of regulars. Their lieutenant arrived yesterday – but you'll know that already.' He watched the poacher calmly grooming his pet. 'Is there to be trouble at the fairs, Duffin?'

'There's always trouble at t'fairs. It's tradition. The heelanders – wild men that works the lead up over the tops – they come down for a set to with the townsfolk every fair. It's tradition. But anything more – nay.' Duffin's negative was derisive.

'Colonel Ison claims there are foreign agitators at work. He says he's been given information.'

The poacher shot him a sudden look. His eyes dropped.

'That's fanciful. Dale folk don't like foreigners.' Duffin put the ferret down. 'You know that.'

Indeed he did. When he had first arrived in the neighbourhood he had found himself accused of murder principally because he was a foreigner with no one to vouch for him. Duffin had helped him out of that tangle; the countryman had become a firm friend in the process.

Moving like a piece of quicksilver Queenie jumped up onto the pile of sacks and curled herself into a smooth ball in the imprint left by Jarrett's recent presence.

'Settled folk don't like incomers,' Duffin elaborated. 'When you're settled you know your neighbours from cradle to grave – or you're kin with someone that does. If nobody knows a man, how can you weigh what he is?'

'Like me, you mean?'

'You?' There was a glimmer of mischief somewhere in the countryman's unsmiling face. 'Well now, I'm not so settled I can't take a risk. What's the hour?' he asked. Jarrett checked his pocket watch.

'Just past eight. Why?'

'Just past eight on a Wednesday.' The poacher got to his feet. 'There's a song club meet up at the Red Angel Wednesday nights; there's weavers among 'em. Not that you're to go suspecting them,' he added severely, scooping up his ferret and returning Queenie to her cage. 'I fancy a drink in company.'

Collecting a disreputable-looking garment that proved to be a bottle-green coat from a pile on the floor, Duffin pulled it on. His yellow dog rose up and moved to the door.

'Comin'?' the poacher asked without looking back. 'It's near an hour's walk.'

'Quicker if you ride up behind me,' responded Jarrett, following him out.

'That'll have folk talking,' the poacher's lugubrious voice rose out of the shadows beyond the door. 'Ezekial Duffin riding up behind the duke's man.'

The track climbed up into the wind. The sky had cleared and the waxing moon threw its light on the moving grasses that rustled portentously in the expanse around them as if pregnant with some secret. Duffin's bulk was warm and solid at his back. Walcheren took the extra weight stoically.

'Fine strong beasts these chapman horses,' the poacher remarked.

'Chapman horses!' Jarrett protested, stung. 'I'll have you know that Walcheren's veins flow with the blood of the Byerley Turk – a true Arab!'

'Told you that, did he, the one that sold him you?'

Up ahead the black density of walls and roofs rose stark and misplaced against the moorscape. Once there had been a medieval manor on this wild moor. Four centuries past, houses had grown up around it to form a small village of dressed stone. But times had changed. The lords of the manor had died out; people drifted away until only a couple of families remained eking a living from sheep and poaching on the richer lands in the valley below. The buildings, weathered and battered by the elements, still retained ghosts of their former decencies in odd wind-bitten fragments of carved stone. At night, with the wind pulling at shutters and loose timbers, it was an eerie place. Approaching from the eastern side, it was hard to tell which buildings were abandoned and which were not. Indeed, with the wind whistling between the walls, a fanciful man might wonder if the remaining inhabitants were still of this world.

'Up there.' Duffin's arm advanced into his vision, pointing to the right.

Jarrett saw a lantern hung above a door. It illuminated

an old swinging sign painted with a figure obscured in layers of red varnish. The Red Angel.

The door opened and two men stepped out. They lingered, talking. Through the lit space behind them a melodic male voice slipped into the night, carrying an air that caught the heart.

I've seen snow float down Bradford Beck
As black as ebony.
From Hunslet, Holbeck, Windsey Stack, good Lord deliver me.

They entered by a side door. Turning the elbow of a short passage they encountered a hard-hewn woman in a man's shirt over a dark red cloth skirt, with a collection of tankards gripped in each fist.

'Ezekial,' she said, her eyes fixed on Jarrett. Her voice was gruff. He had a sudden impression of a half-tame creature threatening to bite.

'He's all right Jeannie.'

'If you say,' responded Jeannie and stomped off.

They followed her into a fug of tobacco smoke mixed with the stink of wet wool and warmed muck and the sweet reek of malted barley. The bar was crowded but quiet. The singer was sitting upright on a bench, his hands on his knees as he sang. He finished to a kind of stillness. Then his listeners broke into muted applause, knocking tankards on tables and shuffling their feet. The hubbub of mass conversation resumed.

'That was good, Jo,' a broad-set youth in gaiters called

out above the din. 'Now, how's about a jig, Sim, to liven us up?' A fiddle scraped. It was joined by a squeeze box from somewhere in the crowd. Together they embarked on a fast tune with a strong beat.

Jarrett paid for two tankards of homebrew. Duffin fell in with a couple of acquaintances. Jarrett spotted a party moving from a settle by the passage, in the shadows away from the fire. As he made for it he knocked elbows with the singer. He recognized the servant who had accompanied Miss Lippett before the magistrate.

'You're in fine voice,' he complimented. Jonas Farr tossed his head in a bashful manner.

'There's many a good voice here,' he replied. Jarrett's ears pricked up at the rhythm of his speech.

'You're not a local man?' The brown eyes were watchful but not yet hostile.

'Nor you neither.'

'Another incomer,' Jarrett responded cheerfully. He tilted his head. 'West Riding?' he suggested with a disarmingly wry expression. He sensed more than saw the young man stiffen. For a moment he thought he would not answer but when he did his tone was easy.

'Born just outside Leeds. You?'

'Oh! I'm a wanderer. Been all over. How do you find it here?' Jonas looked him up and down.

'They're fine honest folk, sir,' he said. 'Once they trust you.' He moved away to rejoin his friends.

That's me put in my place, thought Jarrett. He settled down to observe from his corner. He scanned the room, fixing each group and cluster in his mind as if he had a commission to paint them: the two farmers listening to Duffin tell a tale by the bar; the young men in a circle about the singer with their clean weavers' hands; the two sitting with their heads together in the furthest recess – a tow-headed youth with a foolish face and a bright blue handkerchief tied around his neck listening to a companion whose back was turned. The picture might be called 'The Conversation'. The vignette was framed by the long coat tossed over the speaker's chair, the dark cloth punctuated by a lighter flash of a hand-kerchief or a pair of gloves hanging from a pocket.

Given his previous line of work, Jarrett had trained himself to look for patterns and pieces that didn't fit. Nothing jarred here. What were you expecting to find? he chided himself. Men with secrets don't dangle them before strangers. He listened to the convivial voices about him. It was the rumour of ordinary men enjoying the company of their friends and neighbours; hardly the stuff of foreign agents and secret societies. He watched Duffin spinning his tales. His audience had grown.

That's why Duffin brought me here – to see them like this, at ease on their own ground. It was pleasing to think he was so trusted. Then it dawned on him. Duffin hoped he could protect these people. That thought made him uneasy. How in God's name could he protect any one of them from the colonel's fearful fancies?

A familiar voice glanced out of the mix of voices. He leant forward. The press of people parted a moment and he saw young Favian Adley sitting in profile to him with a notebook open on his knee. He was laughing at some joke being shared by his circle. He had never seen Grub so assured. It was a glimpse of the man he was to become. Jarrett sat back, caught out by an odd twinge of pride. So the boy had found friends already. He did not want to disturb his enjoyment.

He was aware of movement by his right shoulder. Someone walked behind the high back of the settle towards the passage. As they brushed past, Jarrett's nostrils caught a whiff of sandalwood. He leant out, craning to see beyond his high-backed seat. He felt a blast of cold air on his face. The corridor was empty. He saw nothing but shadows.

CHAPTER NINE

His painting box stood on an old square table. Next to it, dominating everything, was the canvas on its easel. Charles had ordered him up a standard fifty by forty from London, ready-primed in a soft off-white. It gleamed at him, a vast reproachful blank.

He lifted the lid of the mahogany chest feeling the familiar thrill of anticipation at the sight of its cork-stoppered glass bottles with their rainbow of dried pigments. There was a world of enchanting associations in that box: Venetian blue and Indian yellow, terra sienna and indigo; sepia from a cuttlefish and carmine from a thousand South American beetles. His colourman, Massoul, kept him well supplied from his factory on New Bond Street. The small bladders of prepared oils lay in the dividers at the back like the exotic fruit of some Asiatic tree. His paints were one of Raif Jarrett's few extravagances.

He might try the new chromate of lead. Massoul had recommended it – a pure bright yellow conjured up by the chemist Davy for Benjamin West. He squeezed out a dollop on to his palette, sealing up the leathery pouch with a tack. He scanned the room. It was well lit by northern light. The walls had been recently plastered and painted a pleasing yellow. A chaise-longue upholstered in an unfortunate shade of puce blocked one corner. In the middle of the floor a couple of chairs with curving backs and broad rush seats stood stranded, facing one another like guests come early for a party. He would have his sitter there with the light of the window falling obliquely on him. He placed one of the chairs and took a step back. Favian entered. He was wearing a dark coat and blue trousers, his cravat correctly tied, his hair smoothed down with water.

'Where shall I be?' he asked.

'Here, if you will.'

Favian squirmed on the rush seat, his eyes on the threatening canvas. He turned this way and that trying for a comfortable pose.

'And I should turn towards you . . . ?' He propped an elbow on the rail to support his head, folding the opposite arm across his chest to brace himself, his hand gripping the chair back. It was fortuitous but it made a good shape. 'How long will this take, cousin?'

'The masters prescribe three sittings in a northern light,' Jarrett murmured absently, adjusting the position of his model's right leg.

'But you will work faster than that, won't you?' Favian asked anxiously. He had had no idea of sitting so long.

'Gladly. I bore as easily as you.'

In a draught of air Charles appeared in waistcoat and shirt sleeves with a bottle in one hand and a glass in the other. He paused before the purple chaise-longue. Looping one foot about the nearest leg, he dragged it to an angle that satisfied him and collapsed full length upon it.

'Have you any idea how many hours a canvas of this size will take?' Jarrett asked him in an exasperated tone.

'Want me to find you a smaller one?' Charles responded genially, filling his glass.

Jarrett sighed. He threw a clean piece of linen across one shoulder, dipped his long brush in a pool of brownish lake and began to cross the white surface with swift strokes, his eyes seeing in shapes and colours and shadows. The pale blob that was to be the head spoke.

'Oh! I near forgot, cousin. I am to give you Mr Strickland's compliments. I ran into him while waiting for the coach in Leeds. Tall fellow; beak of a nose. You know him, I think? I was at school with his brother.' Jarrett grunted.

'Strickland?' queried Charles.

'Francis Strickland. Yorkshire family,' Jarrett responded. Charles frowned.

'Say, isn't he . . . ?' he began.

'They have a place near Leeds,' Jarrett cut across him. 'Yes, Tip, what is it?' The valet emerged from the doorway.

'I am worried about Master Favian, Master Raif. There's a dreadful draught from that window and you know how he's poorly in his chest.' Tiplady pouted out his own chest like an aggressive fowl. He was a small man with a magnificent head that seemed too large for his body – the creation of a satirical God. 'Mrs Adley, she wrote to me herself, seeing as gentlemen can be careless. As I know as well as any, for did I not go all the way to Greta Bridge in a blessed trap on a freezing cold day to find nothing but Master Adley's trunk left for collection?' The servant paused for breath. 'I don't complain for I never do,' he said with emphasis. 'It was a good joke, no doubt, but didn't I have the most dreadful fancies of what might have befallen? For you know he is weak in the chest,' he repeated reproachfully. Beyond him Favian was half out of his chair in outrage.

Pressure built in Jarrett's veins. The pleasure of painting lay in peaceful communion between himself and his subject. This was about as restful as setting up in a barnyard at feeding time. He waved his brush in the direction of the door.

'Out!' he commanded. 'Out! Or this will never be done!'

A less established servant might have taken offence, but Tiplady cherished his martyrdom. He crossed the room at a measured pace, deliberately threw another log on the fire burning in the grate and returned in silence. His eyes fixed on his ungrateful master, he conveyed an age of suffering in his bow. He exited to the accompaniment of a sing-song commentary that faded with his retreat.

'He's not like you. He's sensitive. He don't go round nosing out corpses this way and that and doing other things a gentleman shouldn't, not even in the provinces.'

Charles flung a leg to dangle over the back of his chaise.

'Poor fellow,' he remarked to his glass. 'I know it is tiresome to be sickly, Grub, but old Tip does like to have someone to fuss over – especially now this one won't let him,' he elaborated with a jerk of his head in their artist's direction.

'I'm not an invalid!' cried Favian.

'Am I supposed to be here for my own amusement?' asked Jarrett plaintively.

Favian resumed his position with an apologetic grimace.

'How does that business go?' he asked in a conciliatory tone. 'I heard about the fellow at the Bucket and Broom.'

'It's not my business,' Jarrett answered curtly. 'It's the colonel's.' His brushstroke slipped and he caught the smear of paint with his cloth. He never could handle the man aright. It seemed that the very sight of him put Ison's hackles up: *You are the Duke of Penrith's agent, sir, and new to these parts. I have been magistrate here some years. Allow that my judgement is likely better than yours.*

'Though had I had the lordling here with me it might have been a different affair,' he heard himself add aloud. Charles looked over with a fleeting expression of brotherly sympathy.

'Can't think how you manage to be civil to that fellow. Every time I see him it's all I can do to prevent myself yawning in his face. Do you know, the other day, it was

142

coming down in torrents and I saw him order his coachman and linkboy to stay catching their deaths waiting for him while he went into Bedford's?'

'I fear the colonel lacks your radical sensibilities, Charles,' Jarrett murmured. The law resided with the magistrate. And he had no evidence. One couldn't accuse a man with a piece of toffee and a window opened on a winter night merely because one didn't take to him.

'Who is this Colonel Ison?' Favian piped up in a fair imitation of a man who knew everyone that mattered.

'Colonel Ison, Member of Parliament, His Majesty's Justice and honourable commander of our militia!' Charles toasted with a satirical flourish of his glass.

'A significant man these parts.' Jarrett jabbed a touch of paint along the jaw line of his sketch.

'That brisk and martial air! I heard his service only lasted four months,' Charles remarked. 'He went to Ireland at the time of the rebellion of '90. It so alarmed him he retreated all the way to a half-pay post in the provinces. And this colonel, Grub, fears our peasantry are revolting. Or on the verge of it – though precisely why he should think so is not entirely clear.' He emptied his glass and poured himself another drink.

Jarrett took a step back to contemplate his composition. The colonel's comment about a great conspiracy nagged him. *Nottingham stocking knitters and West Yorkshire croppers singing songs of General Ludd* . . . Weavers gathering in corners, Duffin had said. The dead man Pritchard was a wool buyer. The fairs had to figure in it. Something had stirred the colonel up. What if he had an informant? Being, himself, at one time in the military branch of the trade, Jarrett had heard rumours of domestic agents at work at home.

'I smell an informant,' he stated. Charles snorted, a derisive, dismissive sound.

He had sketched in his outline. Now for the wash – and then the real work to come; building colour and modelling shape in layer upon layer of paint. At one time he had run a whole network of informants back in Spain. His mind prodded the edges of the dark blank of what he did not know. The fairs brought an influx of strangers – a hunting ground perhaps? Imported, he said to himself as he thinned his paint with poppy oil. An outsider. But if he was right, imported as an agent of whom and to what end? His hand hesitated over the canvas.

Capturing a likeness: to grasp a fleeting recognition of one being in the eyes and brain of another and fix it so others might see. Part of him relished the mapping, the planning, the exercise of wit required to overcome the small treacheries of this medium – the dirty oil, the unstable tint, the dripping brush – to reproduce in mechanical labour some semblance of what he glimpsed. But in sum – what folly! All that striving, to end, at best, with a taunting parody of your first conception: a caricature of life. He looked to his left. Charles stood at his shoulder. He was leaning his head back, examining the pallid likeness emerging from the canvas.

'Look at our little Grub. He's a man – well, a little

man,' Charles commented. The impression stared back at them as if it knew more than they.

'You do not take this seriously?'

Favian's voice recalled their attention. He was leaning forward, his whole body tense.

Charles cast him an idle glance.

'And what must I take seriously, young Grub?'

'There are good men out there without work who fear they cannot feed their families. Don't you see it?'

'What rot!' Charles scoffed, reclining once more on his couch. 'There's none of that here.'

'Honest working men have the right to defend the customs of their trade.' A carmine flush stained Grub's cheekbones. 'How can you not see that a man, a good man; a decent, hard-working man, who cannot earn enough to feed his family and fears for the future – how can you not see that such a man might grow desperate? These are unjust times – there is no justice.'

Jarrett had never seen the boy so animated. He had broken his pose again. The composition was too bland. It lacked something – a vibrant splash of colour to focus the eye. Blue. Something blue . . .

'You are too dramatic,' said Charles. 'Too much poetry, I dare say.' He glanced at Jarrett and waved a white hand. 'The pose, the pose, Grub,' he chided.

Favian resumed his position with a little huff of breath. A mischievous expression crossed Charles's face as he lolled against the sofa back. 'Who would imagine that our little scholar should turn out to be such a firebrand?'

he pondered. Jarrett shot him a questioning look. Charles waved his glass in an airy gesture. 'Thinking of what brought him here . . .'

'That was an accident, a misunderstanding,' Favian protested.

'A misunderstanding, Grub?' Charles lifted his brows in exaggerated surprise. 'You assaulted the Warden's lodgings with an incendiary device!'

'I was making a poetic offering and by an unlucky chance the wind caught the balloon. I'll admit I was drunk but what were the servants thinking of, leaving the window wide open in the middle of February?'

'One might have thought the Warden wanted his guests to catch cold,' murmured Raif. 'He should have secured his defences.'

'It was an inventive form of attack,' conceded Charles. Favian's blush deepened.

'I hope my poetry may inflame men's hearts but it was never my intention to cause an actual conflagration,' he stated with dignity.

'Ah! But consequences, my dear Grub! Your poetic flame consumed half a brocade curtain and the Warden's second-best table cloth. You are lucky it was not his best linen – you might have been sent down.'

'Peace, Charles. Let us accept that it was ill-fortune that turned Grub's bark of poesy into a Congreve rocket.' Jarrett looked up and met the boy's eyes. They glowed with such affection and trust, it was unnerving. The sensitive mouth curved in a playful expression.

'Miss Lonsdale is a fine woman, isn't she?' he piped up irrelevantly. 'She's not married, I understand? She seems a very intelligent woman and a warm nature too; interested in others. We spoke of you, cousin, the other day while we drank our tea.'

'She is a fine woman,' Charles chimed in from his sofa, 'though rather too much character for my taste. I swear I did my best to draw her off, Raif, but she had already spied your bird of paradise. Those plump partridges are like magnets to respectable women; they pretend to dis-approve but they are as curious as cats. You're sure to be condemned over the tea cups. Never mind. In their hearts the ladies love a rogue.'

'Miss Lonsdale is no gossip,' Raif reproved him. He could see just the right blue in his mind's eye – a cross between cornflower and Venetian.

'Poor fool! As if it isn't the nature of the sex to tell each other everything.'

'We need some colour. A handkerchief about the neck maybe – do you have one?'

Favian blinked. His hand slipped inside the breast of his coat, white against the dark. He drew out a freshly laundered scarlet handkerchief and held it out tenta-tively.

'Wrong colour; I need blue, I think.'

Favian looked down at the handkerchief in his hand a moment then folded it tenderly. He tucked it up one sleeve and resumed his pose, gazing studiously into the middle distance.

If he used the view through the window beyond – substituted a summer sky for the winter one – that would give him the blue. Jarrett pencilled a note on the margin of a paper lying on the table beside him and picked up his brush again.

'So much about women baffles me,' Favian was saying, 'even their very names. Well, Miss Lonsdale is Henrietta, I think. That's simple enough. But Molly for instance, or Lally,' his tongue stuttered a little over the word. 'I heard that name for the first time the other day and I can't for the life of me think where it might come from.'

Charles lifted himself up on one elbow to stare at him.

'Adelaide, I should imagine,' Jarrett supplied, adding a murmured, 'Down Charles!' My lord shut his mouth and lay back against the upholstered velvet.

Favian broke his pose to stretch a little. He fiddled with his cuff and resumed his position.

'What's another word for yellow?' he asked. 'I have been through corn and straw and sun. None will do.'

'Piss,' offered Charles, gazing at the way his wine tilted in the bowl of his glass.

Jarrett was contemplating the shadows behind Favian's left ear.

'Citrine, mustard, ochre,' he suggested.

'I have a new composition in mind,' Favian confessed. 'Not a classical form but a ballad. A poem for the people. I happened to meet a singer, cousin Raif, a local man, on my way here. You should hear them sing, here in Woolbridge. I have never heard such singing. It speaks to the heart with a directness . . .' His words failed him. He dropped his bracing arm to etch an expressive sweep with his hand.

'Can you sing?' asked Charles.

'I hum a little.'

Jarrett made an impatient sound.

'Sorry, cousin.' Favian resumed his pose. 'I have set about a new work,' he went on, his eyes fixed dutifully forward, the rest of his face animated. 'William Wordsworth speaks of his songs, but my desire is to write real songs – songs to rouse everyman's heart. A ballad, you see. I am working on a ballad . . .'

'A noble ambition,' Jarrett murmured absently, his mind still on the Bucket and Broom. The mystery visitors – they were likely to know something. A bearded man, smelling of sandalwood . . . He could hardly spend his time lurking in crowded places hoping to nose him out.

'What do you know of everyman's heart, young Grub?' demanded Charles. '*He's a dull and empty ass, who will not drain a foaming glass!*' he sang in a reasonably melodious baritone. 'Now there's a song for you.'

'I am learning, cousin,' Favian said with dignity. 'I have begun some acquaintance here among the weavers. *You* must know,' he appealed to Raif. 'They tell me such things. In the old days the work was spread between the families but now the big manufacturers would have it all. Full-fashioned work at an old-fashioned price, that's all the weavers ask. There are rumours of machines. They say wherever the machines arrive the masters want more for less. They will put all the small men out of work. It's happened other places. Something must be done. I tell them the independent men should form an association. If they combine together they can stand against Bedford and the rest.'

'Who's been telling you this?' demanded his lordship, half sitting up on his sofa. 'Keep to your poetry if you must but don't meddle in such things. You know nothing of the matter!'

Favian's neat features took on a stubborn cast. He expected as much from Charles. Charles had everything his way and there was nothing he cared for so deeply as his own comfort. But cousin Raif was different. As an officer he had cared for his men – men of all degrees and none. He moved with ease in all companies and listened to what was said. Raif understood justice and had the strength of character to stand up for it. He focused his attention on the artist behind the canvas.

'What is your opinion, cousin? Should the weavers not have justice?'

Jarrett narrowed his eyes at the painted figure emerging from his canvas.

'I think any man must give his mind to consequences as well as action, Grub. With your connections you may kick a lieutenant with impunity – you may even set light to a warden's lodgings, but a man who does not share your privileges risks much more.'

'What can you mean?' Favian demanded. His face was burning.

Jarrett gave him a sober look. 'You know what I mean. It's all very well to make friends among men of different degrees but you should never forget the responsibilities of your station.'

'My station!' Favian protested. Raif continued over him.

'You don't want your new friends to come to regret the acquaintance,' he finished dryly.

Favian swallowed hard. His throat felt stiff. Raif spoke as if he were an unruly puppy to be slapped down. He had always thought that they understood one another – that they shared a natural sympathy without elaboration or explanation.

Charles swung his boots to the floor.

'Grub used to be such a compliant little chap,' he mocked. He walked round to peer again at the canvas. 'Don't you remember the way he used to follow us about with that trusting little face? Not a scrap of trouble – and now look at him!'

'You're in my light,' said Jarrett.

Favian moved his supporting hand and rolled his head to loosen his neck. Raif stood three-quarters turned to his canvas. The light from the window highlighted the athletic line of his body and the planes of his face. When Favian was a boy no tales thrilled him more than Raif's stories of soldiering. He used to spend hours dreaming of accompanying him on his adventures. Favian shrugged his shoulders to dispel the tension. He resumed his pose.

'You were at Walcheren, weren't you, cousin?' he asked.

'I was.'

'I have been longing to speak to you about how it was. Your experiences . . .'

The brown ochre flowed from his brush. For a moment Jarrett could feel the bark at his back. He saw himself once more under the tree where the officers hung their gear. He would write to the boy when he could, illustrating his letters with little sketches – the mule that fell through the roof of the barn; the fat sergeant losing his boot in the bog. As if telling amusing tales of soldiering to a sick boy who rarely left his room was proof of his own humanity. A preservative against the suspicion that the savagery, the burnt villages, the mud and the blood and the stench of death had made him a monster. The wash was threatening to flood the line. He caught it with his brush.

'Will you tell me about it? Walcheren, I mean.' The boy's voice was insistent.

'Very little to tell. Mosquitoes, marshes, boredom and men dying of fever.'

Favian thought of his verses. That was not how he imagined it. His cousin's tone was flat; a wall thrown up against further prying. The strokes of rough bristle caught against the weave of the canvas.

'But you came through all your campaigns. I think nothing can hurt you, cousin.'

Jarrett's eyes met his, startling in their intensity. There was a sadness there that chilled him. The connection broke.

'There was no glory in Walcheren, Grub.'

'But you were an honourable soldier.'

'I tried.'

'And you did your duty.' There was beauty in the exercise of duty – to protect and serve others.

'I hope so.'

'You did your duty for the good of others . . .' Favian forged on stubbornly. Raif made a derisive noise.

'Soldiering is about following orders, Grub. I followed orders and tried to keep my men alive. A contradictory pair of duties, as often as not,' he added.

Favian stared at him. Could the man he had once thought so admirable be merely ordinary?

'But why did you take to soldiering if not for honour or something fine?' he demanded indignantly.

Jarrett thought fleetingly of how he had sailed from England all those years ago. He was very young at the time; he probably had dreamt of a noble death in distant lands but now he was older he knew better. That youth had fled rather than face the dilemmas of his life. No honour there.

'So why?' Favian's voice was shrill. 'Why did you soldier then – you must have thought you were good for something!'

It was not something he liked to speak about. Jarrett focused on the canvas before him.

'For necessity,' he replied casually. 'The army would take me and a man has to eat.'

There, sitting in that sunny room, his body twisted in that tortuous pose, Favian Adley's idolatry shattered.

The scales fell from his eyes and Raif Jarrett stood before him a mere soldier; a fine physical specimen who took orders, risked his life and took others, so that he might eat.

'You would support the colonel,' he demanded, 'a man you despise – even if he brings in soldiers to crush local men, these weavers?'

Jarrett shot him a glance. He could see the boy was upset. Raif Jarrett had been raised by a proud English-woman who had spent many years in exile on the continent among foreigners. From childhood he had been schooled in the belief that British liberties, and the system of king and parliament that sustained them, were the envy of the world. Time had tempered his convictions but some residue remained. The boy had been out in the world so little, he thought sadly.

'If men don't break the law, the colonel can do nothing – for all his wild suspicions,' he reassured him. 'Ison cannot act alone.'

Favian snorted indignantly. 'So you would do nothing!'

'I did not say that.'

'Then what?'

'You've barely arrived, Grub. You need to get a better sense of things.' Favian had turned pale. Jarrett thought he caught the glint of tears in his eyes. He smiled coax-ingly at him. 'Besides, any man of action should scout a problem thoroughly before he attacks it. Go in blind and you are likely to come to grief.'

'An honourable man stands behind his beliefs – you taught me that,' the youth protested.

'It's never that simple, Grub. Taking violent action in support of beliefs leads to their betrayal more often than not. Imperfect order is better than anarchy.' Jarrett paused; his voice deepened. 'I have been in places where men operate without order and believe me, humanity does not flourish.'

A clock struck in the hall below.

'Have you enough for now, cousin? The fairs open at noon.'

Jarrett put aside his brush and wiped his hands. 'Enough for now. Go. You are at liberty!'

Favian nodded. With an uncomfortable half-smile and lowered eyes he left.

Jarrett watched the empty doorway a moment.

'I've disappointed him.'

'Nonsense. You're his hero!' blustered Charles with just a touch of envy. 'What better man to emulate than our Raif?'

'I'm no one's hero.' Jarrett repudiated the notion in disgust.

'You're my hero!' trilled Charles, clasping his hands before him and fluttering his eyelashes like some trollop in a play. Jarrett buffeted him with his spare hand.

'I know I was young once, but I was never *that* young,' said Charles.

'You have never felt such passion?'

'You *know* I am quite without enthusiasm,' Charles

responded. A glimpse of self-knowing amusement crossed his face. 'A gentleman should never be too passionate – it is unsettling.'

'For you or for the order of things?'

'Precisely.'

Jarrett snorted.

'Don't it strike you as odd,' Charles continued, 'that the family should have chosen the pair of us to set the little fellow back on the path to righteousness and sobriety? I don't know as I like being cast as a dull, preachy fellow.'

Jarrett turned his back, busying himself with his brushes at the table.

'Mrs Adley does not ask for sobriety. She is content with all the manly vices. It is the exaltations of the poet that unsettle her.'

Charles's eyes were on the portrait. 'What father would not take pleasure in looking upon the image of such a son?' He remarked ironically. 'But I fear canvas is the nearest Grub's parent shall come to it.' He stilled. 'The shape of his head,' he said, 'don't he remind you of . . . ?'

Jarrett was caught out. It surprised him that after all these years the pain of one child's loss could still catch him in the heart.

'I sometimes think of what little brother Ferdy might have been,' Charles went on quietly, 'had he not been taken from us.'

'I know.'

'Instead we are left with this brat!' he exclaimed.

They stood side by side surveying the image taking

shape on the canvas. Favian sat in a cloudy form of darks and lights and through the window behind him a sweep of land and big sky.

'Is it safe to let him roam like this – full as he is with his new wondrous notions?'

In his mind's eye Jarrett saw Favian surrounded by his new acquaintances at the Red Angel the night before. They seemed a decent group of men. He liked what he had seen of Miss Lippett's oddly independent servant. For all Favian's outrage at his glimpse of the conditions of the working man Jarrett knew of no acute distress among the weavers – certainly none of the kind likely to fuel real dissent. Let the boy explore this new world. Perhaps his singing companions would teach him sense.

'A cousin of the mighty Duke of Penrith?' he said lightly. 'What harm can he come to in this neighbourhood?'

CHAPTER TEN

The whole population of Woolbridge, it seemed, and that of quite some miles beyond, had braved the chill to gather along the route of the fair. Booths choked Cripplegate down to the bottom of the hill where the wool and leather goods were displayed in front of Bedford's mill. By law nothing could be sold before the opening rituals but here and there stallkeepers struck bargains behind counters and awnings while keeping a weather eye out for the constable. Favian spotted a free space by the railings in front of Bedford's house. As he was making for it his breath caught. It was the same neat figure, the glossy hair, the pink cheeks. There, sitting in an open window, was the young girl who had befriended him in the coach.

He crossed the space between them. There was a half-basement. His eyes were on a level with her waist. He tilted up his face.

'Remember me?' he asked.

She stood up in a fluster and took a step back into the safety of the room.

'Sir! We have not been introduced.'

'F-Favian Vere Adley at your service,' he stammered. He recalled his wits, thinking of their journey north together. 'But we *have* been introduced,' he said.

'By a stranger!' she protested, as if he had cheated at a parlour game.

'Well, I certainly wouldn't want that frightful woman's acquaintance,' he responded, shuddering at the memory of the importunate milliner. His companion stifled a giggle.

'If we've been introduced, you must remember my name,' she said boldly.

'Miss B—' he stumbled as the significance of her family name struck him. 'Bedford,' he pronounced, sounding startled. 'You see, we are old acquaintances.'

She held out her hand. She wasn't wearing any gloves. Her hand was small and rounded with the neatest little nails imaginable. He took it carefully and bowed over it. She made a soft sound halfway between a cough and a sigh.

'I'm a poet,' he announced, straightening up. Now why had he said that? he thought to himself, appalled.

'I thought you might be something of the sort,' Miss Bedford responded matter-of-factly. 'You are the first poet I ever met.' They gazed at one another in bashful silence. He cleared his throat.

'You must be very clever,' said Lally in a rush. 'I wonder where you find your ideas!' She stopped abruptly and bit her bottom lip as if embarrassed by the sound of her own words.

'From all around,' he replied, recovering himself. 'A man meets inspiration everywhere. In the street,' he waved a hand to encompass the scene before them. Then inspired at that very moment, he turned back to her. 'Or in a window.'

Her lashes fluttered. She looked down and blushed. He teased the edge of the red handkerchief that protruded from his cuff.

'I have something I should return to you.' He drew her handkerchief from its hiding place and held it out. She looked at him as if he had just produced a toad. 'It is laundered,' he said quickly, 'just a little crushed.'

'Oh!' she leant forward a fraction.

'I shall always remember your kindness to me,' he blurted out. 'I hope I did not distress you.' In the coach he had thought – just for an instant – that he might die. It seemed to him that that moment had created an intimacy between them. His very skin glowed in the warmth of her dark brown eyes.

'Are you recovered?'

Her solicitous enquiry made him realize that his chest had not felt tight all day.

'Perfectly recovered,' he replied energetically. 'This country air, you know, it does one a power of good.' There was a butcher's stall up wind. The drain flowing behind it was clogged with pungent blood and guts. Miss Bedford wrinkled her nose sceptically. He caught the joke a step behind her and for a moment there were just the two of them bound together in the shared humour of it.

She reached down tentatively to take the handkerchief. He pulled his hand back.

'May I keep it?'

'Why?'

'For inspiration.' She cocked her head like a curious kitten.

'Keep it then,' she said.

'I shall cherish it as a token . . .' He stopped himself. He didn't want her to think him an ass. 'A reminder of your kindness,' he amended. 'I shall write a sonnet in its honour.' His mind raced ahead to a delicate, witty composition playing on the sentiment of how a heart might be snared in a simple square of cloth.

'Hey Book Boy!'

Favian glanced over his shoulder. His companions from the night before had emerged from the crowd at the mouth of Powcher's Lane. Dickon Watson towered above the rest.

'Your friends are calling you,' said Miss Bedford briskly. He looked up at her.

'Why not come down and join me?' he asked.

She hesitated, doubt and inclination at odds in her expressive face.

'My aunt . . .'

'Come with me,' he coaxed. He swept his best London bow. 'Miss Bedford, may I beg your company for a tour of the fairs? I dare say you would find it amusing.'

The lady darted a look behind her and made up her mind.

'I shall fetch my things,' she said and disappeared.

Dickon strolled up on his long legs. He dropped his chin.

'All right?' he greeted Favian. 'Who's that?'

Favian wondered if he looked any different. He knew he was not the same man Dickon had seen the night before.

'Miss Bedford!'

'Bedford?' Dickon's eyes narrowed.

'I am to escort Miss Bedford around the fair.'

Dickon scowled. 'I thought you were with us on this!' he said belligerently.

The old Favian might have been intimidated. The new one floated, buoyed up on a cloud of fresh emotion.

'I am!' he protested.

A sly grin dawned on Dickon's face.

'Bedford's niece! Quick thinking, Book Boy,' he said approvingly. 'We'll walk ahead of yous.' He backed away to rejoin his friends. 'Got plenty of coin?' he called. 'You're going to have to buy her things, know that, don't you?'

'Ribbons at the very least,' Jo agreed.

'Or fairings. My Nancy likes fairings,' chimed in Harry Aitken. Dickon jerked his head at the tousle-headed weaver.

'And Hen's married, so he'd know,' he said, mock solemn, and they walked on up the hill laughing.

Jarrett shrugged his shoulders, drawing his heavy cloak about him. The wind was blowing from the east. He detected a yellow tinge to the solid lid of cloud. There would be snow by nightfall. He had taken up a post at the top of a small flight of worn steps overlooking the tollbooth. The marketplace, filled with pens and beasts, stretched out to his right and Cripplegate Hill, crammed with its people and stalls, dropped down to his left. A clutch of excited young girls – no more than twelve or thirteen years old – stood below him exercising their lungs calling out as a group of adolescent boys passed by. His eye travelled on in their wake. Half-concealed behind an ample mother checking her rampant charges, just to the left of the burly father uncomfortable in his unaccustomed bindings, he spotted two soldiers. They were wearing greatcoats buttoned up over their red jackets, their eyes on watch. One glanced over as if to check a position. Jarrett followed the line of sight and picked out another soldier. Soon he had identified a good half-dozen men posted up and down the crowd.

Up by the market cross a fife and drum were heard and then the ringing of a hand-bell. The press heaved and shifted as a haphazard procession pushed its way past the pens. Out of the corner of his eye he caught sight of something bright standing out against the winter colours of the scene. A woman dressed in a striking costume chevroned in bands of lemon and black had just emerged from the Queen's Head. The sweeping black brim of the hat turned to reveal the unmistakable profile of Miss Lonsdale. A liveried footman stood beside her at the rail of a bath chair. The chair contained a hunched, frail-looking being swaddled in an Indian shawl. So the fairs had drawn out Lady Catherine, Sir Thomas's close relative and companion at Oakdene Hall. The old lady rarely left the Hall in winter. There was a white and tan terrier at her feet. The creature carried a walking stick that protruded at least a foot either side of its mouth. It trotted before its mistress's chair mowing a path through the crowd with an absurd air of self-importance.

The procession approached. Thaddaeus Bone led the way with the white staff of his office as Borough Constable. By his side walked a young boy carrying a brass hand-bell. They were followed by a group of constables dressed in the ill-fitting jackets of their ancestors, bearing ancient halberds from the town armoury. Then came an irregular gap that swelled and narrowed in relation to the perseverance of the fifteen jurymen of the Borough Court who trailed after them. They grouped by habit in their various degrees. The publican, Jasper Bedlington, walking alongside Mr McKenzie, the shopkeeper, and Captain Adams keeping company with Mr Bedford, the mill owner. The magistrates brought up the rear wearing the expressions of public men doing their duty. It felt strange to recognize so many faces. He could attach histories and connections to nearly every participant. It was almost as if he were a settled man. The thought made him uneasy. He filled his lungs with chill air.

The boy rang his bell with enthusiasm and Constable

Bone proclaimed the rules of the fair. The officials processed down the narrow channel between the stalls to repeat the proclamation at the farthest boundary and then marched back up to the marketplace and dispersed. The Easter Fairs had begun.

He should pay his respects to Lady Catherine. Jarrett abandoned his perch and plunged into the crowd. He spied Miss Lonsdale's yellow and black further down Cripplegate. The old lady was no longer with her. Miss Henrietta was bending over a stall in company with her odd acquaintance, Miss Lippett. He stopped, concealed amid the customers pressed round a hot sausage stand.

Miss Lippett was hesitating over a particularly offensive pottery cherub with bulbous cheeks. For all he found the woman uncongenial, he would not have suspected a gentlewoman of such appalling taste. He wondered what could have led Miss Lonsdale to make such a tiresome friend. As he considered the question, a farmer's daughter with the vacant, milksop look of a sentimental print of a milkmaid dropped her handkerchief in the path of some young men. Jarrett recognized faces from the Red Angel song club. He watched as Miss Lippett's singing servant sprang forward. His employer's expression as the man returned the scrap of cloth to the girl was a sight to behold. Could it be that the absurd spinster cherished a penchant for her sturdy serving man?

He had almost made up his mind to step out of cover when Charles came into view. He was labouring to push Lady Catherine up the steep incline in her chair as the old lady emphasized something with an expressive twist of her mittened hand. Jarrett could see Charles was quite out of breath. Miss Lonsdale turned to greet the pair. Something snagged in his chest at the warmth of her expression.

'Why Mr Jarrett, I thought it were you. I were hoping to catch a word ...'

Mr Hilton of High Top barred his way. Bulky and beaming, the farmer settled his weight with the air of a man expecting to bide. Jarrett's eyes flicked left and right. The queue at the sausage stall blocked his escape – it would be undignified to push them aside like ninepins. At his back he was pinned by a trio of goodwives catching up on a winter's worth of news. There was nothing for it – he was cornered.

If cattle could speak they would no doubt converse in the manner of Mr Hilton. His philosophy was of a domestic nature, resting on his deep appreciation of the simple necessities of life.

'Now I took a fancy to a piece of fish,' he declared, clearly convinced that others would find his choice of supper as interesting as he. 'You know how it is, Mr Jarrett. My dear said, Husband, if it is fish you want it is fish you shall have, though I have to send our Margaret ten miles for it ...'

A gap opened in the press before the sausage stand.

'The Marquess of Earewith expects me. Forgive me—' he said in a rush. Darting through the narrowing chink, the duke's agent made his escape.

'As to the eating of fish, I'm as happy with a bit of bacon or a beef stew meself,' said a voice in his left ear.

'Duffin! So you're here. Trouble?'

'Won't be long, I reckon. Heelanders should be kicking off soon. Better than a play, t'fairs.'

'Any idea where?'

Duffin jerked his head in the direction of the market-place. Jarrett saw Lieutenant Roberts, waist high above the crowd on the back of his black mare.

'As pretty as a picture!' the stallkeeper wheedled, holding up a handful of coloured ribbons against her customer's dark hair.

'But which might go best with peach satin?' Miss Bedford's expression was serious.

'Peach now – would you be thinking more yellow or pink?'

Barely an hour previously Favian would have scoffed at the very idea that he could be content to watch anyone expend so much effort on the choice of a ribbon. Now he was transfixed. The little moue she made when she considered; the enchanting attitude she took as she held the ribbons against her hair to see the effect in the stall-holder's mirror. He stamped his icy feet. It was a good deal colder here than it had been down in London but it was a small price to pay. Since he had come north, he had become a different being. His eyes wandered over the market, gloriously content.

He stiffened. Across by the tollbooth he saw Lieutenant

Roberts. He was up on his high horse again, looking down. A familiar figure stood by the mare's shoulder – Raif! Favian shook his head to dislodge the ghost of a corrupt smell. Why should he remember that now?

The last time they'd met Raif had not known him. A twelvemonth since, when Charles first brought him back, they had thought he would die of his wounds. Favian's mother had written him so in a letter that had brought him all the way to Ravensworth, praying with every mile to the God he did not know that Raif should not die. He had barely recognized the restless, sweating feeble being lying in that darkened room. Across the barrens of his own sickness it had been Raif Jarrett – constant, all enduring – who had given him the courage to hope in-better things. Looking down at the lost soul in that bed he had felt cheated. Now the doubt that blossomed that day seemed a portent. In his boyish idolatry he had made a hero, as wise as he was fair in form – something impossible. He could see that now. It had been a shock, of course, to see his boyhood idol exposed as a mere agent of others, but he was the better for it, he told himself. He glanced at the girl beside him, her head bent over the rainbow of ribbons. In the past days he had taken steps of significance in his life. He had a purpose all his own.

'What do you think?' Miss Bedford held out her choices for inspection.

'I think they are nearly as pretty as you,' he said gallantly. He paid for the ribbons feeling exhilarated and a little light-headed.

Up ahead he spotted Dickon moving through the crowd, head and shoulders above the rest. A lad with a mess of light hair that stood up like a dandelion clock around his head was approaching from the opposite direction. Favian tucked Miss Bedford's gloved hand more securely under his arm.

'Eh up!' Dickon acknowledged the lad with a slight toss of the head.

Without a word the newcomer grabbed Harry Aitken's hat off his head.

'Give it him back!' Jo's hand darted out, missing its object by a whisker. The newcomer tossed the hat to Dickon, who danced back kicking up his heels like a pugilist in the ring.

'Need to do better than that,' he taunted. With a casual flick of the wrist he sent the hat spinning. It sailed through the air in a graceful arc to be caught by Sim Cullen who, clutching the prize to his chest, darted through the crowd as swift as a deer. Harry hallooed and raced after him, the others at his heels.

Jarrett's attention was drawn by a joyous shout. He swung up onto the stone balustrade of the tollbooth to get a better view. A collection of youths were weaving in and out of the passers-by. It took him a moment to see that they were playing a game – like a football match without teams and a hat for a ball. The atmosphere was good-humoured – the various players vying with one another in their exuberant displays.

The current possessor of the hat found a pen blocking his path. He vaulted over the rail and crossed the press of cattle, stepping from back to back. Bounding from a convenient barrel he threw in an effortless somersault for all as if he were a Chinese acrobat at Vauxhall Gardens. The pack descending on him, he threw the hat over to a confederate who caught it in a springing turn. As he landed he snatched a kiss from a pretty girl, to the evident delight of the passers-by who stopped to watch. Jarrett spied Favian on the far side of the street. He had a girl on his arm. He was hurrying her off towards the Queen's Head. Jarrett smiled at the boy's protective air. What a dark horse Grub was turning out to be.

Harry Aitken's hat travelled high above the press of heads, gliding on the air beneath its brim. Dickon sprang out of the crowd and caught it again in one neat movement. He came to earth, colliding with a passer-by, sending him sprawling into a group of visiting miners from up the Dale. Dickon rolled round them with a shouted apology and was off again. The heelanders' expressions were stormy. Forged by heavy work under and over the ground, they were furnished with as much muscle as you could decently pack into a man. One clenched his fists and a townsman hit him. The group disappeared in a pack of weavers. The sounds of fists meeting flesh and bone, grunts of effort and yelps of pain rose as decent folk scattered.

By decree of the Borough Court, should any argument at the fair come to violence the constable and his assistants were to arrest the culprits, confining them in the tollbooth lock-up until payment was made of a deposit to ensure future good behaviour. In anticipation of such occurrences, on fair days Constable Thaddaeus provided himself with three sturdy fellows, mature men like him, who had been scrappers in their youth and had solidified into something formidable. Jarrett watched this group making their way towards the dense patch of humanity that seethed with staccato blows and grunts. There were others ahead of them. Lieutenant Roberts was pushing his fretful mare through the crowd and his men, distinguished by their coats, were suddenly visible gathering from their different posts.

Jarrett jostled against the tide of folk moving away. Ahead of him soldiers reached the fight. For a moment it flared up; then, just as quickly, Jarrett felt the energy dissipate. He was about to break through the dense crowd when a familiar flash of blue caught his attention. Just for an instant he saw the tow-headed youth with the blue neckerchief from the Red Angel – the one that had been sitting listening so intently to his companion in the alcove at the back. He was half twisted about, his face turned to the seat of the fight and his body facing away, as if he were caught between fascination and the desire to flee. The expression on his face was striking – part eager astonishment, part fearful; a vignette from some old master's painting of the Last Judgement. A substantial matron carrying a large basket collided with Jarrett and he almost lost his balance. When he recovered his footing the youth with the blue neckerchief had moved on.

Constable Thaddaeus and his men stood grouped to one side as the fair-goers flowed past, affecting a studious indifference now that the action was over. Lieutenant Roberts sat on his horse at the centre of a clearing. His men held between them a couple of miners and a man with a shaved head and a grey wig hanging half-out of his pocket. The latter seemed drunk. He leant away from the restraining hand on his coat.

'I'll have ya!' he yelled, arms flailing.

It seemed a poor catch, given all the drama.

'Take them down to the barracks,' the lieutenant commanded, all business. 'Lock 'em in the storehouse and post a guard.'

Thaddaeus Bone advanced with square shoulders and a stubborn look. 'We puts them in the town lock-up,' he stated. 'These men are my charge by rights.' The lieutenant looked down briefly from the heights of his saddle.

'Colonel Ison's orders,' he snapped. 'You four, bring them. The rest of you, resume positions. This won't be the last of it.' He rode off, using his mare's superior bulk to push aside the constable's men.

Thaddaeus Bone turned to the duke's agent as if he had seen him for the first time.

'Has he the right, Mr Jarrett?' the constable demanded. 'Brawlers in the market go before the Pie Powder court. That's the way it's done – always has been.'

'I'll find the colonel and see what it's all about. They

won't be taken out of town,' the agent reassured him. Jarrett felt a hand on his arm. Charles had appeared at his side.

'The colonel wants us. Something's happened,' he said in a low voice.

'Where is he?'

'Bedford's.'

A sulky housemaid received them. The interior of the house was still against the noise of the fair outside. The maid led them to a half-open door, tapped on it and slipped away. Jarrett pushed the door open to reveal the edge of a mirror-polished mahogany dining table and the vicar, Mr Prattman, standing at the window beside Sir Thomas. They were watching the soldiers march their prisoners down to the warehouse that served as barracks.

'Isn't that Bedford's new coachman?' The vicar frowned. 'Not another drinker,' he murmured sadly.

'Last one burnt himself to death in a stupor,' Sir Thomas supplied, addressing Lord Charles with the mournful expression of an inveterate gossip. 'Bedford's unlucky in his choice of people.'

'My lord!' Colonel Ison hurried up with a chubby man in a rust-brown suit in tow. He introduced the stranger briefly as Mr Kelso, a visiting magistrate from Richmond.

'And our host?' enquired Charles, looking about the room.

'Bedford?' the colonel responded impatiently, as if the whereabouts of the householder were an irrelevance.

'Had business. It is I who have called you here. See this!' He held out a dirty scrap of paper towards Lord Charles and shot a triumphant look at Jarrett. 'I said there was no time for complacency!'

'Oh, I am afraid I am not your man, colonel.' Charles clasped his hands behind his back with a frank, open smile. 'Raif is the one you want.'

'Mr Jarrett.' The colonel, frowning, thrust his paper towards the agent, a dull red flushing the apple of his cheeks. Jarrett took the scrap. Turning it to the light he deciphered a message scratched in foul ink.

'*At the great trybunal Day even justices shal be juged. Onest Men eat swil and you grow fat Have a Care the hogs rise in jugement aganst you and you shal surley go to hell.* Imaginative penmanship.' He turned the scrap over. 'No direction. Where ... ?'

'It was found on the seat of my carriage!'

'I see.' Jarrett made an effort not to meet Charles's eye for fear he might laugh. He tried for diplomacy. 'A few ill-spelt words, colonel, even ones so shocking ...' Charles made an involuntary noise in his throat. Colonel Ison's colour deepened to puce.

'When do you suppose it was done?' his lordship asked hurriedly. 'Was your carriage unattended? Surely some-one must have seen the perpetrator?'

'The carriage was parked up in Bedlington's yard. I had barely been gone ten minutes. My coachman heard the disturbance in the marketplace outside and went with the rest out into the street to look. He found the paper in the carriage on his return. He swears he was not gone long.'

'And you're sure of your man?' asked Mr Kelso.

'No question about him! Been with me for years.' It seemed there were some among the lower sort the colonel trusted.

'Well, this is very troubling . . .' Charles began. Colonel Ison interrupted him.

'It is more than that, my lord! As I have been trying to tell his Grace's man here . . .' The colonel extended his lips in a thin line. 'I do not sound the alarm on a personal whim,' he said between his teeth.

'But who among us has perceived any material signs of disaffection?' protested Jarrett. 'I have heard not a whisper – in town nor up the Dale.'

'Of course not! These villains have a serious purpose. They have been gathering for some time.' Colonel Ison drew out a letter from his pocket and shook it, shoulder high. 'I tried to warn you, Mr Jarrett – but I see I must be more particular. I have been warned, sir, of meetings. Meetings where . . .' He straightened the pages and holding them at a distance to focus, read out: '*An orator in a mask harangues the people and reads letters from distant societies by the light of a candle and immediately burns them.*'

Jarrett leant forward, intrigued. From what he could see the words ran square across the page. There seemed to be no salutation. The paper was covered in a painstaking hand fitted between ruled pencil lines.

'What is the source of this information, colonel?'

The colonel tucked away his letter with the furtive gesture of a greedy child hiding his sweets.

'I am not at liberty to say – my word should suffice,' he said haughtily. 'There is documented evidence of the administration of unlawful and secret oaths . . .'

'Twisting in,' supplied Mr Kelso knowledgeably, nodding his head with a solemn expression. The colonel shivered his shoulders as if shaking off a fly.

'There is a canker spreading,' he declared, 'and we must cut it out.'

'Canker, colonel? And what is this canker that must be cut out?' Mr Raistrick strolled into the room.

'You are late, Raistrick,' the colonel said.

The lawyer bowed ironically. He too held a paper, this one a printed ballad sheet.

'I bring entertainment. Picked it off the ground out there.' Advancing one foot before the other, one hand on his hip, he began to declaim in an ironic tone:

> *Corruption tells me homicide*
> *Is wilful murder justified.*
> *A striking precedent was tried*
> *In August 'ninety-five'*
> *When arm'd assassins dress'd in blue*

'Oh dear!' exclaimed Mr Prattman. Raistrick shot him a contemptuous glance. Jarrett's imagination drew a picture of an urchin taunting an elderly maiden aunt with gory tales.

> *'Most wantonly their townsmen slew,*
> *And magistrates and juries too*
> *At murder did connive.'*

'Murder! Magistrates! Oh dear, oh dear!' repeated the vicar, his eyes wide.

'An old song!' said Jarrett dismissively.

'What do you make of it, Mr Raistrick?' asked Charles curiously.

'What does it matter what songs they sing so long as the mills turn?' the lawyer replied lightly, his tone at variance with his watchful eyes.

'Drink!' said Sir Thomas, breaking through the surface of his habitual anonymity to remind his companions of his presence.

'Drink, Sir Thomas?' faltered Mr Prattman.

Sir Thomas dipped his head to gaze up over his delicate pince-nez.

'The magistrates should warn the publicans not to allow the people to remain in their houses tippling during the fairs.' His voice was soft. 'On pain of losing their licences,' he added helpfully. Then, appalled by the silence that met this contribution, the baronet retreated within the shell of his clothes.

'An excellent suggestion, Sir Thomas.' Mr Prattman looked around the company, vigorously bobbing his head like a puppet. 'Indeed. Indeed. An excellent suggestion. We can post notices.'

'Much good that'll do,' jeered Raistrick. He lounged

against the papered wall as if to mark himself out from the group.

'There are God-fearing people in Woolbridge, Mr Raistrick,' reproved the cleric. 'Strange though that may seem to some,' he added tartly, looking faintly smug at his own daring.

'Perhaps so, parson, but those aren't the troublemakers.'

The vicar didn't appear to hear this riposte; his expression was thoughtful.

'Two of those three arrested just now were miners from the workings up the Dale.' He frowned into the middle distance. 'Woolbridge men aren't likely to make common cause with,' he paused, '*heelanders*,' giving an arch emphasis to his use of the local term.

'Miners!' exclaimed Colonel Ison.

'No,' Raistrick said baldly. 'There's no such foolishness up there.' He intercepted Lord Charles's silent enquiry to Jarrett. 'I'd know of it,' he stated.

Jarrett surveyed the lawyer's bold features. His assurance was no doubt justified. There wasn't a mine in those parts where Raistrick's bullies did not control the workings.

'My information comes from the highest authorities,' Colonel Ison insisted.

'A government agent?' Jarrett pounced.

'I would think that you would take heed, Mr Jarrett!' blustered the colonel. 'As his Grace's steward you have much to defend – as we all do here.' Jarrett felt a vein pulse at his temple.

'Spying on our own countrymen? Are we in France?' he demanded.

'Pish posh!' responded the colonel surprisingly. 'How else, pray, are we to be forewarned? Forewarned is forearmed ...'

'I heard you were a spy yourself once, Mr Jarrett,' the lawyer's voice slipped in. What did he know? Jarrett thought of Bess and momentarily the ground shifted beneath him, although he could be sure neither his face nor posture betrayed him. He had been at the game too long for that. Fortunately the colonel had the bit between his teeth.

'My information is quite precise,' he was saying. 'Men are named. The tailor's son, John Blackwell, and William Dewsnap from Quarry Fell ...'

'But what manner of man denounces them?' Jarrett demanded. 'His Majesty's subjects cannot be condemned by mere accusation!' Charles shifted his position and shot him a warning look.

'This is not a philosophical society, Mr Jarrett! Property and lives are at stake,' scolded the colonel.

'Since it is a question of lives and property, should we not be certain of our information?' the duke's agent responded vigorously. 'Is there any corroborating evidence?'

Mr Prattman leant forward to interpose himself. 'Indeed colonel, I too should like to know who accuses John Blackwell. I always thought him a thoughtful young man. His father has been a member of my congregation for nigh on thirty years; why, he was my parish clerk and sexton for six until his good wife passed away and—'

'If only every son was a pattern of his father, Mr Prattman!' Ison raised his hand to wave the anonymous note in a rhetorical gesture. 'Will you ignore the evidence?'

'Anonymous accusations.' The parson shook his head. 'I do not like them. Wicked things. They lead to all sorts of mischief.'

Bravo Mr Prattman! Jarrett contemplated the man's moonish face; there was a stubborn morality there he had not perceived before. Perhaps there was more to the parson than he'd suspected.

'Enough!' Colonel Ison smacked his hand against the table top. 'There is a dangerous conspiracy afoot, gentlemen. I know my duty and I will do it!'

CHAPTER ELEVEN

'Remind me what the hell we're doing here?' muttered Jarrett as they descended from the carriage to face Bedford's front door for the second time that day.

'Because we've been invited; there are few enough amusements in the country.' Charles glanced sideways at him with the ghost of a smile. 'Think of it as intelligence gathering – how better to keep an eye on the colonel? He's bound to be here.'

The day had closed with that still, expectant light that promised snow. Jarrett could feel the icy pavement beneath his feet. As he reflected on the absurdity of evening pumps masquerading as shoes, a flake of snow landed on his forehead. He glanced up at the night.

'That was snow.'

'Nonsense,' responded his lordship.

Jarrett tugged impatiently at the impeccably folded cravat confining his throat. Ever since Tiplady had resumed command of his domestic life, he was insistent that his master attend social functions properly attired.

'What do you make of that note the colonel found pinned to his carriage?' Charles asked as they climbed the steps. 'A disaffected servant perhaps?'

'I wonder.'

'Ison seemed mighty put out.'

'No doubt he was offended by the sentiment that in the end even justices shall be judged.' Jarrett snorted. 'An unlikely enough event in this life!' The door swung open to reveal an interior full of warmth and candle-light.

'By the by, where's Grub?' asked Charles, handing the servant his cloak and hat.

'He said he'd make his own way.'

'Oh! I see.'

Jarrett turned to follow the meaning in Charles's voice. There, framed in an open doorway, was Favian. He was standing by a sofa talking to a short young lady in figured muslin over peach-coloured silk and matching ribbons in her thick dark hair. Jarrett recognized the young woman Grub had been squiring at the fair that afternoon. He was holding forth in the way of flattered young men while his companion looked up at him attentively.

'Not bad,' said the marquess, running a practised eye over the girl's figure.

'She's much too young for you,' responded Jarrett mechanically, coining over in his head the various excuses he might make to withdraw before the theatrical portion of the evening. He used to enjoy watching Bess perform, but in those days there was no question of mixed company. The room was packed with what passed for good society in Woolbridge. Half of them were staring at the new arrivals with the avid curiosity that always followed Lord Charles in the provinces. He caught a glimpse of their hostess in pink figured silk wearing a Spanish hat of rose sarcenet with three large ostrich feathers bobbing over it. She had her arm locked around the blue sleeve of Lieutenant Roberts's soldierly arm. As she flitted between her guests the young officer moved a beat behind her as if uncertain of his cue. Jarrett shifted irritably. He should never have let Charles persuade him to turn out.

'I see they've arrived.' Mrs Adams craned her head to look round the intervening guests. The ladies had managed to secure one of the rare sofas. Mrs Bedford believed that a successful party rested in pressing all her guests into one room. 'From the old manor,' she elaborated. Mrs Eustace moved to one side and Henrietta saw Mr Jarrett. 'I will say, you can always tell a London gentleman,' Mrs Adams added with a sentimental sigh. Her husband, Captain Adams, had his suits cut for comfort in York.

Mr Jarrett's dark blue coat had been expertly fitted. It lay across his shoulders without a tuck or crease, the figured waistcoat was just what was proper and his pale knee-breeches moulded to his skin. (His valet, Mr Tiplady, was secretly very proud of the shape of his master's legs.)

As she walked about the fairs that afternoon, Miss Lonsdale had seen the duke's agent more than once. She had thought he might come up and speak to her. Lord Charles had been his usual convivial self. Had she so offended Mr Jarrett by interrupting his conversation with that actress? If that were the case, Henrietta thought crossly, Mr Jarrett had more to apologize for than she; she wasn't the one keeping company with strolling players. She felt the sting of the scene in Bedlington's yard and her face grew hot.

'He is so much more of a *gentleman* than poor Mr Crotter.' Mrs Adams was openly staring at the man.

Mr Crotter had been the Duke of Penrith's previous agent whose untimely demise had brought them Mr Jarrett. Why, it was nearly a year ago now, Henrietta recollected. In small towns people soon become familiar with their neighbours and yet Mr Jarrett remained a mystery. For one thing he neither looked nor behaved like an agent; then there was his unexplained connection to the duke's family. Ever since she had heard the marquess's young relative greet Mr Jarrett as 'cousin' in Bedlington's yard Miss Henrietta had been puzzling at the meaning of it. She had even snatched an opportunity to consult Lady Catherine's copy of the *Almanach de Gotha*. She had found no mention of Mr Jarrett. She had closed the book feeling ashamed. What did it matter? If Mr Jarrett and the duke's family did not wish to speak of the nature of their connection, it was no one's business but their own. She wondered if he would turn his head and see her.

Mrs Parry, the surgeon's wife, stepped over to talk to Mrs Eustace and her view was blocked by an ample expanse of turquoise silk.

'Mr Jarrett! Come join us!' Mr Prattman hailed him from a group standing by the fireplace. Jarrett identified Captain Adams, a career soldier who had retired to the town on a modest inheritance, the Richmond magistrate, Mr Kelso, their host, the mill owner, Mr Bedford, and standing at Mr Bedford's elbow, Mr George, his acquaintance from the Bucket and Broom. The civil servant's eyes slipped away as Jarrett's crossed his.

'I was saying that there's considerable distress in the parish . . .' the vicar continued. Raistrick was over by the buffet table just to the left of them. The lawyer yawned and helped himself to a handful of nuts.

'A subscription,' Mr Prattman announced. 'We should raise a subscription among our neighbours to buy wheat and staples to be offered to those in distress at a reduced price. A little late, perhaps, but an appropriate Easter charity.' Jarrett heard the lawyer snort. The vicar picked up his pace. His round face was sincere and flushed under his wig. 'Every other week some poor woman makes application to me. If the women of Woolbridge are prepared to accept charity their distress must be real indeed.'

'Soup kitchens and Easter subsidies! Sop to the consciences of the rich!' sneered Mr Raistrick, cracking a nut between his back teeth.

'Charity is a gift, Mr Raistrick, and a Christian duty!'

responded the parson, twisting his neck uncomfortably to cast a severe glance at the man standing behind him.

'But is there enough to buy? That's the difficulty,' said Mr Kelso with a philosophical shake of his head. 'What with dealers taking up whatever they can find at well over the odds – I've heard they've been travelling from as far afield as Manchester.'

'There's plenty of oats!' scoffed Raistrick. 'Townsfolk grow soft. Want everything handed to them easy.'

Over the hot hubbub of the room Jarrett heard the mantel-clock strike seven. He'd give it a half-hour more.

As the last chime of the church clock resounded, Mr Prattman's curate turned the lock and withdrew the massive iron key from the door. He picked up his lantern, gathering his thick wool cloak about him, and paused a moment, listening to the peaceful stillness. There would be snow soon. If he hurried he could catch most of the farce. He liked a good comic. As he made his way down the path towards the marketplace he heard nailed clogs scuff stone on the other side of the church. The path through the churchyard was a popular short-cut down the backs to the river. More than one person was walking with the firm energetic tread of youth.

'What's the hurry?' a voice said. 'They'll all be at Bedford's or t'play.'

'It'll take a good hour and I want us there before eight,' came the curt reply.

It was only as he crossed by the tollbooth, negotiating his way between the pens, that it occurred to Mr Prattman's curate to wonder what business might cause a person to walk such a distance out of town on a cold night like this.

Favian felt tall and capable and splendidly alive. Miss Bedford was an excellent listener. He fancied he could see his every meaning reflected in her mobile face. In a few snatched moments while dressing he had made a promising beginning on his sonnet. It was on the tip of his tongue to tell her about it when an alarming matron in pink descended upon them, feathers bobbing above her head. Keeping her voice low, she addressed Lally passionately.

'I'll have you know, young miss, this is not your house that you may invite any Tom, Dick or Harry that takes your fancy. I've never seen this young man in my life!' she hissed. The hard blue orbs ran over him as if she were tallying up the cost of his evening dress in her head. The bill must have added up to a consideration, because she appeared to check herself. 'Well?'

Lally's dark brows drew together in a stubborn expression.

'Aunt Amelia, may I present Mr Favian Adley. Mr Adley, my aunt, Mrs Bedford, your hostess.' Lally's self-possessed tone surprised him. Favian felt a flush of pride in his diminutive companion. He imitated the saloon bow perfected by his most dandyish Oxford friend, a graceful inclination from the waist with left foot advanced before the right.

'Madam,' he said, looking up into his hostess's cross face. 'My apologies; I would not intrude. It is a misunderstanding. My cousin, Lord Charles, swore I was invited—'

'Lord Charles?' said Mrs Bedford sharply. One of the ostrich feathers in her hat slipped out of place and quivered slyly over her left eye. He bit his lip for fear he might laugh. Her eyes narrowed. She appeared to swell with indignation. Favian wondered in a panicked way what one was supposed to do if one's hostess boxed one's ears.

'I see you've arrived before us!' Charles's voice washed over him with the cooling sensation of relief. The marquess laid a casual hand on Favian's shoulder. 'How rude of me to arrive after my guest!' he declared with the cheerful confidence of a man who is welcomed wherever he goes. 'You must forgive me, Mrs Bedford. I see you've already met my young cousin Mr Adley – but then you will have noticed the family resemblance, I'm sure.'

Mrs Bedford's expression switched from startled to flirtatious in a blink. She smacked her niece's arm none too gently with her fan.

'Our young people have stolen a march on me, Lord Charles. My husband's naughty niece never told me they were acquainted!'

'What are young girls coming to these days!' exclaimed Charles comically, with a smile to Lally that invited her to join in the joke. Mrs Bedford's eyes snapped.

'Adelaide, your uncle wants you!' she commanded.

'Let me escort you, Miss Bedford,' said Favian quick as a flash, offering his arm.

Charles watched the couple depart.

'Ah the young,' he said sentimentally.

Mrs Bedford was glaring at a point in middle distance, as if burning to tell it some home truths. With a convulsive twitch of her gloved hand she summoned a servant. The nervous girl curtsied and offered up thin biscuits piped with pastoral scenes in gold arranged on a painted porcelain charger.

'Gold leaf,' his hostess informed him.

'Thank you,' Charles replied, sweetening his negative with a smile for the maid. 'I find precious metals set my teeth on edge.'

Mr Sugden surveyed his theatre, chewing the side of his nail as was his nervous habit on such occasions. Well past seven o'clock and the pit barely three-quarters full. Profits were made in the boxes. They were woefully bare. Just an old bent hunchback of a gentlewoman with her maid.

Jasper Bedlington's barn had been transformed. Platforms ran down each of the long sides at breast height, tapering towards the front and flaring out towards the back, so that the seats faced the stage on a rough curve. The well between formed the pit where the sixpenny ticket holders were accommodated on long benches. The side platforms were divided into stalls with painted boards. Here the box patrons were offered chairs with backs for two shillings (*cushions obtained at the pay table, thruppence a time*). Jefferies, the comic, was wooing the pit over the stage lamps with his trademark song 'Tidi didi lol-lol-lol, kiss and ti-ti-lara'. His squints and lewd gestures were causing much merriment among the country folks. There was none better than Jefferies in low comedy. He was well worth his two pounds a week – when there was the money to pay him. Sugden threw a disconsolate look over to the pay table by the door. Mrs Monk, in her make-up and the apple-green dress with orange sleeves, ready for her part as the thief-taker's wife Mrs Peachum, sat, her face abstracted as she counted sixpences. If Justice Raistrick's friends took much longer they'd arrive after the halfway mark and that meant half price; then there'd be no profit in the night at all. He'd have to send the call boy to the bar for Dick Greenwood and the others for the opera soon. He touched the rabbit's foot he kept in his watch pocket. A poor start meant a troublesome engagement, he thought gloomily.

Favian stared at the smooth back of Lieutenant Roberts's nut-brown head across the room; the preposterous feathers of the pink hat beside him were brushing his cheek. The lads would be on their way by now. At first he had meant to join them, until it was pointed out that his absence from the play might draw suspicion. He was eager to discover what progress the others had made. He would have to wait until tomorrow to find out. In the meantime, Favian consoled himself, he had the happy prospect of Miss Bedford's company. He thought how he might engineer an opportunity to sit by her at the play.

'Tell me – what of this afternoon's disturbances?' It was Raif's voice. Favian drew closer to the group by the fireplace. 'Have there been more arrests?'

'A bullock escaped from the pens,' answered the vicar, Mr Prattman. 'And Dan Whittle called Geordie Munsen a thief in the presence of witnesses. He refused to retract for at least an hour ...'

'There's been bad blood between them over a diseased hen Geordie supplied Dan last Michaelmas,' explained Captain Adams. He was a middle-aged man with an air of boyish sincerity lingering about his fleshy face.

'Other than that,' the parson shrugged, 'to my mind there's been less trouble this opening day than some other years.'

'Remember the time in '08 when the heelanders met the townsmen in pitched battle in the marketplace? Almost closed the fairs that time,' Captain Adams reminisced fondly.

'I believe that was '07 ...'

'Surely not. I had just purchased my good Welsh cob – it was '08 for sure.'

'My dear Adams ...'

'What about the colonel's radicals? The men the lieutenant took up?' Jarrett looked across at his host. Mr Bedford had a square head on square shoulders and a watchful stillness about him. 'The vicar says one of them was your coachman, Bedford – is that true?'

'Man was drunk.' The manufacturer's speech was truncated as if unnecessary syllables were a waste of his time. 'On his own time; gave him the afternoon off.' He seemed unmoved by his servant's misdemeanours. 'Leave him overnight. Learn his lesson.'

'I applaud you, sir!' chimed in Mr George delightedly. 'A firm hand's the thing. Servants are forever taking advantage without it.' Jarrett considered Mr George, wondering how many servants the civil servant kept. He looked like a man who lived in lodgings. Mr George's attention was fixed on their host, he noted, like a faithful hound.

'So the other two were the radicals?' he suggested.

'Just miners,' replied Mr Kelso.

'It is early days, Mr Jarrett.' Colonel Ison breezed up. He shook hands with his host and nodded to the rest. 'Apologies. I was detained.'

When they'd last met, he had been irritable, even alarmed. Now he seemed almost jovial. Jarrett wondered what might have occurred in the few intervening hours. Ison rubbed shoulders with Favian and glanced down at him.

'Colonel Ison! How do you do, sir?' The youth greeted him with a smile. 'How goes the investigation into the death at the Bucket and Broom?'

'Investigation? There is no investigation!' responded the colonel with a touch of his old irascibility. ''Twas a natural death. Body's been sent to London for burial.'

'I understood there were signs of foul play . . .' Favian said.

'Who told you that?' The colonel flicked a glance in Jarrett's direction. He harrumphed. 'Nonsense! I have lived in this district all my life. Perhaps I may be allowed to judge matters better than those who've not been here a twelvemonth!'

It was oppressive here by the fire. Too much hot air. Jarrett's thoughts slipped to the Tewards and their inn on the cold, clear moor. The snow should be falling up there by now. Hadn't Duffin mentioned he would be rabbiting out that way tonight? He searched the press of heads for his hostess's ostrich feathers, planning his exit. The party should be leaving for the theatre soon.

Charles was over by the buffet. Mrs Bedford had supplied an extravagant collection of desserts to tempt her guests. The centrepiece of the table was a vaguely off-centre pyramid of crystal dishes holding coloured blancmanges and jellies moulded in fanciful shapes. It gave the uneasy impression it might come tumbling down if anyone disturbed it by helping themselves to a dish. Every substance was pulled and moulded into the semblance of what it was not – flowers, fish, birds, leaves. The nap of Charles's black superfine coat gleamed rich in the light of the candelabra held aloft by a gilded nymph on a polished pink marble plinth. He leant forward to select a pastry piped into the shape of a plump dove glazed with raspberry jam.

'That's bound to ooze when you bite into it and ten

to one it tastes of warmed wax,' Jarrett murmured, coming up behind him. Such displays were made to impress the eye, not the palate. Charles cast a look down at his handsome waistcoat of embroidered Florentine silk and withdrew his hand with a small reluctant sigh.

'There's Miss Lonsdale! Good company at last!' Charles checked himself, noting the ladies filling the seats around her. 'Oh lord! What a tedious collection of old cats!' he said, and wandered off in the opposite direction.

She was looking right at him. It would be rude to leave without paying his respects. Tonight she was dressed in a claret-coloured velvet bodice cut low at the neck and cinched at the waist with a mother-of-pearl clasp. Her back was straight and her long legs made an elegant line as the fabric fell in rich velvety folds over an underdress of white satin. A ribbon of matching velvet confined her soft curls, and jewels in her necklace picked up the same tint. Miss Lonsdale had an instinct for colour. She drew the eye. Miss Lippett, sitting at her side, in contrast, was a poor counterfeit of a woman. She was wearing dull black satin up to her neck and a sour expression. The eccentric spinster flicked a glance in his direction and quite deliberately turned her back to him.

'The colonel says there is a foreign agent at work among us . . .' The speaker was a flush-faced woman in yellow he had never seen before. Was the colonel taking everyone into his confidence? So much for his vaunted discretion.

'Among us, Mrs Eustace?' cried Mrs Adams, leaning

forward and darting a nervous glance about the room.

'Not among *us*,' corrected Mrs Eustace, 'among the lower sort.'

'One would have thought one might notice a Frenchman.'

'Not a Frenchman!' exclaimed Mrs Eustace, fanning herself. 'I heard it from my cook, who had it from her cousin's niece – she's one of the colonel's maids up at North Park. She was laying fires and heard them talking. They're looking for an Englishman—'

'I don't believe it!' Mrs Adams exclaimed.

'A traitor of that sort is no Englishman!' stated Miss Lippett vehemently. 'Hanging's too good for them.'

'Or one that passes for such – a Yorkshireman, like one of them as is coming up for trial at York,' finished Mrs Eustace triumphantly, pleased with the effect of her piece of news.

Jarrett marvelled at this example of the efficiency of small-town gossip. Really, the spymasters of this world were missing a trick when they overlooked the natural talents of the opposite sex. He wondered idly if he were able to track down the niece of Mrs Eustace's cook's cousin whether that person might be able to tell him to whom the colonel had been talking.

'It is almost eight – should we not be thinking of going over to the play?' It was Miss Lonsdale who spoke.

'I do not mean to go,' announced Miss Lippett.

Henrietta had arrived alone at Mrs Bedford's entertainment, her aunt, Mrs Lonsdale, having taken to her bed pleading a headache, as was her wont to do when faced with the prospect of leaving her comfortable home on a winter's night. Aunt Lonsdale had been reluctant to let her niece attend that evening, alarmed by the thought of Henrietta stepping foot in a theatre without her chaperonage. Only Henrietta's assurance that Miss Lippett – whom Aunt Lonsdale respected for her pedigree – would make one of the party had quietened her objections.

'Miss Josephine,' Henrietta coaxed, hoping to persuade her. 'I shall miss your company. Why, the royal family, I hear, is very fond of the theatre; even her Majesty the Queen.' Miss Lippett, a hot Tory, had the greatest respect for the royal family, most particularly the poor benighted king and his good queen (their sons, for all they were princes, being, it could not be denied, rather wild).

'I have not heard that,' Miss Josephine said grudgingly. 'My father, God rest his soul, abhorred the playhouse. Others may shift and compromise, but the old families have a duty to uphold what is proper.'

'But Lady Catherine has a passion for the playhouse,' said Miss Lonsdale. Lady Catherine's pedigree was even longer than Miss Lippett's. Indeed, Lady Catherine's breeding was much too refined for her to set foot in Amelia Bedford's house (besides which, as she frequently reminded anyone who would listen, she couldn't abide fools).

'*She* has always been peculiar,' stated Miss Lippett with

the splendid intolerance of one eccentric for another. 'Romish,' she added, as if that explained it all.

Miss Lonsdale closed her mouth over the retort that rose to her lips. She was very fond of Lady Catherine and her religion was nothing to do with the case. At times Josephine Lippett was a remarkably silly woman for all her extensive reading. Mr Jarrett was watching them. His eyes met hers with a sympathetic expression. She broke the connection, feeling a little flustered.

'I confess I am eager to see *The Beggar's Opera*. I'm told it is most amusing,' she said lightly.

'Strolling players impersonating thieves and whores!' exclaimed Miss Josephine.

'Miss Lippett! Language, pray!' cried Mrs Eustace, fanning herself with an excess of propriety. Miss Lippett threw her a contemptuous glance that amply conveyed her opinion that Mrs Eustace was only the butcher's wife and therefore beneath her consideration.

'I speak as I find.'

'Why, Mr Jarrett,' Miss Henrietta said, her smile leaping the barrier between them, 'do come join us – we are too much women here.'

Miss Josephine Lippett stood up abruptly.

'I have a headache,' she announced. With a ghost of a nod to the ladies she stalked past Mr Jarrett.

A gong sounded from the hall and Mr Bedford's voice was heard announcing the departure for the theatre. Jarrett blinked. Mrs Adams and Mrs Eustace were gazing at him in silence, as if they expected him to do something extraordinary. Henrietta rose to her feet like a naiad arising from frozen water.

'Mr Jarrett, may I take your arm?'

It was only as he helped Miss Lonsdale on with her cloak that Mr Jarrett remembered his intention to make his excuses and avoid the play.

Outside in the cold night, the spy looked out from the shelter of the tollbooth. The moon was hidden behind cloud. He could just make out the pens and backs of the beasts that shifted and murmured in their sleep. At the top of the marketplace a fire flared. The watchmen guarding the cattle were clustered around a brazier. A couple of soldiers had joined them. It was early yet. He would be safe enough here. He settled himself, concealed in the shadows.

He was well paid. He made sure of that, but there was more to it. He liked the parts he played. When he assumed his part he was invisible. He could stand right next to any one of them and not one would recognize his importance. Once upon a time he had resented his anonymity, then he learnt how it could be turned to his advantage. He was a valuable man. They had no idea. Some days he held their lives in his hands. He went over his part, preparing himself for the night's work.

CHAPTER TWELVE

'No madam.' The voice had a Londoner's nasal intonation overlaid with an upper servant's propriety.

'What you saying, woman?' Mrs Eustace responded truculently. She was out of sight above. Mrs Adams, who followed her, had stopped at the top of the short flight of stairs that led to the boxes. Henrietta craned her neck to peek around Mrs Adams's bulk. At that angle she could just see a slice of Mrs Eustace's head. The butcher's wife was halted halfway down the narrow walkway behind the boxes. Lady Catherine occupied the stall nearest the stage. Mrs Eustace and Mrs Adams were hoping to occupy the next.

'This is a private box.' The statement was made in a tone of immovable politeness. Mrs Eustace twitched in fury and Henrietta glimpsed a sharp-faced middle-aged woman with a prominent bust. Fancy, Lady Catherine's maid. Fancy was formidable. Mrs Eustace was red-faced but retreating.

'This box, madam, I believe is free,' the servant said firmly.

The box places were limited and the ladies of Woolbridge were competing to secure a seat. Mr Jarrett had been shouldered aside in the rush through the door. Henrietta, pulled along in the wake of Mrs Adams, found herself stranded there, at the bottom of the left-hand stair. The barn was chilly and damp. She pulled her velvet evening cloak around her. Men on the back row of the pit had turned round to stare. They were eating sausages and nuts and one had a cup of ale. She felt exposed and out of place. Miss Josephine, for all her excessively stiff-backed morality, was right not to come.

At a signal from the manager, the musicians to the side of the stage began the overture again. The latecomers were holding up the opera.

'Fancy, where are my guests?' Lady Catherine's patrician tones cut across the noise. Fancy appeared at the top of the stairs. She beckoned Henrietta up.

'Just here my lady.'

Relieved and a little bewildered, Henrietta followed the maid past Mrs Adams and Mrs Eustace, who sat like a pair of outraged hens in the back box. They turned their faces resolutely away from her polite smile.

'I wouldn't like to guess what that young woman spends on her clothes,' she heard Mrs Eustace say. 'I saw that silk velvet at twelve shillings a yard . . .'

In an oasis of clear space, Lady Catherine sat enveloped in an olive-green silk counterpane gorgeously embroidered with oriental flowers and birds of paradise. She had before her a short ebony crutch with an upholstered top upon which she rested her arms to relieve the weight of her hunched back. At her feet, her white and tan terrier lay curled up on a large tasselled cushion covered in scarlet brocade. The curve of the old lady's spine was such she was forced to twist her head to the side to see out. Her expression was alive with puckish intelligence.

'Come! Come! Tell me about the Bedford woman. She has a new toy, I hear. Likes to play with soldiers, eh?'

Henrietta slid a glance to her right. Mrs Eustace glared at her across the vacant chairs. The rest of the theatre was almost full.

'I believe there are some coming in, Lady Catherine, who might be grateful for those seats,' she suggested tactfully.

'Paid the man a guinea for them,' the old lady said with supreme lack of concern. 'They're for me guests.'

His foot disturbed straw. The stink of the strollers' playhouse filled his nostrils – pressed humanity mixed with turpentine, cattle and warmed animal grease. He had paid for his ticket. That didn't mean he had to use it. He'd let the rush subside, Jarrett thought to himself. Mrs Bedford's principal guests were dividing up the stairs, left and right. The sheep and the goats. Justice Raistrick, as befitted the patron of that night's entertainment, occupied the right-hand box nearest the stage. He had Bedford with him. And Mr George. So the army buyer had filled his contract, had he? The groundlings were getting restless. The opera had been held up long enough. It wouldn't be long before those lads in the pit started throwing the nut shells and other debris that littered the floor. He heard Charles arguing with Grub behind him.

'So you're saying you would rather save an archbishop from the fire in preference to your mother?'

'You know my mother, cousin. Then again, I don't know any archbishops.'

'Damned puppy!' exclaimed Charles, laughing.

Jarrett grinned across at Grub, but the boy dropped his eyes.

'Excuse me,' he said and slipped away towards the right-hand stairs.

'What? Isn't Grub talking to me?'

An uneasy expression flickered across Charles's smooth face.

'Nonsense,' he said with a little too much emphasis. 'It'll be the girl. You know how that goes.' Mrs Bedford pushed past on the lieutenant's arm. 'Lieutenant!' Charles hailed him. 'You're settled, I see. And where are you billeted?'

A faint blush stole over the officer's smooth cheek.

'Mr and Mrs Bedford have been so kind as to offer me a room.'

'Silly boy! I tell him not to make so much of it. It is our duty to support our noble defenders!' Mrs Bedford trilled with a roguish look.

'Indeed.' Charles gazed back at the pair politely.

'Thank you for your hospitality this evening, Mrs Bedford,' Jarrett said, just to be saying something. 'You do your guests proud.'

'And why wouldn't I?' the manufacturer's wife demanded. Her hand twitched the immense pearls that hung around her neck like so many beads. 'Woolbridge may be far from London and other grand places but I still know how things are done!' She tugged her escort's arm and stepped up the right-hand stairs, the swing of her skirts reminiscent of an angry cat swishing its tail.

'What ever did I do to that woman?' Jarrett enquired plaintively.

'Never gave her a second look's my guess,' said Charles.

'So why are you spared the cut direct?'

'*I'm* a marquess!' he said smugly. 'Don't hit me,' he added, cheerfully. 'Yes?' A middle-aged woman encased in a close-weaved wool gabardine that spoke of the well-paid servant stood at his elbow.

'Mrs Fancy,' Jarrett greeted her, recognizing Lady Catherine's maid.

Fancy acknowledged him with an incline of her head. 'My mistress asks, will you join her in her box?'

The orchestra – if a fiddle, a cello, a flute, a tabor player and a hurdy-gurdy man deserved the name – were nearing the end of the overture for the second time. Charles and Raif found Lady Catherine with Henrietta Lonsdale in the left-hand box overlooking the stage, sipping wine from crystal glasses, a large box of chocolates balanced on a chair between them.

'There you are. Lord Charles, come sit by me,' the old lady greeted them. 'I want conversation. Henrietta here knows nothing of the theatre. Go on girl – take that seat over there.' Lady Catherine waved to the next box. 'Escort her, Mr Jarrett; they're about to begin.'

Charles bowed to Miss Lonsdale with a rueful look, as if to say grandes dames must be obeyed. Henrietta bobbed a curtsey and removed herself to the seat on the other side of the low partition. As she gazed resolutely at the scene below she sensed Mr Jarrett draw the seat beside her back a little. She turned to him.

'Am I blocking your view?'

'No. I am quite comfortable.' Indeed, she thought. Mr Jarrett looked remarkably at ease. She wished she felt the same.

'I enjoy a good Macheath,' Lady Catherine remarked to Lord Charles. 'Did y'ever see Kelly in the part? Too genteel by half. A dull, insipid sort of highwayman! Macheath should be a proper rogue. Fancy! Pour Lord Charles and Mr Jarrett some wine.'

The colonel was sitting across on the other side, his lieutenant behind him and Kelso the Richmond magistrate at his side. There were soldiers in the pit and more stood along the back wall. If there were insurgents about they'd hardly be gathered in this hall. Now would be the time to make mischief elsewhere, Jarrett thought. His eyes met Raistrick's. The lawyer sat barely twenty feet away. The barn theatre was an intimate space. Jarrett winced internally. When Bess stood this side of the stage, she'd be less than three feet from him. He flashed a glance at Miss Lonsdale by his side. She was examining the scene before her with every appearance of enjoyment.

There was excitement, she reflected, in being one among so many waiting, in anticipation of being entertained. The last time Henrietta had attended a play, she had had to travel to Richmond. The shifting light of the flaring tapers threw shadows on the faces below, making the ordinary magical. For all she counted herself a rational being, Miss Lonsdale found herself caught up in the childish pleasure of it all.

A middle-aged man with a comical mobile face, dressed in the style of the previous century, walked on stage.

'Hogarth, by God!' declared Lady Catherine with relish.

'Do you have a playbill, Mr Jarrett?' Henrietta asked. 'Who is that?'

'Mr Jefferies – I believe he was once at Astley's. He will be Mr Peachum, the thief-taker,' Mr Jarrett answered.

In his character as a receiver of stolen goods, the comic went through his book enumerating villains he might have hanged for a price, raising appreciative laughter in the pit by the sly insertion of worthy local names in the list. When he was joined by his playwife, Mrs Peachum, Henrietta found herself liking despite herself the companionable couple who thought nothing of murder for self-interest. The songs, too, were good. The opera's author had turned half the familiar tunes of her childhood to his use. Then Polly Peachum appeared.

The bold redhead from Bedlington's yard was transformed. Bess Tallentyre portrayed the author's heroine with such fresh innocence Miss Lonsdale was quite bewildered. And her singing! If truth and feeling could be a sound, it was embodied in that voice. Mr Jarrett was leaning back in his chair with an air of quizzical detachment. Polly advanced to the front of the stage. She stood barely an arm's breadth away. In the light of the oil lamps at her feet her eyes seemed huge in her white-painted face. She turned them to Mr Jarrett.

'*But he so teased me and he so pleased me,*' she sang poignantly.

The notes undulated through the house enchanting every ear. She seemed to be singing just for him. As the lady who happened by circumstance to be sitting at the gentleman's side, Henrietta didn't know where to look.

Bess was up to her old tricks. What had he been thinking to allow himself to be trapped in such a situation! Jarrett shifted his position and looked across the audience, resolutely thinking of other things. He noted that Lieutenant Roberts was no longer sitting in his place behind the colonel. At the back of the box nearest the door, Favian wasn't paying attention to the stage at all. His eyes were fixed on the girl in peach. Jarrett thought of Grub's friends from the Red Angel. Given their interest in ballad singing, surely they would be here somewhere. He scanned the pit. Bess finished her song and was drawn into dialogue further off. He caught Miss Lonsdale's grey eyes watching him.

'The singing is rather fine, do you not think?' she asked.

'Indeed.'

Favian pushed the heavy door to behind him. He had watched her slip out, but where was she? A horse whickered and he saw a pale figure over by the stables. Lally was stroking the nose of a roan poking its head over a half-door. She smiled at him as he approached.

'My seat is directly over some of those tapers. The smell of hot tallow!' she pulled a comical face. 'I was near dying for lack of a breath of clean air.'

'Do you like the play?'

'I like the songs.'

'And the highwayman?' asked Favian, thinking that Mr Greenwood cut quite a dash in the part.

'He is rather old,' she replied, her attention on the horse she was petting. The roan was an old nag with a rough coat, mixed with grey.

'Your glove . . .' he warned.

Lally looked at her hand. There was a greasy smudge on the palm of her kid glove.

'Oh dear! You need a bath,' she told the roan severely.

The sounds of the opera were muffled within the barn. There were just a couple of lamps burning in the yard. In the night it seemed an entirely private place. She cast a glance back to the barn door.

'Shall we take a turn round the yard?' he suggested quickly. 'Before we go in. The air is so crisp and fresh.'

Through the archway the vista of cattle pens stretched out beside the tollbooth. All was shadow and quiet. It was as if they were the only ones awake in a sleeping world. She turned up her face and he forgot himself in the sweetness of her expression. He felt the startled intake of her breath as his mouth touched hers. His hands slid about her waist.

A horse whinnied over by the church.

'There's someone coming.' Lally broke away, alarmed. Footsteps were approaching. A brisk manly tread. Favian drew her into a darkened doorway just in time. The man strode past them. He could feel her heart beating against his. Her hair smelt of roses.

'The coast is clear,' he said, smiling down at her. She wrinkled her nose, her eyes mischievous.

'We should go back,' she said.

'Do we have to?' he protested, and kissed her again. He raised his head.

'What?' she asked.

'There's someone there, over by the tollbooth.'

She turned in that direction, responding to the intensity of his expression. Favian was peering through the dark, a small frown creasing his forehead. At first she saw nothing, then a group of shadows shifted and she glimpsed a silhouette, its edges silvered in the moonlight.

'I know that—' he began.

'Adelaide!'

'Dear Lord! That's my uncle calling me!' Lally slipped

out of his arms, pulling her shawl about her. 'Stay here. He must not see you.'

The door to the barn theatre was open and in the shaft of light Mr Bedford stood looking about. Her light slippers pattering on the stone, Lally ran along the shadows back to the roan horse, who watched her, twitching its ears.

'I'm here uncle,' Favian heard her say. Her voice was light and unconcerned. 'I was feeling faint and came out for a breath of air.'

'You come in now,' came the abrupt reply.

He heard the door slam. His heart was pounding. It couldn't be and yet . . . Suddenly it all made sense. His first thought was to consult Raif, then he steadied himself. That was no longer possible. He must act alone.

Henrietta wondered at herself for laughing. This Newgate comedy was an outrageous combination of the most blatant immorality blended with true feeling. Polly's plight had become real to her. Her heart was moved despite herself. The heroine's singing was sweetness itself, although Polly's innocent bloom was a little rubbed once her lover stepped on stage. Dressed in a red, waisted coat, long black boots and a tricorn hat, Mr Greenwood's highwayman was a picture of gallantry. Indeed Macheath's deluding charm was so persuasive that Miss Lonsdale found herself torn between enchantment and disgust. Miss Polly, she thought, was a little too easy with her highwayman's intimacies. As Macheath wrapped his arm about his lover's waist and kissed her neck, Henrietta was uncomfortably conscious of Mr Jarrett's presence beside her.

'*Were I laid on Greenland's Coast*,' sang the highwayman, tracing his inamorata's neckline with his finger. '*And in my Arms embrac'd my Lass / Warm amidst eternal Frost / Too soon the Half Year's Night would pass*.'

Out of the corner of his eye Jarrett saw Miss Lonsdale blush. The pearl drop that hung from her ear quivered. Her dress was cut to the new fashion with nothing but a thin scarlet strap across the shoulders, leaving a hand's breadth of pearly skin exposed before it met the kid of her long white gloves. The necklace resting on her bosom caught the light as it rose and fell with the gentle swell of her breath. It had an antique, Italian look about it; filigree gold-wire flowers with deep red garnets for petals and pearls at their hearts. They showed to advantage against her skin. Her eyes met his with an enquiring look.

'May I compliment you on your necklace? It is Italian, I think?' he murmured.

'Indeed it is. It was my grandmother's. Do you know Italy, Mr Jarrett?'

'My mother has resided there some years.'

Lord Charles leant towards Lady Catherine.

'What do you make of our Macheath?' he asked.

'A fine rogue!' answered Lady Catherine with relish. 'A proper, red-blooded man!'

*

He had taken his horse from the stables unhindered. With their customers at the play, the ostlers were gathered in Bedlington's bar. The wind had specks of ice in it. As he rode they stung his face. He covered his mouth and nose with his muffler and pulled down his hat. A thin, otherworldly strength whipped his blood through his veins. He had never felt so tremblingly alive. There was a sort of coldness about his extremities but in his core he was sustained by the radiating certainty that he, Favian Vere Adley, was at last engaged in action of real consequence. He was in possession of information that only he could communicate. His friends depended on him. He strained his ears to listen for a rider ahead, urging his horse on.

A good mile away as the bird flies, up across on the moor, nets lay like shadows on the ground. The moon, a bright disc in the sky, illuminated the crisp tracks in the light covering of snow.

'Done?' Duffin called out low. Queenie twisted in the poacher's large hands, her nose quivering.

'That's the last one,' answered the boy, knocking in the peg. He opened the wooden box he carried slung around him. Duffin placed Queenie on the ground.

'Now you go to it.'

The ferret chirruped and slipped down the hole.

When *The Beggar's Opera* was performed at the Theatre Royal, Covent Garden, it was usual for the tavern scene with the ladies of the town to be played much reduced, with the worst indecencies being excised for the sake of the morals of the town and the sensibilities of gentlewomen. Mr Sugden's company played the scene as the author meant it. A chair had been provided mid-stage for Macheath to sit on while he enjoyed the company of his doxies. Bess, dressed in brown curls and a remarkably low-cut dress as the amorous Dolly, one of the ladies of easy virtue, dragged the chair over to the left-hand side of the stage. Macheath, thereby, was forced to follow and sit just below Lady Catherine's box. The gentlewoman and her guests, therefore, had the best view as 'Dolly' and Jenny Diver (Mrs Sugden in a red wig) competed to occupy Mr Greenwood's lap, exchanging banter of a decidedly lewd nature.

Lady Catherine and Lord Charles gave every appearance of being well entertained. Beside her, Mr Jarrett seemed to have gone to sleep with his eyes open. Henrietta stared at her gloves. She was profoundly relieved when the manager Sugden, masquerading as the bawd, Mrs Coaxer, took centre stage with his comedy.

Jarrett slid a side-glance under his lashes. Miss Lonsdale sat very straight. She had grown strangely familiar to him over the last few months. He was easy in her company. She had a calm poise about her that did not make demands of him, unlike some other women of his acquaintance. The candlelight played on the soft velvet of her bodice. It moulded pleasingly to the curve of her breast.

With an extravagant toss of her curls, her hips

swinging, Bess crossed the stage. Now she was playing to Justice Raistrick. Jarrett let out a slow breath.

'Women are decoy ducks, who can trust 'em?' the betrayed Macheath exclaimed.

Charles, who had been enjoying Lady Catherine's excellent claret, rocked back in his chair and shot Jarrett a look under raised eyebrows.

As he was dragged off in pasteboard chains, Mr Greenwood cut such a noble figure he had the entire sympathy of the pit. They booed the treacherous whores until they were hoarse.

He was getting tired. The specks of ice had turned into a flurry of snow. Shadows distorted the land around him but there was enough moonlight to make out the road. There was a fork up ahead marked by a thorn bush. His chest was tight. His mind had been so happily occupied he had not thought once of his chest all day. In his previous existence he would never have thought of being able to put himself to such exertion. *'Try to refrain from snivelling, Grub, it disturbs the game,'* he muttered to encourage himself. His mission spurred him on. Time to rest later.

He heard a horse blow through its lips behind the thorn bush. He turned towards the sound and was struck by a great weight. He slid from the saddle.

'Which way shall I turn me – How can I decide?' sang the besieged Macheath, holding his ears.

'One Wife is too much for most Husbands to hear,
But two at a time there's no mortal can bear.
This way, and that way, and which way I will,
What would comfort the one, t'other Wife would take ill.'

The self-assured rogue who played with women's hearts was getting his come-uppance.

Mrs Sugden, a neat, rounded, brown-haired woman with speaking dark eyes and a surprising turn for spite, was Lucy Lockit, Macheath's discarded lover. She made an excellent foil to the sentimental Polly. The two women's rivalry had the spice of truth to it. Lucy was particularly good at dissembling sympathy, her expression shifting to pure malice out of her rival's sight. It was alarming how short a time it took for morals to be corrupted. Henrietta forgot to be shocked at Lucy, with her padded belly, singing of how she had been 'kissed by the parson, the squire and the sot', and laughed along with the rest. Lucy was preparing to poison Polly, the pair circling each other like two wary cats, pretending to be civil while disguising their sharpened claws.

Lord Charles rested his arm on the partition between them.

'So who's your money on, Miss Lonsdale?' he asked.

'Lucy, I think,' she answered in the same spirit. Her prejudice against Bess had not entirely dissipated, however enchanting her performance. 'I feel for the poor girl. Polly is pretty, 'tis true, but surely Lucy has the greater claim. Macheath should be responsible for his child.'

'If I recall the play,' Lord Charles murmured, 'that belly does not make Lucy so singular.'

'I beg your pardon?'

'I think you'll find the highwayman has other wives.'

It was a good catch. Duffin folded his bag over the warm rabbit corpses. Queenie, sleepy after her exertions, was curled up in her box. His dog barked a little way off.

'What is it, Bob?'

The hound was hard to discern against the purple and grey land but he picked out the outline of Bob's pricked-up ears. They were turned towards the brow of the hill. The poacher stood listening. By rights they were on Grateley land, but the estate had no real gamekeeper. He thought he heard horses not far off. Sounds carried on a cold night like this. The cross lane to Pennygill was over that hill.

'Got a lay up,' the boy called out disgustedly behind him.

'Your Badger again?'

'Aye.'

'Any notion where?'

'Round here maybe.' The boy was lying full length, his ear pressed to the frosty earth, listening. His ferret had stopped in the burrow below to eat a kill. The only way to reach him was to dig – if they could find him.

'We'll have to send the old hob down on a line then. Get your spade out. It's your bloody weasel.'

*

The audience was well pleased with their entertainment. The ale consumed had loosened tongues and collars. Macheath in chains, condemned, stood alone facing his fate at the hangman's noose. His gallant demeanour and the lilting regret of his song – *'Oh Cruel, cruel case; must I suffer this disgrace?'* – brought tears to many an eye. The highwayman rallied his courage. Mr Greenwood advanced to the front of the boards, a handsome manly figure, and sang with open-hearted disdain for the law that sought to crush him:

> *'Since Laws were made for ev'ry Degree,*
> *To curb Vice in others, as well as me,*
> *I wonder we han't better Company,*
> *Upon Tyburn Tree!*
> *But Gold from Law can take out the Sting;*
> *And if rich Men like us were to swing,*
> *'Twould then the Land, such Numbers to string*
> *Upon Tyburn Tree!'*

The pit rose to its feet. They liked the song so much they demanded encore after encore. Weavers and apprentices and other working men sang along, stamping their feet to the beat. The colonel, with a dark face, leant back to speak to Lieutenant Roberts. In the boxes worthy husbands reassured their ladies. Henrietta began to fear a riot.

The struggle was heroic. Here was the enemy, solid and palpable. In that one moment he had never felt so alive.

But the moment fled. He couldn't breathe. Heavy wool cloth enveloped him, robbing him of air. Pummelled and buffeted, he grasped something. It loosened and tore off in his hand. If only he could hold on to it. He was losing consciousness. Panic overwhelmed him.

Breath didn't matter any more. Not so much pain, not so much cold, just a flicker of consciousness in the grey. He heard a distant sound like panes of glass clattering in their frames – or perhaps it was just an echo in his head. The cold hard ground seeped into him and Favian Vere Adley drifted down into a wilderness of night.

CHAPTER THIRTEEN

The boy had his ferret back in its box. It had taken them more than an hour to dig down the line to where they found the old hob, still tearing meat from a bloody mess of fur and bones. They were approaching the overhang that ran above the pack-horse trail that cut across by Grateley Manor and down Quarry Fell, when they heard the protesting creak of a metal handle rubbing against a tin socket and saw a glow moving along the track. There was a figure in the shadows below. The lantern the man carried illuminated his feet, throwing the rest of him into black relief. The broad brim of a hat tilted and a pale shape glimmered a moment. Quickening his pace, the man hastened off into the gloom at a startled half-run.

A few minutes later they found the horse standing, tacked up and forlorn.

'Eh up,' said the boy. 'Belongs to the gentleman, do y'think? But why leave him?'

'He wasn't dressed for ridin'.' As Duffin approached

the animal it rolled its eyes and stamped its front foot. 'Easy, boy.' With a deft movement he caught the reins, making low, soothing noises. 'He's not happy. What's up?' The horse dropped its head and sighed. He stood quivering as Duffin checked him over for signs of harm. 'You look familiar.' The poacher picked up a foot and ran the pad of his thumb over the iron shoe. 'I know that mark. You're one of Mr Jarrett's down at the Old Manor, you are.'

'How did you like the play, Miss Lonsdale?'

They stood in Bedlington's yard waiting for the carriages to come round. The cobbles wore a fresh coverlet of snow. A few picturesque flakes drifted down, catching the light of the lamps.

'Quite as amusing as I had been told, Mr Jarrett.' The play had ended with a dance and a rousing chorus of 'God Save the King'. Macheath had been reprieved. Such was the skill of author and actors, it would not have seemed justice to have seen the highwayman hanged. 'Tho it presents a sorry view of both sexes,' she added, 'every man and woman set on betraying the other.'

'Save perhaps for poor Polly,' he suggested.

'Poor Polly indeed. I should pity her were she a real woman shackled in truth to such a man.'

'You do not believe love may reform a man, then?'

'I should like to believe it, Mr Jarrett, though I have yet to come across an example of it myself.' She smiled at him. 'Perhaps such things only occur in novels – or in the light of the stage lamps.'

'You do not believe in redemption?'

'I should say rather that a person must redeem themselves, Mr Jarrett. Love alone cannot do it for them.'

'You are a philosopher ma'am.'

She looked up at the flakes falling white against the night sky. Her face lit up with pleasure.

'I love snow as it falls. There is something so peaceful, on a still night, when there is no wind to drive it. It makes everything so clean and fine.' She slid him a humorous look. 'But once it falls to earth it is only a matter of time before people trample it and everyone is complaining of the mud.'

'I think I have mud on my shoes now,' he said absurdly, looking down at the thin leather of his evening shoes.

'So have we all,' responded Miss Lonsdale. 'But it is a pretty illusion.'

'There you are, girl.' Lady Catherine's voice was thin but penetrating. 'I am chilled to the bone. Come give me your arm to the carriage. I have a horror of snow. Wretched slippery stuff!'

'Mr Jarrett, sir!' He turned to find Tiplady behind him. His manservant was packed tight within the numerous layers he had donned as a preservative against the cold. His roman features lent his expression of alarm a histrionic grandeur. 'There's foot warmers filled in the carriage and blankets – it is a bitter night – but I can't find Master Favian! I am fearful, what with the young master's chest.'

Charles approached them humming an air from the

opera: *'Tis Woman That Seduces All Mankind.* His foot slipped. Jarrett grabbed his arm. Charles leant into him.

'What?' his lordship asked.

'Tiplady's lost Grub.' Charles looked about the yard.

'Rode over, didn't he? Where's his horse?'

'Good point.' Jarrett beckoned to a stable-hand. 'Can you show us Mr Adley's mount?' he asked. The man led them to an empty stall.

'Dear Lord!' exclaimed Tiplady, nervously patting his mittened hands together.

'Don't fuss,' Jarrett responded shortly. 'He's not a boy any more.'

'But where could he be?' Tiplady asked piteously.

Jarrett's foot disturbed something foreign in the straw. He bent down to pick up a folded square of scarlet cloth. He thought of the girl in peach.

'He has his own affairs – let him be. He'll make his own way home.'

Lulled by his consumption of Lady Catherine's wine, Charles was fast asleep by the time they reached the old manor. They left him in the care of his valet. Tiplady was still fretting about Grub. Jarrett dismissed him to his quarters, suppressing a blossoming sense of unease. He found himself standing at the window of his chamber staring out towards the moors. The boy must be on his way back by now. He had no desire for sleep. Why not ride out and meet him? He changed his clothes and pulled on his boots.

There is something about the combination of moonlight

on fresh snow. It is unsettling; as if normality is suspended in the silver light. He made an effort to mock the sensation of doom lurking at the back of his neck. You'll be believing in fairies next, he chided himself. They were passing a plantation of trees. Beyond the land opened out, smoothed and simplified in its shroud of snow. A group of figures moved against the blank canvas: a dog, a boy and a man leading a horse. His heart thudded. Duffin waved. He raised his hand in acknowledgement and Walcheren sprang forward, throwing up plumes of white snow.

'Here's where we found him,' said Duffin. Favian's horse snorted as if in agreement. Jarrett looked about. They were above the cross lane that led up from the Carlisle road towards Pennygill.

'He was with us at the play.'

'When did you see him last?' the poacher asked.

When had he seen him last? Bess was singing and Grub was watching the girl in peach. When was that? With a jolt he realized it must have been during the first act.

'Four, five hours ago now.'

'What could've taken him all the way out here?'

'Lord knows.'

'We can cut down this way.' Duffin moved swiftly over the rough land; this was his natural habitat. 'What with snow, there'll be tracks in t'lane if he rode by there.'

On the cross lane they found a sequence of shod hoof prints cut into the covering of fresh snow.

'Keep off!' Duffin shouted, as the boy slid on the verge. 'Tread clean ground! Where's your head?' He crouched over the tracks. 'There's been more than one horse this way this night; snow was still falling,' he said, pointing. 'There's a smattering over the tracks. Two horses. One after t'other. Then this one's come back after snow stopped.'

'Back, you say?' Duffin straightened up, meeting Jarrett's look.

'Just one back.' They were coming to a fork in the road marked by a thick thorn bush.

'Is that the track to Dewsnap's farm?' Jarrett pointed to the left.

'Aye, and the Anderses' place,' Duffin answered, 'or a back way up to High Top.'

Mr Hilton's farm. All three were tenants of the duke. He had ridden out this way before.

At the foot of the thorn there was a mess of bruised and frosted grass. A horse had stamped with sufficient force to turn up the earth beneath. Jarrett bent down to finger the curved indentation. The hoof had cut deep.

'A horse stood here a while.' Duffin's voice came from behind the bush. Jarrett followed, watching where he placed his feet. A set of four hoof prints, evenly spaced, showed dimly against a patch of scuffed snow. Beyond, the ground was covered with heather. It stretched out into the distance, a mysterious blend of shadows in the pewter light. Duffin's dog pushed its head under his arm. The poacher rubbed its coat absently.

'Got anything with his smell on it?' he asked. Jarrett remembered the scarlet handkerchief in his pocket.

'It's been on a stable floor but he carried it up his sleeve some time.'

'Worth a try. How's about this, Bob?' The poacher held out the fabric. The hound sniffed at it. He looked up at his master with pricked-up ears. 'Go on. Find it!'

Bob set his nose to the ground, darted hither and thither a moment and then headed out across the moor.

At first it was just a shape, long and low, maybe fifteen yards ahead. Bob barked, a sharp, urgent sound. Favian lay straight on his back, his pale face luminous in the moonlight. One arm rested across his breast. The snow lay over him as if it sought to absorb him into the land.

Jarrett fell to his knees in the springy heather and picked him up, brushing the snow from him with feverish hands. He was so light. He leant close, ear to mouth, listening, but the rush of blood in his own ears drowned out all else. He pulled off a glove and pressed a finger tip. There seemed to be no blood in the boy. He bundled the fingers in his palm and brought them to his lips, seeking to warm them with his breath. Under the pale lids the eyes were slits of glass. The mannequin spasmed. A soft, grotesque sound bubbled from its mouth. The brief, slight spurt of energy expired. The blind eyes focused. A glimmer of Favian flickered out.

'Raif,' he said, looking straight at him. 'I knew you would come.'

'I'm here now,' he heard his own voice answer, calm and casual as if it were the most normal thing in the world to find each other like this in the icy wilderness. 'What's all this, eh?'

He was gone again. The eyes were open but there was no sign of Grub in them. The muscles of the boy's face were relaxed, all expression smoothed out. At least he didn't seem to be in pain. Grub frowned.

'Take it.' The sound was as insubstantial as a wisp of air.

Jarrett felt the boy's free hand move under his. He looked down. Favian uncurled his fingers. On the palm of his glove lay a button. He had held it so tight, its edges had pierced the leather. From somewhere in front of him Jarrett heard Duffin speaking low.

'I've sent the boy for help.'

What help? They were so far from warmth or light out here. Jarrett tugged the heavy wool of his cloak around them both. Grub's left temple was stained with blood. There was a cut in his hairline; it was barely a scratch. He fumbled in his pocket for a handkerchief. The boy turned his face into his shoulder like a sleepy child.

'Now I am comfortable,' Grub said and he sighed. Jarrett's breath suspended white in the cold air before him.

If nothing moved, time could be held here, like this. There need be nothing next. He was hollow under the vast sky. His one purpose was to hold on to the white-faced boy in his arms. There was a church tower chiming the hour down in the valley. One. Two. Three, and no more.

A rough, warm tongue dragged the skin of his cheek. Time was churning again. He was powerless to stop it. A yellow muzzle rested on his forearm. Bob's golden eyes looked up at him. The poacher crouched between him and the sky.

'Let me take him,' he said. Jarrett brushed his eyes with the back of his hand.

'I'll do it.' He made as if to stand and lost his balance. 'Yes, take him a moment, if you will,' he conceded. Duffin lifted the weight from him and he stood up, his head feeling oddly far from the alien earth. He took off his cloak and spread it out on a piece of level ground near the thorn bush. Carefully, decently, Duffin laid the earthly remains of Favian Adley upon it.

There was a whitening at the horizon. A bitter, insistent breeze had sprung up. Dawn was coming. He felt in his pockets. Taking out a pencil and paper, mechanically he began to sketch a map of the ground. Grub had ridden out from town. Just there, before the fork in the road, someone had waited for him . . . His fingers were numb. He couldn't control the scratches of his pencil properly. He shook himself like a dog.

They had found him fifteen to twenty yards from the road, out of sight of the casual passer-by – even by daylight – but not buried or hidden. The attacker had been short of time. Jarrett was aware of warmth to one side. He looked up. Duffin was staring at him.

'Someone did this.' It surprised him, the effort it took to speak. It was as if the sound of his voice drove the whole world to turn. Deep within his hollow self anger flickered. It built and filled him like a thirst – a cold, pinching rage. *I will know him and he will pay.* 'Where were you?' he demanded.

'Knot Hill,' Duffin answered as if he had been asked a civil question. 'Grateley land – over the rise there.' Jarrett pulled back his fury, feeling ashamed. He stared at the markings on the ground. The story they told was plain as day.

One rider followed the other. Where was Grub going? Why had the boy come out here in the middle of the night? Was he followed? No. The attacker waited concealed behind this thorn. Grub had been following and someone caught him unawares. Was it robbery? He'd have to check the body.

Grub was a 'body'. He swallowed hard against the bitter regret. The button. The button Grub gave him; where was it? Feverishly he felt in his pockets. He had no recollection. He saw it on the boy's palm, nestled in the indentation it had cut into the leather glove.

I knew you would come.

But he had come too late. What if he had listened to Tiplady and his fussing? What if he had ridden straight out then; could he have prevented this? Duffin's big hand trapped his arm and held it steady like a vice.

'What you looking for?'

'The button. The boy had a button in his hand . . .'

'So we'll find it.' The poacher glanced over at the shape on the ground. 'Maybe it's in t'cloak.'

He didn't want to go near the shape on the ground. What was this womanly foolishness? It was a husk, that's all. He'd seen enough of them before. It would rot and stink and melt away and the remains dry up into dust.

That fork of the road curved round to William Dewsnap's place. There was the Anderses' farm opposite it and higher up, Mr Hilton's High Top. He had seen Hilton at the play with his wife and the Anders men too. They must be home by now. Why hadn't they passed this way? They would have taken the low way home. It was a better road for a cart in the dark. Duffin was watching him closely, waiting.

'He was jumped, here,' Jarrett said, just to fill the silence. 'Dragged off his horse.' He could see it played out in his head. 'Whoever did it didn't want him to be seen from the road so he carried him over there, but not too far.'

'Short on time, y'think?'

'Or not so strong – tho the boy's hardly heavy.' The words caught in his throat. This was no good. He started again. 'You heard nothing?' Duffin glanced at his dog.

'Reckon I heard horses one time.' He passed a grimy hand over his lower face. 'It was just as the boy called out his jill was laid up.'

'You heard no one cry out? No sounds of a struggle?' The older man shook his head.

'But there was someone. After. Before we come upon t'horse.'

'Where?'

'On t'pack trail by Grateley Manor. We was up high, he was down below. Had the hat and coat of a gentleman. On foot with a lantern.'

'But you'd know every gentleman these parts.'

Duffin shrugged. 'Coming from the east, over by Anderses' farm – or High Top maybe, heading out by Grateley Manor.' Beyond Grateley there was nothing but the open moor deep into Yorkshire.

Torches were moving fast up the left-hand fork. A group of young men came into sight with the boy leading them. One youth towered over the rest. Jarrett recognized the young giant he had first seen at the Red Angel. As the group came closer he picked out at least two more members of the song club.

'What's this the boy's been sayin'?' the young giant demanded. He saw the shape laid on the cloak by the thorn tree. 'What this?' He stumbled across the ground to Favian's still form. He reached out a hand to touch his chest. 'He was supposed to be at the play,' he said in a stunned voice. 'What's he doin' here?'

'Who are you?' The newcomer stared up at the duke's agent. He was a big lad with a thick neck and shoulders fit to lift a young ox but, Jarrett thought in some detached corner of his brain, he's not unintelligent.

'Dickon Watson. And you're Mr Jarrett. You meant something to him.'

A hand reached in and squeezed Jarrett's heart.

'Family,' he said. 'A cousin. He used to follow me

around when he was nothing but a scrap of a boy.' He caught himself and started again. 'I saw you with him at the Red Angel Wednesday night.' Dickon sat back on his heels, his rough working hands resting on his broad thighs. He stared down at the body that lay between them.

'Met him the first day he came. He was bad – poorly chest. Jonas made him a brew in me mam's kitchen.'

'Jonas?' Jarrett asked. Dickon blinked as if he had something in his eyes.

'Friend – works for the old bat up at Grateley Manor. You've heard him sing.' He stared down at Favian's lifeless body. 'He said it made him better.'

Jarrett thought of how Grub had fought his frailties. His spirit had never bowed to his ill health. No more fighting for him now; his struggles were over.

'Was it his chest, do y'think?' Dickon reached out a hand and touched the blood on Grub's forehead.

'There's more to it than that,' Jarrett said. 'You said he was supposed to be at the play?'

Dickon Watson searched his face. His answer was guarded. 'Saw him at the fair. Heard he'd be going.'

For the first time Jarrett paid attention to the others, who stood back at a respectful distance. Harry Aitken he knew by sight. There was a long streak of a lad with a fuzz of fair hair standing up around his head. He'd seen him about town. He was a participant in the hat chase at the fair – was he the tailor's son? John Blackwell, that's it. Then there was a compact, dark-haired lad and

Dewsnap's red-headed boy. But no sign of Miss Lippett's oddly independent servant.

'Your friend Jonas, he's not with you?'

'Had business. His mistress wanted him.'

The members of the Red Angel song club carried Favian Adley down from the fell on an old gate covered with his cousin's cloak. Jarrett led the way. The compact, dark-haired youth – they called him Sim – volunteered to run ahead to warn the household. As they descended into the tree line the branches were thick with crystal hoar frost. Everywhere was silent but for the crunch of their footfall in the snow.

Charles was standing at the gate of the old manor dressed in black, every hair in place. He always had had a sense of occasion. Favian Adley passed through the gate on his wooden bier.

'There's been a letter.' Charles's voice was compressed and strange. He cleared his throat. 'Mrs Adley's at Ravensworth. She's come to visit her son.'

CHAPTER FOURTEEN

'I knew it, I knew it!' Tiplady was white-faced and wailing. 'I had the most dreadful fancies, but this! Dear Lord, I never dreamt . . . It was his chest, wasn't it? I told you to have a care, but would you listen? Out on such a night! Why didn't you hear me? What tragedy has visited us!'

They brought a trestle table into a room on the ground floor darkened by the yew tree growing outside its windows. They set Favian down upon it. Frost blossomed like icy mould on the inside of the window panes. To preserve the body there could be no fire so Charles, at his lordly best, summoned up hot cider to warm the men who had brought his cousin down from the fell.

They gave him back his cloak. Jarrett found the button, as Duffin predicted, in a pocket. It lay on his palm. A white metal button with a chased border, too small to serve a coat. There was a yellowish thread attached to it and clinging to that a tiny flake of soft leather. Grub's purse was still on him, along with his watch. Whatever the motive for the attack, it was not simple robbery. Two murders in a week. That couldn't be a coincidence; not in a place like this. He thought of the colonel and his hunt for his radicals. He had not believed in them and yet ... He looked across at the red-headed William Dewsnap and the tailor's son, John Blackwell, sipping their cider by the door. What were Dickon Watson and his friends doing while the whole town was at the play? He watched them under his lashes. They stood close to one another in silence, eyes lowered.

'You weren't at the play.' His remark was met with blank expressions.

'Need money to see a play.' Dickon Watson, it seemed, was their spokesman. 'We was over at Billy Dewsnap's. His ma brews a tidy ale.' It seemed far to go for a drink on a winter's night but then, these were country folk.

'Where's your Leeds friend?'

'Jo? Told you; he were working this night. Mistress wanted him.'

Jarrett thought of Mrs Bedford's entertainment; Miss Lippett had left before the play.

Charles came in from the hall, his movements controlled and his eyes distracted. He addressed Jarrett as if they were alone.

'They're bringing the carriage round. I must set out.'

'We'll leave you then, sir.' The members of the song club retreated to the door, offering disjointed phrases of respect and regret. Dickon Watson loomed at the rear.

'A sorry day, my lord.'

'Thank you.' Charles's closed hand advanced at waist

height. He was offering money. Jarrett noted the shift in posture as the youth bristled. 'To drink to my cousin's memory,' the marquess said gently. Dickon took the money and held it in his hand. Jarrett watched them as they crossed to the front door. Harry Aitken, the solid married man, fell in alongside Watson. Without turning his head he spoke low. Jarrett caught a few snatched phrases.

'Dinna think—'

'Hush!' Watson responded.

'Duke's man's all right,' insisted Harry. They were almost out of the door.

'Less his kind knows of us the better.'

Jarrett and Charles stood side by side looking down at Grub. It was his image and yet not him.

'This was murder, you know.'

'That cannot be!' Charles swung his head briefly towards Jarrett without looking directly at him. 'Perhaps his horse stumbled and threw him . . .'

'There's more to it than that.'

'How can you—?'

'Tracks. Grub was carried – left for dead away from the road.' Charles looked dazed.

'Left for dead,' he repeated blankly. 'He was alive?'

'Barely.'

'But you were with him?' Charles's voice was insistent, almost pleading.

'He died in my arms.' Charles put his hand out, an involuntary gesture. The warmth of it was an intrusion.

The contact seemed to join and amplify their grief. Jarrett took a step away, averting his eyes with a conciliatory grimace. The marquess cleared his throat.

'He said nothing to you?' he asked.

'Almost nothing.'

'Raif!' Jarrett could feel the appeal of Charles's eyes. He knew he wanted comfort. He could think of none. 'But he knew you were there?' Jarrett nodded.

'He wasn't robbed,' he said absently. His own voice sounded distant to him. 'Perhaps he saw something he shouldn't—'

'I can't believe it!' Charles's energetic exclamation cut him off. 'Murder a kinsman of the duke's? Who would risk such a thing? No!' the marquess protested. 'His horse must have thrown him,' he reasoned stubbornly. 'A countryman passing by found him. He could not carry him – the horse had run off . . .'

'So he left him and said nothing?'

'Perhaps he went for help and you came upon the boy first.'

Jarrett leant down and loosened the crushed cravat around Grub's neck. Beneath there was a mottled bar of a bruise perhaps an inch wide crossing his throat.

'Raif!' Charles exclaimed helplessly. There was movement in the hall. Tiplady appeared in the doorway. His face was wet with tears. Charles stared at him blankly. 'It's four hours or more to Ravensworth this weather. His mother must be told. If I leave now I should make it by noon.' His face spasmed. He clamped his lips together and composed himself. 'You'll stay with him?' he asked. Jarrett nodded. He did not want to face Mrs Adley.

'You'll fetch her here?'

'I'll send word if not.' Charles took a last backward glance at the body. He enveloped Jarrett in a fierce hug. 'I cannot believe this,' he said.

He shaved to make himself more human while Tiplady prepared a hot bath by the fire in his room. He was chilled to the bone.

Dickon and his friends had been over at Dewsnap's farm and Grub was stopped just before the lane that led to that farm. What were those lads doing over there? Could their circle conceal the colonel's radicals? He tried to think of what he knew of Dickon Watson and his friends. He did not even know Watson's trade. He had weaver's hands – strong but clean. Harry Aitken was a weaver; he knew that much. He knew something of Aitken from the affair last summer. He had thought him an honest man.

What was he to make of the colonel's evidence? He had seen nothing material save that poxy note left in Ison's carriage. If he knew who put it there, that might lead to something. But murder! A conspiracy fermenting in the Dale? Something dangerous enough to risk the extermination of two lives? He was all but certain that the same hand that had laid out Mr Pritchard at the Bucket and Broom had dispatched young Favian. What could link Grub to an army cloth buyer? Wool. Weavers

– was he back to the colonel's damned radicals again? He thought of Charles, so completely the nobleman in attire and bearing, and his wayward face betraying his emotion. In Charles's eyes, any local man who risked murdering a kinsman of the Duke of Penrith must be mad or desperate. He had not been home for long, but from what he had seen of the locality respect of rank was strong. Did that make the villain an outsider? The murderer was determined and practised – he was almost certain of that. He closed his eyes. The image of the mottled mark on Grub's throat sprang up.

Get behind, and once the forearm slips in place under the chin, you have him. Pull it back, levering it tight in the crook of the opposing arm. Given the element of surprise, it was an efficient way to subdue an opponent – especially a weaker one. He saw Grub's fingers scrabbling against a gloved wrist.

The water was cold. It was as if it had congealed with his weariness. He forced himself into movement. Tiplady's woeful face as he dressed irritated him. With an awkward pat on his manservant's shoulder, he made his escape. Aiming for the stables, he cut down the side of the house. There was a solid little figure standing by the gate in the cold morning light. The girl in peach. His first impulse was to pretend that he had not seen her, but her searching eyes found his.

'Mr Jarrett!'

'Miss Bedford.' The doleful mask of sadness sat oddly on her girlish features. He thought of how the young like to dramatize and felt a stab of annoyance. She stopped a couple of feet from him, gathering her cloak more tightly about her.

'I have come from town,' she began hesitantly. 'They said Mr Adley ...'

'Is dead,' he said. Tears welled up in her wide-opened eyes. He was ashamed of his brutality. 'Forgive me ...' She reached out her gloved hand and touched his arm.

'Please don't think me strange coming here like this, but I had to know.' She looked as if she were about to give way to emotion. He ushered her over to a sheltered bench.

'Come, let's sit here a moment.' Miss Bedford produced a handkerchief and blew her nose efficiently.

'Was it his chest? Did he suffer an attack?'

'You knew of his condition?'

'We travelled up north together on the Leeds flyer. He had an attack in the coach.'

'You became acquainted at the coaching inn?' She shook her head vigorously.

'Oh no! I was in Miss Price's care – my old governess. She was on her way to take up a very good place outside Wakefield. She hired us a private parlour,' she explained. 'I saw Mr Adley sitting in a bay window down below.' Fond reminiscence flushed her face and her pupils widened. 'He pretended to be busy, taking out a bit of paper and his pencil – all so that I should not think he had noticed me watching.' Her voice caught and she stopped.

'I saw you on his arm at the fair.' She nodded politely, her lips compressed. 'You went into the yard of the Queen's Head.' That must have been around the time the note found its way into the colonel's carriage. He thought of the lads playing their game with the hat in the marketplace. 'Did you see anyone else in the yard?' His tone succeeded in distracting her. She gave him a sharp look. She considered the matter.

'There were ostlers and serving men gathered under the arch watching the disturbance. Mr Adley said we should go into Mrs Bedlington's parlour until the soldiers made order. I did see my uncle's coachman by the stables ...' She checked herself as if the recollection embarrassed her.

'He'd been drinking,' he supplied sympathetically, thinking her an innocent. Lally looked at him, surprised.

'Had he?'

'The man was arrested blind drunk minutes later.' She drew her brows together and wrinkled her neat nose.

'I did not particularly look at him. I did not wish him to see me.' She blushed again. Her skin was a barometer of her emotions.

'While you were with him, did Mr Adley speak to any other friends?'

She pursed up her lips. 'Friends?' she queried doubtfully. 'There were some young men – weavers. Not my uncle's men. Independents, I think.'

'Can you describe them?'

'There were four or five maybe.'

'And Mr Adley spoke to them?'

'To the great tall one – he stood head and shoulders above the rest.'

'Fairish hair and a red complexion?' Miss Bedford nodded. 'And what did they speak of?'

'I didn't hear. Well, not really.' Either Miss Bedford had not been interested – which, to Jarrett, seemed unlikely – or her efforts at eavesdropping had been frustrated. 'I thought there was someone they were looking for – Lem or some such name.' Her eyes were fixed on her fingers twisting the handkerchief in her lap.

'This Lem, do you think he was a friend?'

'If so they weren't very happy with him. The big one said, "Just wait till I get my hands on him," or something like that,' she tailed off. 'But perhaps they were just funning.'

'So Mr Adley took you into the Queen's Head . . .'

'We had tea in Mrs Bedlington's parlour.'

'How long were you there?'

'I do not recall,' she replied evasively. 'An hour perhaps.'

'And Mr Adley never left you all that time?'

'We left the door open and Mrs Bedlington came in and out. It was quite proper!'

'I am sure it was,' he responded mechanically. 'Then Mr Adley escorted you home.'

'Yes.'

'And you saw him next . . .'

'At my aunt's.' Her eyes grew misty. 'He was early.'

'And at the play I saw you in the box at the end across the way,' he said in a cheerful tone, hoping to move her past a fresh wave of emotion. He had to know the sequence of events that led Grub to ride up the fell that night. 'Mr Adley was standing at the back, behind you. Did you observe him leave?' Miss Bedford's colour ebbed then returned a hot pink. 'Perhaps you left the theatre together?'

'I did not!' she protested. She turned in her seat to address him directly, her manner half guilty, half defiant. 'I was feeling faint. I just went into the yard to breathe some air. My aunt was enjoying the opera; besides she was sitting *seats* away. I couldn't catch her eye and,' she ended lamely, 'I did not wish to disturb her.'

'Mr Adley followed you out?'

'He was concerned about me,' she insisted with a touch of pride.

It seemed there had been romance in the air that night. Gradually he coaxed an account of the scene from her. It was a little blurred in parts – a rosy tale of two young people enjoying each other's company away from the eyes of the world.

'So you left the theatre towards the end of the first act. Mr Adley joined you there and you took a turn about the yard together. You remember nothing else? Mr Adley mentioned he was going somewhere after the play, perhaps?' Miss Bedford shook her head. They each stared out at their portion of the frosty landscape in silence. She hugged her cloak closely about herself. It was cold. He should offer her shelter, but that might be considered improper. He was on the verge of proposing that he should call a groom to drive her back into town.

'There was the man in the marketplace,' she said suddenly.

'What man?'

'There were two of them, I suppose, if you think about it,' she went on, debating with herself. 'One after the other, but it was the *other* one.' Jarrett reined back the blasphemy that strained to break from his mouth. She was distressed and young and her species were not known for their reasoning.

'I am afraid I don't follow you,' he said mildly.

'We were standing under the arch that leads to the marketplace.' She hesitated. 'Talking. And Mr Adley saw someone, out by that round stone building.'

'The tollbooth? Who?'

'I don't know. I saw nothing clearly. But Mr Adley knew him, I think.'

'Why?'

Miss Bedford stared at him, startled by his passionate tone. 'Why do you think he recognized someone?' he elaborated impatiently. Her expression changed to one of sympathy beyond her years.

'He made an exclamation,' she said patiently. She's humouring me, he thought fleetingly. 'You know – the kind that one makes when one is surprised to see someone; but my uncle called me.' Miss Bedford looked over towards the gate as if she half expected her relative to appear again. 'I had to go. Uncle John would have been very cross had he seen us together.' Her face fell suddenly. 'That is the last time I saw Mr Adley.' A tear ran down her cheek.

'And you saw nothing else?' he pressed. She looked at him piteously through watery eyes. 'The man by the tollbooth,' he insisted. She dabbed her eyes with her handkerchief.

'Just an outline – he stood in shadow. It was just a man, that's all!'

'Was he wearing a hat?'

'Of course he was!' Miss Bedford responded acerbically.

'What kind?'

'It was just a hat; that's all.'

'And there was nothing else you remember about him? What was he doing?'

'Pulling on his gloves,' she replied and burst into noisy tears. He leant back against the bench. It was at moments like these a man could do with a wife. After a moment she blew her nose. He risked a side glance. She was sitting very straight. She had a neat way of disposing her limbs. She reminded him of a little brindle cat. The impression was reinforced when she turned her head and gazed at him steadily with her dark golden eyes.

'You said there were two men – one after the other. Who was the other man, Miss Bedford? Did you know *him*?'

Lally was thinking of the moment Favian had held her,

heart to heart in the darkness. She would, she told herself fervently, cherish the memory for the rest of her life. Mr Jarrett was waiting for her answer. She nodded.

'Lieutenant Roberts,' she said.

His left hand lay flat against the grain of the oak panel; his right hand encompassed the smooth, cool brass. This was foolishness. He turned the door knob. Cheerful sky-blue curtains were pulled back around the four-poster bed. The slippers embroidered by his mother's hand were set neatly on the rug beside it. A table had been placed in the light of the tall, narrow-paned windows. It was disordered, as if the untidy scholar had just stepped away a moment. Scraps of notes were pinned into the soft plaster of the wall above it. The little vandal! No thought to housekeeping. That would have to be replastered.

There was a black leather-bound book a hand's span high lying on the desk. He frowned. What was Grub doing with *his* notebook? He would never have thought the boy a thief. As he picked it up, he realized it was not his after all – there were gold initials tooled into the leather: F V A. It was the twin of the notebooks he himself had carried for years. A paper label stuck into the inside cover declared it supplied by the very stationer he patronized in Paternoster Row. Odd to think Grub had been carrying about the same notebook as he. He flicked through it. A third of the pages were covered in Grub's thin, erratic hand. It was not a journal but a scattering of notes – thoughts, ideas, tumbled down one after the other. The passages in ink were blotted and smudged where Grub's fingers lagged behind his thoughts. The pattern was strangely familiar. His own notebooks were punctuated with sketches. Grub's were peppered with snatches of poetry – quotations that pleased him and other lines of his own. Grub was not a particularly good poet. He inclined towards the kind of contrived, overblown sentiment Jarrett found tiresome. Perhaps he might have improved had he lived.

The boy's prose was more lively. Jarrett came upon an entry marked with the date of Favian's journey up north. It seemed he had taken against a fellow passenger – a woman whom he depicted as a troll of loathsome habits. A piece of paper slid out. It was a receipt from the Royal Hotel, Leeds, for a pint of porter and a dish of broiled pigeon. There was a raised mark on the surface that caused him to turn it over. Grub had pencilled two words heavily underscored on the back: *yellow gloves.* What was it Miss Bedford had said? *He pretended to be busy, taking out a bit of paper and his pencil – all so that I should not think he had noticed me watching* . . . But why yellow gloves? He slid the bill back into place and turned the page. A quartered sheet dropped to the floor. He picked it up. It was a cheaply printed ballad, 'The Weaver's Lament'. '*Your mouth is shut and you cannot unlock it,*' he read. '*The masters they carry the key in their pockets.*' He heard an echo of Grub's eager voice in the painting room: *My desire is to write real songs – songs to rouse everyman's heart. A ballad, you see. I am working on a ballad* . . .

Grub's verse changed. There were a few fragments in the old style – a half-formed sonnet, 'The Snare', about a scarlet handkerchief belonging to a lady with tresses of night and eyes that pierced the soul. He smiled, thinking of young Miss Bedford. There were word combinations, some impatiently scored through, others circled, and verses of another kind, verses with more life to them: the beginnings of a fresh composition, 'The Hand in the Glove'.

> *There's not a mechanic throughout the whole land*
> *But what more or less feels the weight of his hand.*
> *That creature of tyranny, baseness and pride*
> *Mangles men crying Progress! And other such lies.*

If Watson and his friends were in truth the colonel's radicals, Grub would have been no threat to them. He would have offered his whole-hearted support.

As he laid the notebook aside, his eye was caught by a single sheet of paper. He picked it up.

My dear Sticks –
A chance encounter with your brother in Leeds the other day put me in mind of the letter I owe you . . .

He had never finished it. Grub must have begun the letter soon after his arrival. The first paragraph mentioned 'cousin Raif' three times. The boy had been so very young. He thought of how Grub had cut him in the theatre the previous night and a lump rose in his throat.

The boy had told him of this encounter in the painting room. *Mr Strickland's compliments* . . . Francis Strickland. That Grub should have run into *him*. Then again, the region was unsettled. He thought of the colonel's informant. It came to him in a flash of memory: standing in the yard when Mrs Bedford had issued invitations to her deathly 'entertainment'. There had been another Woolbridge connection in Leeds with Grub that day. He would have come to the Royal Hotel to collect his niece. Jarrett dropped the letter back on the desk and left the room.

Half an hour later Matt the footman answered the bell ringing in the morning room. Mr Jarrett handed him a letter.

'Get this to the post as quick as you can.' He put his hand in his coat and drew out a shilling. 'Go now,' he urged. 'There's another for you if you catch the down stage.'

CHAPTER FIFTEEN

He rode up Quarry Fell with the button Grub gave him wrapped in a clean handkerchief in his breast pocket. He fancied he could feel it over his heart. A pure world of virgin snow spread out left and right highlighted by delicate strokes of copper where dried grasses broke the surface. If he stood again where they had found the boy perhaps, in the daylight, he could discern something more of what had happened there. They made good time. Despite being dragged out of his warm stall with the taste of barely digested feed in his mouth, Walcheren was on his best behaviour. They jumped down a bank into the cross lane to Pennygill. The thorn tree was up ahead. The pristine snow was soiled. Miss Lonsdale's words in the courtyard, the night before, came to mind: *Once it falls to earth it is only a matter of time before people trample it and everyone is complaining of the mud . . .*

The man Duffin saw on the pack-horse trail: where had he come from? He stood up in his stirrups examining the lie of the land. Knot Hill was to his right. The pack-horse trail crossed the lane behind him, running on around the foot of the hill towards Grateley Manor. Thanks to the shadows thrown by the lantern the man carried, Duffin's impression had been restricted to clothes and build. A gentleman's clothes and hat; the poacher had been adamant about that. Not many with clothes like that came up here – though a man might borrow or steal, of course. He looked north, tracing in his mind's eye the line of the pack-horse trail curving down to join the Carlisle road. In this isolated neighbourhood a man on foot would have most likely come from Dewsnap's farm, or the Anderses' place or perhaps High Top. He thought of Mr Hilton and his strapping sons. Their bulk ruled them out. Duffin had described a slimmish man of average height. He heard voices and the rumble of cart wheels. Over the branches of the thorn tree a familiar head was bumping up the lane towards him.

'I was only sayin' . . .' Mr Hilton's voice had a hard-done-by lilt. Beside him on the bench sat a woman whose small face looked out resentfully from a carapace of efficiently wrapped shawls.

'Tsk!' responded his wife impatiently. Their two great sons rode in the bed of the cart behind them. One had his face turned away, staring across the moor. The other watched his parents.

'Now da . . .' the youth contributed sheepishly. Mr Hilton pushed out his lips. Jarrett was reminded of an offended baby. Mrs Hilton glanced over and jabbed her husband under her shawls.

'Why, Mr Jarrett!' Mr Hilton hailed the duke's agent in a joyful voice. He hauled on the reins and the cart came to a halt. His face composed itself into a ludicrously solemn expression. 'We heard,' he said dramatically, 'of your great loss.' Jarrett inclined his head, embarrassed to be the object of such sympathy. 'He was something to you, eh?' The duke's agent glanced down in a sort of acknowledgement. 'That's hard, that is.' The farmer paused decently. A glint entered Mr Hilton's eye. 'I'm told it were murder.' His wife twitched beside him. 'Now, Mrs H. There's no call to be botherin' yourself.' He gave his wife's shawl a pat. 'She's not feelin' too clever,' he confided. 'I'm not happy her riding out this weather but she do love the fairs. She's a powerful decided woman this one,' he ended proudly. His wife looked faintly scornful. The cart rocked as their sons shifted their weight.

'Now da!' they chorused.

'So was it murder?' Mr Hilton prompted, ignoring them.

'I fear so, Mr Hilton. Perhaps you may help me,' said Jarrett, continuing over the farmer's excited exclamation. 'There was a man seen in this neighbourhood last night. An average-sized man dressed genteelly, wearing a low-crowned hat.' He swung round in his saddle, pointing behind him. 'Over there, on the pack-horse trail.'

'A gentlemanly man, you say?' responded the farmer. 'Well, there's none of that sort up here, not since old Mr Lippett passed. He was a well-dressed man. Nothing but the best for him. Everything neat and proper to the day he died.' Behind Mr Hilton, Jarrett saw a thought cross the face of the younger son. His brother caught it too and widened his eyes. The younger boy tipped his head sideways towards his brother and mumbled something.

'What is it, Thomas? Speak up!' their mother cut in.

'Her?' responded the elder boy to his sibling. He pulled the corners of his mouth down around his bunched-up chin in a dubious expression. 'Could be right,' he agreed. Jarrett looked to Mrs Hilton for clarification.

'The Anders girl,' she translated. 'Has a gentleman caller – well, that's what's said.' She tilted her head back and spoke down her nose disparagingly. 'Not that any o' us ever laid eyes on him. Comes at odd times when there's none about.'

'Whist woman!' exclaimed her husband, astounded. 'Mary Anne Anders! What you sayin'? Matthew Anders and his brothers would never have that! Powerful careful of that lass they are.' He leant towards Jarrett to make his point. 'She's all they've got since her brother died. Chopped his hand in the spring of '09 and went with a putrefaction, just like that. Grand send-off, mind. Whole Dale turned out. 'Twas before your time, Mr Jarrett,' he added consolingly, as if the duke's agent might feel cheated to have had no part in such a funeral.

'And no one has any notion who this gentleman caller might be? How curious,' Jarrett said. 'How long has this been going on?' The sons shrugged in unison. Their father puffed out his cheeks and declared it all a piece of fool-ishness but Mrs Hilton pursed her lips as if there was something else that might be said in different company. Alerted by his posture that Mr Hilton was winding himself up to deliver one of his endless monologues, Jarrett collected his reins.

'I must not detain you,' he declared. 'Mrs Hilton will be growing chilled. Good day to you all.' He touched his hat and rode on.

Dewsnap's farm squatted like a comfortable hen in the curve of the land at the end of an open track. He rode up into the deserted yard. Not even a dog barked. He dismounted.

'Anyone at home?' he called. No one answered. Were they all at the fairs? He turned towards the house. A sense of movement behind him made him swing round. Red-headed Billy Dewsnap was standing in the door of a stone shed with a stick in his hands. Jarrett walked towards him. The youth's face was white against the shadows. The muscles in his neck moved as he swallowed.

'Mr Jarrett,' he said. He filled the low doorway. Jarrett did not check his pace. At the last moment the lad fell back a step and let him by.

'Billy. Has everyone gone to the fairs and left you on your own?'

The smell suggested the shed had once been a byre but it was at present untenanted. Strips of light slanted through a roughly boarded window. At some point in its history a wooden partition had divided the room. The strut that once supported it remained in the centre of the space. A rope was secured to it at breast height. The ends dangled to the floor. Billy moved in front of the post.

'Dogs,' he said by way of explanation. There was a scatter of dark marks on the flags. Billy scuffed straw over the stains with his booted foot. Jarrett looked steadily at him. 'Brought in a rabbit,' Billy said. He turned aside to set the stick he carried against the wall. 'What can I do for you, Mr Jarrett? Folks are all gone to town. I'm to follow quick as I can.'

'I am trying to trace a man, Billy. He was seen on the pack-horse trail last night. He was coming from this way. Dressed in a gentleman's coat and a low-crowned hat – know anything about it?' Billy shook his head.

'Nay.' His broad Dalesman's features were placid. His previous tension had dissipated. They watched one another a moment. Billy, it seemed, was prepared to wait him out.

'I'll let you get off to town then.'

As he rode out of the yard Jarrett thought of the shed. That good strong rope was tied too high for dogs. And a dog ripping a rabbit would have left smears not splashes on the stone. Had more than drink been dispensed at Dewsnap's farm the previous night? He might believe in an interrogation, had there been more marks on Grub's body. He thought of Dickon Watson's response on the fell. There had been tears in his eyes; but, then again, he had seen guilty men cry before. This business had him suspicious of everyone. He imagined a child using that rope in the shed to swing around the post like a merry-go-round. It could be no more than a game. So what if Billy had been wary when he first rode up? Tenants were often uneasy when the agent came to call – and Billy was alone in the place. He turned Walcheren's head towards the Dewsnaps' neighbours, the Anderses. Miss Anders's gentleman caller intrigued him. Perhaps there were answers to be found there.

A view opened out down the sweep of the valley. The sky was a delicate confection of oyster pink and blue shaded with featherings of grey. All around the ground sparkled under the sun. The air was so clear he could distinguish individual roofs in Woolbridge across the shining ribbon of the river. There was movement on the Carlisle road. A troop of tiny horsemen were turning up the cross lane to Pennygill. He whisked Walcheren about.

He caught up with them just as they were taking the spur round to Grateley Manor – four troopers riding behind two officers. Lieutenant Roberts raised his hand and his troop came to an orderly halt.

'Mr Jarrett!' It was Colonel Ison, all bundled up with watery eyes and wind-chapped cheeks. He wore fur-lined gauntlets that made his reins difficult to manage. He slipped in his saddle as his horse fretted. With an effort, he righted himself.

'Colonel, Lieutenant,' Jarrett greeted them, 'what brings you out here?'

Colonel Ison struggled to compose his expression into something approaching cordiality. 'My condolences on your . . .' he stopped, recalling that he had no formal knowledge of what the victim had been to Mr Jarrett. He began again. 'Mr Adley, a foul crime. A tragedy. I will, naturally, be calling on the marquess to express my personal regrets. I would have done so before now but that there is business that cannot be delayed.' He pulled back his shoulders. 'We are on our way to arrest the man,' he declared astonishingly.

'The man, sir?' The colonel could not conceal his satisfaction at Mr Jarrett's reaction.

'Mr Adley's murderer,' he replied smugly. 'We go to arrest him now.' The colonel clapped his heels to his horse. 'You follow if you will,' he called back over his shoulder. The troop fell in behind him with a clatter of shod hooves.

The party advanced at a brisk trot. Grateley Manor appeared on a rise above a plantation of trees. It was a desolate location, its sparseness accentuated by the blanket of snow. The riders hunched themselves against a knifing wind. The house was forbidding from this aspect, showing almost windowless walls built to withstand attack in a time when marauders swept down from the border. The approach brought them round to a more recent frontage, barely softened by a portico and a couple of beds planted with hardy shrubs.

The door was opened by a servant, whose skirts hung bell-like over her ample hips. They stopped short of the floor to reveal surprisingly small stockinged feet thrust into grey felt slippers. The maidservant's eyes drifted over the colonel's shoulder to the troopers. One was a fine-looking young fellow. The colonel reclaimed her attention.

'Colonel Ison to see your mistress.' Arethusa looked down at his muddy boots.

'She's suppin' tea in t'parlour. Are you comin' in?' she asked dubiously. 'I've just washed t'floor.' Colonel Ison glared at her from under his fierce eyebrows.

'Damn your impertinence! Tell your mistress, woman!' He turned to Lieutenant Roberts. 'Have the men search the outbuildings,' he commanded and swept in after the affronted maid. Jarrett followed. The passageway was so dark the lamps were still lit. The maid's slippers clung loosely to her feet. They slapped along the flags. She knocked on a door and opened it.

His first impression was of comfort. Although the windows set in the thick walls were small, clear light streamed in from the snowy landscape outside. Before a good fire, a sofa and a wing chair were drawn together on a fine Indian carpet woven in rich reds and blues. The fireplace was very old. It bore a stone cartouche with a painted crest featuring a sheaf of corn tied with blue cornflowers. Miss Lippett sat in the wing chair, a piece of sewing in her hands. On the sofa, dressed in a sage-green riding habit, her skin bright from her recent exercise, was Miss Henrietta Lonsdale. She was in the act of raising a wide-bowled teacup to her lips. She set it on its saucer, holding it before her, an expression of the liveliest curiosity on her face. A patch of sun illuminated the graceful arch of her hand as she held the cup in its place. The contrast between the subtle tones of her skin and the gleaming blue and white of the porcelain cup pleased him.

'Gentleman to see you,' the servant said. 'M'um,' she added as an afterthought and withdrew with her slapping step.

'What's the meaning of this?' demanded Miss Lippett.

'Miss Lippett. Good morning. I come on official business, I regret—' began the colonel.

'Sit down then!' interrupted his hostess. Colonel Ison looked about him. The sofa and wing chair were drawn together. The two remaining straight-backed seats stood between the windows in the cold outreaches of the room. The sofa was quite large enough to accommodate two persons with propriety, but the second place was occupied by a large tortoiseshell cat that faced Miss Lippett as if it were party to the conversation. The animal turned round yellow eyes on Jarrett and twitched its ears. Jarrett bowed.

'Miss Lippett, Miss Lonsdale. Good morning.' The day and the occasion, he thought, were just too odd for convention. The cat made a protesting mew as he scooped it up and sat down in its place. Miss Lippett bristled.

'Mrs Pussypaws does not like to be handled by strangers!' Jarrett scratched the cat's head, lost for words at Miss Lippett's choice of so arch a name. Truly, she was a most unexpected person. The animal purred, rubbing itself against him as it reached up to his caressing hand. Tiplady wouldn't thank him for the hairs it was transferring to his coat. '*Why* are *you* here?' his hostess demanded, sitting forward in her seat as if she might spring up and forcibly reclaim her pet.

'I am at a loss, ma'am. The colonel has not confided in me.' Jarrett looked over at the magistrate who remained standing by the door. 'I believe he is in search of Mr Adley's murderer,' he said conversationally. Out of the corner of his eye he saw Miss Lonsdale go white.

'Mr Adley? Murdered!' she exclaimed. Jarrett instantly regretted his flippant demeanour. He wasn't himself. This business had made him mad. The cased clock in the corner gave the hour as just past two. Grub hadn't been dead a day yet.

'I do beg your pardon, Miss Lonsdale. I thought you knew . . .' She looked at him so directly he felt the impact in his chest.

'I am so sorry.' Her compassion almost unmanned him. 'What . . . how did it happen? He was at the play last night. I saw him.' She blinked back tears. The damn cat on his lap made him feel a fool. Mrs Pussypaws jumped to the floor and scuttled under the sofa as the colonel stepped forward to reclaim their attention.

'Last night Mr Adley, the marquess's young cousin, was foully murdered on Quarry Fell,' he projected. His voice was too loud for the room. The man was enjoying himself. A surge of anger caught Jarrett unawares. For a second he saw himself leaping up from the sofa and his hands closing around the colonel's throat . . . He encountered Miss Lippett's eyes. They were bashful.

'I am sorry the young man is dead,' she said gruffly. 'You have my condolences, Mr Jarrett.' Picking up the piece of linen in her lap she began to set workmanlike stitches in a seam. The colonel raised his voice.

'I regret Miss Josephine, but I have received information that implicates a man I understand you have in your employ here at Grateley Manor.' The flashing needle stilled but Miss Lippett did not raise her head. 'One Jonas Farr.' Miss Lippett looked up. The colonel expanded with satisfaction. He settled his weight on his heels and lifted his chin. His voice took on a narrative lilt. 'Some time ago I was informed that a known conspirator had infiltrated our neighbourhood.'

'A conspirator, colonel?' repeated Henrietta Lonsdale with a little gasp. Colonel Ison favoured her with a paternal glance. He thought Miss Lonsdale a comely and ladylike woman.

'A dangerous man, ma'am, known to the authorities,' he assured her.

'And you've decided that this Jonas Farr is that man,' Jarrett cut in. The colonel gave him a look of pure distaste.

'I have information.'

'Information!' Jarrett repeated. The colonel adjusted his position to address the ladies.

'Jonas Farr,' he announced, 'is the grandson of one Thomas William Farr – a known Jacobin, twice imprisoned for distributing seditious literature.' Colonel Ison straightened his neck and bowed out his chest, well satisfied with the effect of his pronouncement. Jarrett thought of the open-faced singer in the Red Angel and the self-sufficient servant standing against the wall while Miss Lippett laid her complaint before the Reverend Prattman. His impression had been of a decent, respectable man and he was a good judge of character – wasn't he?

'Why should you suspect Farr of Mr Adley's murder?' he demanded.

'I have learnt that Farr was expected at a clandestine meeting on Quarry Fell last night while the town was at the play,' replied the colonel complacently. 'He did not arrive. It is my conjecture that Mr Adley discovered the wretch's secret and threatened to expose him.'

'More information from your anonymous informant?'

Colonel Ison smiled at the duke's agent. 'Your trouble, Mr Jarrett,' he declared almost jovially, 'is that you cannot bear for me to be in the right!'

That was uncommonly perceptive of the man, conceded Jarrett to himself. He had worked with spies half his life. He, of all men, knew better than to take a person for his outward appearance. He considered the colonel. Someone among the Red Angel circle must be feeding information to the authorities. If Jonas Farr were the man the colonel thought him, and Farr suspected as much, he might well light on Grub as a likely informant. Might not such a suspicion lead to murder? The weakness in that line of reasoning was that it failed to take into account Grub's compassion for the working man. Even if Farr was this radical agitator, he had spent time in Adley's company. He would have known that Grub was a sympathizer, not an enemy. Jonas Farr had no need to kill Favian Adley. And besides, there was Pritchard, the wool buyer. That murder had been calculated and cold-blooded in its execution. He had sensed nothing in Jonas Farr's manner that hinted at a nature capable of such an act.

Miss Lippett was sitting very straight in her wing chair. With the family crest hovering by her head, she was the picture of the proud descendant of an ancient line. Her expression was haughty outrage.

'I do not believe it,' she stated.

'What?' queried the colonel, confused.

'Farr's grandfather! And what's that to the purpose? I had a great-aunt on my mother's side who was quite mad. Does that mean *I* should be assigned to the mad-house?'

Jarrett stared. He had taken the spinster for a country Tory, the kind for whom the very whisper of 'Jacobin' was enough to light the torches and call out the dogs. What was she doing defending a virtual stranger from such a charge? It was not as if Jonas Farr were an old family servant. Miss Lippett's colour changed from pale to rose pink.

'Nonsense! I know my servant to be a good, sober man,' she declared. 'Young Farr is thoughtful. He reads.'

'That in itself,' Jarrett suggested mildly, 'is not neces-sarily a persuasive argument against his being the man Colonel Ison describes.'

'But I,' stated Miss Josephine loftily, 'am a good judge of character!'

And he, apparently, reflected Jarrett, was not. The woman had surprised him again. He looked over at Miss Lonsdale. Her eyes were fixed on her friend with a faintly abstracted air.

'I will not believe it,' Miss Lippett repeated. She stared at the colonel, daring him to challenge her.

There was a smart rap on the door and Lieutenant Roberts appeared. He saluted his superior and bowed briefly to the ladies.

'Do you have him?' snapped the colonel.

'No sir. There is no sign. The cook says he left for town with his mistress yesterday and must have returned later – she cannot say when. He sleeps in the barn, she says, not in the house. But she saw him leave early this morning as she was laying the fires; she swears to that.'

'Have a description?' The lieutenant consulted a pocket book. His buttons gleamed; his coat fitted to perfection; not a hair was out of place. His manner towards his superior officer was so very correct, Jarrett (who had some experience of military men) wondered whether behind his perfect bearing Roberts despised his colonel.

'Farr – forename Jonas; twenty years of age or thereabouts,' read the lieutenant. 'Brown hair, average size, wearing a serge coat, brown corduroy breeches and a soft hat.' Over by the fireplace Jarrett thought he saw a tinge of complacency in Miss Lippett's expression. She caught him looking at her and glared.

'Have bills posted,' ordered the colonel. 'Farr will be arrested,' he informed the company. 'He won't get far.' He heard the absurdity of the repetition and harrumphed.

'My man has gone into town,' Miss Lippett insisted loudly. 'I sent him. He will return and you will discover that you are mistaken in these absurd accusations.'

The interview broke up the ladies' tea party. Miss Lonsdale rose with the gentlemen and said her farewells. The colonel, having made his exit from his hostess's immediate presence, wished to depart in form. Jarrett found himself lingering at Miss Lonsdale's side as the troop rode out in parade-ground order.

'You are well acquainted with Miss Lippett, are you not?' he asked privately.

'I have known her most of my life, Mr Jarrett. I count her my friend.'

The duke's agent watched the troopers as they trotted down the hill. He was not a conventionally handsome man, Henrietta thought. His skin was neither pale nor fine, and his nose could not be described as classical, but his person was undeniably charming. She couldn't put her finger on it. Perhaps it was the way he held himself. Her mind brushed the edges of the dreadful news about Mr Adley. She could not comprehend it. Poor Mr Jarrett. He was being so brave about it. She wanted to offer some words of comfort but what could one say to a man whose close connection had just been found murdered? He must be so sad. He looked distracted. She was caught unawares by his question.

'You do not find your friend remarkably adamant on the subject of Farr's innocence?' he asked. Jarrett was thinking of the moment when young Farr had picked up that country maid's handkerchief at the fair, and the expression on his mistress's face. 'Could it be, do you think . . .' He hesitated delicately. How to put this? Ladies could be remarkably sensitive on these subjects. 'Does Miss Josephine,' he searched for an appropriate phrase, 'have a tender heart?'

There was a short silence. Miss Lonsdale's grey-green eyes were fixed on his. He began to fear he had offended her. A hiccup of laughter broke from her lips.

'Oh no! Mr Jarrett. That won't be it at all!' Henrietta clapped a hand over her mouth. 'I'm so sorry,' she said, blushing. 'I don't know what came over me.' She turned away a little, running a hand down the waist of her habit as if straightening it. 'Miss Josephine does like to read. Living isolated as she does,' she continued. Her voice quivered. She bit her bottom lip. 'I believe she has often felt the lack of company, someone with whom to share her passion. For books, Mr Jarrett!' she added looking up into his face with an oddly intense sincerity. 'For books!'

CHAPTER SIXTEEN

Charles must have near killed his horses. The marquess's travelling carriage stood in the yard, the crest on its side-panel barely visible under the mud. Through the wide stable door he caught a glimpse of foam-flecked flanks and drooping heads. Jarrett slipped in through the kitchen. Servants were running this way and that. He would change his clothes first. A fresh shirt and a cravat with sharp creases made a man feel better-prepared to meet emotion. As he opened the baize-covered door leading from the back stairs, he heard wailing. Against his better judgement, he followed the noise.

The door to Grub's room stood open. A figure was framed by the four-poster bed. It was a woman, dressed head to toe in black. A voluminous veil thrown back from the face fell in a sooty train behind her. He hadn't seen anything like it since Mrs Siddons played the faithful widow Isabella in Southerne's tragedy at Drury Lane. A fragment of a review he had read at that time drifted up: *there was scarce a dry eye in the whole house.* The woman was pressing Grub's nightshirt to her lips and sobbing. He took a step forward and saw Charles standing by the desk. He looked nearly as weary as his horses.

The mourning figure turned her head. Grub's mother. There was a lack of definition about her features: sandy eyebrows blended into white and pink skin, an insignificant little nose and a fleshy chin. Her eyes were red-rimmed and swollen. Mrs Adley stretched out her arm. She pointed directly at him.

'I left him in *your* care,' she declared. Charles jolted forward.

'In both our cares, madam,' he amended. 'Your charge was to me.'

'My boy is dead!'

'You cannot say this tragedy is of Raif's making ...' Charles's protest had a sing-song lilt, as if he had repeated himself more than once.

'My boy lies murdered!'

'We don't know that – it may be he fell ... An accident ...' Charles appealed to Jarrett. His cousin cleared his throat.

'I will find who did this.' Jarrett spoke as much for himself as for her.

Grub's mother advanced on him, pressing him with her weeds and black cloth.

'What good is that? I want my boy!' It was as if his presence set her free from restraint. She beat her hands against her breast. They were babyish hands – like a cherub's in black lace mittens. Jarrett had the ugly feeling

266

she was taking some kind of enjoyment in her grief. He forced himself to look down into the reddened eyes, reminding himself that her loss was genuine.

'It was you!' she accused him. 'Murder follows you! You're fruit of a poisoned tree. That's what you are. You should never have come back!'

'Madam! Mrs Adley!' Charles exclaimed, outraged. Favian Adley's mother poked forward her commonplace face with its gaping lips.

'How could his Grace forgive you for letting his boy die? I never will!' He must have flinched. An odd look of triumph brightened her eyes. 'Yes. His poor little Ferdinand,' she hissed. 'And now my boy. You should never have come back. Look what you have brought us!'

'Madam!' Charles's voice was commanding but still Mrs Adley did not heed him. Jarrett could feel her hot indignation on his face. There wasn't enough air in the room. He was suffocating.

''Tis you should have died, not my boy!' she cried.

'Enough!' Charles took her arm and forcibly swung the dumpy little fury away. Still she stared back at Jarrett, her red-rimmed eyes opened wide in the white-floured face.

'What are you good for?' she spat.

'Madam!' Charles shouted.

Mrs Adley shrank. Hunched over, she sank onto the bed. She buried her face in her son's nightgown, sobbing with harsh intakes of breath.

'My little Favian. My sweet boy; my only treasure . . .' she moaned.

'With all allowance due your grief, madam,' Charles spoke low to her, 'that is past enough. Tiplady,' he called over to the valet who had appeared outside the door, pallid and shaking. 'Mrs Adley is overcome. Be so kind as to take her to the small parlour and fetch tea – and brandy, I think. Be sure there is a good fire.'

Jarrett felt the weight of Charles's hand on his sleeve. He was trembling.

'My dear, do not pay her any mind. It is the grief talking . . . The woman's gone mad.'

Jarrett backed away, waving off Charles's concern. 'Where are you going?' the marquess called after him.

He wasn't sure where he was going. He just had to get away. He heard Tiplady and that woman below. He climbed the stairs blindly. He saw a door ajar and emptiness beyond. He went in, pulling the door behind him. He dropped the snicket and heard the brass lock into place. He was alone. Silence.

Yellow walls, bare windows and an empty chair; he was in the painting room. Grub's ghostly outline stared out blankly from the canvas on the easel. He leant back against the door, an echo playing in his head. He had stood over his paint table with Charles at his back.

'Is it safe to let him roam like this – full as he is with his new wondrous notions?'

'A cousin of the mighty Duke of Penrith? What harm can he come to in this neighbourhood?'

The air was dusty. He crossed to the window and flung open the sash. There were ice crystals in the air. They pricked his skin. He was trapped, tethered, cornered. Why had he come back?

Henrietta closed the door on the soft snoring and stared at the wooden panels. She considered herself a capable woman but this . . . She had never encountered anything like it. Her heart was racing. A grandfather clock struck the hour in the hall below. The candles had been lit. More than an hour had passed in that room.

She had ordered the carriage fully expecting to drive into town. The Lonsdales having no male relative to represent them, her aunt had not thought it proper to call. The marquess was so very exalted in relation to their own social standing, and a bachelor besides. Henrietta Lonsdale acknowledged the dictates of propriety. She had errands to perform in Woolbridge – not of a pressing nature, perhaps, but errands nonetheless. Half a mile from home, she found herself stopping the carriage to instruct Hartman, the coachman, to call at the Old Manor instead. Her intention had been to leave a short note expressing her aunt's condolences, with her own name signed beneath. Mr Jarrett's demeanour up at Grateley Manor had awakened her sympathy and she wished to express it. But as soon as the carriage drew up outside the door, the marquess himself had appeared to greet her. She had never seen him so distracted. He appealed to her as a woman. Mrs Adley, the murdered boy's mother, was within and quite beside herself. She would have none of the female servants of the house about her and the

maid she had brought with her was proving quite useless.

'She's French,' my lord informed her, in a flash of his
usual manner. 'Said to be excellent at dressing hair but
quite the wrong temperament in a crisis.'

Henrietta Lonsdale was a compassionate woman. She
liked to be of use. Lord Charles appeared so pitifully
harassed, she had felt it impossible to refuse him. And
that is how it came to pass that Henrietta Lonsdale, spinster of marriageable age (more or less), found herself un-
chaperoned in a household of bachelors.

The things she had heard! She stared at the closed
door as if the truth might be discovered in its wooden
grain. She did not know what to believe. Of course, these
noble families were bound to be different from ordinary
folk, but still . . . She was at a loss as to what to do next.
She looked up to find Lord Charles observing her.

'How is she?' he asked. His expression was conspira-
torial, as if they had known each other for years.

'She's sleeping,' Miss Lonsdale replied. 'I gave her a
draught of Mr Tiplady's tonic.'

'Sensible,' he said, taking her arm in a brotherly
manner and steering her towards the stairs. 'What's in
it?' he asked conversationally. She suspected he did so to
fill a gap. She was grateful.

'Tincture of laudanum, I believe. Dr Parry has pre-
scribed my aunt something similar. It soothes her when
she is hysterical.' She checked herself. That was hardly
polite. She had just implied Mrs Adley – a stranger to her

and the marquess's relative – was hysterical. But what other word could properly describe the lady's behaviour? Lord Charles had fallen silent. She slid a glance at his profile under her lashes. He held her hand in the crook of his arm, lightly covered by his own cool fingers. Apart from a faintly set look about his jaw, they might have been entering a ballroom. The staircase creaked as they descended. There must be servants about but not one was in sight. You are a respectable spinster, she told herself forcefully; Lord Charles is a gentleman and you are doing your Christian duty. They stepped off the bottom stair and she slid her hand free.

'Mr Jarrett.' A voice sounding remarkably like her own resonated in the panelled hallway. 'Is he at home?' The marquess crooked an eyebrow at her. 'I-I saw him earlier,' she stammered, grateful for the blending cover of the candlelight as colour flooded her face. 'I was visiting Miss Lippett. Mr Jarrett arrived with the colonel. That is how I learnt the dreadful news about Mr Adley. At Grateley Manor.' Lord Charles took a moment to react.

'What was he doing up there?' he demanded. Henrietta moistened her lips. Had Mr Jarrett not told him? Wouldn't he think her a dreadful gossip?

'I understand that Colonel Ison believes he has identified the culprit responsible for ... for last night's tragedy,' she explained, picking her words with care. 'He rode up to Grateley to arrest a man in Miss Lippett's employ. He did not find him.' That was the bare truth. Lord Charles stared back at her, his expression blank. For a foolish moment she wondered whether she should repeat herself.

'Good God!' he exclaimed. 'I need a drink.' Leaving her standing, he led the way into the library.

'Did Mr Jarrett not tell you?' she asked unnecessarily, as she followed him.

'He is keeping out of the way. I can't blame him. That woman—' Lord Charles broke off and rang the bell. 'Tea?' he asked.

She was grateful for the tea when it came. The marquess seemed to have forgotten her. He stood over the mantelpiece. Leaning an arm against the marble shelf, he nursed his whisky, contemplating the flames below. Henrietta examined the room about her. The library lacked the sense of comfort that came from family use. The curtains, she noted, looked newly hung and the paintwork was fresh. A taint of turpentine and linseed touched with vinegar mixed with the taste of her tea. Apart from the yellowing perspective of the old manor, as it had been in Queen Anne's day, hanging over the fire, there was a sparseness in the decorations. There were no porcelain vases or curiosities dotted about. None of the usual hunting prints, family portraits or interesting peeps from some ancestor's tour added interest to the walls. Miss Lonsdale felt as if she trespassed. Her acquaintance with the marquess, in truth, was slight. It rested solely on the fact that they had been thrown together in an isolated neighbourhood. Were they in London, or even in York, she would never have had an opportunity for such an encounter. They belonged to such different spheres. She was out of her depth. Her interview with Mrs Adley had troubled her deeply. She told herself that the woman was half mad and malicious with it, but she could not forget what she had heard.

'Mr Adley's mother is dreadfully shocked,' she said. Lord Charles lifted his head.

'Has she blamed poor Raif for the boy's death?'

Henrietta was nonplussed. She had not anticipated so direct a response. 'She has said many things. I did not . . .' Henrietta tried to find the proper compassion for a mother's grief and came up wanting. She cast about for some way to change the subject.

'Come now, what did she say?'

Henrietta resorted to a sip of the dregs of her cold tea. The marquess's mouth curved upwards as if it smiled despite him. He came and sat down beside her. Gently he took the cup from her hands and set it aside. He picked up her hand and held it between his.

'Miss Lonsdale – Henrietta,' he said coaxingly. 'I appreciate your delicacy but I should like to know what Mrs Adley said.' His brown eyes were warm and generous. You do want to know the truth of it, thought Henrietta to herself. She gathered her courage.

'Mrs Adley mentioned Mr Jarrett. She . . .' Henrietta hesitated then pushed herself on, speaking in her most matter-of-fact style. 'She charges him with responsibility for her son's death and she spoke of another boy.' The marquess dropped her hand.

'Little brother Ferdy.' Henrietta felt cold. Charles read her expression. 'It was an accident!' he protested. 'We were boys, playing on ice.' He got up and crossed to the window. Drawing a curtain aside, he looked out. The snowy landscape glimmered in the dark. 'Much this time of year, as I remember. The ice broke and Ferdy fell under it. It was Raif who pulled him out. He was our hero that day.'

'Then why should Mrs Adley ... ?' Charles made an impatient sound. He let the curtain drop back into place.

'Raif pulled Ferdy out,' he repeated, 'but my brother did not recover. He was taken by a fever. There was nothing to be done. Raif blamed himself – we never did.' Charles had resumed his contemplation of the fire. 'Raif has a noble heart.' He spoke so quietly, his manner so abstracted, that Henrietta wondered if he remembered to whom he spoke. 'He thinks it his duty to protect us. Mother calls him our centurion.' She thought of that boy with a noble heart who could not save someone he loved; and of that same boy, grown to be a man, somewhere above in this house, alone, facing this new loss. Her throat constricted.

'How old was he?' she asked.

'Who? Raif? Then? Twelve years old, or thereabouts.' The man before her straightened up. He seemed to fill out and harden. He, a marquess, turned to face her. 'You, ma'am, have a way of winning confidences,' he said lightly. He crossed to the bell and rang it. 'But I am remiss. I have imposed on your good nature too long. Your aunt will be wondering what has become of you. Let me call for your carriage.'

The servant came and the carriage was brought to the door. Lord Charles escorted her to it, his polished manner marking the distance between them. At the steps, he bowed over her hand.

'I cannot thank you enough for your kindness, ma'am,' he said, his voice suddenly intimate. Henrietta took her seat, fussing with her skirts to cover her embarrassment.

'What will you do?' she asked before he could close the door. The marquess's expression softened. He answered her readily enough.

'Mrs Adley wants to remove her son as soon as possible. Her husband is on a visit with friends in Kent. He will meet us in London.'

'And Mr Jarrett, will he accompany you?'

'No. Raif will stay here. He will discover what happened to poor Grub,' responded Lord Charles with utter assurance. The carriage door swung closed on her with a decisive click.

The idea of his own death had never troubled him. He did not imagine there was any means to worry once you were dead. He did not believe in an afterlife. He hoped for a clean death, other than that ... But this was different. Grub should have been safe.

Murder follows you! As if death were a plague he carried from place to place.

He was almost through the bottle Charles had so

considerately left behind him. The brandy filled him with rage. Damn him! Damn Charles to hell for his interfering, well-meaning ways. If he hadn't dragged him back, this would never have happened. He listened to the old house creaking around him. It was at Charles's urging that the place had been cleared out, plastered and painted, as if it would make him a home. He thought of the library beneath him as it was the first time he set eyes on it – broken, vile and uncared for, like its previous inhabitant, the last duke's agent, who had died there. It's still the same shell that housed Crotter, he thought. Paint and plaster will not disguise that. Your kind has no home.

What are you good for?

His box cut a familiar outline against a window of stars winking in the night. His paints had always been his pleasure, a means to create form and order. He stood up, catching himself on the corner of the table. He could capture Grub's image and leave a likeness to remember him by. He needed light.

He opened the door to deeper darkness. He felt his way down the wall to the attic door. He pulled it open and yelled for light. Bare feet thudded on boards overhead. A pause and then a door opened. Light wavered round the corner, gradually filling the stairwell. At its centre appeared a young footman Tiplady had engaged. He lifted the lamp. Its light fell on his master's face.

'The house is asleep, sir.' The youth's feet were bare. He wore breeches with his nightshirt half tucked into them.

'Why aren't you, then?' Jarrett put a hand on the wall to steady himself, squinting a little against the dazzle.

'You called, sir,' the youth answered patiently.

'I want light. Tip!' Jarrett roared, demonstrating the lung power of an officer in the field. 'Tiplady!'

The footman was intrigued. It was the first time he had seen Mr Jarrett proper lit. He'd only been at the manor for eight months but, like the rest of the household, he was proud of his dashing master.

'Hush sir,' he said urgently. If Mr Jarrett carried on like this, he'd wake the old witch downstairs. 'Mr Tiplady's taken his tonic.' His master waved a hand.

'You'll do. Matthew, isn't it? Fetch me straw.'

'Straw, sir?'

'You heard me. Straw. Fetch it.' Jarrett pushed himself off the wall. 'A bale from the stables.' He looked back over his shoulder. The boy had not moved. 'Go on. Fetch!'

'It's the middle of the night, sir.'

'Do you think me blind?' his master enquired without heat. 'I want straw – at least half a bale and that roll of wire in the tack room by the feed bin. And light. Lots of light.' He moved towards the stairs. 'And brandy,' he added as an afterthought: 'I'll fetch the rest,' he said and disappeared.

'What's he up to?' Jinnie the little housemaid peered over Matt's shoulder, holding a shawl tight over her nightgown.

'He's gonna burn us out! The master's gone mad!' squealed Maggie, who had followed her roommate.

'Get on with you!' scoffed Matt. Maggie was known as a worrier. Although he was barely sixteen years old, Matt had a presence about him. Girls looked up to him.

'Where you goin'?' demanded Maggie, watching Matt head towards the back stairs.

'I'm fetching t'bale and wire,' he answered. 'Yous get off to bed.'

'If master's gonna burn the place down,' responded Maggie, 'I'm sleeping in the kitchen by the yard door.'

'What about you?' Jinnie called softly after Matt. He looked back up at her.

'I'll get me a chair and wait out the night by the door in case he needs me.'

'You smell smoke, you come warn us,' urged Maggie and turned back up the stairs to bed.

The candles had burnt out. Pink dawn light filled the room. It was almost done. The door opened behind him and he smelt coffee.

'Fine fellow you are, hiding away and leaving me alone with that wretched woman!' Charles was actually holding a tray. Jarrett blinked at the unaccustomed sight.

'What?'

His cousin put down his burden. 'The boy brought it up.' Charles saw the chair and its occupant. 'What the devil!'

Favian's clothes, stuffed with straw, occupied the chair where Grub once sat. The rough mannequin posed in parody of its original, one arm bent up along the back of the chair and pantalooned legs stretched out in counterpoint. Charles advanced on the gruesome doll as if he would throw it to the ground.

'Don't! The balance is precarious.' The artist looked up from his canvas. 'I needed the clothes,' he said simply.

The portrait was almost complete. Favian Adley leant his head on his hand. His pale face glowed, delicate and translucent, but it was a blind face. The eyes were blurred as if blank. Charles stared, transfixed, as Jarrett's steady brush traced a single fine line of grey paint down the shadowed side of the nose. The artist took a step back. He flicked a rueful glance towards his companion.

'I could not bear him looking at me . . .'

Charles opened his mouth as if to say something. Instead, he closed it again and turned to pour two cups of coffee.

'Sky's a good colour,' he commented. The window to the side of the figure framed an Italianate summer sky of pure blue highlighted with scumbles of cloud.

'It's a new tint. Field calls it Dumont's Blue.' He liked to think of Grub under a cheerful sky. 'It's a touch more purple than ultramarine. Works tolerably in oil.' Picking up a fresh brush, Jarrett gave substance to the white cravat with a few sparse touches of black.

'You missed Miss Lonsdale.' Charles leant against the table drinking his coffee. 'The blessed creature happened by and settled the gorgon before she left. She told me of the colonel's hunt for this man Farr.' Jarrett's hand stilled.

'Do you blame me?'

'No. I never thought of blaming you,' Charles answered as if they were talking of an overturned jug. Jarrett faced him.

'How can you say that? He would never have come here but for me and this!' He jabbed with his brush in the direction of the canvas, barely missing its surface.

'Vain speculation and quite useless!' Charles exclaimed impatiently. Raif's one weakness was to think too much. He took things too much to heart. Always had. The marquess frowned down at the cup in his hands, remembering the last time the three of them had been together – the last time they would ever meet – that evening in the barn theatre when the foolish boy had snubbed Raif. 'He loved you.' His voice was soft. 'I know – for he and I were not so different when it came to you. As boys you were our model. It was your actions, your temper we most wished to emulate.'

Jarrett moved impatiently and winced. His head was aching from the brandy.

'You and I are not suited to melodrama!' he said with a lopsided smile.

'Be booed off the stage,' Charles agreed. He resumed with an air of defying their mutual embarrassment. 'Some villain robbed the boy of his life. You could not protect him from that, but I know you. You will find this man and you will avenge our Grub.'

Mrs Adley reached up her plump mittened hands and pulled the veil over her face. She passed by without the slightest acknowledgement of his presence. Jarrett stood to attention, shaved and correct. His head was throbbing. Whatever the woman did, he would see Grub off. The men loaded the coffin onto a waiting cart drawn by a matched team of black horses. Lord knows where Tiplady had found those. It occurred to him he did not appreciate his valet's skills sufficiently. He should thank him later. Charles had elected to ride. His showy grey stallion was playing up, tossing its head and fretting to be off. Mrs Adley took her place in the carriage. She leant forward and addressed the marquess through the window.

'He knows he will not be welcome at the funeral?' she said distinctly. 'Let him stay away. *He* has done his part!' The grey stallion curveted and spun its rider away. Mastering his mount, Charles brought him round to Jarrett. He leant down from the saddle.

'Pray for me,' he murmured. Jarrett rested his hand on the horse's muscular flank.

'Good luck.'

'I'll need it,' responded the marquess gloomily.

The little procession set out – the coffin cart leading the way with the carriage and its outrider following. In the middle distance, along the road, a smart travelling carriage had drawn up on the verge. Blinds covered its windows. The coachman and his assistant waited, hats in hand, for the coffin to pass. All at once Jarrett felt overwhelmingly hungry. He could not recall when he had last taken food.

A short time later, Matt the footman found him in the kitchen eating some of Mrs Martin's game pie.

'There's a visitor, sir; a gentleman to see you.' Matt handed his master a rectangle of board. Jarrett glanced down at the card and rose to his feet, his food forgotten.

CHAPTER SEVENTEEN

A tall man with grey hair stood with his back turned, outlined against the window. He swung about.

'Frederick Jarrett!' Grasping Jarrett's hand he shook it vigorously, baring thin, grey teeth. 'A pleasure, a pleasure. Heard good things.'

'Sir. You have caught me unawares.'

''Twas fortunate your letter found me at home. Dreadful news about young Adley! Dreadful! Sympathies. Understood, eh?'

'Thank you for responding swiftly – and in person.' The man must have travelled through the night. 'This is an unexpected courtesy. Do sit down, Mr Strickland.' Mr Strickland settled himself. He bore none of the signs of urgency. His linen appeared freshly laundered. His clothes were unobtrusive but fine. Their expert cut spoke of Stulze, the Duke of Wellington's tailor.

'Only saw him a week or two back. Was at school with me little brother, don't ye know.' The visitor paused, giving due weight to the melancholy thought. 'Ran into him in Leeds. On his way up here, as it happens.'

Jarrett indicated a carved cabinet. 'May I offer you refreshment?'

'You were in Portugal, were you not? Under McCloud, I think? Sherry if you have it.'

Jarrett picked up a decanter. 'Is the Royal Hotel a regular rendez-vous?' he asked.

'Coaching inns are convenient,' responded Mr Strickland ambiguously. He held his glass up to the light. He sniffed then tasted the amber liquid and made an approving face. 'Passable.'

'What can you tell me, Mr Strickland?' Jarrett sat across from his guest. Light from the window gilded Mr Strickland's profile, highlighting his hawkish nose.

'What do you think you know, Mr Jarrett?'

'That there is an agent active in this neighbourhood. I suspect he is one of yours.' The spymaster inclined his head in a courtly manner. 'Speculative mission, or particular?'

'Bit of one, bit of the other. Why should you need to know more?' Mr Strickland paused. His eyes widened. 'You think my man may know something about the boy's death? No, no! That's quite the wrong track.'

'How so?'

Mr Strickland leant forward. 'We are talking murder?' Taking Jarrett's slight tilt of the chin as confirmation, he continued. 'In this case,' he positioned his glass with precision in the centre of the mahogany table beside his chair, 'my man was entirely otherwise engaged.'

'You were with him?'

'No, but he is accounted for. All night. He is a fruit-less pursuit.' They contemplated one another in silence a moment.

'If your man is hunting insurgents, he may have infor-mation to my purpose,' Jarrett said.

'You expect to find young Adley's murderer in that quarter?'

'Perhaps. Colonel Ison certainly thinks so.'

'The magistrate hereabouts? You disagree?'

'I have insufficient intelligence.'

'Hence your desire to interview my man?' Mr Strick-land stared at the ceiling a moment. 'My man is well placed,' he mused.

'In a substantial home in the manufacturing quarter, I'll venture.' Jarrett was almost certain he had scored a hit. Mr Strickland's eyes reacted with an infinitesimal flicker. His lips curved upwards in a painted smile.

'You'll forgive me if I cannot comment.'

'Do you trust your man?'

'He has proven himself.' Mr Strickland took a mouthful of sherry, holding it on his tongue a moment before swal-lowing. 'He was useful in rolling up the Ludlow gang,' he expanded, 'and he uncovered an assassination attempt on precious Prinny in 1810.'

Jarrett's attention sharpened. Surely that must exclude Bedford – and the other Woolbridge men in the case. But what did he know of their individual histories? He had only been here a year himself. Then again, Strickland was not above direct deceit.

Mr Strickland tapped his glass against his lower lip.

'I would say my man was sound.'

'A good man?' Jarrett rolled the stem of his glass idly between forefinger and thumb.

'Now we can't expect *that* in our line of work,' replied Mr Strickland archly. 'But he's expert. Not one to stray from the brief.'

'And his brief in this case?'

'To track an agitator said to have fled Leeds a while back, active in corresponding societies.'

'I thought the corresponding societies were all disbanded after '93?'

''Tis true, the execution of King Louis did bring many to their senses, but we've been keeping our eye on an active remnant. For a time now there've been tales of recruiting.'

'Tales?'

'Information,' corrected Strickland gently. 'Reports of clandestine meetings, the administration of illegal oaths to disaffected apprentices – that sort of thing.'

'And you think this Leeds man a recruiter? The candidate in this case seems very young to be of importance. He must have been in leading strings in '93.' Mr Strickland raised his eyebrows and pursed up his mouth. 'I have come across him,' Jarrett replied in answer to the look. 'This is not a populous place.'

And that being so, he thought to himself, what of Colonel Ison in all this? And what of Mr Raistrick?

'What do the magistrates know?' he asked out loud.

'As little as possible.' Strickland brushed a speck of dirt from his cuff. 'Small-town men lack finesse,' he drawled. 'Best to avoid them if one can.'

Jarrett experienced a spurt of ill-temper. His head was sore and dull from the fumes of last night's brandy. It was hard work guarding his expression. There was a time when he had enjoyed such fencing. He had lost his taste for it.

'Your man's been feeding reports to Ison,' he stated baldly. Mr Strickland met the challenge with a benign, blank look.

In his mind's eye Jarrett saw a chair, a travelling bag beside it, and a pair of worn buckled shoes placed neatly beneath. The memory reproached him.

'And what of Pritchard?' he asked abruptly.

'Pritchard? Who is this Pritchard?' Mr Strickland was hardly given to transparency, but he gave a convincing show of surprise.

'He came to town with a colleague, a Mr George: a pair of buyers looking to fill a wool order for the army. He died at an inn called the Bucket and Broom.'

'What's that to the purpose? People die.'

'They do,' Jarrett conceded. 'But in this case it was murder, and my cousin was likely killed by the same hand.' Mr Strickland's gaze intensified.

'And what does the colonel think?' he asked mildly. 'Ison. He is the law in these parts, I believe?'

No mention of Raistrick. Was that significant? Jarrett marshalled what he knew of the man before him. They had never worked together but Strickland was well known in the service for running tight operations at a gentlemanly distance. From what he had heard, Francis Strickland was not one to involve himself with boot-strap bullies like Raistrick. They were too independent as a type.

'The colonel does not think,' Jarrett said out loud.

'But you do?'

'I am persuaded.'

Mr Strickland searched his host's face. 'You are persuaded,' he repeated.

Jarrett nodded.

'Very well.' Mr Strickland tilted his head in an echo of the gesture. He stood up and returned to the window. 'I shall arrange a meeting,' he said, looking out. 'On one condition.' Jarrett held his peace. 'My man will answer your questions; he will share any relevant information; but in return you will engage,' here Strickland cast a pointed look over his shoulder, 'upon your word of honour, not to use the encounter as a means to penetrate his disguise.' He turned back wearing a collegial smile. 'You know how important anonymity is in this line of work. I must protect my operatives.'

Outside the snow was beginning to melt. In the silence of the room they could hear the dripping trees.

'Agreed,' Jarrett replied.

'Bleak country, this,' Mr Strickland remarked.

'It is winter.'

'Even so.' Mr Strickland shivered. 'God knows how you stand it.' He cocked his head to one side. With his length and his hard, bright eyes, he reminded Jarrett of a giant heron. 'There's always work for a man like you. Glad to put a word in.'

'Thank you but no. Those days are behind me.'

'As you will.' Mr Strickland picked up his cloak and hat. 'Change your mind. Happy to be of service. Give me a few hours to contact my man. I'll send word.'

They took their leave. The older man's grip was iron. Jarrett matched it.

'Forgive me, but I cannot wait long,' he said firmly. 'A matter of family, you understand.'

The brush trailed symmetrical tracks through Walcheren's thick winter pelt. It was cosy here, wrapped in the miasma of sweet straw and warm hide. The big bay vibrated his velvet lips contentedly as dust and loose hair flew from Jarrett's brush. At least this was one task he was sufficient to. If only he could separate truth from deceit so easily.

Who was Strickland's man? In such a small neighbourhood, it was likely he had met him already. He thought of Bedford and his watchful stillness. He discarded him. The manufacturer was too high-placed. This sort of operation needed an agent who blended in among the little men – someone who could mix with weavers in the manufacturing quarter. That would be an agitator's hunting ground, the place to find the disaffected and fearful. One might have thought that a foreigner like that would stand out these parts. The fairs were insufficient cover. They would be over in a day. Then again, there were always folk passing through – merchants, drovers, pedlars, labourers on the tramp ... A sudden thought struck him, absurd in its simplicity. He had gone along with the colonel's casting of Jonas Farr as the radical in the case. But what if *he* were Strickland's man? He was a stranger, come from Leeds, and in tight with the song club ...

When was that affair with the Ludlow gang? He was almost certain he had heard talk of it when he had been in London on leave in 1806. Six years ago now. He checked himself impatiently. Farr was much too young. At best, he could only have been in his mid-teens then; a mere stripling.

The rhythmic slap and draw of the brush across Walcheren's hide was soothing. Farr intrigued him. He needed to get closer to the man. He wondered if Colonel Ison had managed to run him to ground yet. He rather hoped he hadn't. He ducked under Walcheren's neck.

What did he know, from his own observations? He thought back to Grub that first day at the Queen's Head, squirming in the grip of Lieutenant Roberts. The lieutenant had been in pursuit of the distributors of inflammatory songs. That small puzzle was answered. The song sheet he had found interleaved in Grub's notebook convinced him that Dickon Watson and his friends from the Red Angel were the source of the ballads papering the town. But those were just songs. They were no real threat. The note in the colonel's carriage – that was the one piece of evidence that suggested something more: a direct threat of violence. It had found its way onto the seat of the colonel's carriage during the hat game played in the marketplace by Watson and his friends. Did it follow that the Red Angel song club were responsible? That game was a convenient diversion. And yet, the note troubled him. What could be the purpose of it? If there were a conspiracy brewing, why risk the attention? Unless some wider plan had misfired and been abandoned.

He thought of the colonel, blustering and red-faced as he waved that dirty piece of paper. It was a good joke, if one was there to see it ... His hand stilled, the brush idle in its track. Raistrick? The lawyer had swaggered in late to that meeting at Bedford's. Had there been an extra touch of mischief in his manner that day? Walcheren looked back at his master reproachfully.

'My apologies.' Jarrett resumed his rhythmic task. 'But in truth that note is a mystery.'

It might appeal to Raistrick's humour but he couldn't picture the lawyer going to the trouble of forging and placing such a note for so small a return. *I need more information*, he told himself. *I need a weaver* ... The snatched exchange between Harry Aitken and Watson he had overheard as they left the Old Manor eddied up from his memory. Harry Aitken had been inclined to confide in him, he was almost certain of that. If he could just put himself in the way of a private conversation . . .

An awareness pricked his skin. He looked up. Duffin stood in a halo of winter daylight just within the door.

'Ezekial!' he greeted him. Duffin's outline was still against the pearly light. Jarrett tensed. A shadow loomed just outside. Duffin jerked his head.

'Come on now!' he urged the concealed presence. 'Step up!'

The shape coalesced into the spokesman of the Red Angel song club, the young giant, Dickon Watson.

'Dickon here's got summat to tell yous,' the poacher announced. Jarrett knew him well enough by now to discern the tinge of satisfaction in the countryman's voice. 'Out with it, lad.'

Dalesmen, as a breed, were stocky and square to the ground. Dickon Watson was constructed to similar proportions but on a massive scale. He loomed, like an idol or dolmen. He seemed ill at ease. He cast a wary eye over the line of stalls. Walcheren bent his sleek neck, observing the newcomer with mild interest. Jarrett kept up his brushstrokes, concentrating on his horse's front legs. So Duffin had been busy, had he? He had wondered where the poacher vanished to after they brought Grub down from the fell.

'Ezekial Duffin says you're to be trusted,' the young giant declared abruptly. He paused and started again, his voice swelling with truculence. 'Soldiers are looking to take up Jonas for Book Boy's murder. I come to tell yous, he never done it.' Walcheren stamped a back foot restlessly. The young giant flinched. 'Jonas would never hurt Book Boy,' he continued in a milder tone. 'None of us would. He was a good soul.'

Jarrett surveyed his visitor over Walcheren's broad flank.

'What's your trade, Mr Watson?' he asked.

'Weavin', when I had one,' answered Dickon, startled.

'Had?'

Dickon advanced further into the stable, keeping to the outer wall.

'Me da was a partner in Cullen's shop – did well enough when I was a bairn. But then da took a consumption and died and me ma couldn't keep up wi' debts . . .' His voice trailed off, his attention focused on Jarrett's hands. The duke's man was detaching the rope that secured the big bay's head collar to an iron ring set in the wall. Jarrett turned Walcheren about.

'Here, take his head will you?' He addressed Dickon, handing him the rope. For a moment it looked as if the man might flee; instead he took the rope. He stood stiffly, eyes front, as Walcheren pulled back his head and looked down on him from his greatest height.

'Stepped on as a bairn, was you?' Duffin asked mockingly. Dickon scowled and hunched his shoulders.

'Where's that tail comb got to . . . ? Go on,' Jarrett prompted the youth. 'What happened then?'

'Ma had to sell out to Cullen so as we could eat,'

answered Dickon, watching Jarrett search the straw around his horse's feet. 'Cullen apprenticed me and I served me time. Now I'm a daytal man.' Jarrett shot a questioning look at Duffin.

'Paid by the day,' the poacher explained.

'I save what I can,' Dickon elaborated. 'I'll buy me back in one day.'

Walcheren sighed and dropped his head, inspecting the ground for stray oats. Dickon looked down at him and breathed out through his nose. 'Sim Cullen and me, we have plans – if his da can hold on t'shop.'

'Times are bad?' asked Jarrett.

'They're bitter, Mr Jarrett. I haven't had work at t'looms for months.' Dickon changed the rope from hand to hand, flexing his freed fingers.

'But you've been busy, nonetheless. You and your friends have been handing round those songs, have you not?' Jarrett said. Dickon stared at him blankly for a moment.

'What's a man, Mr Jarrett?' he burst out, suddenly rhetorical. 'A man must be worth more than to work himself out for the profit of rich men and never himself. Working men need their eyes opened.'

'And once men's eyes are opened, what then?' Jarrett spied the missing comb half under Walcheren's hoof and gave him a shove. Dickon started as Walcheren moved his foot and settled again. The large weaver widened his stance.

'I'll tell you what, Mr Jarrett. Material things,' he said,

leaning forward a little, as if impelled by his urgency to make his point. 'A few weeks back we heard word of these army buyers coming to Woolbridge fairs with a big order to fill – work for the whole town, maybe. It's been a bad winter. Price has come down tuppence a piece on last year. Bedford can't fill an order like that alone. We heard these buyers were stopping in Penrith, Sim Cullen and me. We goes over. We found one of them buyers, going from shop to shop looking at cloth, talking prices. We had words. He made himself out an honest man. We would have our chance to make our bid, he said, at the fairs – all straight and above board.' He paused significantly.

'And,' prompted Jarrett obligingly.

'Them buyers stops at an inn outside town. Next we hear, our man's dead.' Dickon swept his widened eyes between Jarrett and Duffin and back again.

'Pritchard. The man you spoke to in Penrith was Pritchard?' demanded Jarrett. Dickon nodded.

'And the deal's been struck – with Bedford and no other.' The weaver stood closer now, the sheer breadth and height of his frame adding force to his words. 'And here's a thing, Mr Jarrett. All through winter there's been talk of Bedford's mill failing but what diz ta think? He's bringing in machines – and them's not got for naught. When Bedford has machines, he'll have no more need of piecework. Then a man'll slave for him or starve.'

Jarrett finished combing Walcheren's mane. He gave the bay's neck a pat.

'So, no more independents,' he remarked.

'There won't be if we can't find redress. I'm telling you, Mr Jarrett: not Jonas, not I, nor any of us, had a reason to harm your boy.' Nor Pritchard, neither, thought Jarrett to himself, if what you say is true.

Walcheren was staring off through the open yard door with an abstracted air. Dickon was more at ease than when he first made his entrance. He met Jarrett's gaze with unwavering eyes. Jarrett took the rope from him and led his horse down the narrow walkway to his stall.

'I believe you,' he said over his shoulder. 'But what of Farr? He's not accounted for the night of the play – for he wasn't with you, was he?' Dickon followed in their wake, his hands thrust deep in his pockets. He shrugged.

'I'm not his keeper,' he said.

Jarrett regarded him thoughtfully, pondering what kind of man this Jonas Farr must be to elicit such loyalty on so short an acquaintance.

'Why are you so sure of him?' he asked. 'A month or so ago you must have been strangers.' Dickon shrugged again.

'With some men, you know,' he said simply. He looked away, his skin reddening. 'You've heard him sing,' he said. 'No liar ever sung that true.'

'My dear fellow,' Jarrett began, but Dickon looked back at him with such a steady assurance in the simplicity of basic truths, he stopped. He remembered the transparency and meaning in that voice he had heard at the Red Angel. He found to his surprise that he wished he could share Dickon's simple faith, so he left it at that.

'You don't know where Farr was that night?' he pressed, instead.

'Not know,' Dickon said grudgingly. For all his formidable height and bulk, he took on the look of a truculent schoolboy.

'But you have an idea?'

'Reckon it's a woman.'

'You've seen him with her?' The young giant shook his head in slow motion, keeping his eyes boldly fixed on Jarrett's as if daring him to challenge him.

'But there will be a witness as to his whereabouts that night while my cousin was murdered on the fell?' Dickon shrugged.

Jarrett thought of the tale the Hiltons had told him that morning about Miss Anders and her mysterious caller. The night of the play seemed so distant. It took him a moment to recall, but he was certain he had seen the Anders men down in the pit. He could not picture a woman sitting with them. Mrs Hilton had left him with the impression that she thought Miss Anders's mysterious visitor was not the gentleman he purported to be. Might Farr have taken the opportunity to go a-wooing while his lover's family was at the play?

'Tell him the rest,' prompted Duffin. The poacher had been standing so silent and still, as was his habit, Jarrett had almost forgotten his presence. 'Tell 'im about t'stranger.'

'What stranger is this?' asked Jarrett.

297

'There's been a stranger slippin' about trying to catch up young fools in secret oaths and the like,' Duffin supplied before the weaver could answer.

'Someone's out to make trouble,' Dickon chimed in. He seemed eager enough to confide now.

'Twisting in, don't they call it?' Jarrett responded. 'You don't favour it then?'

'I'm not a fool nor a traitor neither!' exclaimed Dickon. 'That's sedition, that is. I'm a loyal subject of King George,' he declared indignantly, 'and I don't know any that aren't.'

'You've no notion who this stranger might be, then?' asked Jarrett. The weaver turned down his mouth.

'He's a dark 'un,' he said dubiously. 'Moved over from Lake country, by all accounts. First heard tell of him over the tops. Secret meetings. Came and went at night. Some say he wore a mask as he made his speeches. Don't rightly know but one who's seen him.'

An orator in a mask harangues the people – wasn't that what the colonel's report said?

'And what does that one have to say?' asked Jarrett.

Dickon folded his massive arms across his chest. He looked up under low brows.

'He's a halfwit.'

'He's not named Lem, by any chance?'

Watson's mouth dropped open. 'How does yous know that?' he demanded incredulously. That was a piece of luck, Jarrett congratulated himself.

'You were looking for him at the opening of the fairs,'

he pressed on, feeling his way from what Miss Bedford had told him. He had a flash of inspiration. He saw the boy with the blue neckerchief, fleeing the action just as the soldiers closed in. 'Was that the purpose of your hat game?' he asked. 'Did you catch him?' Dickon was utterly still.

'No,' he said but there was a fracture in his denial. Jarrett sensed Duffin shift his position just at the edge of his eye-line. He risked another leap.

'But Billy Dewsnap had him in that byre the other night,' he said. The silence stretched out between them. 'Do you deny it?' The weaver looked away for a fraction of a second. 'So tell me about it,' Jarrett said quietly. Dickon sighed. He unfolded his arms.

'Lem's a fool,' he began, 'but he's never been one to know it. Clever-daft, that's Lem. Always out to prove himself. This one got a hold of him – I don't know how they met – had him take some fancy oath an' all.' Dickon's voice was scornful. 'Tried to get Lem to read it at first but little Lem don't have his letters, so fellow had to repeat for him. Lem was cock o' t'midden.'

'He told you this?'

'Not him. Lem's none too fond o' me. Told Jinnie – boasted about it. Lem's sweet on Jinnie,' he explained. 'Follows her about like a little dog. She's found him looking in at her window before now. She weren't best pleased. Billy neither,' he added as an afterthought.

'Billy Dewsnap? Is Jinnie his sister?' Jarrett ventured. Dickon shook his head.

'Walkin' out,' he said.

Jarrett thought of the stone shed on Dewsnap's farm and the rope and the blood drops Billy had tried to conceal with straw.

'So Lem's been pestering Billy's girl and Billy got a hold of him later that day, after the fight in the marketplace?'

'Stepped in, like, once we got there,' Dickon said, a touch shamefaced. 'Bill was in a bait – gave Lem a pastin' – nothing broken but Lem was in no mood to confide. Took us all night to get Bill to see sense. Then we was called out by t'lad with news of . . .' he tapered off, casting Jarrett an uncomfortable look. 'Anyhow, while we was gone Jinnie came in and let Lem out. He scarpered. But we'll find him,' he wound up confidently. 'Lives with his gran; has no place else to be.'

They were both watching him, Duffin and that overgrown lad. Duffin believed him; but did he? Jarrett examined Dickon's stoic Dalesman's face. There was no tension in the line of his shoulders. His hands were relaxed. Walcheren was at ease around him.

'Do you know the whereabouts of Jonas Farr?' Dickon's eyes went opaque.

'I won't betray him.'

'Understand me,' Jarrett said. 'You say Jonas Farr is a decent man. If the colonel lays hands on him, that will mean nothing; he will see him condemned.' He paused a beat. 'Is Farr still in Woolbridge?'

The weaver folded his massive arms once more. He looked to Duffin.

'You can trust him,' the poacher urged. Dickon

scowled. 'What did you come here for, but to ask his help!' Duffin dealt him an exasperated swipe with the back of one hand. 'Go on with ya!'

'Perhaps you're waiting for Farr to contact you?' suggested Jarrett.

'Time I went,' Dickon announced, making for the door. With his massive bulk, stopping him hardly seemed an option.

'What of Lem?' Jarrett's question turned him back. 'This stranger – I want to know who he is.'

'You and me both,' said Dickon. 'I want this meddler more than you, Mr Jarrett.' He stared stone-faced at the duke's agent a moment. 'Tell you what,' he said finally. 'You come find me after sundown. May be I'll have news.'

'Where?' Jarrett called after him as the young giant moved off into the winter light.

'Powcher's Lane,' came the reply and he was gone.

'Everyone knows the Watsons in Powcher's Lane,' said Duffin.

'The alley down by Bedford's stable yard?'

'That's it.' The poacher watched as Jarrett threaded a bridle over Walcheren's head and fetched his saddle. 'What now?' he asked.

'If anyone can nose Farr out, you can, Ezekial. Will you go to town?'

The poacher tossed his head. 'And what will you do?'

Jarrett tightened the girth and swung into the saddle. 'I have a visit to make – meet you at the Queen's Head. Five o'clock? I'll buy you a drink.'

CHAPTER EIGHTEEN

'Men are all at t'fair.' Old Mrs Anders advanced towards him in a sort of crab-wise shuffle, cradling at her waist gnarled hands twisted into hooks. Her eyes, under her smart starched cap, were sharp and her expression cheerful. 'Come in, come in, Mr Jarrett. 'Tis an honour to have a visit from the duke's man. I'm a prisoner to me joints and company's a rare pleasure this time of year. Sue! Fetch tea,' she called out to a servant girl hovering in the background. 'Best cups, mind! My granddaughter, Mary-Anne, Mr Jarrett. Ooff!' The old lady dropped herself into a chair, expelling a little puff of dust from the patchwork cushions.

'Miss Anders,' Jarrett acknowledged with a half-bow. Sitting before him was the girl with the milkmaid charms and the wayward handkerchief he had spotted at the fair. Mary-Anne Anders had rosy cheeks, a sturdy white neck and the placid demeanour of a cow. She held the obligatory piece of sewing in her hands. Her thick fingers were surprisingly neat and delicate in their movements. The old lady beamed at him from her chair.

'This is a comfortable room,' he remarked, looking about. 'A good size, without being so large as to be draughty.' Had Miss Henrietta Lonsdale seen him at that moment, she would have been astonished by Mr Jarrett's cosy impersonation of a gossip. It was a woman's room, crowded with mementoes – carved spoons and painted boxes, and pressed flowers in frames. Against one wall a table was arranged with dried grasses flanking a crudely coloured picture draped in black. The image was of a broad-faced young man with an uncertain mouth and one eye larger than the other.

'Our John. Her brother.' Old Mrs Anders jerked her head towards her granddaughter. 'The good Lord took him from us near three years ago now.' The echo of her loss was so poignant Mr Jarrett found himself embarrassed. Mary-Anne sewed on as if she heard nothing.

'A great sadness,' he murmured.

'Lord's will be done.' The clock ticked and dust motes danced in the sunlight. The door creaked and to his relief the serving girl appeared with tea. Mr Jarrett was grateful for the prop. He and the old lady smiled and nodded at one another over their cups, he marvelling privately at the dexterity of her tortured hands.

'You do not attend the fairs today, Miss Anders?' he asked. The girl raised her head. He fancied her expression was wistful. It was mirrored on the bulbous face of a hideous pottery cherub that peeped over her left shoulder from a shelf. He recognized the offending object at once. It was one of the fairings for sale on the stall just by the spot where he had observed her encounter with Jonas Farr.

'I saw you in town on opening day, I think.' He nodded towards the fairing, remembering how the farmer's daughter had simpered as the young man returned her handkerchief. 'I see your memento. A token from a gentleman admirer, perhaps?'

His teasing remark elicited a strange response. Mary-Anne Anders stared. Her eyes were of a limpid, washed-out blue that suggested thoughts rarely clouded the possessor's mind. It was almost as if she ruminated. Her grandmamma, on the other hand, fell into a fit of coughing. Mary-Anne leapt up and went to bend over the old lady, mumbling soothing noises. He averted his eyes so that they might be private. Miss Anders's sewing lay face up on the seat she had vacated. A mop of vivid sky-blue petals sang out amid a ghostly pencilled pattern of flowers twined in a harvest sheaf. Old Mrs Anders regained her composure and Mary-Anne resumed her place.

'Perhaps not a gentleman admirer in the strict sense,' Jarrett amended meditatively, continuing as if there had been no interruption, 'but gentlemanly in spirit, I dare say. I saw you together at the fair,' he explained. Miss Anders threw a wary look at her chaperone. It occurred to him belatedly that perhaps she was fearful of speaking of her mysterious admirer before her grandmother. But then, if Old Mrs Anders rarely left the house, how could she be ignorant of his visits?

'*He* spoke to you at the fair?' demanded the old lady.

'Not *him*,' responded her granddaughter. The tone of this exchange perplexed him. Old Mrs Anders did not sound angry or even displeased. The pair seemed mutually astonished, if anything. Jarrett forged on.

'It was when you dropped your handkerchief. I saw him pick it up,' he confided to Miss Anders apologetically, adding a flirtatious half-smile. In the past young ladies had been known to melt and become quite giddy when Mr Jarrett deployed his charm. Miss Anders, however, goggled at him as if he were speaking Chinese. Her eyebrows drew together.

'He picked it up,' she repeated slowly.

'Miss Lippett's man, Jonas Farr; he returned your handkerchief to you,' he said. Miss Anders went rigid.

'Miss Josephine's serving man?' she exclaimed, outraged. 'What can you mean?'

'A serving man! The very thought!' hooted the old woman. 'Mary-Anne Anders knows her due better than that! I should think so!' An improper noise broke from the old woman's mouth. He looked at her astonished. She had chuckled. Miss Anders was sitting bolt upright in her chair, her expression affronted.

'I take that unkindly, Mr Jarrett,' she told him roundly. 'What have I done that you should suggest such a thing? I am always perfectly proper and refined.'

*

He looked back at the Anderses' farm, puzzling over the scene he had just witnessed. The girl's repudiation of Jonas Farr had seemed sincere. He would have wagered his horse that Miss Anders lacked the wit to counterfeit such a performance. Could Farr have been courting her in disguise? He should have liked to have asked her directly about her mysterious visitor, but Miss Anders had fallen into such a sulk at his supposed insult, he had been forced to give up the visit and take his leave. The smoke curling up from the farmhouse chimneys hung in insubstantial twists in the chill air. Had he learnt anything to the purpose?

The low winter sun declared the hour advancing into the afternoon. He thought fondly of Mrs Martin's pie and of his interrupted breakfast. There was time for a decent meal before he set out again to meet Duffin. Walcheren was just stepping through the gates of the Old Manor when young Matt ran up wearing mittens and a thick woollen scarf.

'I was coming to find you, sir,' he called out. He held up a sealed paper. 'This was brought for you. Man said it were urgent.'

'How long ago?'

'No more than forty minutes. 'Would have set out earlier but none of us knew which direction you took, then, Mr Tiplady, he said to try town.'

Jarrett did not recognize the device pressed into the wax – an elaborate affair like an Irish knot. He broke the seal and unfolded a single sheet of thick, smooth writing paper. There was no greeting, just two lines executed in a precise black hand with forceful downstrokes: *Be at the split beech, a hundred yards up stream from the old ford, town-side, 3 o'clock, today. S.*

Strickland worked fast. Jarrett consulted his pocket-watch and turned Walcheren about with a sigh. His stomach would have to wait.

'When are we to expect you, sir? Cook, you know ...' Matt called after him. Jarrett thought fleetingly of the excellent Mrs Martin waiting in her kitchen with the makings of another spoiled dinner. He turned back in his saddle with a regretful grimace.

'My apologies to cook. Tell her she has my full permission to curse me. I'll find dinner in town. If I'm required, send word to the Queen's Head.'

Winter was retreating, the bright, frozen light dissolving towards drear grey. At the edge of the wood giant moth holes of dark earth punctured the blanket of white. He had no difficulty following Strickland's directions to the split beech. As a clandestine meeting place, it was well chosen. In five minutes, a man could be lost among the crowded lower town, but with the rush of the swollen river to one side and the steep woods hiding the town above, it was an isolated, secret spot. The split beech stood on rising ground a few yards back from a small clearing where three paths met.

He was on edge, all his senses alert. Would he recognize the man he had come to meet? He would be disguised no doubt – a hat pulled down low and an all-concealing cloak at least. But there were identifying marks that were difficult to conceal: voice, intonation, build and posture, especially if you could catch sight of your man on the move. And if you could but glimpse an ungloved hand or the shape of an ear – they were as good as a portrait. His promise to Strickland, he told himself, did not preclude him from using his senses.

Somewhere up above the barrier of trees, the church clock struck three. He heard the protesting cry of a rook and looked up. A figure had appeared on the rise above him, enveloped, as anticipated, in a cloak. There was a flour bag over the head. Eyeholes had been cut in the hessian and a slash gaped in the region of the mouth. He had once had an encounter on the road to Arruda with a band of Portuguese partisans who disguised them-selves with sacks like that. Theirs had been stained with blood.

He made his way between the spindly, close-pressed trees under the gaze of the silent watcher. The wood had grown up on a thin layer of soil overlying fissured rock. The steeply rising ground was run through with trenches, disguised under thick vegetation, and unexpected stony outcrops. He came to a fallen tree. The figure was standing maybe ten feet away across a gully.

'Close enough!' the voice was an amplified whisper. A man's voice, deliberately distorted. Jarrett scanned the broken ground between them. There was no immediate way across. The gully was dense with undergrowth and too wide to jump. The eyes were no more than glints of light in a pair of black holes. Through the slitted fabric he saw the pale lips move, bare and pink against fairish skin.

'Captain Jarrett. Heard of you. You've a reputation.' So he's interested in me, Jarrett thought. If I have met him before in recent days, I missed any hint of that. 'Foreign service. You'll have stories to tell.' The tone was an uncertain mix of truculence and grudging respect.

'Maybe another time,' responded Jarrett briskly. 'You know why I asked for this meeting?'

'Young gentleman's accident.'

'It was no accident,' Jarrett replied. Moisture dripped from the black trees.

'A Yorkshireman – call him Jonas Farr,' the voice started up again. 'Taken up with a group of weavers – a song club.'

'That's old news.'

'Farr comes from a line of troublemakers,' said the harsh whisper. 'Prominent in a clandestine society in Dewsbury.' It was hard work disguising one's voice. The longer you talked, the more words you used, the better the chance you gave the listener of latching on to the real voice behind the mask. *Clandestine*, Jarrett noted. He shifted his position and sharpened his ears.

'You have evidence of insurgency?' he queried a touch impatiently.

'In Dewsbury. Raising money and support of strikers; printing and distribution of unstamped material,' listed the voice monotonously.

'The intent?'

'Riot and disorder.'

'And you have clear evidence of Farr's involvement? Enough to convict in a court of law?'

'I just write the report.' Something personal had slipped into the intonation there – a spark that just failed to ignite.

'What do you believe to be Farr's purpose in Woolbridge?'

'Recruit weavers.'

'For what?'

'Plot.'

'A plot? What kind of plot?'

'Sabotage.'

'Of what? There are no machines in Woolbridge.'

'Not yet.'

The fellow was well disciplined with his monotone brevity and immobility. He stood so still he might have been a scarecrow on a pole rather than a man.

'What do you know of the night Mr Adley died? Where were you?'

'Called away.'

'So you have no information about that night?'

'Farr went astray.'

'What do you mean?'

'Song club had a meeting on Quarry Fell near where the young gentleman was found. Farr was expected but never came.'

'You say he was expected? I heard he had a girl.'

'A girl!' A touch of emotion tainted the contrived anonymity of the voice. 'Farr had a meeting at a hut on the fell not far from where the body was found.'

'Who was he meeting?'

'A recruit – but Farr never got there neither.' Jarrett thought of the barren moor where he had found Grub. So much traffic for a cold winter's night.

'How do you know all this?' asked Jarrett. It occurred to him that Strickland's man himself might have been playing the recruit in question.

'Sources.'

'Can you be more precise?'

'No.' The grotesque bag swung away a moment. 'Time's up,' said the voice.

'What do you know of the death up at the Bucket and Broom?' Jarrett's question arrested him. The dark emptiness of the eye-holes fixed him. 'A wool buyer for the army, a guest, died there a few days ago.'

'So?'

'He was murderered too.' The blank parody of a head seemed to tilt a fraction. The pink lips moved.

'Was he?' Jarrett fancied the whole wood was leaning in to listen. Even the sound of the river seemed to have hushed.

'The suspect in that case had an accomplice.' Jarrett felt, as much as saw, the infinitesimal pause. The figure shrugged.

'Farr was the one astray that night.' The voice repeated its refrain. 'Your boy ran across him ...'

'The boy had no reason to be up there,' argued Jarrett.

'Saw the man in town by chance, then, and followed him.' The figure shifted. Across the still, cold air Jarrett caught a whiff of a smell, woody yet out of place – too exotic for a northern winter. 'Wrong place at the wrong time.' The figure bent and dropped out of sight.

Jarrett stood a moment, staring between the black tree trunks. There was no sound save the rush of the water below and the dripping trees. Moving swiftly, his boots slipping on the icy ground, he found his way to the head of the gully and followed it back down the other side to the tree where the man had stood. Hidden from his previous vantage point, he discovered a shallow trench, deep enough for a man to retreat out of sight. It ran to a rocky outcrop on the other side of which was a path that led back up to the cottages and gardens at the edge of town.

He retraced his steps to the place where the figure had stood. The leafy mulch covering the earth held no prints. He ran a hand over a knobbly protrusion he had noted during their interview hovering in line with the eyeholes of the mask. Mr Strickland's man stood five foot five inches, or thereabouts. The fellow's arms, when hanging by his sides, were a touch longer than average. He was skilled at concealing his native accents – although he had slipped in that final phrase. He had shaped the combination of 'r' and 'o' in a manner that betrayed Lancastrian birth. For all the good that piece of deduction did him. Behind the mask, he suspected, this man was quite proficient enough to bend his voice and person to any character he wished to adopt. He thought of Bess, redolent with innocence, as she was in her first entrance as Polly Peachum. The man was an actor. He paused a moment. Could that be the answer? A member of Sugden's troupe?

He slithered back down the damp hill to where he had left Walcheren tied to a branch. At least he had confirmation of machines coming into Woolbridge – Bedford no doubt. They might be here already. The traffic of the fair could provide useful cover. Was that what it was all about? Could Ison have used the government's preoccupation with radical insurgency to acquire soldiers merely to guard a commercial venture? There was that stink of corruption clinging to Mr George and his army contract. Because of that contract, Bedford's mill had the prospect of turning pretty profits – but not yet. Everyone knew how long it took the government to pay its dues. The money from that contract might not appear for a year or more. If Bedford's finances were as precarious as Dickon Watson suggested, whose investment had paid for the machines? Was Ison in partnership with Bedford? It would take thousands. Did Ison have thousands of pounds? The river below him glinted with rosy lights in the late afternoon sun. He thought of Duffin and wondered how he was getting on.

Ezekial Duffin was half-blind and struggling to keep upright. If the good Lord was indeed a loving God, as the parson pretended, he would have reserved snow for open country, he grumbled to himself. It was nothing but a trial in the town. The mercury in the thermometer hanging in Jasper Bedlington's stable yard had hovered just above freezing all day. Mud overlaid the slick ice. He cursed as his foot lost its purchase yet again. A day spent working his way through half the taverns and front room snugs in the lower town had loosened his balance. He had been to all the usual places, sitting in the corner with his pint pot and his dog, listening. He was up to date with all the current gossip. Folk were full of how the colonel's borrowed soldiers were out looking for the stranger who had murdered the duke's kin and interfering with decent citizens in the pursuit of their legitimate business in the process. But not a whisper of Jonas Farr. He tugged at the brim of his hat. The glare of the low winter sun reduced the street to a slice of frozen ground at his feet and a disorientating dazzle. A hazy presence passing by hailed him: 'Now then young man!' Duffin grunted in response. He turned a corner into the full path of the setting sun and collided with a living wall.

'Beg pardon,' said a male voice.

As the fellow slipped out of sight, Duffin saw an outline in black and shadow: a coat, long in the waist, and a broad-brimmed, low-crowned hat.

There were soldiers on the bridge stopping young men of average size and examining every wagon that passed. The fairs were winding down and the line of traffic waiting to leave the town extended back as far as Bedford's mill. The Queen's Head was seething, some guests making their departure, others seizing the final opportunity to meet business acquaintances before they scattered for another year. The yard and the bar beyond were full. Jarrett entered the inn through the front door to avoid the press. Down a perspective, through an open door, he saw Miss Henrietta Lonsdale. Ice sparkled in her hair. She was flapping the edges of her open coat with both hands while Miss Josephine Lippett ran a handkerchief over the bare skin of her friend's neck. Had both ladies been equally good looking he might privately have thought it a pretty picture, but Miss Lippett's part in the scene repelled him. He did not like the attentive way she applied herself to her task. There is something unseemly in her manner, he thought distastefully. He rapped his knuckles on the door jamb. Henrietta Lonsdale turned her head.

'We were caught in an avalanche, Mr Jarrett!' she greeted him, laughing. 'From the roof! I fancy the snow must be thawing.'

'So you have come to town, ladies,' he responded lamely. Miss Lippett shot him a haughty look and turned her back, shaking her handkerchief out before the fire.

'There are always bargains to be had on the last day of the fairs,' Henrietta replied with a smile that made up for her companion's coldness. Her expression sobered. 'And Miss Lippett is eager to discover news of her manservant.'

'I have come to offer the testimony of my good opinion before the authorities,' stated Miss Lippett. 'I have no confidence in Colonel Ison's justice.'

'I applaud you, ma'am.'

Miss Lippett looked at him suspiciously out of the corner of her eye. Henrietta took a step towards him.

'And will you help this unfortunate young man, Mr Jarrett?' she appealed. She searched his face. They stood quite close. Henrietta was suddenly conscious of Mr Jarrett's gaze resting on her hair, her eyes, her mouth. How admirably the black lashes set off the smoky green of the eyes, Mr Jarrett thought, distracted. He watched her expression grow quizzical.

'If I can, Miss Londsale,' he answered hurriedly.

'You do not believe him guilty of Mr Adley's murder?' she insisted.

'Mr Farr's guilt is certainly not proven to me. I am eager to speak with the man—'

'I do not know where he is!' Miss Lippett interrupted loudly.

All at once a question occurred to him, so simple and obvious he felt a fool not to have considered it before.

'How long has this Jonas Farr been in your employ, Miss Lippett?' he asked. The spinster blinked.

'Six weeks ... more than a month at least,' she amended dismissively.

'You hired him on references? He was recommended to you perhaps?' Miss Lippett straightened her back, conveying by that gesture that her patience was being severely tried. 'I wonder how you came to employ a weaver from Yorkshire, ma'am.'

'A weaver? Farr is not a weaver.' Miss Lippett's inflection was smug, as if she had bested him. 'Shoe-making is his trade, but he could do better,' she added. 'He has a very neat hand. He restored a folder of soft Italian leather for me, an antique. It was torn, I thought beyond repair; and yet with his fine stitching he made it like new. And he will turn his hand to anything. It is rare to find so useful and sober a servant. I always say—' Miss Lippett was prevented from sharing her wisdom by an uncouth noise.

'Hisst!'

Jack, the landlord's young son, stood imperfectly concealed beyond the door jamb. He poked the upper half of his head through the aperture, widening his eyes significantly in Jarrett's direction.

'Yes, Jack?' he asked, amused.

'Mr Duffin asks if you might meet him by the barn, Mr Jarrett, where the players is,' the boy informed him in a strident whisper.

'Now?' queried Jarrett. Jack nodded. His innocent face was alive with excitement. 'If you'll excuse us, ladies.'

Jarrett thought he perceived a glint of triumph in Miss Lippett's eye. All at once he had had enough of her unmannerly eccentricities. He was loath to leave her in possession of the field. He paused before Miss Henrietta. Taking her hand, he bowed over it, grazing the soft skin with his lips. 'Miss Lonsdale,' he said, warm and low. For a moment Miss Lippett was quite excluded. Then he followed the boy out.

He found the poacher lurking under low-hanging eaves at the far end of the stable yard. He was watching the closed door of the grey barn where so recently the whole town had watched Bess play.

'In there?' asked Jarrett.

'Recognized the hat,' Duffin replied.

CHAPTER NINETEEN

Grey light filtering down from slits set high in the massive stone walls touched rolls of scenery piled alongside an assemblage of props and flats. By daylight the true nature of Jasper Bedlington's barn reasserted itself. The theatrical trappings intruded, tawdry and ephemeral, within its sturdy carcass. A handful of people were gathered on the stage. Jarrett recognized five principal members of Mr Sugden's company, looking strangely colourless in their everyday clothes. Bess, he noted, was not among them – nor the comic, Mr Jefferies. The actress who played Lucy Lockit in the opera sat on a large hamper cutting an apple into neat slices with a folding knife. By her side was the older lady who had played Mrs Peachum. Both held their bodies self-consciously, like dancers. At their feet, reclining in a romantic posture, accepting tit-bits from Lucy's hand, was the handsome youth who had played Filch to the delight of the country maidens. A large painted screen, of the sort that concealed duped husbands and foolish wives in farces, formed a backdrop

319

behind them. The three were watching the manager in debate with the leading man – as if waiting for their scene, thought Jarrett. The picture intrigued him. Each one of the persons before him displayed themselves to the empty seats. He wondered if that was the mark of their profession – always to be looking to the audience.

'He says he will not attend, being unwell from his anxiety of last night . . .' Mr Sugden, the manager, was saying, his face creased in a worried expression.

'Anxiety!' scoffed Dick Greenwood, the gallant Macheath. 'Too much brandy, more like. Thank God he's leaving, I say!' As if they responded to a cue, the two men turned in a synchronized movement in Jarrett's direction. Mr Sugden peered into the dim light.

'Yes?'

Jarrett climbed the short ladder that led to the stage. The sole of his boot slid a little on the step. The wooden treads were wet as if someone had recently come in from the muddy snow outside.

'Mr Sugden, isn't it?'

Mr Sugden regarded him speculatively. His thinning dark hair was cropped close, accentuating liquid, emotional eyes. He was a compact man. Barely five foot four, Jarrett estimated, making a quick comparison with his own height. Dick Greenwood, on the other hand, was quite tall. Perhaps five foot nine inches. Cordiality transformed the manager's expression. The scene has begun, thought Jarrett.

'Mr Jarrett, isn't it?' Mr Sugden pumped the visitor's

hand up and down with an excess of enthusiasm. 'Bess's friend? Agent for the Duke of Penrith, if I am not mistaken,' he pronounced gaily. Jarrett winced a little at this public advertisement of his connection to Miss Tallentyre. He wondered where Bess might be.

'Let me introduce Dick Greenwood.' The little manager moved lightly on his feet. 'Dick takes our first line of business, both tragic and comic . . .' Up close, Greenwood was a well-preserved fifty. He had a cynical air of detachment, as if he were well accustomed to life and it mildly amused him.

'You made an admirable Macheath, Mr Greenwood,' Jarrett complimented.

With the flourish of a magician producing a bunch of flowers from his sleeve, Mr Sugden directed his guest's attention to the lady with the apple.

'My heart's delight, Mrs Sugden!' he declared. 'Mrs Clarice Hickson, to give her stage name,' he confided, low-voiced. 'You'll have admired her Lucy, I'm sure.' The lady flashed her dimples in a roguish smile. The Ganymede at her knee tilted up his handsome face. 'Will Vaughan, our walking gentleman – he takes our Romeos, Young Norval in *Douglas*, that sort of thing,' explained Sugden. The boy was about Grub's age. His features bore that unknitted look before character coalesces into maturity. 'And this,' Sugden beamed companionably at the final member of the party, 'is Mrs Monk, our Mrs Peachum. She takes our character parts. Her nurse in *Romeo* is one of the best in the business.'

'Your Mr Peachum – he is not here?' Jarrett enquired. The ladies gazed at him without moving a muscle of their faces. Mr Sugden's mobile mouth turned down.

'Ah, Mr Jefferies!' he said.

'Incapacitated.' With a quick movement of his hand, Greenwood mimed tipping a cup to his lips. 'Frequently under the necessity of eating anchovy toasts behind the scenes,' he mouthed in comic parody of a prim old maid.

Jarrett grinned. 'To alleviate the fumes of the liquor . . . ? What a pity. He is a fine comic.'

'When he turns up,' Greenwood replied sourly. Jarrett sensed a long-running dispute.

'Mr Jefferies is unreliable?'

Greenwood grimaced.

'But you can't deny his talent, Dick,' protested Sugden. 'He's a very fine clown, even in his cups. His tricks are excellently comic. That way he has of eating cabbage! It rivals Bullock's fabled mode of devouring asparagus. He'll try anything to amuse an audience, even sleight of hand. He pulls them in better than any clown I have met with . . .' Mr Sugden's attention shifted. He took a step back as if struck by a sudden thought. 'Bess says you've a singing voice.' His bright black eyes swept Jarrett head to toe. 'And a fine figure too, if I may be so bold. Just the right degree of military bearing. A very Captain Absolute! And I dare to think, a beguiling Macheath. I don't suppose . . . ?' Jarrett saw Mr Greenwood stiffen.

'No,' he replied firmly. 'No. I thank you, Mr Sugden, but that is not my line.'

'Pity,' said the manager without resentment. 'We could do with a novelty.'

Jarrett crossed over to the pile of scenery and props. He lifted the edge of a heavy roll of canvas. It depicted a sand-coloured building with Roman pillars. His new position gave him a partial side view of the hamper and the figures grouped around it. He wondered why the screen was deployed in the middle of the stage rather than folded ready for transport like the rest. He felt the eyes of the cast upon him. He took a step towards the back of the stage. His foot disturbed an oversized ring of gaoler's keys lying on the floor. Their iron clank resounded up to the rafters of the barn. In a swift movement, Mrs Sugden stood up with a rustle of skirts. Mr Sugden's mouth hung half open a moment.

'You are leaving us already?' Jarrett asked idly.

'Ah! Sadly, yes!' The manager darted over to him. 'Last night there was not a single person in the boxes! This business of the murder of that young man . . .' He slipped a hand under Jarrett's elbow, gently steering him back to the others. 'Such a tragedy. Dreadful,' he chattered. 'And of course these soldiers everywhere. It's not good for business. The *joie de vivre* of the fairs is quite gone. And what with Mr Jefferies having declared his intention to leave us, we plan to head for Manchester. I have a business acquaintance there who will find us a stage.'

'And where will Mr Jefferies go?' enquired Jarrett.

'He's had a better offer.' Lucy – for he could not help thinking of Mrs Sugden in that part – had a trick of making the simplest sentence sound suggestive. 'He has high ambitions.' The actress laughed, displaying her plump bosom before him in a preening movement.

'He's played Astley's, in London, you know,' contributed Mrs Monk.

'In the old days, when he could hold his liquor,' murmured Greenwood.

'Perhaps you can help me with a wager,' said Jarrett. 'The other night, while we were watching your opera, I bet my friend that Jefferies was a Lancastrian. He thought him a Yorkshireman but I think I have the better ear.'

'Jefferies?' Sugden looked puzzled. 'Can't say I know where he was born.' He appealed to his companions.

'Liverpool,' Mrs Monk frowned thoughtfully. 'Yes. He was born in Liverpool; he once told me a story about his boyhood there.'

'So do you win your wager, Mr Jarrett?' asked Mrs Sugden in her arch way.

'Perhaps.' Jarrett changed the subject. 'Have you been together long? As a company I mean.'

'Our little family?' Sugden surveyed his cast with the air of a complacent papa. 'We've been together near three years now.' The others nodded and murmured in agreement. 'I hesitate to boast, but I don't believe the company has changed a member of it for more than a twelve-month. We are a happy band.'

'Except for Jefferies of course,' said Greenwood.

'Is he a recent addition?'

'He played a season with us a couple of years ago. He

met us again here when we arrived for the fairs. We've been up in Newcastle,' the manager replied.

'A successful engagement?'

'Three weeks of decent houses.'

'So Mr Jefferies rejoined you only for this engagement?' asked Jarrett curiously.

'He was to stay with us for a northern tour, but he has changed his mind.' Mr Sugden cast a quick glance at Greenwood. His tone turned brisk. 'So what can we do for you, Mr Jarrett? In truth, we were hoping to make a last sally before the fairs are entirely packed up. I spotted a smart jacket with military togs on a second-hand stall. A perfect fit for a lady. The theatrical wardrobe, you know, it must be kept up.' *It's now or never*, thought Jarrett to himself. He took the plunge.

'The night my cousin was found murdered,' he began, 'your company was playing *The Beggar's Opera*.' It was as if a steel rope circled those present and he had tightened it.

'Of course, of course,' murmured Mr Sugden.

'The performance, as I recall, ended at eleven o'clock, or thereabouts. I was wondering, what did your people do after that?'

'Do?' asked Sugden airily.

'Did you go to your beds?'

'Well, no.' The manager tucked his thumbs in his waistcoat. He seemed to plump up, like a bird under threat. 'It may seem odd to those not familiar with our profession but an actor leaves the stage exhilarated,' he expounded. 'Even when exhausted by giving one's all, sleep does not beckon directly.' Out of the corner of his eye Jarrett saw Mrs Sugden and Greenwood exchange a glance, half impatient, half indulgent. 'On Thursday night, however,' continued the manager, oblivious, 'our generous patron treated us to a dinner.'

'Justice Raistrick? A dinner?'

'Here. At the Queen's Head, in Mr Bedlington's assembly room.'

'You were all present?'

'The entire company: every one of us down to the call boy.' They all nodded in unison.

'We keep ourselves pretty close in towns like this,' Dick Greenwood explained. 'You can never be sure of your reception in out-of-the-way places. You cannot count on a welcome from the natives. If you happen to stray into the wrong tavern there's always the danger of someone picking a fight. And it detracts from the art, you know, if Romeo must make love with a black eye.'

'So Justice Raistrick entertained you. Did he stay long?'

'Quite late.'

'And when did these festivities end?'

'Oh the early hours,' Mr Sugden replied off-handedly. 'I seem to remember the church tower striking three as we made our way to our beds. Is that not right, my dearest?'

'Sugden always likes to be the last one up,' returned his heart's delight, dimpling.

'And you?' Jarrett asked Greenwood.

'Will and I carried Jefferies to his room. He was insensible.'

'Around the same time?' Greenwood shrugged.

'Maybe quarter of an hour earlier. I had drunk quite liberally myself.'

'Can anyone outside your company confirm this?'

'Well, there was Jo ...' Will Vaughan spoke up from the floor. The others started as if they had forgotten him.

'Jo?' demanded Jarrett.

'A Yorkshire youth,' Mr Sugden waxed sentimental, 'another young spark who rubbed against the flats and smelt the lamps and lost his heart,' he declared, tapping his breast in the region of his heart with blunt, white fingers.

'To our Bess, more like ...' murmured Greenwood. Mrs Sugden flashed him a warning look.

'He spent the night in the wings,' continued Mr Sugden, ignoring the interruption. 'Do you remember his name, my love?'

'Jonas Farr,' replied Mrs Sugden serenely.

'I beg your pardon?' exclaimed Jarrett.

'A moth gathered to Miss Tallentyre's flame.' Greenwood's manner was playful. He seemed to be teasing someone. Jarrett thought of the last time he had laid eyes on Bess, Thursday night at the play; the night Grub died. He saw himself attempting to keep his countenance while she postured and ogled him an arm's breadth away, making a laughing stock of them both. Mrs Monk shifted her weight and the wicker hamper creaked in protest.

'This Yorkshireman, Farr – he was with you during the whole performance?' Jarrett pressed.

'Watched from the wings,' repeated the manager, slipping him a curious look. 'Was quite helpful, in fact. Lockit's shoe sprang a seam and he made an excellent repair during one of my exits,' he reminisced, speaking of his part as if the character were a separate entity.

'And Farr remained in attendance throughout the dinner afterwards? What time did he leave?' The actors looked at one another.

'Can't say I noticed,' responded Sugden. 'I was entertaining the Justice.'

'And when did the magistrate leave?'

'About midnight.'

'A disappointed man,' chuckled Greenwood. Mrs Sugden glared at him. Greenwood smiled back. 'Like many others, he had hopes of our leading lady,' he explained jauntily.

Bess was playing hard to get, was she? So Raistrick had not bedded her yet. At least there was some satisfaction in that.

'And when did Jonas Farr leave?' Jarrett asked. He had a flash of memory. Miss Lippett's servant turning up his face as Bess made her entrance on the gallery in the yard outside. Mischief hitched up the corners of Greenwood's mouth and eyes.

'We-ell,' he began.

'Dick Greenwood!' Bess's voice rang out. 'That's more than enough from you!' The screen wobbled and folded back upon itself. Her cheeks flushed and arms akimbo, Mr Sugden's leading lady confronted her mischievous Macheath. Her eyes slid to Jarrett. She bit her lip.

'La!' she exclaimed, with an exaggerated gesture, as if they were playing a scene from some farce. 'We are discovered!'

'Now that's what I call an entrance,' murmured Dick Greenwood.

Jarrett was staring at the figure that stood a step behind her: a medium-sized young man, dressed in a low-crowned hat and a long-waisted coat.

'Mr Jarrett,' Miss Lippett's manservant greeted him.

'Mr Farr. I've been looking for you.'

Jarrett sought some privacy at the back of the barn by the door, where Duffin joined them. Bess tucked her hand under Jonas's arm and would not be separated from him. The rest of the company, left behind on the stage, clustered, with their backs turned, around the hamper murmuring to one another. Farr glanced at the woman at his side now and then; a mild astonishment glossed his face, like a man in a dream he did not care to wake up from.

'The magistrate, Colonel Ison, is looking for you, Mr Farr,' Jarrett said. His breath misted in the cold air between them.

'Looking to arrest me. I know it, Mr Jarrett. But you must believe me: I am no murderer.'

'Of course he's not! He never left this inn that night.'

Bess tossed her copper curls over her shoulder, holding Jarrett's eye defiantly. He noticed her squeeze Farr's arm. 'He was with me. All night.'

'All night,' echoed Jarrett. Bess always had had a tender spot for lost dogs.

'All night,' she repeated defiantly. He turned back to Farr.

'Your mistress left the evening's entertainment early. She had a headache. She did not go to the play but returned home by Quarry Fell. Surely you escorted her?'

'Miss Lippett dismissed me,' he said with an uneasy glance at Bess. 'She'd hired a coach. She gave me permission to stay at the play.'

'You are a playgoer?' Jarrett's manner was sceptical.

'When I can, sir.'

'I did not see you.'

'And yet I was there. They can all vouch for me.' He indicated the actors huddled on the stage.

'And will,' stated Bess violently. Farr flicked a startled look at her then back to Jarrett. 'What is it, Captain Fred?' Bess's voice was sugar sweet. 'After all we've been to one another, don't you trust my word?'

'Stay out of this, Bess. This is not one of your games,' Jarrett said low. He had rolled naked with this woman. How could he ever have been so unguarded? She heard the iron in his voice. Her jaw tensed, almost as if she was going to spit at him, then she subsided.

Farr was staring down at the hat he held in his hands. It was of good quality, with a fine glossy nap. It had been well cared for although the shape was a bygone fashion. The cut of the coat, too, was out of style but well made. Jarrett glanced at Duffin.

'These are the clothes the man wore?'

'Aye,' replied the poacher.

'So how do you explain that?' Jarrett asked Farr. 'Mr Duffin here saw a man on Quarry Fell that night not far from where my cousin lay dying. That man wore the clothes you wear. That hat, that coat . . .'

'That is a lie!' Bess's face flushed red. 'He was with me!' she insisted.

'So you say,' Jarrett threw out dismissively. 'But how can you answer that, Mr Farr?'

'I cannot, but I tell you—'

'Hold on, now,' Duffin interrupted. 'Hold a piece.'

'What is it?' snapped Jarrett. The poacher leant forward. He reached out grimy fingers and pinched the lapel of Farr's coat.

'Man I saw had his coat buttoned tight. It was a bitter night as you'll recall. And his sleeves covered half his hands. I saw that from the way he held the lamp. Now look at this young fella here, and look at them sleeves.'

The coat hung open over Farr's chest. He made no complaint as Jarrett attempted to draw the coat together. It would not button up – and the sleeves were tight. They stopped at his wrists.

'Where did you get these clothes?' Jarrett demanded. The young man met his eye.

'I cannot tell you that, sir,' he replied.

Jarrett thought of Mr Hilton sitting on the cart bench speaking of old Mr Lippett, Miss Josephine's father – *He was a well-dressed man. Nothing but the best for him. Everything neat and proper to the day he died.* The garments were of a style that had been in fashion thirty years ago. Had someone kept old Mr Lippett's clothes?

'Did a friend give them to you? Did you find them?'

'I will not say.' For a young man of twenty he was remarkable in his self-possession. It seemed unshakeable.

'Did you steal them?'

'No!' Jonas Farr lowered his head, as if he bent it before a storm. He did not raise his voice or protest. 'I am sorry to disoblige you, Mr Jarrett,' he said steadily. 'I cannot in good conscience say more.'

'Good conscience!' exclaimed Jarrett.

'Only believe me, this suit of clothes has nothing to do with the murder of young Favian,' he said sincerely.

Jarrett frowned at him, perplexed. 'You know but you will not tell,' he repeated softly. 'Very well. Tell me this – why are you accused of this murder, do you think?'

'I know I am accused, but I do not know why.'

'I've heard a lot of things: talk of radicals and insurgency and Luddite plots. What do you say to that?'

'Nothing. I know nothing of such things.'

'I was warned about a Yorkshireman, come from Leeds – a known conspirator.'

'That must be some other man.'

'Is your grandfather not a convicted Jacobin?'

Farr's open face twisted in a resigned look. He sighed.

'He was twice imprisoned for distributing unstamped material,' he conceded. His words followed one another evenly, as if he had repeated himself many times and no longer expected to be believed. The attentive way Jarrett listened gave him courage, and his voice warmed. 'It was back at the start of the French wars. My grandfather published works of Thomas Paine and others. A local magistrate was hot against him ... They never saw eye to eye.'

Jarrett leant back in his seat contemplating the sturdy young man wearing his borrowed clothes with his head held high. His life had often depended on his judgement of men. He relied on it. His every instinct told him the youth was honest.

'So you swear to me that you have carried no messages to workers here in Woolbridge?' he asked. 'You have administered no illegal oaths, or attended secret meetings, nor otherwise made attempts to promote combinations or dissent against the legitimate authorities?'

'Listen to you!' jeered Bess. 'I remember you when—' Farr put his hand over hers a moment. She fell silent. He gave her a sideways, private smile. *Poor fool!* thought Jarrett fleetingly.

'No sir,' Farr answered. He leant forward, meeting his eyes directly, his hands on his knees. 'I have sung ballads – and I will do so again. But that is not against any law. God created man as a creature of reason – I believe that; and I believe every man, be he pauper or a lord, has the right to inform himself. It is knowledge mends injustice. When men are pushed to riot, it is them that suffer. The high are too mighty and they will not abide it. No.' He paused and took a breath as if such extended exposition was unnatural to him. 'Decency cannot exist without law.'

'And if the law is unjust?' asked Jarrett.

'Then I will raise my voice against it, if I can.'

'I have heard you charged with taking part in seditious combinations in Dewsbury.'

Farr snorted. 'I was no more than five years old when my family moved from Dewsbury. My grandfather, he belonged to a Friendly Society there and was active in it; it was a charitable association. But that was many a year ago now. We've lived in Leeds since then.'

They were quiet. The sun had almost gone. They sat in twilight. Duffin caught Jarrett's eye and signalled with a jerk of his head. They were expected in Powcher's Lane. There was a clatter of movement from the stage. Mr Sugden led his band towards them. He pulled a conciliatory face.

'Not wishing to disturb, but we must get on. There's packing to be done. The wagons go out tonight, after the fair traffic has died down.' The actors clustered about their leading lady and her protégé. Greenwood stood behind Bess, one hand on her shoulder. She covered it with her own.

'What will you do?' Farr asked Jarrett.

'Do? He'll let you be,' declared Bess. The actors stared at him defiantly.

Jarrett got up. 'Do you go with them?' he asked Farr.

Farr nodded. 'How do you plan to get him past the soldiers?' Jarrett asked Bess. 'They are searching wagons on the roads out of town.'

It was Greenwood who replied. 'We have a false-bottomed trunk – phantasmagoria and other optical illusions . . .'

'It's been Dick's salvation more than once,' Mrs Sugden chuckled, 'when pursued by cuckolded husbands and love-mad spinsters.'

'And this time there's no reward posted, so no one will be tempted to betray him,' returned Greenwood, meeting her eye significantly. They both laughed.

They were right about there being no reward posted, thought Jarrett. That was odd, given Ison's apparent determination to pursue his culprit. Either the colonel was uncertain of his ground or too mean to pledge his funds.

Jarrett reached out his hand and Farr took it. A grin transformed Jarrett's face. An answering one dawned in Farr's.

'Maybe I shall hear you sing again one day, Mr Farr.'

'May be so, Mr Jarrett.' Jonas's face turned solemn. 'And I hope you find your cousin's murderer. He was a good lad, that Book Boy.'

'Thank you. And I will find the villain. You can be sure of that.'

335

CHAPTER TWENTY

Dusk filled the alley. The fading sky above blended into the shadow of the walls. Duffin indicated a half-court to the left. They climbed stone steps to a door standing half open to the pale grey light. Through it, lit by a fire burning in the hearth, Jarrett saw a woman sitting at a table with her arm about a young boy. Their heads were bent together, his soft cheek resting against her coarsened one. The woman looked up with laughing, youthful eyes. They darkened warily as they fell on him.

'Mrs Watson?' Jarrett ventured. 'Your son Dickon said we might find him here.'

'You are Mr Jarrett, then,' she said.

'Yes. And this . . .' He turned back to Duffin who followed him. Her face lit up.

'I know him,' Mrs Watson responded. 'How are you, Ezekial?'

'As well as ever, Sara.' The boy flung his arms about the poacher's bulky waist. 'Now then young man,' said Duffin, ruffling the child's hair. 'Let me just . . .' He opened his coat and produced a dead rabbit. Taking a piece of string from another pocket he tied it neatly about the back legs and hung it from a hook by the door. Sara kissed his cheek.

'You're a good friend,' she said. 'Now sit you down. Dickon said you'd be by. He'll not be long, if you don't mind waiting.' The boy stared at Jarrett. 'My youngest, Saul, Mr Jarrett,' his mother said, the affection plain on her face. She went to the fire and lit a candle and brought it to the table, sheltering its flame with her hand. The light caught the grey threads deadening the brown of her hair. Jarrett smiled at the boy. Saul stood by Duffin's chair, leaning against the poacher's solid shoulder, his eyes downcast. Jarrett was reminded of Walcheren leaning over a fence; his horse would sometimes rest against him like that, when he was feeling affectionate. The boy was fiddling with something, rolling it between his fingers.

'What you got there?' asked Duffin. He boy held out his trophy. 'Your Burned Man's button, eh? That's quite a thing, that is. What do you think of that, Mr Jarrett?' Duffin glanced at Jarrett with a twinkle in his eye. Saul approached with his hand outstretched. Jarrett looked down at the scorched button. He became very still. The candlelight fell on his face. It caught the movement of his hand as it went to his breast and felt in a pocket.

'What is it?' asked Sara, her voice sharp with concern.

Jarrett drew out a wadded handkerchief. He unfolded it on the table. He laid Saul's button beside the first. The

337

scorching had dulled its tooling but it had the same cable border. He picked each button up and peered at the back, leaning in to the candlelight. The flame flickered over tiny maker's marks scratched in the metal. They matched. Saul edged closer, peering over Jarrett's arm.

'Where did you get the other?'

'It was given to me. Why do you call it the Burned Man's button?' Jarrett responded in an oddly distant voice. The boy leant closer.

'Found it in t'loft after t'fire,' he said.

'The fire in Mr Bedford's stable loft, a few weeks back,' Sara Watson explained. 'Michael White, him that was coachman before this one, he died there. Saul was helping the carpenter afterwards and he found that.'

'This Michael White – he was known to you?'

'He was a stranger these parts. Mr Bedford hired him in Leeds. He was a drinker, poor man. Irish. And not happy Irish. More melancholy and solitary. They found him with a bottle at his side and an overturned candle. It was a straw mattress, you see. Must have knocked the candle over, I suppose, and set light to it, when he was too drunk to help himself.' Jarrett heard the doubt in her voice.

'Must have?'

'We-ell, my Dickon, he was one of the first there to put the fire out and he thought it strange the man was not more burnt. They put the fire out before the mattress was completely gone and the man just lay there on his back—'

'On his back?' Jarrett queried.

Sara frowned slightly at his urgency. 'Dickon can tell you himself; here he is now.' Rapid feet mounted the outer steps. 'Son,' she greeted him as Dickon came through the door, 'Mr Jarrett wants to know about the night Mr Bedford's coachman burned in his loft. How was it you found him?'

Dickon dropped a kiss on the top of his mother's head. He looked well satisfied with himself.

'Flat on his back, staring up at t'ceiling,' Dickon answered.

'His eyes were open?' demanded Jarrett, startled.

'Aye. Doctor said it were heat; muscles draw back the lids. Give me the shivers – along with the smell, of course,' the young giant added meditatively.

Jarrett met his eyes. 'I've never heard that,' he said.

Dickon stiffened.

'Damn me! You don't mean another one?'

'Three deaths,' Jarrett replied, staring down at the two buttons in his hand. 'Three murders, that's my guess – that wool buyer, Pritchard, my cousin and Bedford's coachman.'

'Never! What the hell's going on?' Dickon exclaimed. His mother dealt him a smart smack.

'I'll not have swearing in my house!'

'Beg pardon, ma,' he responded sheepishly.

'I wish I knew,' Jarrett said. 'What about Lem? Have you found him, by any chance?'

Dickon's mouth broadened into a gleeful grin. He

339

turned a chair about and sat astride, resting his muscled forearms on the back. 'Summat.'

'What?' invited Jarrett, amused.

'Well, it was Jinnie that found him. She and me, we talked to young Lem Porter together. The man in question's not tall. Well, Lem's a longshanks; he said about Sim's height.'

'That would make him five foot four or five?' asked Jarrett. Duffin grunted.

'Round about,' agreed Dickon, 'and he's got a black beard, curly like, and works in town. Or at least, so the lad thinks.'

'That's it?' Jarrett was disappointed.

'He could be holding something back.' Dickon shrugged. 'I almost knocked his block off, the way he kept sniggering and muttering how we didn't know the half of it. He was going to meet the fella again tomorrow, but Jinnie's talked him out of it.'

'Why did you let her do that?' Jarrett was exasperated. 'We could have used the opportunity to find this villain.'

'Lem's daft, Mr Jarrett,' protested Dickon. 'He'll speak out of turn, say summat he shouldn't. He's neither quick nor strong and if this man is what we think him, he's murdered three already. Lem'll get hurt. You need to find another way.'

'You're right, of course,' Jarrett apologized ruefully.

'Besides,' Dickon went on. 'I've got summat better. Lem told Jinnie who it was that brought him to this bearded man.'

'Oh yes? Who?'

'A poisonous piece of piss they call Nat Broom.'

'Him!'

'You know him?'

'Oh yes.' Jarrett exchanged a look with Duffin. He was thinking of his stolen boots. 'And you know where to find him?'

'Harry Aitken does. He's heard Nat has a room in a passage behind Wharton's yard.'

'So what are we waiting for? Let's go see the man,' Duffin said.

'Read my mind.' Dickon raised his bulk from the chair. 'He don't have friends, so we should find him in. Let me just fetch a couple of lanterns. It's dark down there.'

Dickon led them down the hill towards the tanneries by the river. He turned down a ginnel and then into a passage hardly wider than he was. It ran between two buildings and bent around the back. Jarrett turned the blind corner and saw Dickon stopped ahead.

'Up here,' he called back over his shoulder. 'On the first floor.' A pale patch of light flickered on to the blank wall of the building opposite from a window above. There was a doorway and a staircase beyond.

'Let me go first,' Jarrett said. The weaver stood back to let him pass. The staircase was narrow and dusty. The treads creaked and cracked under his feet. The light bobbing ahead of him touched a landing. He heard scuttling and saw a rat with red whiskers. It looked at him briefly, then vanished into the shadows. The pool of light illuminated a rusty trail of tiny footprints. He followed them to a lake of blood. His nose and mouth were filled with the sickly iron smell of it. The room was small. Sprays of blood arced on the lime-plastered walls. A bloody hand-print faced him. Beneath it lay a hunched shape that made wet, choking sounds. Jarrett crouched down, conscious of the liquid sucking at the soles of his boots. He gripped a bony shoulder and rolled the man over. His head had been battered and broken open. There was so much blood it was a miracle he was still alive. Nat Broom – his good servant's clothes were quite ruined.

They slung him in a blanket and carried him back to the Queen's Head, listening to the sickening noises and waiting for them to stop. But each rasping breath was followed by another, catching and laboured and mixed with deep sighs. The Bedlingtons exclaimed over the blood and the sight. Mrs Bedlington sent her boy for the doctor and her maids running about. They washed Nat Broom and bandaged him and made up a bed by the fire in a small room beside the kitchen.

'All our upstairs rooms are taken. Besides, it's warmer down here and we can keep an eye on him.' Mrs Bedlington's motherly face crumpled suddenly, as if she might cry. 'What is the world coming to? He was never a good man, but who deserves this?'

'I don't know, Mrs B,' Jarrett said gruffly. He looked away to her husband. 'He'll need to be guarded, Jasper. The longer he lives, I fear someone may want to finish him off.' The publican held his eye a moment.

'Is that right?' he responded. 'Oh dear me!' he murmured involuntarily. He wiped his hands nervously on his apron. 'I'll make sure they all know to keep an eye out,' he assured Jarrett. 'I'll go to the lock-up and tell Constable Thaddaeus of this affair, but I wouldn't expect much of him. He has his hands full. He's got six ne'er-do-wells in charge because of the fairs.'

'Bob and me we've nowhere special to be,' said Duffin, rubbing his dog's ears.

'I can take my turn tomorrow,' offered Dickon. Jasper left to inform the constable.

Jarrett looked down at the waxy, absent face. The lids were not fully closed. Slips of eye glinted meaninglessly under the lashes.

'Well, he's not going to tell us anything now. Did Lem say *anything* else about this bearded man?' he asked Dickon. 'Anything else at all?' Dickon shrugged.

'Nothing worth knowing. Only that he liked his clothes.'

Nat Broom's head looked more peaceful rendered in pencil on paper. You could not hear him fetch those heaving sighs and rasping breaths. Jarrett examined his sketch. It was a face reduced to mere architecture. Unconsciousness had wiped away all character. The man on the bed sighed deeply. 'If only they had found him out earlier!' Jarrett thought, in frustration. It was silent. Had he stopped breathing? Jarrett counted eight of his own heartbeats before Nat gasped and sighed again. Jarrett deepened the shading around the left eye socket.

Someone knocked his elbow. Duffin's dog inserted its head under his arm.

'Everyone's a critic,' Jarrett complained, stroking Bob's rough coat. 'Ezekial.'

'Brought you some hot toddy, compliments of the house,' said the poacher. Jarrett took the mug gratefully.

'That reminds me, I must pay the Bedlingtons for his care. Anything to report?'

'The bar's full of soldiers. They've discovered Mrs B's ale.' He propped himself up against the window sill.

'What links an Irish coachman, an army wool buyer and my young cousin, Duffin? Do you see it?'

'No.' Duffin lifted his mug to his lips. 'Can't say as I do.'

'Just as we discover that Nat here was the man who introduced young Lem to this bearded twister in . . .'

'This,' supplied Duffin, with a gesture towards the bed.

'Someone tidying loose ends?'

'If it's connected.'

'True.' Jarrett pulled his shoulders back. 'But when so many acts of unusual violence follow one another in swift succession, it seems reasonable enough to suspect they might be connected.' *Start at the beginning.* 'Why kill a coachman?'

'Maybe he just likes killing,' Duffin suggested. 'Could be no sense to it at all.'

'I don't see it. This man is careful and tidy. The first two murders nearly passed unnoticed – it was Grub's death that tripped him. That was rushed. It looks as if Grub followed him out there to Quarry Fell. If so, why?

What did he suspect? For God's sake! The boy had only been here two days!' He unfolded the handkerchief once more. The button lay in stark relief against the white lawn, the yellowish thread still attached to it and the flake of leather. The tooling of the raised rope border around the pewter button was crisp and delicate. Pewter, not silver. 'Too fancy for a plain man but hardly rich enough for a gentleman,' he murmured to himself. A yellow thread. *Yellow gloves* . . . He saw the words written in Grub's hand heavily underscored on the back of a bill – a bill from the Royal Hotel in Leeds. Grub saw something in Leeds. Someone. He saw Strickland. No. It couldn't be Strickland. But why was Strickland there? *It's a convenient rendez-vous.* He had a meeting – a meeting with one of his men . . .

'My cousin saw someone in Leeds.' Duffin tensed at Jarrett's tone. 'Bedford was there that day; he went to Leeds to collect his niece.'

'You don't mean Bedford—'

'No. His coachman! Just think, Duffin. Why kill the first man; why kill the coachman?' Duffin looked at him blankly. 'For his job!' Jarrett exclaimed impatiently. 'He wanted his job.' Duffin sucked his teeth thoughtfully.

'Trouble is Bedford's coachman is one man who couldn't have killed your boy.'

'What do you mean?'

'He was arrested that afternoon, at the fair. The colonel's soldiers had him in lock-up all night.'

*

He listened to Duffin snoring gently in counterpoint to Nat Broom's rasping breaths and sighs. He had not slept for days. He was beyond the boundaries of sleep. Nat Broom and he were two sides of the same coin: Nat trapped inside a sleeping body and he a waking one. He needed some air. He pulled on his greatcoat and opened the yard door. There was a smell, an intensely familiar smell. There was someone in the yard. He saw a dim patch of red, white facings and the glow of a pipe bowl. A sergeant sat on a barrel under the eaves smoking Spanish tobacco. His head was tipped back, his face turned up to the stars.

'That brings back memories,' Jarrett said. 'The smell of your pipe.' The sergeant shifted his head slightly to cast him an idle glance. An angry puckered scar ran from his left temple, skewing the corner of his eye on its way down to his chin. This, along with his flat nose and a drooping moustache gave him a truculent, melancholy air. Jarrett looked up at the sky. The moon peeped coyly over a wisp of cloud.

'It's getting warmer. Been cold enough of late.'

The sergeant grunted. He took his pipe from his mouth. 'Nothing to the bitter chill of the mountains of the peninsula,' he declared and resumed his puffing.

'That's the truth. I've spent winter in the Portuguese hills.'

'Thought you might have,' the sergeant said with some satisfaction. He tilted his bulk to reach in a pocket.

'Share a pipe?' he offered.

'No. Thank you. Just like the smell.' He had never taken

to the habit. He had found it bad for the health. When a man spent much time on the wrong side of enemy lines he soon learnt that the smell of burning tobacco carried in open country.

'Got this in the retreat from Corunna,' the sergeant said, indicating the scar on his cheek. He cocked his good eye at Jarrett speculatively. 'You?'

'I'd just got back from Walcheren then.'

'Fever posting! Rather you than me.'

'That retreat wasn't so easy either.'

The sergeant grunted.'There were so few of us left, they parcelled us out all over. I ended up here. Recruiting party, or supposed to be!' he spat in disgust. He pulled on his pipe.

'Made many arrests, then, with the fairs?' Jarrett asked. The sergeant snorted.

'Not likely! Don't know what we're bloody here for.'

'What happened to those three taken up on opening day? Someone told me they were out to murder the magistrates.'

'No such luck. Just drunks. Magistrate let them all out the next day.' He fussed with his pipe bowl and sucked the stem industriously.

'Two miners and a townsman, fighting drunk, as I recall,' Jarrett mused. 'That should have been a lively night in the lock-up.'

'You would have thought, wouldn't ya? The lads were all set to lay bets. The townsman was a scrappy little chap. Full of vigour and ready to have at it but colonel shoved his oar in. Scrappy, you see, is in the employ of one of the big noises these parts. He was to be kept safe and quiet away from the others by colonel's direct orders.'

'Undisturbed.'

'Locked up in his very own accommodations out back.' Jarrett thought of the duke's warehouse the soldiers were using for their barracks. There was one lockable shed. It stood some yards off, on its own by the river. It was cold that night. If he knew soldiers, with their officers at the play, they would stay by the fire.

'That was troublesome, having to check on him through the night.'

'No need.' The sergeant shook his head. 'Colonel said he should be left to sleep undisturbed. And I always obeys my officers. Colonel came back himself in the morning and let the man out. Scrappy must have been servant to a friend of his.' He leant back his head and stared up into the infinite night. 'Christ!' he said. 'Bloody home postings! Much more of this and I shall grow moss.'

CHAPTER TWENTY-ONE

Nat Broom was still breathing – a little more calmly now. The Reverend Prattman's bell-ringers had begun to warm up their bells. Sunday. Another day and night gone by and no nearer to Grub's murderer.

'Down this way, you say? Well, if you don't think I'll disturb him, we'll just say good morning.' A skipping step pranced down the corridor. Jarrett moved swiftly to the door just in time. Hester's bright face smiled up at him. She had a Sunday ribbon tied fetchingly in her curls. Concerned that she should not see the ugliness in the bed, he swept her giggling into his arms.

'Good morning, Hester,' he said. 'You're remarkably clean.' They stepped out into the corridor. Meg Teward waited to greet him. Her bonnet was tied with a large lilac bow under one ear. Her elfin head tilted as if the weight of the ribbons pulled it down.

'Mr Jarrett! We're on our way to church; we'll not stay.' She dropped a shy look at the parcel she held in her gloved hands. A flush of carmine touched her cheek-bones. 'You were such a comfort that day, when . . .' she trailed off.

'Please don't mention it!' he responded, rather more robustly than he had intended. Her pale eyebrows drew together in a little frown. Hester squirmed. He released her and she went to take her mother's hand.

'We've brought you curran wigs,' Meg Teward said. 'Hester had me bake them special, just for you.'

'Why, thank you!' He was touched. As he took the parcel he thought of his sketch. He slipped back into the room to fetch it from the window sill, leaving the parcel in its place.

'I wonder if . . .' He held it out with one hand, pulling the door to behind him. 'You don't by chance recognize this man, Mrs Teward?' She examined the sketch carefully, her face as a solemn as a stained-glass angel.

'Is he sleeping?' she asked. 'He doesn't look well.'

'Do you know him?'

'I *think* . . .' She worried her lower lip with her teeth. 'Yes!' Jarrett felt the blood pump a little faster through his veins. 'Last Tuesday! The two men that come visiting Mr George. This is like the smaller one, the one with the bearded man.'

'Is Mr George still with you at the Bucket and Broom?'

'Oh no! He was only booked in for t'fairs.'

Damn! Too late! He could hardly chase Mr George to London to ask him about his contract and his visitors.

'There's the bells again.' Mrs Teward was distracted. 'We

must be going.' She bobbed a curtsey. Hester gave him a little wave as they turned to leave. 'We dropped Mr George off on our way,' Meg Teward said. 'He's booked a place on the York flyer; it passes through at half past ten.'

He dismounted, exhilarated. If his pocket watch kept its time, it was twelve minutes after ten. He glanced into the coffee room. It was like many others in country coaching inns up and down the north road – stuffy and dim, with robust furnishings and a tired, rubbed look. The landlord hurried out from a back room.

'Mr Jarrett; it's been a time since we've had the pleasure,' he greeted him. 'You've something for t'mail? I'm just doing up bags.'

'I've no need to trouble you, landlord. I was hoping to catch an acquaintance; he has a seat on the flyer, I believe.'

'Mr George, would that be?' There was the urgent sound of a chair scraped back and the shadow of movement in the room beyond.

'Never mind, I think I see him.' Jarrett brushed past the innkeeper into the coffee room.

Mr George was standing by a table just to the left of the door. He had been tucked out of sight eating a plate of beef and bread.

'Mr Jarrett. I take the stage at any minute.' He took a hurried side-step. His foot knocked against a small leather trunk stowed beside the table and he almost fell.

'We need to talk, Mr George.' Jarrett advanced on him.

'About what?' Mr George's eyes darted this way and that about the empty room. They were alone. The landlord had returned to his mailbags and the duke's agent blocked the path to the door.

'About corruption, sir, and murder.'

Mr George suddenly resumed his seat. He glanced irritably at his half-eaten food and pushed the plate away.

'What is all this?' he demanded petulantly. 'What do you mean coming here in this unmannerly fashion?'

Jarrett pulled out a chair to sit facing him.

'Tell me about the men who came to see you at the Bucket and Broom the night you arrived.' When they had first met, Mr George had seemed such a cheerful man. Now his expression was frankly sulky. After a moment Jarrett realized that he was attempting an air of haughty indifference, but his neck and shoulders were too stiff for nonchalance. 'One of them was this man.' Jarrett put his sketch of Nat Broom on the table between them. Mr George rolled his eyes down to it reluctantly. Tiny drops of sweat beaded on his upper lip. 'Who was the other?'

'By what right do you ask me? You have no authority . . .' Jarrett leant across the table. The fat man flinched.

'The secret's out, Mr George.' Jarrett spoke low and deliberate. 'Your colleague was murdered.'

'Pritchard died of natural causes! The magistrate himself said so!' Mr George took out his handkerchief and wiped his hands. He looked down at them as if they had a life of their own. He tucked his handkerchief up his sleeve in a furtive movement.

'But you and I know he was killed. Two more murdered men have been found – and one of them was kin to the Duke of Penrith.' Mr George's chubby fingers went to his cravat. 'And as you know, I am agent to the Duke of Penrith.'

'What can you want of me?' the buyer asked plaintively. Jarrett tapped the sketch that lay between them.

'This man and another, a bearded man, came to see you at the Bucket and Broom last Tuesday night; what did they want with you?' Mr George opened his mouth. His denial withered before the intensity of Jarrett's blue-grey stare. 'Tell me about the contract.' It was as if an inflated bladder had been pricked by a pin. Jarrett watched the defiance seep out of Mr George.

'He . . .'

'The bearded man?' The buyer nodded, jerkily, like a mechanical doll with a faulty spring.

'He suggested that Mr Bedford's mill should be awarded the contract, that's all.' The first words having slipped out, more followed at a gathering pace. 'Bedford was on the preferred list, in any event. I was assured that there were machines ready to be installed. With them Bedford may fill the entire order without difficulty. It is simpler to deal with one contractor—'

'Not if he fails to deliver,' interrupted Jarrett. 'If he meets with some difficulty or accident, how then is the army to clothe its soldiers?'

'I received assurances,' Mr George insisted.

'You received more than that. I hope they were

generous.' Mr George's neck seemed to retract between his shoulders, as if he were a tortoise that would hide its head. 'Who was his principal?' Jarrett demanded.

'His principal?' Mr George faltered.

'The bearded man spoke for someone. Who was it?'

'I don't know. I do not know.'

'How can you not know?'

'I did not ask! They offered cash – and threats of violence if I did not comply.'

'And Pritchard?'

'He would have none of it.' Mr George turned petulant. 'Silly, moralizing fool! He had been sent as my watchman, he said. There is a new man come in, you see. Taken over the department; wants to make a name for himself. For all my years in the service, *my* patron is gone and I am left unprotected. Twisting in the wind.' His voice was moist with self-pity. He dabbed his handkerchief over his face.

'So you connived at your colleague Pritchard's murder so that you might collect a retirement bonus?'

'I take offence at your tone, sir!' Mr George rallied. 'I did no such thing. I knew nothing . . .' Jarrett thought of the fading footprint in the frost below Mr George's window and the two pairs of open shutters, and the hole where the post of a ladder might have slipped into loose dirt.

'But you opened the window. You let the murderer in.'

'I was never in Pritchard's room!' Mr George's lips spoke his denial stiffly from a frozen face.

'I don't believe you.'

354

Mr George turned his head away. 'Pritchard wasn't well.' His voice slid about the scale. 'He was ill. Who's to say how long he should have lived . . .? He was forever anxious. *He* did not believe he was well – with his sleeping draughts and his complaints.'

'But someone hurried his death.'

'I did not do that!'

'You opened the window.' Mr George's full red mouth hung open and fear shifted in his eyes.

'You cannot prove a thing. This is a monstrous lie!'

'Monstrous!' Jarrett repeated. 'So tell me about the murderer, this bearded man.'

'I don't know. I don't know,' Mr George repeated desperately. 'He had a beard. He was muffled up. He wouldn't take off his hat. He did not want to be seen. And I did not see his face. He hardly stayed a moment—'

'And yet he arranged to come back later . . .'

'He threatened me! I was fearful for my life—'

'So you let him take Pritchard's instead.'

'That is not how it was! He . . . he was just supposed to talk to Pritchard. To persuade him.'

Jarrett watched with distaste as the man squirmed this way and that. He was weary of it all. He imagined Mr George wakeful in his own room as the deed was done; listening to the noises through the wall; clutching his bribe in the dark.

'It was never supposed to be like this.' Mr George kneaded his handkerchief fretfully. The square of linen was by now quite damp. 'I only wanted a little comfort.

I am alone in the world, you know, since my mother died. I never did find a wife.' His fleshy face was a ludicrous mask of melancholy. 'Bedford will supply the order just as well as another. His price is good enough. I am not a bad man, Mr Jarrett. I am not. This business went far beyond anything I anticipated.'

'So help me catch the murderer.'

'I cannot.' He pushed the thought away with plump, white hands. 'I know nothing and you see how dangerous he is . . . I am insignificant. I cannot help you.'

A distant post horn sounded. The landlord poked his head round the door. Mr George swung towards him eagerly as if to his salvation.

'Stage is here, Mr George!' The thunder of carriage wheels and horses approached at a canter. Mr George snatched up his trunk. Outside the window, the coach rattled to a halt in a crescendo of movement and sound. At the door, Mr George hesitated. He looked back.

'What will you do, Mr Jarrett?' Jarrett contemplated him coldly for a moment, then he shrugged.

'I hope your bounty was worth Pritchard's life.' He picked up his sketch of Nat Broom and stowed it away. 'This bearded man doesn't like loose ends. He did for this one just last night. I'd advise you to watch your back, Mr George.' The terror on the man's face was some satisfaction. Not much, but some.

He was back in Powcher's Lane. He turned in through the gates of Bedford's stable yard. The kitchen door was closed. He crossed the open space conscious of the wall of windows rising up to his right. No one called out. No one challenged him. At the entrance to the stable, a cat sat on a feed sack licking its paws. It glanced up briefly. Finding him insignificant, it returned to its task. Two stalls were occupied by a showy bay hunter and a plump pony. The others were empty. The carriage was out. The household was still at church.

A wide flight of open-tread stairs rose up to the loft. His eyes breached floor level. He saw space, clean lines and tawny wood. A single attic room ran the length of the stable. Four windows, two along each long side, let in plenty of light. The wooden ribs of the roof soared overhead.

As he rose step by step, a simple iron bed came into view down the vista of boards. The fourth tread from the top of the stair was loose. It protested under his weight. The bed seemed to rest in a pool of light until he realized that the wood around it had been recently replaced. The bed was covered by a horse blanket. A canvas satchel rested on top.

He circled the room like a cat, keeping to the walls where the boards were firm and did not creak. The floor was simple planks laid over joists. Through the chinks he glimpsed the backs of the horses below. The wall behind the stairs was covered with leather reins and carriage harnesses suspended from large hooks. Apart from a stool and a broom leaning against the bricks between the windows there was nothing else. The neatness was familiar. It spoke of a man who might pack up and remove all trace of himself in a minute. He paused by the bed to make a cursory examination of the contents of the satchel: some spare linen and shaving gear; nothing of interest. He left it as he found it. He ran his eyes about the space, examining it section by section. A beam crossed the room over the stairwell. At the far end a large cobweb stretched up into the roof. Its bottom edge flapped loose. He fetched the stool. Standing on it, he reached along the beam to where it joined the bricks of the wall. He touched crumbs of mortar, the sharp edge of brick and a void. He stretched a little further. His fingertips encountered a crumpled, foreign surface. His nail snagged on a piece of curved metal. Crumbs of mortar pattered to the floor as he pulled out wadded leather the size of a man's fist. A pair of men's gloves. Yellow gloves. *Citrine, mustard, ochre* . . . he murmured to himself. They were stiff with dried blood. When they were new-made, each glove had been secured at the wrist by three pewter buttons with tooled cable borders. Now there was a button missing on each. On the left-hand glove, two pinpricks indicated where the missing fastening had once been secured; on the right-hand glove it had been torn away along with a scrap of leather.

So now he knew. These had clothed the hands that strangled Grub's life. Grub's fingers had torn the button from that wrist and held on to it unto death so that it might lead him here. He crumpled the gloves up in his fist.

He returned them to their hiding place. He brushed his clothes and swept up the crumbs of masonry that dusted the boards. As he replaced the stool, he noticed smoke drifting outside. There was an orchard behind the stable bordered by a high wall that hid it from prying eyes. A bonfire smouldered by the wall, its smoke drifting picturesquely in the crisp air. He heard the fourth tread before the top of the stairs creak.

There was a man watching him. It was hard to determine his features. He wore a hat and long coat with the collar turned up. The lower part of his face was covered with a curly black beard. With one hand he swept off his hat revealing a shaved head; the other he lifted to his ear. With one steady movement he peeled off his beard.

'Itches like the clap,' he said. 'Glad to be rid of it. It's the gum.' Taking a round tin from his pocket he laid the false beard inside and stowed it away. 'So you've found me, Captain Jarrett. The chief said you might come by.'

Mr Strickland's man was unremarkable: a smallish man with a sharpish nose and pale eyes under sandy eyebrows. He carried his head a little forward in a manner that seemed to supplicate the world's indulgence. He held out his hand. Jarrett shook it, feeling the long bones and the strength in the wrist.

'You have me at a disadvantage. What should I call you?'

'Go by the name of Judkin these parts; Matthew Judkin. Coachman. I'd offer you refreshment but as you'll have seen, I've nothing to hand,' he said with a ghost of a wink. 'Mr Bedford doesn't like it, having had difficulty with drinkers in the past.' His voice was soft and flat and his expression tended towards the bland as if he had disciplined his muscles to anonymity. He was very clean for a coachman.

He turned his back, taking off his coat. Jarrett automatically adjusted his position to make himself a smaller target, paying close attention to the movement of the man's back and shoulders. The coachman hung his coat up on a hook by the bed, his hands in plain sight. 'Well, this is pleasant. I've heard talk of your work – Spain, wasn't it?' He turned back. His face wore a mild expression but his pale eyes were acute.

'Farr's slipped away from you,' Jarrett said. 'Your information against him was false. He was never party to any conspiracy in Dewsbury. He left that place when he was a boy.'

'Never!' Judkin mouthed incredulously.

'You knew.'

The spy snorted. 'You know the game, captain! All they require is plots averted and culprits tied up all pretty and neat. They don't concern themselves with details. They want reports, they get reports.' The man seemed to think they belonged to the same corps. Curiosity blossomed in counterpoint to the cold anger seething through Jarrett's veins.

'So you've no need of proof?' he asked lightly.

'Proof? Proof's what they are willing to believe!'

There was something Lally Bedford had said. Something about the time Grub took her into the Queen's Head that day, at the opening of the fairs, as the fight erupted in the marketplace. It tugged at his brain. She had mentioned her uncle's coachman ...

'The note in the colonel's carriage; you planted it,' Jarrett stated. Judkin preened himself, like a country wag whose audience had finally got the joke.

'The hogs first rose up in Lincolnshire,' he smirked. 'The colonel was losing heart.'

'And the note kept him keen.' Jarrett noted that Judkin liked to boast. A man didn't get much opportunity in the spy trade.

'Did your service abroad but you've retired now?' Judkin enquired, looking his guest up and down. 'I had a fancy for foreign service; never had the connections.' The last had a lilt Jarrett had heard before: it was the sound of a disappointed man. 'But I'm the best at my trade on home ground.'

'Indeed?' Jarrett was sceptically polite. 'Yesterday's outing was on the messy side.'

'Unfortunate circumstances,' Judkin said huffily.

'Really? Bloodshed like that tends to get a man noticed.'

'Do you see any on me?' Judkin gestured to himself. 'Took along an old coat left by the drunken Paddy, didn't I?' Which he no longer needed, since you murdered him, Jarrett observed to himself. A bloodstained coat wasn't so easy to dispose of. He thought of the bonfire burning in the orchard. That might destroy cloth, although it wouldn't dispose of pewter buttons.

'First you make an accomplice of a local villain who could hang you, then you panic and bludgeon him, leaving the man alive. Your chief can't have been happy. I assume Mr Strickland knows?' Judkin's expression confirmed that he did.

'Only just alive,' Judkin muttered. 'And now you've got him safe.' He slid a sly look under his sandy lashes. 'He's not going to talk, is he?'

He had him there. Even if by some miracle Nat Broom did eventually wake up, Jarrett had seen enough severe head wounds to know that the victims almost invariably suffered memory loss.

'We know better than to leave traces in our profession,' Judkin was saying.

'I traced you.'

'So you did, but then you and I are in the same trade.'

'Hardly!' Jarrett snapped. 'I fought as a soldier against foreign enemies in time of war.' The spy's assumption of collegiality caught him off balance. He considered himself a realist but he had always believed, at heart, that the purpose of his soldiering was to defend a peace where justice and order prevailed. 'You are a murderer!'

'Murderer! That's a hard word. I take exception to that, Mr Jarrett.' Judkin was offended. 'I take no pleasure in killing. Can't abide a suffering creature. Why, do you call yourself murderer? You'll have killed plenty in your time and not all neat and tidy on the raging battlefield, I'll

362

be bound. What you and I do, Mr Jarrett, it's not common murder. When we take a life it is of necessity. You can't pursue our line of work without a little quiet killing.'

'A little quiet killing? Of honest men like Pritchard? There is no justice in that.'

Judkin was stung. His native accents began to colour the contrived voice. 'Justice! There's no such thing! It's a matter of means and what is. You've had it easy; my lord's pet all your life – playing the hero. You do your killing in foreign parts; that's the only difference between us – that and you've been blessed with connections. You've no call to be looking down at me. You and I we do what we do and we're good at it. And as for Pritchard,' Judkin exclaimed irritably, 'we all take a job on the side now and then, so long as it's not out of our way. I was only going to talk to him. The silly fool woke up dopey and started creating. Had to silence him quick. He wasn't supposed to go like that. Must have had a weak heart.'

'He was a civil servant, a servant of the Crown.'

'How was I supposed to know he had a weak heart?' Judkin protested, aggrieved. 'There was no unpleasantness. How did you know?' he enquired with sudden equanimity.

'Because of the way you left him. You practically laid him out. What were you thinking?'

'He flayed about a bit and I had to tidy him,' the little spy responded, matter-of-factly.

'But why like that?'

Judkin looked startled a moment, then a secret reminiscent smile settled around his eyes. 'Knew a man once who slept like that, said it made him ready for heaven.' The expression vanished. He pulled the lobe of one ear, thoughtfully. 'Besides, ran out of time and had to leave him. Never thought the bumpkins would notice. How was I to know the likes of you would be passing?' He paused a moment; his mood shifted. 'It's a pleasure to be tested by a fellow professional,' he finished cheerfully.

'I've been meaning to ask,' Jarrett began again after a stunned moment. 'How come you got yourself arrested on fair day?' A shadow passed over the spy's face.

'Those damned weaver boys and their lumping leader,' he said discontentedly. 'They were out to grab that Porter boy. He nearly led them to me.'

'So you get yourself arrested – quick thinking,' Jarrett conceded. Judkin looked pleased.

'I'm hardly a novice. Ready for anything, that's my motto,' he said modestly.

'But you took a risk. How did you know you could get out when you wanted?'

'Like I said, ready for anything. Lady luck tossed me a bone and I made the most of it.'

'Why not stay snug for the night?' Judkin shrugged.

'Needed to make a try for that daft boy Porter and shut his mouth before those weaver lads learnt something they shouldn't. And what a sweet alibi! Who could resist?'

'I'll give you that,' Jarrett said, seasoning his voice with reluctant admiration. 'But how did you arrange it?'

Judkin waited, a playful smile on his lips. Jarrett thought back to Colonel Ison's late entrance at Mrs Bedford's entertainment before the play. He had been surprised at his marked improvement in mood. The magistrate had been positively buoyant. 'You revealed yourself to Colonel Ison that afternoon,' he supplied. 'You revealed yourself as a government agent, the source of those reports, and enlisted his help.'

'It's a pleasure to watch you reason, captain! The magistrate was kind enough to provide me with private accommodations. How pleased was he to be party to business of state!' Judkin's contempt for Ison was clear. 'The rest I could do myself. The lock on that shed was as good as no lock at all.'

Jarrett searched the bland face, wondering how much the spy knew of the closeness of his connection to Grub. He wanted to keep the man talking. He seemed to relish the opportunity to relate his cleverness.

'And Mr Adley?' he prompted. 'You knew the weavers had Lem Porter and you wanted to stop him talking . . .'

Judkin's pupils contracted for a fraction of a second.

'That lily-handed boy!' he spat in a flash of venom. 'I'd seen him with those weavers. What was he doing mixing with them? It's unnatural. If he'd warned them, it'd be all up with me. I can't abide it,' he said, primly. 'Gentry have their privileges because they're above us. When they steps down like that, they're no better than the rest of us.'

To hear Grub discounted so casually! Jarrett choked down the rage that threatened to overwhelm him. Easy now! He clung to his reason; there is more you can learn from him.

'How come Mr Adley recognized you?' he asked, relieved to hear his voice sounding perfectly calm. 'He saw you with Strickland in Leeds?'

Judkin flashed him a razor-sharp look. 'You know about that?' He sniffed and rubbed his nose with the back of his hand. 'Wasn't sure he'd seen us at that inn. But then of course, the chief had to go in and have a chat. Bloody gentry! Every bugger knows the other or *someone they went to school with*,' he parodied bitterly.

'So he recognized you that night and followed you up on to the fell and you murdered him,' stated Jarrett evenly.

'Why do you say murdered?' protested Judkin, half playfully. 'The young gentleman might have fallen and knocked his head. Weather like that and a sickly boy not used to riding.'

'Is that what happened?' Remembering the bruise on Grub's throat, Jarrett thought the words might choke him, but he got them out. 'You were there at least.'

'I left him comfortable. Had to get back; time was getting on.' For the first time, a faint suggestion of nervousness crossed the pale eyes. 'A casualty of war, Mr Jarrett; a casualty of war.'

'Then you went back to your shed and waited for the colonel to release you the next morning. And you took the opportunity to send him after Farr. How could you be sure Ison would not suspect you of Mr Adley's death?

Is the colonel party to all this?'

'That great booby! I had only to whisper in his ear and he'd jump as high as you could wish,' Judkin boasted. 'The colonel's very trusting. I'd told him I had wind of a meeting on Quarry Fell; that's why I needed my liberty while the world thought me stowed away. I was collecting evidence of the administration of illegal oaths that night – all he could wish for. Next morning, all I had to do was bring news that Farr was not where he was supposed to be.'

'But how could you be sure of that?'

'Saw him all over that doxy with the players and took a chance. The way they were going at it, he was fixed for the night. So there I was, sweet as a nut, and the colonel himself comes in with the news of the young gentleman's death. All I had to do was be amazed to hear of it; the colonel he puts two and two together all on his own.' He stopped. They seemed to have exhausted the subject. Judkin regarded him speculatively, as if he were a guest and it was time for him to call for his hat. He seemed to fear no retribution for what he had done.

'We've spoken of enough to hang you.'

'Really? What proof is there?'

'And if I had proof?'

'But you don't, do you? It's nothing personal, captain. It's just a job. It was all for the mission. You go ask the chief.'

'Strickland? Is he still here?' demanded Jarrett.

'You'll likely catch him up at the church if you hurry.

He doesn't attend but he likes to call by on a Sunday. I must be getting going – things to do. The family'll want collecting soon.' He gave a brisk nod, dismissing him. 'I doubt I'll see you again.'

'You are leaving?'

'Just picked up new orders. This seam's exhausted. I'm for Manchester. Something big's brewing there, they say. The kind of thing to make a man's name in the service. Mr Bedford will have Mr Judkin's notice tonight. One more day as Matthew Judkin, then tomorrow I'm off.'

They were singing inside Mr Prattman's church. A travelling carriage waited in the lane. Its blinds drawn and the coachman hunched immobile on the box. Jarrett found the familiar stork-like figure among the tombstones.

'We meet again, Mr Jarrett. You look a trifle peaked.'

'Mr Strickland.'

'The Yorkshire boy has slipped away, I hear. To Manchester . . . ?' Strickland's gaze was probing. 'No matter,' he said with a vague smile.

'Since Farr is innocent of all charges.'

'Ah! Which one of us is truly innocent!' Strickland was in philosophical mood. He tapped a moss-stained tombstone with the tip of his cane. 'I'm fond of graveyards. They have a certain melancholy peace – particularly in the winter. In the warmer months the smell can be unpleasant.'

Jarrett thought of Judkin following Jonas Farr to

Manchester. He tried again. 'Your agent falsely accuses a decent man.'

Mr Strickland made a faint moue of distaste. He lifted his eyes to the far horizon. 'Of course, you have fought your war abroad,' he mused. His tone turned gently chiding. 'It is easier to play the hero on foreign soil. Operations at home can be a dirty business – I'll give you that. But the truth, my dear Jarrett, is that the common Englishman has no more of a heart of oak than your average Frenchman. They are preoccupied with the petty struggles of their little lives. They complain of the tax and how trade suffers and the price of wheat. They grow restless. These little public dramas help keep the spark of their loyalty bright. A traitor hauled from the shadows every now and then – it draws the plebs together. Thus may Britannia and her liberties endure beyond this war.'

'That is how you justify the sacrifice of innocent men?'

Strickland pursed his lips. 'It is an old argument. I am no philosopher. These are proven tactics.'

'Pritchard, the second victim. He was a servant of the Crown.'

The corners of Mr Strickland's mouth turned down sorrowfully. 'There were extenuating circumstances – a weak heart, I believe? But that was indeed bad. The men will take the occasional job on the side – extra money you know. They're always complaining we don't pay them enough. My man was reprimanded, I can assure you.'

Jarrett snorted impatiently. 'And my cousin? Do you dismiss Favian Adley's death so lightly?'

'Indeed, indeed I do not. A great tragedy,' Strickland answered smoothly.

'He was only a boy!'

Mr Strickland wagged his head judiciously, as if weighing up the matter. 'Perhaps so, but a boy who chose poor company.' He sighed. 'It can happen in the best families, but ...' he raised a hand, interrupting Jarrett's retort. 'I must tell you, with regret, when I found him in Leeds young master Adley was reading material of a decidedly seditious nature.' He paused. 'I burnt the pamphlet, of course,' he continued silkily. 'I'm certain his family would not want the scandal.'

They had reached the end of the path. Mr Strickland's servant opened the wicket gate. His master passed through. He tapped Jarrett's shoulder in an avuncular gesture.

'My condolences. My condolences, of course.' He mounted the steps of his carriage and was swallowed by the dim interior. 'A regrettable adventure, but it is over now at least. You should get some sleep, Mr Jarrett. You've had a trying week.' He turned his hawkish profile and knocked the head of his cane briskly on the ceiling above him.

Jarrett watched the carriage roll out of sight. It was all slipping away from him. He had no evidence to bring to law. Mr George wouldn't speak and Nat Broom couldn't. Colonel Ison, the local chairman of the bench, was already convinced of Jonas Farr's guilt. Tomorrow Judkin would be gone. The Marquess of Earewith had money and connections, and Charles, of course, would want Grub avenged; but how far would he go? How far could he go with men like Strickland guarding their interests in the shadows? Charles did not have the temperament for such a fight. The grinding, ugly truth was that Grub's murder would most likely be laid at Farr's door. He saw Jonas Farr's open face and he knew those eyes would haunt him.

He was so tired. His limbs performed their tasks mechanically. He listened to his heart flogging his blood through his veins.

These are unjust times – there is no justice. Grub spoke to him from his painting chair, his face bright with the clear passion of youth. *An honourable man stands by his beliefs. You taught me that.*

And what had he answered? Imperfect order is better than anarchy?

What you and I do, it's not common murder, murmured the spy. *When we take a life it is of necessity. You can't pursue our line of work without a little quiet killing.*

Then Mrs Adley's powdered mouth spat at him: *What are you good for?*

CHAPTER TWENTY-TWO

He lay along the boards framing the void. He caught the length of the reins under the weight of his body, so that there was no danger of them hanging down and giving him away. He waited, cloaked in shadow, regulating his breathing; listening to the sounds of the horses shifting below. It was past eleven. The church clock chimed the quarter-hour. He heard a footfall in the stable below. He tightened the leather strap between his hands.

Light swung up the stairs. The crown of a head rose smooth and bare. The head turned. They looked eye to eye. He saw the surprise in the pale gaze and the recognition – but it was too late. The strap snaked over the head and bit into the soft flesh of the neck. The lantern clattered down a step or two and went out.

Velvet bristles brushed his mouth. He turned his face away to protect his nose. The skin-covered skull knocked hard against his cheek. All the burning intensity within him was concentrated on that moment. Detached, he listened to the harsh, desperate noises in the dark. He felt the weight collapse against his leather reins. Life ebbed between his hands. Beneath the fear and the other effluvia of death, he could smell sandalwood soap.

He ticked off seconds in his head. It was done. He looped the long reins and tossed them over the beam. He heaved the body up. The swollen face bobbed up and up from the darkness. A third of the body was out of the stairwell. He crouched down against the weight, pausing to adjust his grip. The head lolled inches away. The sandy-lashed lids were half closed.

He tied off the leather straps. Sliding past the legs, he retrieved the lantern and lit the candle and shuttered it. By its dim light he arranged things, taking his time, dusting away marks, checking his clothes. Then he left the way he had come, passing through the trees, and over the orchard wall – silent and unseen.

The end of it. Once again he was walking under the arch leading to the yard of the Queen's Head where it had all begun; and now it was done. Grub was avenged. His firm step echoed against the stone as if it belonged to someone else. Pale lines of light glimmered from shuttered windows. He heard the rumour of voices. There were still men in the bar. He did not want company. He wanted oblivion. He climbed the gallery steps as weary as death. He needed a drink. A door opened ahead of him. He smelt a familiar perfume.

'I thought you were gone,' his voice said.

'Company went ahead with the baggage. Principals

follow tomorrow. He's safe on his way to Manchester.'

'But you've not gone with them?' he repeated dully.

'We take the stage tomorrow.' Her hand rested on his breast. It slid up to his face and cradled his cheek. He leant his tired head against it. He felt her warmth on his cold skin. 'You're all tired out, my love.' He looked into the light, knowing eyes. She saw him as he was and she expected nothing more. 'Come with me,' she said. Her small hand clasped his and he followed her into the darkness.

What are you good for?

This?

He woke with a pounding head and a dry mouth. The fire was out. A froth of copper curls lay on his chest. She slept beside him with her mouth open, her milky skin flushed on the cheeks like a child. Her freckled breast seemed somehow more naked in the morning light.

His only thought was to get out. He pulled on his clothes by the door, fearful every second of waking her. Minutes later he swung up onto Walcheren and was heading for open ground.

The snow had melted. The earth was fresh and green under a strengthening sun. The hedgerows were full of birdsong. Henrietta Lonsdale rode up above the Carlisle road light-hearted. The fairs were over and the players departed. She sensed hope in the air among the puffs and wisps of cloud that hung in the blue spring sky. Her mind wandered over the events of the past week. Mr Adley's death was not the first thing she remembered, and she felt a sting of shame when she recalled it. His death was very terrible and she felt deeply for Mr Jarrett, but she herself had hardly known the boy. Her thoughts lingered over other scenes.

Henrietta was conscious of how little she knew of Mr Jarrett and his origins. She was no green girl. She speculated that the mystery obscuring his connection to the duke's family concealed a scandal but she found she did not care. The truth, she told herself boldly (and when she was alone Henrietta could be bold), was that she was bored by the confines of her respectable existence. And Mr Jarrett's company was . . . exhilarating. The even tenor of her life had at last been broken open and she delighted in it.

He could not bear the thought of returning to the Old Manor. He was detached, untethered, as if his actions had broken his recent, fragile moorings. How could he stay on now? What would he do if he left? He had sold his commission; he had few funds. Distracted and part-mesmerized by the rhythm of Walcheren's familiar gait, he hardly noticed that they were heading up the southern slope of Quarry Fell. *You and I, we do what we do because we're good at it* . . . Strickland would probably give him a job. The thought made him heart-sick.

A rider rode towards him out of the sky. With a falling sensation below his sternum, he recognized the pretty black mare and the sage-green habit of the woman on its back.

'We have the same idea, Mr Jarrett,' Miss Lonsdale called out to him as she rode up. 'Spring is come at last!' There were delicate sweeps of shadow under his eyes and his skin was pallid under his tan. How tired he looks, she thought compassionately. She watched him rub the back of his thumb wearily over one eyebrow as if he couldn't think what to say.

'Come,' she said bossily. 'The exercise will do you good.' Before he could answer, she urged her black mare forward into a canter. 'Catch me if you can,' she called over her shoulder like a careless girl. Walcheren stretched out his legs and gave chase.

She had an excellent seat. Her mare was quick and strong. They gave him a good race. Over a short distance at least, it was only Walcheren's longer legs that gave him the edge. Miss Lonsdale brought her mare to a halt on a little outcrop of hill that seemed designed as a viewing platform for the sweeping panorama of the valley below. Jarrett took his bearings. They were near the pack-horse trail, above the Anderses' farm. Blood coursed through his veins and the clear air filled his lungs, refreshing him. He eased back in the saddle, feeling the muscles in his shoulders and neck relax.

After a moment, he began to suspect that Miss Lonsdale was waiting for something. He glanced over. Her profile was serene; she appeared to be admiring the view. She rose a little in the saddle, tilting her head to look downwards. He was intrigued. The movement seemed somehow exaggerated. He followed her eye-line down.

Their platform overlooked a pretty copse nestling in a dip. A path ran to it alongside a field – a field that lay on the outer edge of the Anderses' farm. In punctuation to this thought, a woman came into sight down the path. She was wearing a yellow dress and a straw bonnet, a blue shawl, and most extraordinarily for Quarry Fell on a brisk spring morning, she carried a parasol in white-gloved hands.

'Miss Anders!' he exclaimed under his breath. He glanced at his companion. She was still looking out over the view, with a little smile on her lips.

A gentleman stepped out of the trees: a gentleman dressed like a beau of a generation before in a long-waisted coat. He swept off his low-crowned, broad-brimmed hat and bowed low to Miss Anders. They turned together, arm in arm, and Jarrett saw the gentleman full face. He recognized the curls; hair like black lambs' wool. In a flash he saw the painted insignia of Miss Lippett's family crest, the cornflowers twined in the harvest sheaf, and the pencilled design on Miss Anders's sewing with its vivid blue flower head. If he had been struck by lightning he could not have been more stunned.

Henrietta Lonsdale was watching him closely with a slightly anxious look in her grey-green eyes.

'You were so fixed on discovering the man Mr Duffin saw on the fell that night,' she said astonishingly. 'I had

377

to speak. I knew Jonas Farr was not that man, and that the man Mr Duffin saw was no murderer.'

'Nor man neither,' he countered curtly.

'No,' she agreed. Her eyes danced.

'How can her family be ignorant of *this*?' he demanded.

'It is Monday – the third Monday of the month,' she replied prosaically. 'Matthew Anders and his brothers always attend the Woolbridge agricultural meeting on the third Monday of the month.' Jarrett stared down at the extraordinary couple below.

'And her grandmother? I thought old Mrs Anders never left the house?' Henrietta arched her elegant eyebrows.

'Mrs Anders? She's as deaf as a post.' She leant down abruptly to pat her mare's sleek neck, hiding her face.

'But she can't be blind!' he exclaimed. Miss Lonsdale heard the revulsion in his voice. She coaxed her horse round to face him.

'This is a woman's secret, Mr Jarrett,' she said seriously. 'I believed I might trust you with it. Besides,' she added, trying for a lighter tone, 'I dare say you have seen stranger things.'

'I am not so certain,' he replied. Down on the path below the gentleman presented Miss Anders with a small parcel wrapped in tinsel paper. The farmer's daughter opened her present with every appearance of delight. She placed a chaste kiss on her admirer's cheek and they strolled by the trees arm in arm beneath the joyous sky. A thought struck him and he swung round in his saddle to face his companion. 'You are telling me that others know of this?'

'Other women, yes. Some old friends and neighbours.' He thought of Mrs Hilton sitting among her hulking husband and sons.

'And yet their menfolk are ignorant?'

'Men are inclined to judge uncommon women harshly,' Miss Lonsdale said carefully. He heard a wistful note in her voice. 'Miss Josephine's eccentricities do no one any harm. Mary-Anne is happy to have so genteel an admirer.'

He stared at her.

'She knows?'

'Of course!' she answered, amused. His attention was drawn, fascinated, back to the couple below.

'But why?'

'It is very pleasant to be read to and admired. The country swains would never pay Mary-Anne such pretty attentions. I do not see why Miss Lippett should be pilloried for so harmless an eccentricity. Besides,' she added with a twinkle, 'the Lippetts are one of our oldest families.'

'Eccentricity!'

Henrietta caught the undertone of disgust. 'I *can* trust you?' she asked urgently. He looked into her eyes. He was astounded by her faith in him.

'Yes ma'am,' he answered. 'You can.' He watched her relax. She gathered her reins more securely in her gloved hands.

'I am to meet Lady Catherine at the Queen's Head in

an hour. I must return to town.' He flinched at the thought of the Queen's Head. He fell in beside her, trying to remember if he knew what time Bess was supposed to leave.

'Let me escort you – as far as town at least. Was Farr aware of ...' he waved a hand wordlessly.

'I think Jonas Farr was, beside yourself, perhaps the one member of your sex who was. Somehow he gained Miss Josephine's trust and proved worthy of it.'

'So *that* is why he would not tell me how he came by those clothes! But why would he ... ?'

'I believe – if I have read certain hints aright – Mr Jonas Farr has an aunt who is somewhat similarly inclined.' He felt his jaw drop. He mastered it. Henrietta bit her lip.

'Why, Mr Jarrett,' she said gently, 'I thought you a man of the world.'

They came off the sunlit fell and trotted down the Carlisle road. His sleep-starved brain was reeling. He slid a side-look at the rider beside him. She sat, back straight, perfectly composed, rising and falling neatly on her pretty mare. His eyes drifted down the smooth fabric of her habit as it curved so closely across her breast. The vignette he had glimpsed at the Queen's Head rose in his mind: that ludicrous spinster patting Miss Lonsdale's bare neck with a napkin on the pretext of her having been caught in a shower of snow. He realized she was watching him with an anxious little frown.

'Madam, you astound me,' he said.

'I hope that's a good thing.' She laughed and he found himself laughing with her.

Ahead of them the honeyed light of the sun glazed the curve of the bridge and danced on the surface of the river. Woolbridge rose up the hill on the other side. He tasted Bess in his mouth and felt the weight of her hair against his skin; as his hands held the reins, they seemed to flex with the memory of what they had done. He stopped laughing.

'You do not know me, Miss Lonsdale,' he said abruptly.

'No?' Her head was tilted back a little; the long lashes curtained her green-grey eyes. 'I suppose I must go by appearances.' Although he feared a true answer, he responded in the drawing-room manner.

'And what do you see?' He braced himself for some flippant, foolish bon mot. Instead she answered sincerely.

'I see a man who cares for others; an honourable man; a man who can be trusted.' He was warmed by a sudden surge of hope. Henrietta Lonsdale spurred her horse over the bridge. 'And I,' she said, humour lifting her voice, 'am an *excellent* judge of character.'

They turned up Cripplegate Hill. Dickon Watson ran out from Powcher's Lane.

'Mr Jarrett! You should come see this!'

'Perhaps you'd best go on to the Queen's Head, Miss Lonsdale.'

'Nonsense!' she responded briskly, following him.

'It's Bedford's coachman. He's only gone and hung himself!'

Mr Bedford, Colonel Ison and Constable Thaddaeus were clustered at the bottom of the stairs to the stable loft staring up at a pair of suspended feet.

'There's a beam that runs above the stairs over the well,' Constable Thaddaeus pointed upwards with his staff of office. 'He must have meant to do it. He could have kicked out and taken purchase on a stair if he'd had a mind.' He craned his neck. 'Used a pair of your carriage reins, looks like, Mr Bedford.'

'What's the meaning of these, do you suppose?' Mr Bedford held a pair of bloodstained gloves. 'They were lying on the stairs as if he wanted them found.'

Jarrett cast a glance at Miss Lonsdale. Her face was pale. She met his eyes and raised her chin defiantly, but she dropped back and left the stable. She stayed in view. He could feel her watching him from the yard.

His hand went to his breast pocket. He unfolded the white handkerchief.

'When I found Mr Adley dying he could not speak of his attacker,' he said. 'He had only the strength left to give me this.' His listeners shuffled nearer to see the button. 'He held it in his fist – it was torn from his murderer.'

'A glove button,' said Mr Bedford.

'If you'll permit . . .' Jarrett took the right-hand glove from him. He held out the button with its thread and flake of leather and the glove with the tear at the wrist.

'The buttons match,' said Mr Bedford. Colonel Ison looked up at the hanged man.

'He must have given way to his conscience. Well. Take him down.' Dickon Watson climbed the stairs and took hold of the legs while Constable Thaddaeus went above.

'But why the blood?' queried Bedford, turning over the gloves.

'There was a man, Nat Broom,' said Jarrett, 'who was brutally attacked on Saturday night.' The colonel's eyebrows climbed further up his forehead.

'You don't mean?' Judkin's feet swung and rapped against wood. There was a grunt and a thud as Dickon heaved the body onto the boards above.

'Silencing an accomplice, you think?' Constable Thaddaeus's voice called down from above.

'See this!' Dickon's face appeared in the stairwell. He handed down a circular tin containing a mess of black hair. 'Found it in his coat.'

'What's this?' asked the magistrate.

'False beard, I should say,' replied Mr Bedford dispassionately, as if nothing in the world could surprise him.

'Nat Broom was seen with a bearded man up at the Bucket and Broom visiting the wool-buyers – just before that Pritchard died,' Dickon chipped in. The colonel made a strangled noise.

'Good Lord!' He did not seem to want to meet Jarrett's eyes.

'He was always a secret and solitary sort of man,' commented Constable Thaddaeus comfortably above them. Through the boards Jarrett could see the soles of his boots. He appeared to be looking down at the body. 'They are the ones, aren't they? For this sort of thing.'

Mr Bedford was still examining the gloves.

'There's another button missing.'

'Young Saul, me brother, found that some weeks ago, sir; here in this very loft,' Dickon said.

'What was he doing here?' demanded the manufacturer.

'Saul? He was helping the carpenter you had repair the loft, Mr Bedford – after him that was coachman before died in that fire.'

'And the buttons match?' The colonel glanced upwards. He swallowed and turned away. Mr Bedford's face was unreadable.

'Strange,' he said, drawing out a paper. 'I have his resignation.' Colonel Ison half snatched it from him.

'Says he found himself unhappy in his place. Well, that explains it. Unhappy,' repeated the colonel. He pocketed the paper. He put his hands behind his back and rocked on his feet. 'An end to a melancholy affair. Eh?' He flicked a side-glance at Jarrett under lowered lids.

'If you say so,' responded Mr Bedford with a shadow of a shrug.

'The end of it,' repeated the magistrate with a firm nod.

'Well, the man's dead,' the manufacturer said. 'I suppose I must look for another coachman.' He left the loft.

*

'But wasn't Bedford's coachman arrested at the fairs?' demanded Lady Catherine blowing gustily on her tea.

'I think so,' Henrietta answered vaguely. She stood with her cup by the window. 'He must have got out somehow.'

'Unsatisfactory!' complained the old woman. Her little dog barked. 'Yes,' she nodded down at it. 'Unsatisfactory.'

'As Sir Thomas has remarked,' said Henrietta, 'Mr Bedford is unlucky in his choice of servants.' Her eyes were fixed on Mr Jarrett. He had stopped in the street below beside a coach she did not recognize. She leant towards the glass. That was a woman's hand. She saw copper curls.

'What is it?' piped Lady Catherine, tapping the floor with her cane to draw her attention. 'What do you see?'

'I thought you'd gone,' he said.

'You've said that before.' Bess was as brittle as spun glass. 'I've had another offer.'

'What about the boy?'

Her smile was bitter. 'It's many a year since I dreamt of you every night, captain. I take my rest where I will.' She waited as if she expected him to say something. He did not. All he wished was to be somewhere else. He fancied he could see the shell forming around her. He looked into the pale blue eyes and felt nothing. He was disgusted with himself.

'You liked me well enough in the shadows, but now you want to be in the light, is that it?' she said. His hand opened towards her a moment, then retracted. He turned his face away. 'Well, then,' her voice was harsh. 'I've accepted an offer from Mr Wilkinson's management in Richmond,' she said brightly in her old manner. 'Very advantageous terms. I'm to have the pick of First Tragedy and genteel comedy too.'

'Richmond,' he repeated.

'Aye. Mrs Siddons had her start there! You must come see me, lover. If you don't, I'll be visiting you. There's always the summer tour and I'll make sure this old barn is on the circuit. I've grown quite fond.' She waved gaily and was gone.

A few days later, the Marquess of Earewith returned. Charles was glad to hear of the death of Grub's murderer. Jarrett never told him the details of it, but sometimes he thought he suspected the truth.

'There is one thing that puzzles me,' Charles said. 'Who had this Pritchard killed?' They were driving out of town towards home. 'Surely not Bedford? You're not telling me I've dined with a man who has people murdered for profit?' Jarrett noted the delicate distinction and was grateful for it.

'He might have done, but from what I hear, he lacked the money. He must have borrowed heavily for the new machinery. My guess is he has a partner.' They were nearing the bridge. The carriage halted.

'What's the matter?' asked Charles. Jarrett craned his head out of the window.

'Construction. There are wagons bringing in materials.

It looks as if they are getting ready to tear down the old black and white house on that plot over the road from Bedford's mill.' The plot was large – larger than might be expected once the old house was cleared. It was a fine situation on rising ground, overlooking Bedford's mill and the lower town and the river curving round it. The wagons ahead were moving again. They turned into the site one by one. Jarrett spotted a familiar figure.

'Dickon Watson,' he called out. 'What do you do here?' The light in the carriage dimmed as Dickon filled the frame of the window.

'Day labourer, now,' he replied. 'The machines are in at Bedford's and Cullen's selling up. I'm a weaver no more.'

'I am sorry.'

Dickon shrugged. 'Shouldn't complain. Justice Raistrick pays good wages.'

'Mr Raistrick? This is to be his house?'

'Aye.' Dickon surveyed the site with a certain proprietorial pride. 'Job'll last a while too. I've seen the plans. They're grand enough. Hey!' His face brightened with a thought. 'Have you heard about Nat Broom?'

'Only that a relative has taken over his care.'

'Relative! Nat's not got relatives! His master, more like!'

'His master?'

'Aye,' Dickon responded, slyly deadpan. 'The magistrate has a reputation for looking after his men.' He tossed his head meaningfully.

'What does he mean?' complained Charles, bewildered. 'Ison?'

'No,' answered Jarrett, his eyes locked on Dickon's. 'Raistrick. Have you seen the Justice? Is he in town?'

'Hang about, I'll ask. Lads!' Dickon called over the enquiry.

'Heard he's gone to Richmond,' came the reply.

'Word is, he's got a new woman there,' said Dickon. 'Well, I must get back. Pleasure to see you, Mr Jarrett.' Jarrett nodded. His jaw was tight. He knocked briskly on the roof of the carriage.

'Drive on!'

'Mr Raistrick!' Charles was astonished. 'He's Bedford's partner? And he had a man killed!' Jarrett was looking back at the plot. Labourers had grappling hooks into the plaster wall of the stately old house, ready to pull it down. So Justice Raistrick was moving up the hill.

'Monstrous! This is monstrous!' Charles was indignant. 'The man cannot be allowed to get away with it!'

'Do I hear passion, Charles? You'll find it unsettling.'

'I may be a gentleman, but I am also an Englishman.' As far as the elegance of his person would allow, the Marquess of Earewith squared himself belligerently. 'So what's to be done?'

'For the present? Nothing. But there shall be other engagements with Mr Justice Raistrick; you can be sure of that.'

EPILOGUE

Mrs Adley never liked Jarrett's portrait of her son. There was something about the eyes, she said. Mr Adley donated the picture to his son's college where it was hung over the fire in a junior fellow's study. The new French tint, Dumont's Blue, recommended by Field, the colourman, proved fugitive. The colourman cut it from his lists that same year. As the months passed, the summer sky Jarrett painted to shine down on Grub turned black in the acid smoke of the coke fires. The lights dimmed until only a pale face and hands glimmered out of the dark. But Favian Adley was not forgotten. Jarrett remembered him each time he opened his paint box, and Book Boy was the toast of the Red Angel song club every Wednesday night for many a year. And, throughout a long life, Lally Bedford never forgot the gentle, eager youth who once held her close to his heart.

ACKNOWLEDGEMENTS

Writers aren't supposed to work in real time, but, due to the vicissitudes of life, this book has taken almost the length of Jarrett's foreign campaigns to complete. It owes its existence to the patience and indulgence of many. I am deeply grateful for the financial support of a New Writing North Writers' Award provided by the Leighton Group, the Society of Authors and the Royal Literary Fund. Thank you too, to Quercus and my admirable editor, Charlotte Clerk; and, of course, Caroline Montgomery – it could not have been done without you.